THE SHIELD
OF
SHAMBALA

BY
CHEN TZU

ISBN 978-0-557-06017-7

Author's notes and acknowledgments: *The Shield of Shambala* was inspired by the wonderfully rich myths, traditions and beliefs of Tibetan Buddhism. The names of deities and characters are a mix of Sanskrit and Tibetan origin. Numerous sources were consulted, ranging from Nicholas Roerich's *Shambhala* (1930) to Thomas Laird's *The Story of Tibet: Conversations with the Dalai Lama* (2006). The inclusion of a Dineh (Navajo) physician as a central character helped to demonstrate the many parallels in Tibetan and Navajo spiritualism, likely because both cultures were strongly influenced by shamanic practices. Finally, I wish to acknowledge the fine artistic guidance of Maya Chensue for cover design and layout.

Beyond great snowy peaks there lies a mystical kingdom where a line of Enlightened Kings guards the innermost teachings of Buddhism. When the light of truth falters and evil seems to have prevailed, the warriors of Shambala shall emerge to defeat the forces of ignorance.

Like the myth of Atlantis, Shambala has stirred the hearts and imaginations of those who long for a utopian world. Since rumors of Shambala came to the West, adventurers and mystics have sought this hidden realm but to no avail. For Nicholas Roerich (1874-1947), the Ukranian theosophist, artist and adventurer, Shambala was an obsession. In the early twentieth century, he led an exploratory expedition to Tibet journaled in is book, *Shambhala* (1930). His book recounts the response of a Lama to his query as to the location of that mystical land.

"The Lama studies us with his piercing gaze. Then he says: The great Shambhala is far beyond the ocean. It is the mighty heavenly domain. It has nothing to do with our earth…"

Despite the Lama's response, Roerich refused to accept that Shambala did not have an earthly manifestation. What he did not realize is that such a refusal denies entry to the sacred realm.

*To all dreamers, artists, mystics, lovers and explorers, for you
are the meaning of life.*

CONTENTS

Prologue

Perched upon a wind swept crag like a hellish gargoyle, Mahakala looked across a barren, chasm-scarred plain. His rancor intensified as the growing darkness revealed the faint glow of Shambala beyond a distant range of snow-capped mountains. There, he had been Lord Protector and supreme leader of eight demon-gods avowed to defend the Path of Enlightenment. For more than two thousand years, he had ensured mortals passage to the upper realms, but no longer would he suffer the humiliation. Before the Taming, unshackled by human concerns, they were masters of the middle realms, but they had allowed themselves to be reduced to glorified guard dogs. The Path of Enlightenment offered them nothing. As leader, he took the initiative to restore their dignity. He had risked negotiating a dangerous alliance with Munpa Zerden, the Master of Eighty-thousand Negativities. When he returned from Naraka and presented the offer to his fellow demon-gods, he expected their support, but despite urging and coercion, only three were willing to join him.

Regrettably, four were not enough to wrench Shambala from the grip of its defenders. The fools clung to wishful prophecies and empty promises, denying the fact that Shambala's influence was fading. In the past millennium, the signs had been growing ever more apparent that humans were unworthy. The inevitable truth was that Zerden and his black chaos were destined to swallow Shambala and its defenders. If it had not been for that cursed dakini cow, Palden, his plan would have succeeded. As his former consort, he felt particularly betrayed by her opposition. She argued vehemently against him and denounced his proposition, but the greatest insult was turning the Shield against him. He never suspected that a demon-god would be trusted with the secrets of the Shield. It was the one power that could destroy an immortal. She cleverly used her dakini forces to draw him beyond the Shield where she could shut him out. Now exiled, he and his allies

1

had to fight their way back to the center of power. Although the defeat was disappointing, victory was only postponed. Zerden's forces grew stronger each day and Shambala would fall. Even now, his nagu armies were establishing strongholds near Shambala and he had shown Zerden the means to attack Shambala's defenders on other fronts. Once the Shield was destroyed, human sentients would have but one path, the path to Zerden and the lower realms. It was only a matter of time and as an immortal, he had plenty of that.

While brooding over his circumstance, he noticed movement on the plain. A human-sized figure ran toward him with great speed; flying more than running as it leapt over boulders and chasms. It was not one of his scouts, more likely one of those interfering monks on a mission to defend the outland borders. A glint of light emanating from beneath the robes confirmed his suspicion. The figure was aiming for the main road to Naraka that crossed the plain. Without hesitation, Mahakala leapt from the cliff. In an instant, he was on the plain, the earth quaking under his monstrous weight. His three eyes burned like red coals in pitch as he fixed his attention on the puny human. Without hesitation, he raced to his quarry with impossible speed, wielding a weapon in each of his six arms.

Noticing the demon's approach, the monk abruptly halted on the road and pulled a phurba from his robes, its three-sided blade glowed with an intense blue-white light. In a desperate fury, Mahakala flung his tilug, sending it spinning across the final distance to sweep off the monk's head, but he was too late to stop the phurba from piercing the earth. A dome of light bloomed on the plain. Mahakala's momentum suddenly turned against him and he recoiled half the distance to the cliff base. Spitting and cursing, he stumbled as he tried to regain his footing. To avoid its white-hot field of energy, Zerden's minions would need to build a bypass road. For him, a fixed phurba was another annoyance in this annoying war, a futile gesture of resistance. A thousand phurbas planted in the Asura outlands could not stop the onslaught that he was preparing to unleash. "Let them waste their precious phurbas on the plain," he snarled.

As he made his rounds in the deepest chambers of the lamasery, Tenzin held a butter oil lamp in one hand and an intricately carved jadestone rod in the other. His ancient, weathered face glowed as he navigated a narrow circular passageway giving access to eight windowless cells sealed with disks of stone. Each door bore a silver inlay of one of the Eight Auspicious Symbols, brightly reflecting the circle of light cast by the lamp. Using his stone rod, he tapped three times on each door and waited for a response. Two dull thuds answered from all but the cell marked with the Sign of the Conch. With furrowed brow, Tenzin rolled the silent door aside with a heave of his shoulder. Pushing the lamp into the dark gap with an outstretched arm, he squeezed through the opening, his robes scraping on rough-hewn stone. The lamplight revealed Brother Norbu's headless body slumped on the floor. No blood flowed from the cauterized stump of neck. Nearby, upon a cushion, lay a severed head with Norbu's face bearing a serene smile and half-closed eyes. Tenzin sighed, saddened by the loss of another brother, but Norbu's smile was some consolation; perhaps at least a minor blow had been struck for Shambala's cause. Still, it was a serious loss, as the ranks of the Kalacakra masters grew thinner each day; he doubted there would be another ready soon enough to replace his lost brother. Tenzin set down his lamp and jadestone rod. He lovingly picked up the severed head and recited the Bardo prayers to guide his brother's spirit on the journey to his next incarnation.

"Brother Norbu, listen carefully and without distraction. Now, pure luminosity of Dharmata is shining before you, recognize it. O child of noble family, at this moment your state of mind is by nature pure emptiness. When you recognize this pure nature of your mind as the Buddha, looking into your own mind is resting in the Buddha-mind…"

Shield of Shambala

*Gesar Despa felt as if he had suddenly forgotten where he was. "Where am I?" he thought, tightening his arms about himself in response to a frosty gust of wind. His clothing was not his own. His strange boots stood on a rock strewn path shadowed by a range of snow-capped mountains. A pink glow illuminated the snowy mountaintops, suggesting it was early morning or evening. Nearby, in the midst of the path was an unexpected but familiar structure, a brightly painted choten containing a statue of the Buddha within a carved niche. Beyond the choten, the path wound steadily upward skirting the edge of a chasm between slate-blue mountains. His Tibetan grandfather had described such scenes of choten shrines on remote mountain paths and it struck him that he must be somewhere in the Himalayas.

Confused, he scanned up and down the trail for any clue that might lead him to shelter. A feeling that safety and warmth lay beyond the mountains compelled him to climb toward the gap in the range. Yet, the pass was likely miles away and well above the snow line, an unlikely place for a safe haven. Despite his misgivings, he started upward, passing the shrine on its left as his grandfather had taught him. He had not walked far when he noticed a dark shape about the height of man drop from the shadows of a rocky hillock onto the path ahead. The man-like creature quickly gained its footing and began running toward him. Moving against a background of flint grey rock, it seemed more a ghost than solid flesh, but despite its ethereal appearance there was malevolence in the creature's movement; it was clearly not coming to welcome him. A sharp weapon drawn from beneath its black cloak dispelled any lingering doubts about intentions. On the narrow and exposed path, retreat was not an option; an encounter with the creature was inevitable. Gesar's years of martial arts training were about to be tested in deadly combat. His mind raced, using the seconds to seek a weakness in his attacker, but more importantly, a way to neutralize the weapon. The only weakness he could discern was unbridled speed.

In the next breath, the attacker was upon him. A fearsome war helmet with long fangs carved on each side of the mouth slot hid the attacker's face, but the weapon, a short sword-spear with a double-edged blade, was the main concern. Gesar spun aside and blocked the spear shaft with his right forearm, letting his attacker pass by carried by his own momentum. As he passed, Gesar noticed a grisly shirt of mail made of small bones stained pitch black beneath its cloak. Gesar reset his stance, expecting his opponent to turn and attack again, but instead, the creature adeptly thrust the spear shaft backward jabbing Gesar squarely in the abdomen. After the ease of the initial deflection, Gesar was unprepared for the explosive pain and force of the blow. He stumbled backward and fell to the ground stunned. His attacker turned and raised his weapon to make the final kill, but suddenly there was a blur and flash of shining metal. The attacker's spear and arm fell harmlessly to the ground. Surprised and apparently numb to pain, the wounded creature looked skyward for the source of the strike. Gesar followed the attacker's gaze. Above, riding on the back of a great bird, was a woman in turquoise body armor wielding a sword. Her face, wreathed in wind blown black hair, bore an expression of defiance as she guided her mount to drop for a second attack. With his remaining arm, the creature fumbled among his garments for another weapon, but his awkwardness spent precious time. Before he drew his throwing dagger, his helmeted head tumbled to the ground.

Gesar got back on his feet and leaned against a boulder for support; he had witnessed the bizarre scene with combined awe and disbelief. It required incredible strength to decapitate a man with a single sword blow, yet this strange woman riding on the back of a mythical bird made it look effortless. The great bird with its rider alighted on the path. The woman dismounted, sheathed her sword and strode past her headless victim without a passing glance. At close proximity, she was a classic Hellenic beauty with an athletic body who could easily play the role of the goddess Artemis or an ancient queen of Sparta.

She looked at Gesar with large dark eyes filled with concern. "Are you injured?"

Gesar winced as he drew a breath to speak. "Not seriously. He, or whatever that is, surprised me. He used a tricky move, thrusting backward while moving forward. The blow hurt a lot more than I expected. I'm just bruised, there's no blood."

5

The young woman smiled, enhancing an already striking countenance. "Good. I was worried that you received a mortal blow. You did well avoiding the first attack. That was an elite nagu fang warrior, we call them drons. You're lucky that I noticed him during my fly over. The nagu drons have been watching the chotens waiting for the arrival of new Buddha warriors and killing them while they are disoriented. We try to defend the chotens, but there are more than we can defend and we never know exactly when or where a new warrior will come to us. Before the rebellion, the dron scouts feared the chotens."

The woman's incomprehensible words were only compounding Gesar's confusion. He had not yet recovered from having just seen her step off the back of a mythical creature out of one of his grandfather old stories. None of this is real, he thought. "Who are you and where is this place?"

"Forgive me. I'm Ane and that's my mount, Brug. I forgot how disorienting it is for the newly awakened. I was in a pretty bad state when I arrived. It was at this very choten, but that seems like a long time ago now. As to your second question, that is a little more difficult to explain. You are in Asura, one of the realms of existence. Like you, I had a life in the Human realm, or what you might call the "real world" where there are no kinnaras like Brug. Complex machines can't exist here, but many things in the Human realm are reflected in some way here. I was a helicopter pilot in the Human realm. Here, I'm also sort of a pilot except I have Brug instead of an attack helicopter."

If nothing else, the pain in this realm certainly seemed real. Gesar suppressed an urge to groan as he took another breath to ask, "How did I get here?"

"I don't know. For that matter, I don't know how I got here. All I know is that I have not gone back. Some of the awakened warriors stay permanently, a few are here only briefly and still others come and go. There are monks who come and go at will. They bring messages and have special abilities and weapons. One thing that I am sure of, if you are here then Shambala needs you. I'm sorry if it's not a very satisfying explanation but it's as good as I can offer. Now perhaps, you will tell me your name."

Gesar hesitated. Shambala, he had not heard that word since childhood. Shambala was a myth, a fairytale land. This beautiful woman, her giant bird and strange place had shattered his sense of reality. His vision blurred, resisting this bizarre unreality.

"Are you sure you're okay?" Ane asked.

"Yeah, I'm okay." He lied. "Gesar, my name is Gesar."

"That's a Tibetan name, isn't it?" she asked.

Gesar's head throbbed, but he managed a response. "Yeah, not too many people know that. I got it from my grandfather, he was born there. This place looks like the pictures he showed me. I thought this place might be Tibet."

"Actually it's more accurate to say that Tibet looks like this place," Ane corrected. "A Tibetan grandfather eh? You might be the first Tibetan that I have met here who was not a monk or nun. Most of us are given Tibetan names, but you already have one. Gesar, that's an important name in Tibetan history isn't it? If I remember correctly, he was sort of a King Arthur character, right? Obviously, your grandfather thought you were special."

Gesar felt dizzy. He was beginning to tremble. Emotionally, he was overwhelmed, but he strained to stay focused on the conversation. He purposely avoided looking in the direction of the huge scaly headed bird perched on a rock outcropping, preening itself. "I...I'm half Tibetan and my grandfather spent a lot of time with me before he died. I still don't understand. Why am I here?"

Ane's brow furrowed with concern. "You're shaking. That usually means you need to go back soon. We must return to the choten, but first let me take care of this mess. It's contaminating sacred ground. It's not good to use a choten with dead dron warriors around."

She walked to the headless corpse still sprawled askance on the path. Removing an amulet bearing the image of the Buddha from beneath her turquoise mail, she carefully set it upon the ground next to the body. She then reached into an embroidered pouch hanging from her belt and drew out a pinch of rust-colored sand. Chanting a prayer, she carefully sprinkled the sand in a circle around the body and upon the severed parts. After completing the circle, she stepped back. She clapped her hands together once. Suddenly, there was a flash of white light and the body and all of its weaponry transformed into dust.

"Good, the space has been cleansed. You can use the choten now." Ane announced. She picked up the amulet and returned it to its place under her mail shirt. When she turned around, Gesar was shaking more violently. Quickly, she put an arm around him to support his weight. Remarkably strong, she nearly took all of his weight as she directed him along the trail. In a few moments, they had reached the choten.

"Lean against the choten. Put one hand on the Buddha figure and look into its eyes," she instructed. "Now say, Namo Amida Buddha."

Gesar did as she instructed. The Buddha's eyes had gold irises and black pupils; its captivating gaze calmed his trembling and allowed him to say the words he had first learned from his grandfather, *Namo Amida Buddha. I take refuge in the awakened one.* Gesar's hand warmed and heat flowed through his arm and quickly permeated his whole body. A moment later, he felt as if he was on fire. The Buddha faded into a blinding light and he heard Ane call out.

"I will look for your return!"

Gesar's bedding and tee-shirt were soaked in sweat. Images from his bizarre dream lingered in his mind's eye. Part of him remained on the mountain path staring into the Buddha's golden eyes. For a time, his senses struggled for a footing in waking reality. The cacophony of street traffic leaking through an open window helped bring him to consciousness. He forced his eyes open. Sunlight reflecting from the windows of the high-rise across the street beamed onto his bedroom wall and he suddenly realized he had overslept. Jerking upright, he felt a sharp pain in his abdomen and visions of the spear shaft, the beautiful woman and the mythic bird flashed into his mind.

"Weird dream," he said recalling the kick to his stomach he had received during the kung fu tournament on the previous evening. As he made his way to the bathroom, he became aware of other aches and pains, especially his bruised abdomen. It had been a challenging tourney, but ultimately he did win the trophy and prize money; it was his first international competition. He remembered achieving a perfect state of mind-body harmony in the final bout. He calmly watched his opponent become increasingly frustrated as his blows were constantly blocked. In the end, the man's frustration defeated him. Desperation led to mistakes and mistakes led to defeat.

Gesar reached to turn on the shower tap, numbness and tingling bolted through his right hand. He could barely grip and turn the knob. As he painfully stepped in to shower, he recalled the dream again, the little shrine, the unusual strength in his body. The hot water started to clear his head. That kick under the arm from that Indonesian, he remembered. It must have done some nerve damage. "Damn, I can't go to work like this. I'll have to cancel teaching today!"

Chidag Nagpo, child and minion of Munpa Zerden, woke in his new flesh. Energy surged through his torso, arousing a silent heart and pumping warm blood like waves of dark life to his extremities. Air rushed to fill the emptiness in a chest throbbing with exquisite pain. Unusual odors entered his nostrils. Strange sounds and foreign words entered his consciousness. All of these sensations were unfamiliar to one who had existed as an immortal in the Asura realm. To carry out his mission in this strange realm, he would have to rely on the host that he possessed.

"Nurse, put away the paddles. His pulse is back and he's breathing regularly. The police will be happy to learn that we just saved one of their finest. I really didn't think he'd make it. I was just about to call off the code."

"Look doctor, his wounds have stopped bleeding," the nurse announced.

The doctor examined the wounds with amazement. "That's a first for me. This guy's blood must clot fast. Move him to intensive care and hang two more units of red cells. Those gunshot wounds took a lot of blood out of him."

Chidag felt weakness in this new form. Only moments before, he was in Asura among the wellsprings of suffering and the eighty-thousand negativities. As the oldest and strongest of Zerden's children, he was chosen to make the first journey, but his companions would follow soon. While often tampering with the Human realm through secondary forces, it had been a long time since Zerden's children had manifest directly among mortals. The bodhisattva laws of dimensionality prevented it, or so they had believed. Instead, they discovered their restriction was only a matter of dominance. Shambala had held sway since the Taming and the secret of travel between the realms was known only to a select few. With the shifting of power, the demon-gods, Mahakala, Yama, Kubera and Changpa Karpo, had defected and brought the secret of the passage with them. Mahakala showed them how to find the weak points in the barrier that separated Asura from the human world. Ironically, the mortals created the weak points by their passages between the worlds. Since the beginning, they had moved between the worlds either knowingly or unknowingly, leaving transient points of weakness that could be used to make passage. While a demon-god like Mahakala could not pass through such an opening, a lesser demon like Chidag could, as he had now proved. However, the journey required incarnating a weak and tediously slow piece of flesh. He would test the physical limits of this incarnation, but for now he needed time to adapt to this human body.

Tethered with thin pipes and wires, Chidag's new body was being moved by human attendants. A mask supplying him with metallic flavored air covered his nose and mouth. The smell reminded him of the odor in the air after a battle of fire swords. He cracked open his eyes and quickly closed them. The intense light was unbearable. No longer did he have the nictating membrane that normally protected him from the sunlight of Asura. His new body knew what words to use. "Give me my sunglasses," he ordered, but the plastic mask muffled the sound.

"Doctor, I think he's trying to talk," a nurse pointed out.

"This one's a tough cookie, he should be unconscious. Take off the mask and listen to what he's saying," the doctor ordered.

The nurse lifted the oxygen mask and waited for the patient to speak again. "Give me my sunglasses," Chidag repeated.

"He must be delirious, he's asking for sunglasses," the nurse reported.

The doctor laughed and patted the patient's knee, as he walked alongside the rolling gurney. "I'm sorry Officer Cutter, but it's a little too soon for you to go back out on patrol. If you had sunglasses, they will be among the personal items in your room."

Chidag groaned in frustration. He already despised these mortals. In his world, he would have eaten them alive after a suitable punishment. It was ludicrous that the demon-gods of Shambala had wasted their time serving these beings; they were clearly meant to be slaves. Yet to his vexation and that of the other captains of Zerden's armies, Shambala had successfully defended itself by recruiting from these humans, some of whom were especially troublesome. For that reason, he was given the mission to seek out and destroy them in their own world, stopping the infestation at its source. The rebel demon-gods of Shambala had made this possible by revealing the way to discorporate and pass into the human realm. His true body lay within the walls of Naraka, unconscious and vulnerable but under the watchful eye of Zerden and the protection of elite dron guards. He was free to fulfill his mission. Somewhere in this city slept the helpless bodies of the annoying humans serving as defenders of Shambala. As soon as his human form was ready, he would hunt them.   Fortunately, the body that he possessed had a detailed knowledge of the city, a fact that could only hasten his success.

Chidag flicked his eyes open. At the end of a hallway, a shaven headed human watched him. Quickly, the human averted his gaze, but not before Chidag noticed the bright flash of turquoise behind the pupils. "So, they have found me already. I must be careful." Chidag thought.

ༀ

ulku Lama Jhado Zhangpo's shaven head glowed orange in the morning sunlight as he looked east from his chamber window. In a distant gap between mountain slopes, there was a glimpse of green, the Zhaxika grasslands. On that vast ocean of grass roamed the famed horsemen of the Sun Tribe among which his lamasery had essential allies. A glimpse of the grasslands was discernable only from his chamber, located in the highest point of the lamasery. Carved from a mountainside, the lamasery faced a mostly barren high plateau cut with a river gorge and bordered by steep foothills. It had stood undisturbed for more than two millennia and was so cleverly camouflaged that the Chinese army had literally marched past its front gate without noticing the ancient structure. The secret of the temple's location depended on caution and devotion. Only the most trusted monks, nuns and allies knew the lamasery's location and after the Chinese invasion, many had sought permanent refuge there. Just a selected few on the outside had knowledge of Dagpa Akar, the Sacred White Crystal Temple.

Presently, Jhado made his daily assessment of the mani wall that was under construction. Beyond the lamasery's inner walls, brothers dressed in rust-orange robes were chanting in unison as they stacked a line of flat stones, not ordinary stones, but stones engraved with a six-syllable mantra of protection. Slowly and with deep focus they stacked a low wall around the exposed perimeter of the lamasery. The wall was only as good as the prayer energy that imbued it. A child could easily jump over it, but it would be as impassable as a mountain range for any malevolent force attempting to enter the temple. However, mani walls had not been put to a real test in many lifetimes, a respite that was possibly coming to an end. The mani wall was but one of many levels of protection that the lamasery might need. Jhado had learned recently of a threat to the barrier between realms, a dreadful development, shifting a balance of power that had held for thousands of years. Soon the Kalacakra might be fighting battles in two realms. At any time or place, the minions of Munpa Zerden could incarnate in the human realm and begin hunting the Sleepers and their protectors. Upon receiving the warning, he immediately initiated defensive measures and alerted brothers and sisters around the world to watch for enemy incarnates and move the Sleepers to safer havens.

Satisfied with the progress of the mani wall, Jhado walked to a window that overlooked the inner courtyard and gardens. The gardens were among his greatest joys, reminding him that forces of light still held sway in the universe. The fruit trees were ripening and vegetables were nearing time for harvest. Unfortunately, many of the flowerbeds had been replaced by solar panels in order to provide electrical power to his computer and satellite uplink. Sunlight was plentiful at the lamasery's elevation so the storage batteries were usually well charged. The solar panels, batteries, and computer were another compromise needed in the fight against Munpa Zerden. Transporting them to the lamasery was difficult and risky, potentially revealing the lamasery's location. Horse and camel caravans guided by their allies among the Sun Tribe carried disassembled parts carefully hidden in bags of barley and rice. When the various components were assembled and installed, Jhado was surprised by how easy it was to learn their use. Computer logic seemed to bear a certain clarity that was quite compatible with the disciplined mind of a monk. The major element missing from the computer mind was compassion. His first exploration of the internet reaffirmed his commitment to his cause and religion. Thousands of websites plainly illustrated the struggle between spiritual evolution and chaos. Sadly, the vast majority of the world's population was ignorant of their imminent danger and knew nothing of the small group of Kalacakra monks and nuns that bravely held back the tsunami of chaos. And he, an ordinary stocky monk with deep knowing eyes set above smooth childlike cheeks was their spiritual toehold.

Jhado went to his desk and turned on his computer to check for messages. Due to the risk of discovery, he had no electronic mail address. Instead, he used an independent blog as a proxy messaging board where Kalacakra agents posted messages in the form of Haiku poetry. They communicated regularly from their temples or internet cafés in the countries where they lived. Only he and his personal assistant at the lamasery knew the pseudonyms used by the agents.

After opening the blog site, he scrolled through several pages before recognizing the name of one his agents, Kasa.

Spring rains have started.
The ancient roof is leaking.
Drops snuff our candles.
Kasa

To Jhado the message was clear. His fear had been realized. At least one of Zerden's minions had slipped between realms and incarnated in the human realm. With the ancient barrier breached, the enemy could attack the sleeping Buddha warriors directly. It was critical to cast the interloper back into its realm, but in the meantime, they had to monitor the creature while they prepared. The old manuscripts described the method; it meant getting dangerously close to the demon and it had been millennia since the technique had been put to the test. Kasa's temple was in the United States near San Francisco, California. The demon's place of incarnation was clearly a tactical choice, a large contingent of Sleepers were under Kasa's care. Jhado quickly composed a haiku with instructions.

Spring rains fall early.
Showing the path to oneness.
The silent sea waits.
Dan Poe

For Kasa, the source and meaning of the message should be evident. He would notice that the poem repeated a key part of his original message and know that it was intended as a directed response. More importantly, he would recognize the pseudonym, Dan Poe, a play on the Tibetan word, danpo, meaning "the first". He had instructed Kasa to watch and wait, reporting developments as needed.

Jhado was trained to control negative emotion, but in face of this report, he struggled to suppress his anxiety. Not since before the Taming had the barrier between realms been violated. The Kalacakra adepts monitoring the demon would be in danger, but more worrisome was that the Buddha warriors were sure to be its targets. Strategies and defenses needed to be coordinated between the realms of existence. A messenger needed to be sent immediately to inform Lady Palden. Unfortunately, his first choice, brother Norbu had recently died in the meditation chambers beneath the lamasery.

Finding another messenger to journey to Shambala on short notice would be difficult, only the most skilled adepts could move between existences and their numbers were few. After a brief meditation to purge his fear, Jhado left his chamber to inquire if there were any among the senior Bhikshu who could make the journey. If there were none suitable, he would go himself, despite Tenzin's objections.

Gesar waited patiently in Dr. Hoskie Ashki's examination room. The problem with his right arm did not clear up in a few days, so he reluctantly made an appointment at the University Hospital clinic. After numerous tests involving scans and needles, he was about to get a final diagnosis. The doctor had looked over the test results and left the room, supposedly to get a second opinion from a colleague. The forced smile on the doctor's face as he left the room was distressing. Gesar had not forgotten the vivid dream he had the night after the kung-fu tourney. The pain and weakness in is right arm was a constant reminder of it. Strangely, his subconscious mind had twisted around circumstances. In his dream, his arm was fine, actually better than fine, stronger and nearly impervious to discomfort. It had deflected the bizarre attacker almost effortlessly.

The arm weakness prevented him from practicing kung fu, but at least he could still function at his day job using his left arm. Luckily, teaching was not too physically demanding. He was already largely ambidextrous and could easily write with his left hand. His students had not even questioned the change. Their tall, half-Tibetan instructor with shoulder length black hair had regularly presented them with new challenges, so they assumed his switch to left-handedness was some new self-imposed discipline. They were still reeling from the midterm exam in which they were required to identify Asian statuary by touch alone. Gesar enjoyed watching the surprised expressions when his students stepped into the testing room to find twenty boxes covered by opaque black drapes. Despite the difficulty of his exams, his classes were always full and no one complained of boredom.

Unlike his students, Gesar was getting bored of waiting; he had finished his survey of the various horse breeds displayed in photos on the walls of Dr. Ashki's waiting room. It was easy for him to identify the breeds. Horseback riding was his other passion; it was in his blood. His ancestors were from Kham, known as the Khampa. They

15

were legendary horsemen of eastern Tibet, fiercely independent warriors, who the Chinese could never quite completely subjugate. His grandfather likely would have died fighting in Tibet had he not assisted the escape of a lama and a group of his senior monks. After an arduous trek through the Himalayas, grandfather Despa safely escorted his family and the lama to India. Eventually, his Western educated son brought the old man to the United States to be with his family and to teach his grandson Kham traditions. As a child, Gesar spent many weekends with his grandfather riding rented horses and one day hoped to have one of his own. Depending on the doctor's diagnosis, that was possibly a moot ambition.

Gesar let the depressing thought go and considered doing some meditation to clear his head when he recognized his doctor's footsteps. The step pattern included a slight but distinct drag and shuffle due to an old sports injury. Dr. Ashki was a big man of Navajo descent; he had been a college football star in his youth with million dollar contract offers from professional teams, but that all ended with a serious hip injury in his senior year. The injury motivated him to pursue a career in medicine. A moment later, the door opened and Dr. Ashki entered. His usual broad smile was gone, replaced by a stiff lip girding itself for an unpleasant task

Ashki hesitated. He hated having to deliver bad news, especially to the young ones. "Sorry to keep you waiting Mr. Despa, but I wanted to be absolutely sure before I told you anything. You seem like a man who doesn't like to be patronized, so I'm going to be straight with you. After looking over the test results and getting the opinion of a number of my colleagues, we agree that you have a rare neurodegenerative disorder. In your case, it has started with unilateral upper extremity paralysis, but it will likely progress to involve other limbs. In the worst-case scenario, you could be in a wheel chair by this time next year, but it is impossible to predict the course of the disease. That's basically it, without any sugar coating. I'll try my best to answer any questions that you may have."

Despite expecting bad news, Gesar was unprepared for what he heard. Did he say wheelchair? Automatically, his discipline reacted to the fear; controlled deep breaths tempered an instinctive surge of panic. While he breathed, he focused his attention on Dr. Ashki's turquoise studded silver watchband. Eventually, he relaxed enough to formulate a question. "Is the paralysis permanent?"

"Complete remissions have been reported in some cases and partial remission in others. About half of those affected die of complications within five years, but as I said, it is impossible to

16

predict the exact outcome. The case numbers are few and we have no idea what causes the disease. Since there are similarities to Guillian-Barre syndrome, viruses have been proposed, but again there are just not enough cases to do good research."

"Is there any treatment at all?" Gesar asked.

"I'm afraid nothing with proved benefit," Ashki answered. "If you wish, we could try an empiric course of steroids. There's a possibility it might slow the process, but there will be side effects."

Gesar remembered becoming nearly psychotic after taking steroids for a joint injury. "No. I think I'll pass on the steroids, any other advice?"

In spite of his intimidating defensive lineman-sized frame, Dr. Ashki's manner expressed almost a motherly compassion. "Son, do you have any family in the area?"

"No, they're all dead." Gesar answered. "Grandfather died of old age and my parents died in a car accident while on their way to speak at a Tibetan independence rally. The circumstances of the crash were suspicious. I've always suspected Chinese agents."

Ashki looked into Gesar's eyes and saw the raw pain of personal loss, despite their stoic facade. "I'm sorry to hear that. I was hoping you had some family support. It's going to be tough. These situations are especially hard for young people like you who are used to being active. To have your lifestyle suddenly taken away might make you feel angry and betrayed. My advice is to take one day at time and deal with each disability as it comes. Focus on adapting and keeping to your routine as much as possible. I will set you up with regular neurology appointments to keep track of things. I promise you my full support through this unfortunate event, however it may come out."

Ashki was hitting the mark. He had obviously dealt with similar situations before; Gesar was already feeling anger and self-pity. "I guess the Buddha was right when he said suffering is unavoidable in this world."

Dr. Ashki gently placed one of his large palms on Gesar's shoulder and said, "That may be true, but I thought the Buddha taught a way to go beyond suffering. You don't have to think of it as suffering. My grandfather was a Navajo medicine man. He was blind and crippled by polio, but he became one the greatest healers among the Dineh. He once told me that when we lose a physical capacity in this world, it is meant to be used in the spirit world. He said that in the spirit world, he could fly and see like an eagle. For the Navajo that's a wonderful gift."

"My grandfather was from Tibet, he had some similar notions," Gesar said, recalling the strength he felt in his body in that bizarre dream.

"I'm not surprised," Dr. Ashki replied. "I understand Navajo and Tibetans have a lot in common. Both cultures value turquoise, weaving and sand paintings. Both live in lands occupied by conquerors. Both have sacred mountains and we even look alike. Perhaps, we're long lost brothers. We should compare family albums someday."

Gesar laughed. He appreciated the doctor's attempt to cheer him, but he doubted the feeling would last. He left the clinic intending to marshal all of his physical and spiritual strengths to deal with an uncertain future.

alden Lhamo entered the Jewel Heart of Shambala, the great temple hall of Kalapa Palace. As a demon-god, she once bore a wrathful form, but since the Taming had adopted an angelic persona, which was a divine beauty with flowing black hair, shining dark eyes, high cheekbones, and unblemished golden skin. Her head was crowned with a silver circlet set with a glowing turquoise skull nested within the horns of a crescent moon. Her gown was full-length, dark blue and studded with a myriad of tiny jewels. She floated across the floor, knelt, and prostrated herself before Sangpo Bumtri, whose ethereal image sat in perpetual meditation within a pillar of blue-white flame that rose up from a throne set upon a tiered dais at the center of the hall. The creator existed as pure illumination in neither physical form nor dimension; his energy opened the portal to the higher realms and maintained the power of Shambala's Shield.

Assembled around the throne-altar, fellow demon-gods, captains, and phalanxes of Buddha warriors waited patiently for Palden to speak. After the rebellion, she replaced Mahakala as supreme leader of the Council of Guardians and was responsible for the defense of Shambala. Before speaking, she bowed to each of her fellow faithful demon-gods standing nearby. After the Taming, each had acquired an angelic form and pledged an oath to defend the Path of Enlightenment. Yamantaka, the Enemy of Death, appeared as a kindly ancient hermit attired in rags and holding a white staff topped with a carved bull's head. Hayagriva, the Keeper of Wisdom, took the form of a white-bearded monk dressed in orange robes; his only adornment was a necklace of dzi beads from which hung an ivory amulet carved into the shape of a horse's head. Betsge, the Protector, appeared as a tall horse warrior, dressed in mail decorated with a cuirass of polished copper, a goatskin cloak, and high riding boots. A sheathed sword was at his hip and a bow strapped to his back.

Missing from the assembly were the rebel demon-gods, Mahakala, Yama, Kubera and Changpa Karpo, all of whom had reverted to their wrathful forms upon their exile to the outlands of Asura. After the rebellion, the faithful demon-gods redistributed the former responsibilities of the rebels, such that all of Changpa's tapah cavalry units were under Begtse's command while Hayagriva and Yamantaka assumed the palace operational duties of Yama and Kubera. Palden continued command of the dakini aerial units but acquired Mahakala's title as Defender of the Palace.

As Palden took stock of her audience, she noticed Ane among the captains. Of all of Shambala's defenders, Ane had nearly caused her to succumb to the transgression of attachment. Ane was the best of her dakini warriors and quickly rose to the rank of first-captain. In training sessions, Ane had nearly defeated her demon-god instructor, a feat that elicited a certain pride in Palden. Yet, pride itself was a dangerous state of mind; it was an aspect of attachment that could lead a demon-god to revert to the 'old ways'. Was attachment the weakness that would ultimately undermine her will? Perhaps attachment was a weakness of femininity, she thought. Human females developed strong attachments to their children. She was the only female guardian among the original eight. She had even been consort to Mahakala, but it was unlikely that maternal emotions extended to demon-gods. Before the Taming, she was a monster, indulging in every transgression, slaughtering uncountable numbers of sentient beings without the slightest regret. Despite this, she found herself thinking of Ane as a daughter and it saddened her that Ane's time in Shambala would be as brief as all of the other mortals recruited from the human world over the centuries.

When she finally spoke, Palden's voice emanated from every corner of the great hall. One of her powers as a demon-god was to awaken sound from stone and earth. "Defenders of Shambala, we have thus far held the rebels at bay," she began. "Your selfless acts of courage have thwarted the forces of Zerden, but our enemies are not defeated. Constantly, they probe our borders searching for weakness but the Shield remains intact. I now see the wisdom of the Bodhisattvas in entrusting me with the secret of the Shield, but unfortunately, not all secrets were only mine to keep. The unfaithful rebels, now exiled to the Asura outlands, were also entrusted with important knowledge. This day, a messenger from our Kalacakra allies in the Human realm brings news that at least one of those secrets has been revealed to our enemies. Mahakala has shown the children of Zerden how to enter the Human realm where our allies and warriors are most vulnerable. Zerden's first born, Chidag Nagpo, has successfully made the crossing. All of you know the significance of this news. We were unprepared for this tactic and presently we have no defense. I called this meeting to discuss a response and I ask my fellow guardians to speak first."

There was a prolonged silence while the assembly considered Palden's words. Hayagriva spoke first. "This seems to be a desperate act on the part of our enemies. To incarnate in the Human realm requires leaving their immortal form and then searching for our allies among billions of sentient beings. Even avatars that have gone to work among humankind have not fared well. Most were punished and killed for their teachings."

Begtse's armor clattered as he stepped forward to address the assembly. "My brother, you fail to consider our enemy's purpose. They do not intend expose themselves in order to improve humanity. They intend to hunt and kill by stealth, biding their time and remaining in the shadows until the right moment to strike."

Yamantaka, known for his wisdom, tapped his staff on the stone floor, drawing the assembly's immediate attention. In a commanding voice that belied his ancient form, he said, "Do not forget that demons do not sacrifice all of their power when they incarnate as mortals. The energy they infuse into mortal flesh will enhance healing, strength and prolong life. They cannot be subdued easily."

"They still must find our allies to destroy them," Hayagriva retorted.

Palden raised a palm and all eyes fell upon her. "In that regard, they may have another advantage," she said. "Mahakala knows that the choten portals can lead to a Buddha warrior's place of origin. We know that warriors from similar locations in the Human realm often arrive by the same choten. I suspect that the nagu drons posted at the chotens serve not only to kill new Buddha warriors, but to alert Mahakala when the portals are used."

Begtse responded immediately. "Then there is only one course of action. Our allies must move the Sleepers to defensible locations."

"This is already underway, but it can be done for only some of the Buddha warriors. Some cannot be moved and the location of others is unknown," said Palden.

"Many from my squadron have no memory of where their bodies sleep in the Human realm." Ane shouted.

Palden was surprised by the delight she experienced upon hearing Ane's voice and more surprised by the concern she felt for her safety. I must meditate upon this attachment, she thought.

Begtse continued. "At least we can protect those that can be located and we should set guards upon the chotens."

"I completely agree with your plan my brother, but its success may be difficult to achieve," Palden answered. "The Kalacakra have already anticipated the danger. Even now, they search for enemy incarnations and protect our warriors by whatever means necessary, but they face a daunting task with limited resources. We likewise will have great difficultly guarding the chotens. While the Kalacakra have the skill to enter the Asura realm where they desire, the Buddha warriors arrive without warning and usually beyond the protection of the Shield. The dakinis cannot defend all of the chotens in the Asura outlands. Already our forces are spread thinly, reconnoitering the outlands and attacking enemy columns on the Plain of Deception. If they are stationed at the chotens they will become easy targets for our enemies."

Ane's voice broke in again. "Lady Palden, I have a proposal."

"Please share it captain. We are open to all suggestions."

Ane took a moment to compose her self. She had never fully overcome a certain apprehension at speaking in the presence of immortals. "I have ordered my dakini company to include a sweep of the outer chotens at the end of each patrol. By doing this we have eliminated a respectable number of dron scouts. Each warrior is assigned a choten with instructions to attack only an enemy that they can handle. They are not to challenge any force that might be superior in numbers or strength. We then reassemble on the Kalapa ramparts and count heads. So far, those have only been the heads of dron scouts. I suggest extending this practice to all of the dakini companies. We can at least minimize the number of chotens that are under watch by Zerden's forces."

Palden smiled. "I should have expected such initiative from you Ane. Your independent action may have already hampered our foes. If the other dakini captains agree, I think we should implement Ane's proposal immediately."

There was some additional discussion, but no dissent. All agreed that Ane's plan would require added effort and danger, but the potential impact would far outweigh the risk. Begtse patted Ane on the back, Hayagriva gave her a respectful nod, and she thought she noticed a wink from the old hermit, Yamantaka. Palden avoided direct eye contact. After additional prostrations before Sangpo's altar, she floated out of the hall as she had entered. When Palden and the other demon-gods had left, the warriors remaining in the hall likewise bowed to the altar before leaving. Each squadron followed their captain in ordered formations.

Ane led her squadron of sixty-four women dressed in armor down a wide stair to a windowed causeway that connected directly to the outer wall. The sun was low over the western wall and it was nearing time to begin the night patrols. Due to a distortion of light caused by the Shield, the sun appeared as a slightly flattened orange ball haloed by a sparkling blue mist. The Shield was Shambala's primary metaphysical defense and no malevolent force had ever penetrated it. Its power emanated from the throne in the temple dome at the summit of the island city. Even without the protection of the Shield, Kalapa palace would not fall easily to a siege. Eight enclosed causeways extended spoke-like from the upper plaza to eight towers that stood upon ramparts rising hundreds of feet above the valley floor. A network of gardens, housing, stables and practice fields filled the tiers between the palace summit and the outer walls. Each of the guardians lived in one of the eight towers, of which only four were occupied since the rebellion. After the unfaithful demon-gods were exiled, Palden remained in her eastern tower while the others moved accordingly to restore a four direction defensive balance. Everything about the palace defied the laws of gravity, at least as Ane understood them. The towers were impossibly tall, the causeways spanned too great a distance, and the outer ramparts seemed to challenge the surrounding mountains for altitude. At times, she could see beyond the barrier-mountains from her chamber window. This was an effect of the Shield, which bent light as it passed over the mountains. The purpose was to provide a panorama of lands beyond the mountains when viewed from the sentinel towers, but under certain atmospheric conditions, the strange optical effect extended to the level of the upper ramparts where the dakinis were housed.

Being an island fortress, Kalapa palace was also protected by Lake Shambala which lapped against the base of its ramparts. No bridge allowed passage over the expanse of water. Entrance and exit involved temporarily freezing the lake. Miraculously, an avenue of ice formed as the cavalry rode out of the Vishvamata gate to go on patrols. Finger thick ice supported the weight of a thousand mounted defenders, but it would melt instantly under a single enemy footfall. Ane never learned how the lake discerned friend from foe, but it was rumored that the Eye of Vishvamata mandala carved over Kalapa's only entrance controlled the formation of the ice.

Beside the demon-gods, three human armies defended the palace and valley, the palace guards, tapah cavalries and dakini squadrons.

Eight divisions of palace guards, consisting of men and women, remained in the city. Horse mounted tapah patrolled the circuitous trails that enemies might use to penetrate the valley. More recently, the tapah were striking out onto the Plain of Deception to engage enemy forces, which required crossing the inner and outer barrier mountains. While the tapah were best for dealing with snow and rocky trails, the dakinis were far superior for mountain patrols. Nothing was better that an aerial view for keeping watch on large expanses and maneuvering narrow canyons. Dakinis also had the advantage of being able to descend upon an enemy in silence and with incredible speed. The dakini forces were women while the tapah were comprised of men. Unlike the palace guard, tapah and dakinis were segregated by sex because the kinnaras maneuvered better under the lighter body weight of the women. When combined in a coordinated battle formation, tapah and dakini armies could easily defeat a force twice their number.

Though the responsibility was great, Ane was happy as captain of the Druk dakini squadron. She loved the exhilaration of flight and never tired seeing Shambala's green valley greet her as she topped the barrier mountains on her return from a night patrol. Arising from a series of western tributaries, the silver ribbon of the Shenla River cut the length of the valley before draining into Lake Shambala. The quilted land south of the river was cultivated with crops and orchards, whereas an ancient green forest extended from north bank to the northern mountain range. The rich colors of the valley were a welcome sight after a night in cold grey canyons. The only thing Ane loved more than feeling the wind on her face was her mount, Brug. Like every dakini, she had a close telepathic bond with her kinnara. Any lesser alternative was not an option since the great raptors responded only to their bonded rider and would defend her to the death.

As Ane's squadron reached the halfway point along the causeway, their mounts began singing. The hearts and steps of every dakini hastened as the choir of hundreds of kinnaras joined in a perfect harmony, each calling to its rider. When they sang, the glow of Shambala's Shield brightened in intensity and residents in villages throughout the valley knew the Path of Enlightenment was preserved.

The causeway that Ane's squadron used ended at the base of Palden's tower where it joined the Wheel. The Wheel was a wide passage running through the outer rampart and wrapping the full circumference of Kalapa Palace. Doors along the Wheel marked entrances to personal living spaces and common rooms of the dakinis.

Each dakini shared a simple three-room living space with their respective mounts. The kinnaras roosted in the outer room with a large window that allowed them egress and ingress. When resting, the kinnaras usually perched at the window with their chest and heads projecting gargoyle-like from the upper ramparts.

Ane stopped and turned to face her squadron. The women following her, composed of eight groups of eight, halted in unison. Suddenly, the song of the kinnaras halted. Ane stood in silence on a wide step in front of a huge intricately carved wooden door that was the entrance to Palden's tower. The doors were sized to accommodate the guardians in their wrathful demon-god forms.

Ane pressed her palms together and bowed her head as a gesture of humility. Her squadron did likewise and together they recited the ritual blessing. "Let our souls shine with the Light of Illumination to drown the shadow of ignorance. Let our voices sing with the Harmony of Illumination to fill the emptiness of chaos. Let our eyes see with the Clarity of Illumination to lift the mist of deception. Let our swords burn with the Fire of Illumination to cut through the enemy of desire." Four times, they repeated the mantra, while simultaneously the other dakini squadrons at the other seven towers performed the same ritual.

When the mantra ended, Ane said, "You all heard Lady Palden approve of the strategy that we have been using to defend the chotens. You also know the risk of flying alone. As your captain, I remind you that each of you is of great value to Shambala and I order you not take unnecessary risks. If you encounter a rebel demon-god or one of Zerden's demon offspring get out as fast as you can. No matter how confident you might feel, do not engage. If you have the slightest suspicion of a trap, retreat immediately. Do you understand?"

The dakinis pressed their palms together and bowed their heads in deference.

"Good. Now, go to your mounts!" Ane ordered.

The song of the kinnaras resumed and the teams of dakinis streamed apart to go to their mounts. As first-captain, Ane's chamber was nearest to Palden's tower, so she was first to reach her rooms. Brug stopped singing when she entered his room and he twisted his neck around to nuzzle under her arm. "I love you too, Brug," Ane said, stroking the soft scales on the top of his broad head. His hooked beak was at least three hand lengths long and sharp enough to tear flesh from bones, but Ane had never suffered even the slightest scratch. Since the kinnaras were a blend of bird and reptile, the scales transitioned into feathers across the back creating a natural saddle.

Ane could easily ride Brug bare back, but all the kinnaras were fitted with a knee-well saddle and breast armor decorated with the unit's symbol. Brug bore the dragon symbol, the mark of the Druk dakini.

After making final adjustments to her armor, Ane hung a flask of amrita from her belt. The drink was all the sustenance she needed for her night's work. Not only did it provide a source of energy, it quickened reflexes and conferred excellent night vision. The latter was especially important, as Zerden's armies preferred to move under cover of darkness. Ane secured saddlebags on Brug, who reared and high stepped his taloned feet in anticipation of the coming patrol.

"Be patient Brug, we can't be losing our reserve arrows. Alright, everything is secure, I'm ready now."

Brug knelt to allow Ane to mount, and then stepped to his window perch and awaited the command to take flight. When the last of the kinnaras was similarly perched, Ane gently tugged Brug's reins "Let's go Brug."

Brug's voice sounded in Ane mind, "As you wish, mistress." He spread his wings and leapt from the window. Aglow with golden light, a wave kinnaras and their riders spread away from the palace to assemble into eight triangle formations, each heading to a designated patrol area. As the Druk squadron penetrated the Shield border, Ane felt a brief tingling sensation and then the sting of an icy breeze on her cheeks. Ahead, the snowy mountaintops burned red in the light of a setting sun.

An intense beam of light from an overhead surgical lamp illuminated a shaved patch of Gesar's scalp where a masked operating room nurse applied disinfectant. Using her palm as a fan, she wafted the area dry, then placed a sterile drape around it and announced, "The site is ready doctor."

Stepping away from the operating table, the surgeon took a last glance at the brain scan images on a nearby display monitor. Satisfied as to the location of the dark fusiform mass compressing the brain, he returned to his position.

"That's a lot of blood. It looks like Mr. Despa took quite a hard blow to the head," the doctor observed, his voice muffled by his surgical mask. "Okay let's get started. Knife please."

After making a small incision, he returned the scalpel and said, "Spreaders." Next, he spread the tissue to expose the yellow-white bone of the skull. "I'm ready for the cranial drill."

Positioning the drill bit on the skull, the doctor switched on the motor and the room filled with a high-pitched whir. He advanced the drill slowly while watching the calibration marks to ensure penetration to the proper depth.

The drill was through the skull in about a minute and the bit withdrawn. Blood began to ooze from the hole. "Suction please."

He then placed a suction probe in the hole and a column of dark blood flowed through a plastic tube into a collection bottle.

Gesar opened his eyes to a vast plain lit by a gibbous moon hung upon a star-salted sky. He sat with his back against something hard and smooth. His clothing was strange, a woolen shirt, quilted pants and leather boots. Pulling his knees to his chest, he rose to his feet.

Surprisingly, the act, intended to be gentle, nearly caused him leave the ground. His legs were strong, incredibly strong. He turned around to discover that his backrest was a stone choten fitted with a golden-eyed Buddha much like the one in his first dream, but the location was completely different.

"I'm dreaming again," he said to himself.

Recalling the beautiful woman who promised to await his return, he searched the sky for her great eagle-like mount, but it was empty but for moon and stars. In the distance beyond the little spired choten, he saw a line of jagged snowcapped mountains glowing in the moonlight. The silver outline of a trail wound its way down from the mountains and abruptly ended on the plain about fifty meters below the choten. He was somewhere in the foothills of those mountains. Everything was as vividly real as in his first dream, but this time he felt less distressed because he realized it was only a waking dream, one of those rare times when one becomes conscious of dreaming. All of it would vanish when his head next turned upon his pillow. For the moment, he would accept the experience and hope not to encounter another fang-helmeted nightmare.

"I'll chance a hike." He thought. Again, the mountains called to him and his legs felt more than ready for the climb. Besides, Ane might be up there; that is where she would be looking for him if she were part of this dream. He started up the trail, but almost immediately he halted and turned to the sound of thunder arising from the plain below. In the distance, at least sixty horses pounded the earth in full gallop carrying warriors armed with bows and spears that glinted in the moonlight. They were running for their lives. A moment later, Gesar saw what they were running from. It was a fugitive from hell, a massive six-armed creature, with glowing red eyes and fanged mouth. It was at least ten meters tall and bore a different weapon in each hand. It wildly swung axes, spiked clubs, and barbed swords at the nearest riders, who deftly dodged and turned to avoid the strikes. Compared to this creature, a hundred fang-assassins like the one from his first dream were a welcome alternative.

Familiar with military strategy, Gesar soon recognized the clever ploy used by the horse warriors. The retreat was not the rout that it appeared to be; rather there was a disciplined pattern to their movement. After loosing their arrows, the men at the rear would race forward to be replaced by others who would slow and harry the demon with another shower of arrows. When the demon redirected his attention to his new attackers, they in turn raced forward out of harms reach. The strategy effectively slowed the demon's alarming pace, giving the horses the time to keep ahead of their pursuer. Despite its success on the open plain, the tactic would be useless once the army reached the line of foothills. Slowed by the rising ground, the horse warriors would inevitably be chopped into mincemeat by a blur of demon blades.

Engrossed by the scene on the plain, Gesar failed to notice the figure approaching from his rear. "Move aside boy!" It ordered.

At the unexpected sound, Gesar's new legs instinctively reacted and he leapt nearly four meters from the trail. As his feet touched, Gesar saw a figure in Buddhist monk's robes briefly alight upon trail where he had stood only a heartbeat before. Like an oversized elastic ball, the monk bounced down the hillside in fifty-meter lengths then finally stopped at the trailhead on the plain below where the horse warriors were fast approaching.

"A lung-gom-pa," Gesar whispered to himself. His grandfather had told him stories of Buddhist monks and nuns with supernatural powers. They ran at unbelievable speeds and jumped incredible spans. Gesar watched the monk with intense interest hoping not to wake from his dream before witnessing the outcome of the drama unfolding before him. The monk reached into his robe and withdrew a long glowing blade. Without hesitation, he drove the spike into the ground and from it exploded producing a blue-white dome of light that spread across the plain.

Seeing the beacon appear, the horse warriors pressed hard for it and the demon let out a maddening wail that seemed to discharge from the very earth. A few breaths later, the horses had gathered under the dome of light, while the demon halted at its perimeter, swinging his weapons at the dome, which rejected his blows in a rain of sparks that fell harmlessly upon the ground. Spitting curses, the demon kicked at the earth dislodging rocks and clouds of dust. Ignoring the monster, the horse warriors dismounted and attended to their exhausted mounts that glistened with lather under the dome of light. Eventually, the demon accepted the futility of attempting to penetrate the dome and left in disgust, jogging back across the plain. After resting their horses, the men remounted and started for the trailhead.

"Who are you?"

Startled, Gesar jerked his head around at the sound of the voice. It was the monk. Again, he appeared as an unexpected voice in the dark. Squatting on a large boulder like a wary cat, the monk looked down on Gesar with a piercing gaze. The stocky body and strong square-jawed Asian face reminded Gesar of his Tibetan grandfather and he felt compelled to answer.

"Gesar…Gesar Despa."

"Where are you from?" The monk asked.

"What's that to you?" answered Gesar, thinking this to be a bizarre interrogation from a dream character.

"It's nothing to me, but everything for you. Now, answer my question."

"The United States," Gesar said.

"No, be more specific. What city?"

"San Francisco, California."

"Have you been in this place before?" asked the monk.

"I think so, but it was different, up there in a mountain pass I guess," Gesar said, pointing to the mountains.

"Can you ride a horse?"

"I've been riding since I was a child," answered Gesar.

"Are you familiar with martial arts or traditional weaponry?"

"Yeah, they're kind of a hobby of mine, but why the questions? I'm the one who should be asking the questions. It's my dream." Gesar objected.

"Later. First, I must put you in the care of the captain of those warriors. Come with me," the monk ordered.

"Wait a minute. Who are you and what the heck was that three-eyed nightmare I just saw?"

"That was the demon-god Mahakala and I am Jhado Zhangpo, bearer of the phurba that repelled the demon."

"Phurba! You mean a magical tent stake?" Gesar answered, remembering his grandfather's collection of traditional Tibetan talismans.

"No. I mean a Dagger of Illumination, a Demon Banisher, made at great expense of time and effort by the brothers and sisters of my lamasery. One does not repel a demon-god with a tent stake. Before the rebellion, Mahakala would have been unaffected by the phurba, but he is now an enemy of the Path and fallen from grace. You will learn more about these matters later. Now for your own safety you must join the tapah and ride for Shambala. There is no time. Mahakala might decide to return."

Gesar laughed. "This dream is wilder than the first one. All of this, including you will vanish as soon as I wake up. I don't even know how or why I'm talking with you."

Jhado jumped from his perch and gently landed in front of Gesar. The monk silently inspected the young man's face before speaking. "How do you feel?" he asked.

"A lot better than in the last dream," Gesar answered. "I'm not as dizzy and I feel much stronger. Even my gimpy arm is strong again, but anything can happen in a dream."

"Listen to me boy." Jhado said sternly. "This may seem like a dream, but it is not. You are in real danger. You have projected your sentience into Asura, the Jealous God realm. Your body, like mine, remains in the Human realm. Believe me when I say that you can die in either place. It is only a question of whether your soul will serve the enemy or find the Path of Illumination. As a new Buddha warrior you have much to learn in order to survive here."

As Jhado spoke, the first of the horse warriors approached along the trail. Even in moonlight, Gesar could see that they were extraordinary. Like their riders, the sleek warhorses were fitted with armor made of a combination of stone and metal. The riders wore helms of varied shapes but all were fitted with long horsehair tassels. Quivers affixed to the back of light saddles were mostly empty of arrows and only a few of the men still had spears after the encounter with Mahakala. All had swords hanging from wide belts partially hidden by riding cloaks.

"Who are they?" Gesar asked.

"They are the tapah, horse warriors of Shambala. They will be your escort." Jhado answered.

Before Gesar could raise more questions, the lead horseman rode up to Jhado, dismounted, pressed his palms together and respectfully bowed his head before speaking. "Greetings, venerable master, I am Jigme, captain of the Senge tapah. In the name of the Senge I thank you for your timely and very welcome aid."

"You and your men are deserving of any aid that I can offer, but may I ask how you happened to encounter Mahakala?" Jhado asked.

"Tonight we engaged a company of nagu raiders attempting to make their way into the mountains and successfully drove them back onto the Plain of Deception, but Mahakala was waiting to ambush us and we were forced to retreat. My men were greatly relieved to see the phurba beacon."

"You are fortunate that a Seer in Shambala saw that you were in danger and Lady Palden dispatched me to help you." Jhado replied.

"And more so that you were a phurba bearer. I will be sure to express my gratitude to both the Seer and the blessed lady upon my return. Without your help we would have lost many more men and horses at the trailhead tonight."

"How many men did you lose captain?" Jhado asked.

"We lost three men and their mounts on the plain. They challenged Mahakala while the others regrouped for the retreat."

Jhado pressed his palms together, touched them to his forehead and recited a prayer. "May their minds know the Path of Illumination. May their essence seek the Source of Illumination. May their souls find the Peace of Illumination. May their selflessness brighten the Light of Illumination. Namo Amida Buddha."

"Thank you, your holiness. My men will be gladdened that the Lama of Dagpa Akar himself gave blessing to their lost brothers on their soul journey. They were brave and skilled fighters and will not be easily replaced."

Jhado jutted a chin in direction of Gesar "Well, you may have gained at least one replacement in this man. His name is Gesar Despa. He knows horses and martial arts. Take him to the palace to begin training. I must return to my lamasery immediately." Jhado then turned to Gesar and said, "You are here because you have skills that are needed. It is no coincidence that you are skilled with horses and weapons. You have been given the opportunity to defend Shambala. In a vast dark universe, the Path of Illumination is the only hope for humanity. I pray that your service to Shambala will honor your namesake."

Before Gesar could respond, the monk sprang away, reaching the choten in a single bound. He placed both hands on the shrine and vanished in a flash of light.

"Where did he go?" Gesar asked.

"Tibet," captain Jigme answered.

Still dumbfounded, Gesar continued to stare at the little shrine where the monk had vanished. "My grandfather called it Po," he said absently.

"You can ride behind me," the captain said. "Dawa won't mind as long as you're with me. So, you have you been on horses before?"

"Yes." Gesar answered, returning his attention to the horse warrior captain.

"Good," the captain answered, extending a hand to Gesar. "I'm Ben Wilson."

Gesar shook the young man's hand, surprised to hear so common an occidental name in such an exotic dream. "I thought you said your name was Jigme?"

"Jigme is my Buddha warrior name, it means Fearless One, but Ben was my given name." After taking a swig from a flask that he unhooked from his belt, Ben leapt gracefully back into his saddle, whispered something into his horse's ear, and then said. "Climb up behind me. We need to get going. We have a long ride ahead of us."

Gesar found that his unusually strong legs made it a simple matter to jump onto the large warhorse. He barely needed Ben's hand for support. When Ben urged Dawa forward, Gesar gripped the horse's flanks with his legs. Without spurring, Dawa quickly rejoined the column of riders climbing toward the first mountain pass that would lead them to Shambala. During the remainder of the night, Gesar watched the moon slowly sink behind the range of mountains that grew steadily more imposing in the growing light. The line of men rode warily and did not speak; only the sound of hooves striking stone and scree disturbed the night. It was not until they reached the level of the pass that the men seemed to relax. Ben was first to break the silence.

"Gesar, that's an unusual name. The Buddha warriors come from all over the world. I've been here for years and I'm still learning the origins of names. His holiness seemed to think your name was meaningful."

"I was named after a Tibetan folk hero."

"Then you're from Tibet?"

"No, California," Gesar answered.

"In that case we're practically neighbors," Ben said with a subdued excitement. "I'm a half-breed Crow from Montana. It's all a bit foggy now, but the last thing I remember before coming here is competing in a rodeo in Billings. I think I was quite a hotshot on the rodeo circuit. As you can see, I'm still riding, but now it's for something more important than prize money."

"Just what are you riding for?" Gesar asked.

"Didn't you hear his holiness? We're fighting for the freedom of humanity. All of this probably seems a bit crazy to you now. It certainly was to me. Imagine a Montana cowboy waking up here. I didn't know squat about Buddhism let alone demon-gods. Yamantaka found me at a choten. I'm thankful that he was in his angelic form. He taught me about Shambala and the defenders of The Path. I asked him why I was chosen to be here. He said that Buddha warriors are not chosen; instead, they find their way here by achieving oneness with their particular skill. I guess mine is riding. I knew there were times when I was in the 'zone' and there was nothing on four legs that I couldn't ride, but I never thought it would lead me here. If it was my choice, then it was a good one. I'm glad to be part of this. At least I was lucky enough to come before the rebellion. Now, new arrivals, such as you, risk getting killed by nagu dron scouts."

"Yeah, I've met one of them before," said Gesar recalling the black armored warrior with the fanged helmet.

"So, you've been here before."

"Once before, it was somewhere in the mountains. A girl riding on a giant bird saved me from one of those enemy scouts." Gesar replied.

Ben urged Dawa to step up his pace and said, "That was no girl. That was a dakini and she was riding a kinnara, not a giant bird. Did you learn her name?"

"She said her name was Ane." Gesar answered.

"If nothing else, your Tibetan namesake brings you luck. Ane is first captain to Lady Palden Lhamo, leader and patron of the dakini forces. The Lady herself trained Ane. I'm sure she dispatched the dron handily."

"She did." Gesar confirmed.

"When we reach Shambala you will meet her again. The Druk squadron should be in Shambala when we arrive."

The air grew colder as the tapah unit climbed the trail. Ahead, moon shadows of mountain peaks stretched across an expanse of snow. They were approaching the summit of a high pass. "Is Shambala near?" Gesar asked.

"Not yet," Ben answered. "We have a way to go. There is another pass to cross yet. A double range of mountains encircles Shambala."

Unless his bizarre dream ended soon, he was in for a long cold ride. The possibility of meeting Ane again was some comfort against the cold. Since that first dream, he had often thought of her, but more than the physical attraction, she radiated strength of purpose that roused him to make his own life mean something. He nearly laughed realizing that a product of his unconscious mind had evoked such feelings. Had he conjured an elaborate distraction based on childhood stories to help him deal with his personal losses? He had lost his family and now his health.

The strange monk, Lama Zhangpo, claimed this was Asura, the Jealous God realm. His Tibetan grandfather spoke of the six realms of Buddhism, which until now, he had relegated to allegory. Could they possibly exist? The lama sowed doubts in his mind, but wasn't the monk also the stuff of dreams? Part of him wanted this strange world to be real, but another part feared it might be.

"There's a coat in the saddlebag." Ben said.

"Thanks," answered Gesar as he pulled the coat from the saddlebag. At least the cold seems real, he thought.

After several days, Chidag Nagpo in the flesh of Officer Charles Cutter left the hospital against medical advice. He had endured repeated audiences with several humans, Ur-nurse, Ur-doctor, one named Ek-swife and another called Da-cheef. When he ripped away the assortment of tubes and wires attached to him, Ur-nurse became distressed and said, "Stop that! I'm calling your doctor, right now."

Ur-doctor arrived, looked over the wounds and said with some amazement, "My God! He's a fast healer." He then reassured Ur-nurse that the tethers were no longer needed. To remain concealed in his borrowed flesh, Chidag spoke very little and did not kill any of the humans, although Ek-swife tested his limited patience. She was insolent and provocative, constantly insisting that he remove his sunglasses. He nearly dismembered her but for an intrusion by Ur-nurse.

The audience with Da-cheef was simply tedious. He made strange offerings of plant material and promises of extended sick leave. "Chuck," he said, "you're a tough S.O.B. but after that many bullets to the chest were not expecting you back on patrol for at least a few months. At least the bastard who shot you is dead, so you won't have to appear in court. When you come back to work, there will be a medaling ceremony. There might also be a promotion in this for you."

Chidag remained silent, his eyes hidden under dark glasses. Placing a container of plants on a nearby table, Da-Cheef continued. "Oh yeah, I don't know if you like flowers, but we took up a collection at the station and bought these for you."

Getting progressively uncomfortable by Chidag's stony unresponsiveness, Da-Cheef expressed some meaningless apologies and left the room. "I know you're probably feeling like crap, so I'll quit bothering you and let you get some rest."

Chidag was relieved to see him go and expressed his pent up frustration by casting the container of flowers against a nearby wall.

He hated the bright flowers; they reminded him of this realm's irksome yellow sun. None of these humans were of any consequence except for the watchers with their turquoise eyes. He had recognized them. Disguised as cleaning slaves, they would take surreptitious glances through his doorway or even make unobtrusive entrances under the pretense of moving equipment or cleaning floors. They had made their first fatal error by thinking that he was unaware of them. Apparently, the allies of Shambala were ignorant of the mark that they all carried in the depth of their eyes. He left them to enjoy their false security as it would provide a significant advantage to his mission. With a defiant confidence, he walked out of the hospital.

In this alien realm, Chidag was forced to draw heavily on the knowledge of his host, who obtained objects and fulfilled desires using a small talisman called Vee-Sha. He found transportation to his host's dwelling by choosing one of the brightly colored self-propelled litters that waited near the hospital entrance. The driver was wearisomely chatty as he moved with exhilarating speed among a bewildering number of similar vehicles. Chidag's host reminded him that he had the ability to operate these vehicles, a skill that would prove useful.

Upon reaching his destination, Chidag remained secluded for three days, learning as much as he could about his host and the Human realm. He mostly restrained his anger, destroying only one small box that suddenly emitted the discorporate and insolent voice of Ek-swife. The object called Tee-Vee allowed him to view humans remotely and reaffirmed his contempt for them. It was particularly difficult adapting to artificial lighting, tasteless food, and useless objects. Keeping the lighting low or off helped to temper his frustration and he made several pleasing discoveries.

His host owned a transport vehicle and an impressive collection of projectile weapons as well as a personal practice range. Chidag mastered their use in a few hours. Though noisy, the weapons were far superior to the primitive spears and arrows of Asura. His host flesh had an extensive knowledge of human weapons and as a police officer, a modicum of authority. On the evening of the third day after leaving the hospital, Chidag dressed in the uniform of the San Francisco Police Department and started his mission. His first task was to eliminate the watcher who kept vigil in the small vehicle parked across the street.

Chidag backed the vehicle out of the garage, stopped with a screech of brakes and sped down the street. His host was a trained driver and performed this maneuver with ease. The watcher, surprised by the sudden appearance of vehicle, made pursuit after a clumsy start. Chidag purposely slowed to be certain the watcher would not lose him. Using his host's detailed knowledge of the city, he had chosen the place of the watcher's death. It was a place of chaos and darkness where death had a home on the bay. His host knew the place well; it was Hunter's Point where he had suffered the fatal wounds that allowed Chidag to perform his incarnation.

The odor of fear in the air of Hunter's point was invigorating. It was Chidag's first moment of real pleasure since his incarnation. He had barely taken ten steps away from his vehicle, before the humans on the street began retreating into the shadows at the site of the shining badge on his chest. It was hard to believe that the defenders of Shambala were recruited from among such as these. After walking two blocks, he entered the particular alley that he sought. Melting into the darkest shadows, Chidag removed his sunglasses and waited.

Brother Zak recited a chant under his breath as he followed the creature in the police officer's uniform. The small monk's reluctant steps sharply contrasted with the defiant stroll of the hulking man who turned into the alley ahead. Brother Zak understood the creature was dangerous and had he the proper weapon, he might be able to defend himself, but until those weapons arrived, his instructions were to keep Chidag in sight and to report frequently. Only minutes before, he had given an update of his location by cell phone after parking his car. Chidag's choice to come to this neighborhood was curious. Although, it was the sordid kind of place where one might conceivably meet allies largely unnoticed, a worrying thought, since it meant that Chidag was not the only one of Zerden's children to incarnate in the Human realm. If other minions of Zerden were indeed among them, then it was essential to identify them. Hoping Chidag would reemerge from the alley, Brother Zak waited, but after several minutes, there was still no sign of the creature. Eventually, fear of losing Chidag overcame the fear of encountering him and he ventured into the alley. It reeked of garbage and was soundless except for the faint rhythm of a drum backbeat emanating from an apartment window above. After walking the length of the alley, Brother Zak thought he had lost the demon. He turned to retrace his steps, thinking that perhaps the creature had entered a side door or window. In a dark niche near a dumpster, he noticed a pair of glowing red embers seeming to float in the air. He blinked attempting to bring the odd glows into focus and then stepped toward them. An instant later, the embers dimmed to blackness as he expelled his last breath.

Jhado knocked three times in response to the taps on his cell door and it rolled aside with a resonant grating of stone upon stone. The light of an oil lamp stabbed into his pitch-black cell. Jhado moved toward the light, slipping through the opening as soon as it was wide enough for him to pass through.

"Tenzin, how long was I gone?" he asked the old monk holding the oil lamp; its light accentuated the furrows in an ancient face carved by many years of exposure to sun and wind.

"Your holiness, it has been three days and two nights since you entered the cell," Tenzin answered.

"Three days? That is longer than I intended. I have instructions from Lady Palden, who requests that we locate and protect as many of the Buddha warriors as possible. She is especially concerned for her Druk dakini captain. Unfortunately, we have little to guide us in finding some of them."

Tenzin lowered his lamp and interrupted. "Your holiness, there has been more news since you entered the cell. Chidag has recovered enough to begin his hunt. He left the hospital where he was being watched."

"Is he still in San Francisco?" Jhado asked.

"Yes, Kasa reports that he has learned to use his incarnation well, but he struggles to contain his cruelty."

"I must hurry and contact our agents. Finish your rounds Tenzin and then join me in my chambers."

"Yes, your holiness," said the old monk bowing his head and then returning to his duties.

Jhado's robes rustled as he strode toward the spiral of stone stairs worn smooth by generations of footsteps. As he climbed, the scent of sandalwood hung in the air and a warm glow emanated from sixteen elaborately worked metal oil lamps hung at regular intervals along the stairwell. The staircase was the only access to the meditation chambers deep below the lamasery where there was total silence and darkness. Only the most adept monks and nuns could achieve the prolonged state of meditation needed to create a portal to Shambala.

With only a single cushion for comfort, they sat for days or sometimes weeks without food or water. While in meditation, their bodies were near death and moved only by striking the floor twice with a stone hammer in response to the daily tapping on their cell door. A jade hammer and sometimes a phurba dagger were the only items ever taken into the cell. The hammer's purpose was not only to signal that the adept was still alive, but also to provide an anchor to life. The phurba, its triple-edged blade constructed from a complex metal alloy and imbued with spiritual force, could be moved between realms and served as a weapon for the defense of Shambala.

When Jhado reached the top of the stairs, he opened another stone door that was so carefully camouflaged to match the wall it was invisible to an unknowing eye. After resealing the door, he pushed aside a large cloth thangka with an elaborate depiction of the Buddha surrounded by the eight Wisdom Bodhisattvas. The tapestry covered the secret entrance to the meditation chambers and was the focal point of the temple's main assembly hall or dukhang, which also served as the thekpu where formal ceremonies were performed. Presently, the hall was empty of practitioners, but lamps and urns of incense were still smoldering indicating that morning meditation had recently ended. "The brothers and sisters will be in the workrooms," Jhado thought.

Jhado walked the length of the dukhang then turned to mount another stairway that led to his tower chamber. He passed several workrooms on the way. Through open doorways, he saw groups of monks or nuns mixing scented herbs for incense sticks, crushing colored rocks for sand painting, and weaving carpets or thangkas for meditation rooms. This section of the lamasery was reserved for indoor artistic endeavors. Many of the fine items produced were traded for resources not available locally. In other parts of the lamasery, scholars copied ancient manuscripts, smiths forged phurbas, cooks prepared food, gardeners tended plantings, masons repaired crumbling walls and students practiced martial arts.

A dim grey light filled Jhado's chamber when he entered. The window revealed sky overcast by an ominous bank of clouds. Noting the poor light, Jhado hoped there would be sufficient charge left in the solar powered batteries to execute his task. He went directly to his desk computer and breathed a sigh of relief when the display activated. A few keystrokes later, he was searching among pages of Haiku poetry. He soon found the most recent message from Kasa posted the day before.

Frost hunts in silence
Blossoms closed to bar cruel cold
Await sleeping death
Kasa

It was the news that Tenzin had reported in the passages beneath the lamasery. Chidag was ready to begin stalking the Sleepers. Kasa and the other Kalacakra lamas around the globe needed guidance immediately. No one living had faced a foe such as this before. Jhado quickly composed a poem to provide instructions.

Striking in silence
The white crane thwarts the viper
While nestlings take flight
Dan Poe

The method of communication was both elegant and efficient. A well-constructed poem contained considerable information that was extractable only by the prepared mind. His agents should interpret the message and act accordingly. He advised them to use whatever covert action necessary to protect the Buddha warriors and move them to safe havens. Jhado was about to close his connection when he remembered Lady Palden's request concerning the dakini captain, Ane. The request to protect a particular Sleeper was strange, but he would attempt to comply. He composed another poem and posted it to the Haiku website.

The white crane is blessed
Through dark night, she leads her flock
And rests on gold bridge
Dan Poe

The message was for Kasa. The first line referring to a blessed white crane indicated a dakini warrior of special significance. To lead a flock revealed that she was a captain and the reference to a golden bridge meant her physical body was in the vicinity of San Francisco, the city where Chidag had begun his hunt. Perhaps, Chidag's choice of location was not coincidental. Kasa would need to call upon all the alliances he had forged during his time in the city of the golden bridge. Although Chidag was in a mortal's body, he was dangerous, having greater strength and sharper senses than that of a normal human. His regenerative powers would be superhuman and to kill him would require special techniques. It was fortunate that one of Kasa's monks had recognized him while surveying hospital emergency rooms. Jhado suspected that Zerden's minions would possess a human body that was resuscitated after a near death injury so he had instructed his agents to focus their surveillance on hospitals and emergency rooms.

As Jhado finished his poem, Tenzin entered the room and set a tray bearing a large cup of tea and a bowl of rice on a table near the entrance. He then pressed his palms together and bowed his age-spotted head. "Your holiness, I have completed my rounds of the meditation cells. The remaining brothers and sisters are well. I am now free to serve you."

Jhado bowed in return and said, "That is good news brother. As soon as I finish here, I humbly request that you help me shave my head and face. My hair has grown much during three days of meditation."

"As always your holiness, it is my honor. I will get a shaving bowl and razor immediately." Tenzin bowed again and left the room.

Jhado glanced back at the computer display. In the brief time that Jhado spoke with Tenzin a new poem from Kasa had appeared.

Spiteful serpent strikes
Innocent eyes cloud with death
As slayer seeks grass
Kasa

Jhado's heart sank as he read the poem. Like a snake taking to deep grass, Chidag had disappeared after killing the person assigned to watch him. Now Chidag was free to strike without warning. Kasa's monks and all the Buddha warriors in the San Francisco area were in grave danger.

Jhado turned off the computer and started on the food and drink that Tenzin had left for him. He focused his full attention on the meal, allowing the experience to nourish him fully after the days of fasting. He would need to every grain of energy to face the enemies of Shambala.

Tenzin returned with the shaving bowl and razor. "Are you ready, your holiness?"

"Unfortunately not, my old friend, but we must proceed nevertheless."

The first rays of dawn cut over the mountains as the cavalry descended the southwest pass into Shambala. With their spirits buoyed by the scent of home, the horses stepped up their pace. The morning light reflected from the snow-covered western slopes illuminated the length of the valley. The distant view of a misted lake surrounded by verdant fields and thick forests was as breathtakingly beautiful as it was welcoming, especially after a night of negotiating an incomprehensible web of trails in the dark, so when Ben said, "Prepare yourself, you are about to have your soul tested." Gesar took the comment as purely metaphoric and was unprepared for what occurred.

Suddenly, he experienced a curious tingling that started at the base of his neck and then spread throughout his body. At first, it was almost pleasant, but without warning the tingling became blindingly painful. He felt as if he were engulfed in flame. The view of the valley vanished replaced by searing blue-white light. It took every iota of his will to keep from screaming. Mercifully, the pain ended before his will failed. The scene of the beautiful valley of Shambala reappeared. The experience had lasted only seconds but it had felt like an eternity.

"You have been permitted passage. Now we know you are truly an ally." Ben commented, soberly. "The pain lessens with each passing as your soul is cleansed. You took the passing well, most of the new Buddha warriors scream and tear off their clothing."

"I nearly did." Gesar answered.

"Your self discipline will be an advantage," Ben commented.

"What in hell happened to me?" Gesar asked.

"Not in hell," Ben countered. "More like what in heaven happened? We just passed through the Shield. It protects Shambala against the enemies of enlightenment, like that demon you saw us encounter. Our enemies have recently recruited allies from among the former Guardians of Shambala. The defection has tipped the balance of power and our enemies of have gone on the offensive. Their goal is to defile Kalapa palace and control Asura and the Human realm, but the Shield has turned against them and denies them passage."

"What do they want with humanity?"

"To enslave us and deny us any chance of true freedom. To them we are nothing more than ripe fruit for harvest and consumption. There was a time when demons lived among humankind in the form of conquerors and despots, but through the efforts of many avatars, they were converted or exiled to this realm. It's our job to keep them beyond the Shield. Our armies are a constant annoyance to them and so far, we have kept them at bay, but as you witnessed on the plain, to a demon-god we are of no more significance than a swarm of biting gnats. Unless the balance is regained they might eventually conquer us by attrition."

Gesar unconsciously gripped Dawa's flanks to steady himself. The thought of six-armed demons rampaging through the streets of San Francisco was ludicrous. He had to be dreaming. It was only a question of when he would wake up.

Dr. Ashki stood next to the hospital bed where Gesar lay unconscious. He had been notified of Gesar's emergent admission and made the trip to the intensive care unit as soon as he had finished seeing his clinic patients. Dr. Chandron, a tired looking neurosurgical resident briefed Ashki on Gesar's condition.

"Apparently, he fell in his classroom and hit his head against a desk. His students reported that it seemed like his legs just gave out. He was admitted through the ER this morning. The blow to the head caused a concussion and large subdural hematoma. I can show you the CT scan if you'd like. We trephined the skull and removed the blood clot. Since then, we've kept him in a drug-induced coma until the brain swelling subsides. It might be some time before we can wake him."

"What about his neurological status?" Ashki inquired.

"There seems to be no major brain damage if that's what you're asking. But as far as his underlying neurological disorder, we won't be able to evaluate that until we wake him up. We suspect it has progressed and that's what caused him to fall."

Ashki took Gesar's limp hand and squeezed warmly. "I don't know if you can hear me son, but I'm gonna stick with you through this. Like I said, you got to take it one step at time."

"I doubt if he can hear you. We have him under pretty deep." Chandron commented.

"It doesn't matter if he can hear me. I'm sure part of him is getting the message." Ashki countered.

"Okay, I'll take that as a lesson in bedside manner."

"I hope you will. The difference between a good doctor and a great doctor is that the great doctor never forgets that there is a ghost in the machine. Healing the spirit is as important and healing the body. Be sure to contact me when you start to withdraw the barbiturates." Ashki instructed. "I want to be here when he wakes up. I like this kid and he is going to need a lot of spiritual support. In fact, I'm going to request a special consultation for him back in Navajo country. There's something different about this young man."

Impatiently tapping a reflex hammer in his palm, Chandron said, "Excuse me for being a bit abrupt, but I've got to write some orders before I can go home. It was good meeting you Dr. Ashki. I'll be sure to call you if his condition changes."

After shaking Ashki's hand, Chandron disappeared in a blur of blue scrubs and white lab coat. Ashki remained at Gesar's bedside for a few minutes longer, making his own silent prayers.

Palden's spirit was troubled as she looked from her tower window, facing the great twin peaks of Jetsun and Jetsunmu, the king and queen of the inner ring. Nestled between the royal mountains, the triple strands of Trinity Falls tumbled gracefully into Lake Shambala from a high escarpment that rose abruptly at the eastern end of the valley, but despite the stunning scenery at her threshold, Palden's attention was elsewhere. Her vision was superior to that of any human and with the optical assistance provided by the Shield, she looked beyond the mountains to the desolate plains of Asura. She had been poring over the landscape since dawn when she first received news that the Druk squadron had not returned when expected. A delay could only mean an encounter with a rebel demon-god. Of all of her dakini captains, Ane would be the most likely to survive such a meeting, so Palden did not abandon hope. Despite her confidence, she could not relax enough to forsake her watch. She desperately wanted to mount her own kinnara and search for her missing warriors, but that was out of the question for the Shield would bar her return and without the full complement of the four remaining guardians, Shambala would be at serious risk. Leaving would play into hands of the enemy and the Druk may have been purposely targeted to lure her into a trap. For the sake of Shambala, she had to be prepared to accept the loss of her best captain and the first dakini company. For now, she could only watch, wait and hope. Her vigil had revealed one heartening sight, a returning tapah column wound its way down into valley from the southwest pass. She had recently dispatched a Kalacakra master, Jhado Zhangpo, to give them aid. Apparently, he had succeeded.

She wondered which of the demon-gods would be willing to challenge a full dakini squadron. Any of them had the power to defeat a squadron of dakini but they would pay dearly for the victory. It was most likely Mahakala or Yama; they were the boldest and most committed to Zerden's cause. Changpa was never skilled at dealing with aerial attacks and Kubera was most likely plotting strategies, biding his time, waiting for Shambala's forces to weaken enough for him to join the fray with minimal risk to his personal comfort.

The rift between the demon-gods was difficult for her to accept. She had been Mahakala's consort for millennia but in the centuries after the Taming, they had drifted apart, committing themselves to their duties as guardians. She never imagined he would so easily reject his sworn responsibility. In his angelic form, Mahakala was as strikingly handsome as he was terribly dreadful in his demon form. His angelic persona was that of a gracious prince, tall with dark bronze skin and strong chiseled features. His sky blue eyes invited and the flashing red jewel at his third eye delighted. She enjoyed their conversations as they walked together in the gardens in the morning or on the palace ramparts at sunset. Mahakala exuded passion in every movement and word, but she could see now that he had never learned to feel compassion. That was the most difficult emotion for the demon-gods to experience. To an immortal, the vicissitudes of a mortal life seem prosaic and fleeting. How could a demon-god attach meaning to something as ephemeral as a dayfly? Yet, humans had the advantage of advancement through repeated reincarnations, the ability to shed the confines of an old shell in order to seek a fresh one. Those that ultimately achieved enlightenment attained powers that eclipsed those of the demon-gods, as evidenced by the Taming and the creation of the Shield. Perfect illumination seemed beyond the reach of the demon-gods who were weighted with uncountable centuries of sin and excess. Yet freedom was supposedly possible for them through dedicated service. At least that was the promise made by the bodhisattvas to the eight defeated demon-gods who were growing tired of their own existence. For Palden, the Taming had been a rebirth. She had discovered new feelings and motivations; she enjoyed her new form and purpose. Meaning had come into her existence. There was no going back for her, but Mahakala either had

46

doubts about his role as a guardian or simply lacked the patience to fulfill it.

Suddenly in a flash of insight, Palden realized the truth; Mahakala was afraid. He feared that which he might become and it was likely the same for the other rebels. They had existed as demon-gods for so long that to change must be terrifying for them, especially for those who were the most extreme in their excesses. A great weight of historical baggage held them back. She realized that her sudden insight had arisen from compassion, an emotion that she would never have had experienced in the days before the Taming. She realized too that this new awareness might be useful. To fear change is a weakness, but to fight change is certain defeat. Emptying her mind of negative thoughts, Palden continued to scan the landscape in search of her missing dakini. "May the Buddha protect them," she whispered.

Letting their mounts attend to the trail, the horse column descended a series of winding cutbacks at a dizzying pace. To stave off vertigo, Gesar focused his eyes on the valley or the mountains beyond it. He was relieved when the column finally reached a well-groomed dirt road at the valley floor. Along the road, an assortment of idyllic farmhouses, temples and shrines dotted the hills among neatly groomed fields. To his surprise, none of the occupants was in view, but the peaceful sound of bells and chants resonated from the temples. When he asked about the absence of people, Ben answered, "It is early. Most of the people would be in meditation. The fields and orchards of Shambala will gladly wait until prayers are complete."

"Then more than Buddha warriors live in the valley?"

"Yes, there are many who serve by living in this valley and helping to support the palace. Unlike the Buddha warriors, they are born here. They are beings close to enlightenment that choose to serve in the Asura realm before accepting nirvana. They are a long-lived people some are hundreds of years old. Our stable master is nearing two-hundred fifty years. He has served many Senge in his time."

Gesar remembered his grandfather's description of Shambala as a fertile valley enclosed by snowcapped mountains populated by immortals. It seemed his mind was fabricating a dream from childhood stories, but surely, no dream could feel this real.

Eventually the dirt road ended and joined a paved avenue that paralleled a river. Fed by spring runoff, the river ran deep and fast with the roar of rapids penetrating thick vegetation at its banks. "That is the Shenla." Ben explained. "We follow it to Lake Shambala and Kalapa palace." The avenue weaved back and forth matching the course of the river as it descended at a gentle grade. The palace came into view as they rounded a bend where the river widened at its mouth to offer a panorama.

From the mountain pass at early dawn, the palace had been obscured by a mist that clung to Lake Shambala, so Gesar was unprepared for the sight that met his eyes. Gleaming white, a massive spired dome dominated the top of an island city. A wall with eight towers reaching the height of the dome enclosed the city. Amazingly, the structure seemed to float upon the lake like a great ship. The island was so symmetrical, he wondered if both island and palace had been painstakingly carved from a preexisting mountain. From his present vantage point, it was impossible to estimate the height of the ramparts, but they contained windows at several levels suggesting there were multiple stories.

At its mouth, the Shenla slowed to become a broad expanse of wetlands that merged with Lake Shambala. The column continued along the lakeshore road, which widened and was bordered by high walls on each side, presumably another line defense. Eventually, they reached a main crossroad with an immense golden statue of the Buddha in its midst. At the crossing, the column turned left toward the lake. A paved avenue led steadily down to a wide quay which abruptly ended with waves lapping at its terminus. The entrance of Kalapa palace faced them across an expanse of deep water where the fortress wall extended nearly to lake level. The rectangular opening in the wall was ungated with a beacon of white light shining out of it. Over the entrance was an arch and tympanum supported by columns carved from rock on each side of the portal. The columns were at least the height of ten men and fierce images of guardian dogs sat in vigil at their bases. Elaborate designs carved in relief surrounded the opening, but most striking was the sparkling, jewel-studded mandala in the tympanum. No bridge, boat, or dock was in sight, Gesar saw no means to cross the water short of a cold swim.

"How will you cross?" Gesar asked.

"We cross to the Vishvamata gate on a bridge of humility." Ben replied as he raised his hand to signal his men. In response, the men removed their helmets and riding gauntlets, pressed their bared palms together, bowed their heads and spoke in unison, "Vishvamata, Mother of All. We defend without pride. We fight without hate. We die without fear. We come without karma."

When the brief chant ended, the center of the jeweled mandala briefly flashed with blue-white light. An instant later, the waters of Lake Shambala stilled and Gesar felt a breath of chilled air brush his cheek. Suddenly before him, the shining water crystallized into a complex pattern of interlacing ferns, becoming progressively dense until a sold sheet of ice stretched from quay to island. Ben urged his mount forward and waved his column to follow. Gesar experienced a moment of panic as Dawa's hoof struck the ice, which seemed too thin to take the weight of a horse, let alone one bearing two men. Miraculously, the ice was as solid as the paved avenue. The horses were clearly familiar with the ice-bridge, taking to it without protest or delay. The subdued mood of the men turned to joy as they approached the palace gate. Some started up a song that quickly spread among the ranks.

"Your men seem happy to be home." Gesar observed.

"The missions to the plains of Asura are prolonged and taxing," Ben explained. "But that is only part of it. You will soon find that Kalapa palace has its own rewards."

In front of the palace gate, the ice ended at a ramp that led up to a tunnel entrance that penetrated the full thickness of fortress wall and ramped steadily upward. At close proximity, Gesar realized that the beacon he had seen from the lakeshore was a clever use of light and architecture. The beam of light emanating from the tunnel reflected from a section of floor that was set with polished white stone. Once inside the long narrow tunnel, the feeling of claustrophobia was oppressive, only the light shining directly ahead of them offered any sense of hope. If this was the only entrance to Kalapa palace, a defending force could easily hold off any siege attempt.

"This must be the most impenetrable fortress ever built." Gesar commented.

"Considering what it's protecting, it can't be safe enough." Ben said.

"What is it protecting?" asked Gesar.

"The power of the Shield emanates from the throne of Sangpo Bumtri which sits in the great hall beneath the temple dome. If the throne were destroyed, the Shield would fail and the world of sentient beings would fall back into chaos. It has taken many incarnations to create the avatars that have opened the pathway to enlightenment and freedom. Siddhartha and other avatars proved that the enlightened human could surpass the power of demon-gods. They showed that human destiny is to become more than compost lifetime after lifetime. But it took a very long time for us to get here and we might not get another chance."

Being of Tibetan descent, Gesar understood the significance of the path of spiritual enlightenment to the Tibetan people. It was the very core of the Tibetan culture and spiritual awareness permeated daily life. Incense, prayer beads and prayer wheels were in nearly every household. In the land of his grandfather, the teachings of the

Buddha had merged with ancient Bon shamanic practices, creating a powerful combination of compassionate discipline with the ability to move between realms of existence. Every Tibetan man, woman and child was aware of their "true" goal despite the distractions of the material world and crushing oppression of dictatorial governments.

Having assimilated eclectic American culture, Gesar thought of Tibetan Buddhism as simply another religion, but he now struggled with doubts. Was it possible that it held the key to human spiritual freedom? No, he couldn't accept that. Shambala was a myth and the notion of split existences was impossible. None of this experience could be real, yet his memory of a life in San Francisco was beginning to seem like a dream. The longer he remained in Shambala the more the memories of his waking life faded. His consciousness could not handle living two realities. Which was real? According to the lama, both were.

At the lead of the column, Gesar was among the first to see the source of the beacon that grew brighter as they ascended the Vishvamata passage. Squinting, he looked across an expansive courtyard to where a lens-like concavity of mirrored tiles embedded in a high wall focused sunlight into the passage. As they approached the end of the passage, the light was blinding.

"We are entering the Diamond courtyard. Don't look directly into the light." Ben warned. "On sunny days, the light is blinding. It is another of the island's defenses, an example of the power of illumination. Enemies attempting to enter by way of the tunnel would be at a great disadvantage. Blinded, they would be quickly cut down by what appeared to be only shadows." After the passage through the Shield, Gesar had learned to respect Ben's warnings. He averted his eyes.

The column crossed the courtyard and passed through an arched portal at its western end that led to a paved avenue. Gesar later learned the road paralleled the outer wall and circled the entire island until reaching the east gate of the Diamond courtyard, a distance of nearly ten kilometers. A sense of peace inexplicably came over Gesar once he was within the fortress walls. Doubts regarding his sanity faded away in amazement at the perfect balance of architecture and nature. The dome of Kalapa palace stood as a shining jewel set upon the highest point of the island surrounded by a walled forest. The land below the palace was excavated into a series of tiers with alternating layers of marble-white buildings and green spaces filled with cultivated gardens, fields and orchards. Waterfalls and ponds were bountiful filling the air with happy sounds of splashing water.

Small animals and birds skittered among the vegetation and along the waterways.

As they approached the base of one of the demon-god towers, a shadow enveloped the column of horse warriors. Looking up, Gesar was dumbstruck by the tower's height. The cupola at its top seemed to be fishing for low flying clouds, but at this time of day, the shadow cast upon them was not from the tower, but rather from an elevated causeway that connected the tower to the third level of the city. Gesar surmised there must be eight similar bridges that divided the island in to eight sections, replicating a basic dharma wheel.

Ben raised an arm and pointed beyond a wall toward an enclosed expanse of grassland to the right. "Look Gesar. Those are the horses of the tapah. Your mount will come from among them."

My mount? He's as presumptuous as the monk, Gesar thought, speaking as if I've already volunteered.

Looking to where Ben pointed, Gesar saw a herd of at least twenty horses grazing on a hill. He was familiar with horse breeds and what he saw tempered his irritation. These animals were magnificent. They reminded him of the legendary wild horses that once roamed Mongolia, but the animals were larger with traits of Arabian and American Rocky Mountain breeds. Despite the appearance of wildness, the horses of Shambala were apparently familiar with humans, seeming more curious than wary as the column of warriors passed by. A dark stallion with a blond mane attracted Gesar's eye. While not the largest of the group, he had sleekest lines. The animal shook its head, showing off its long mane and then it separated from the herd and galloped toward Gesar, stopping at the wall that separated the road from the fields. The stallion whinnied as if trying to get Gesar's attention. At the same moment, Gesar heard a voice or rather felt a voice invade his mind.

"Welcome rider. I run with joy to see you. I have been waiting a long time for you to come." Gesar suddenly realized it was the stallion's voice echoing in his head. Shocked, he nearly slipped off Dawa's back.

"Hang on back there. You're going to get thrown making sudden moves like that," Ben chastised.

Gesar was reluctant to say anything about hearing voices, but he felt a need to tell someone. Presently, Ben was his only confidant in this bizarre reality. "I swear I just heard that horse talk to me."

Ben erupted with a knowing chuckle and then waved the other riders to continue on as he turned Dawa toward the blonde-maned stallion standing behind the wall. "Congratulations Gesar, you've been chosen. You're about to meet your closest friend. Sorry I didn't warn you about this, I was intending to explain it later. I didn't think your mount would find you so quickly. It usually takes a suitable period of growing familiar before a freemane chooses his rider, but that one has always been brazen and knows what he wants. When he wishes to speak, only you will hear his voice as Dawa only speaks to me."

"Does he have a name?" Gesar asked.

"All the foals are given names by the stable masters. That one is Goba, which means eagle. He has a small white patch on his forehead in the shape of an eagle and he lives up to his name. Ever since he was a colt, he has attempted to fly rather than run. I think he envies the kinnaras. You will have your hands full with him, but if you're ever in need of speed that one won't fail you."

Ben maneuvered Dawa to the wall where Goba's head was within arm's reach. "Go ahead, get acquainted."

Gesar dismounted and was surprised at how quickly he found his legs after the long ride. "Hey boy," Gesar said reaching out to stroke Goba's forehead and noticing the symmetrical winged patch of white beneath the forelock.

"That feels good. Now get the back of my ears please." Goba's voice echoed. Gesar obeyed immediately and started to massage behind the horse's ears.

"Ahhh! That's the spot. Now under my chin." Gesar complied and started to work on the chin.

"You have good hands rider. Now behind my ears again."

As Goba voiced his satisfaction, Gesar felt a rush of exhilaration. The landscape brightened. An intense odor of sweet grass filled his nostrils. A cacophony of temple bells, buzzing insects and birdsong hammered his eardrums. It was as if he shared the animal's heightened senses. The more he stroked the animal the more his resistance to this reality weakened. His initial offense at Ben's assumptions faded. Not only could he envision himself riding Goba, he had the strange feeling of having always known him. Like every other encounter in Shambala, this was intense and seductive, captivating his awareness and relentlessly stripping him of links to his other reality.

"Gesar, you'd better stop," Ben interrupted. "Dawa tells me that Goba is taking advantage of you. He's attempting to focus all of your attention on him. He knows that you're new and not familiar with the rule."

"What rule is that?"

53

"A warrior and his horse must earn their rewards."

Almost against his will, Gesar came to the animal's defense. "That seems a bit harsh," he said.

"I have chosen wisely," Goba voiced with pleasure.

Suddenly, Dawa whipped his head around and bit Goba on the neck. It was only a harmless nip but Goba reared and whinnied at the insult then turned and galloped away. "We will earn many rewards together, rider." Gesar heard as Goba retreated up the grassy hill.

"He's a spirited horse. I think he was offended." Gesar commented.

Ben stroked his mount's neck and said, "Dawa was the same when he was young and not battle tested. Goba is eager and feeling confident, but that will change when the hot breath of a demon touches his hindquarters. Come and get back on, we must rejoin the column. We are not far from our barracks."

Ben and Gesar were the last to pass through the arched gateway that led to the practice field and barracks of the Senge tapah. The men had spread out, directing their mounts to various stables that were on the same level as the practice field. The apartment for each warrior was directly above his mount's stable so that horse and rider were never far apart. With no urging from Ben, Dawa headed straight for his stable. A stableman ran out, grabbed the halter and led Dawa into the building. Ben and Gesar dismounted in an immaculately clean stable that smelled of fresh cut hay.

"I see that not all have returned," commented the stableman.

Ben replied somberly. "Three men and their mounts were lost. We unexpectedly encountered Mahakala. None of us would be here if not for Lama Zhangpo. He appeared with a phurba just as we were about to be trapped. He also presented us with our latest hindmost. Shingdong this is Gesar. And Gesar, I believe I have already mentioned our stable master to you."

Gesar nodded and extended a hand. After a moment of confusion, the stocky, heavily muscled stable master accepted the hand, gave it a frenetic shake, and returned a broad toothy smile. "Welcome to the Senge tapah and please excuse my hesitation. I am not used to the hand shaking gesture, although Ben has explained it to me." Shingdong apologized.

"Usually, our formal greeting is the traditional pressed palms combined with a head bow," Ben explained.

"You go to the baths before feasting," Shingdong instructed. "I will take care of Dawa. I will give him a good washing and rub down."

As Ben gathered saddlebags and collected his weapons, he gave the stable master an additional task. "Shingdong, when you're finished with Dawa, go to the field and bring in Goba and find some tack that will fit him. Goba has chosen Gesar as his rider. They can begin training together tomorrow."

Shingdong's eyes widened with surprise. "So the wild one has finally chosen. You must be a strong rider, Gesar."

Gesar was at a loss for words. The stable master's reaction was not helping to ease his misgivings.

With his gear slung over his shoulder, Ben stroked Dawa's forehead before making his way toward the stair. "Follow me Gesar, I will show you to your quarters after we clean up." When the two men reached the first landing, Ben stopped, turned and called back to his stableman. "Shingdong, have the Druk dakini returned? Gesar is acquainted with their captain and I believe he would like to to see her again."

Shingdong's expression turned grave. "No, Captain Jigme. They did not arrive when expected this morning. Even now, Lady Palden keeps watch for them from her tower."

One felt uneasy as she signaled her squadron to begin a double helical attack formation against a column of nagu fang warriors spotted marching along a canyon trail. She could not explain her apprehension especially as the situation seemed routine and with minimal risk to her forces. The double helical formation was a proven and effective strategy. It not only surprised the enemy but it was also highly disorienting when viewed from below. The interlacing flight pattern confused enemy archers and it was nearly impossible to fix on a single target, let alone judge its distance.

The well-disciplined squadron of dakini warriors reacted immediately to Ane's signal by drawing their weapons and taking positions. One arm of the helix would rain arrows on the enemy column while the other would sweep in finishing off survivors with swords. Ane led her silent flock of kinnaras into a spiral descent. The squad closed nearly half distance to their target and the enemy had not yet noticed them. It would be an easy strike, Ane thought. The enemy column had no cover to which to retreat. The raid would be over in minutes. In the next moment, she realized what disturbed her; it was the sense of routine and predictability. The scenario was all too easy as if deliberately designed to instill a false sense of security. She suddenly recognized her mistake. The column was bait, which meant it was a trap. A surge of fear snapped her out of complacency. She ignored the enemy column and instead scanned the canyon walls. With her amrita-enhanced vision, it did not take long to locate the real threat. Obscured by the shadow of an overhanging cliff face, she recognized the glowing eyes of the demon-god Yama, also known as the Lord of Death. He was among the most ancient of the demon-gods and had been among the most difficult for the Bodhisattvas to tame. While his angelic persona, the austere ancient judge, was daunting, his demonic form was simply disgusting. Ane was glad that shadows hid the details of his repulsive countenance. Like all of the demon-gods, his eyes glowed ember red, but they were fixed in a face disfigured by pestilence and dripping with black pus. A crown of human skulls decorated his horned head. Unlike Mahakala, he had only two arms but these bore his favored weapons, a spiked iron club and a lasso of twisted razor wire. A closer inspection of the canyon walls revealed they were dotted with hundreds of archers concealed in caves and crannies, ready to loose their arrows the moment the bulk of squadron had dropped below them. How did the enemy entrench so many nagu warriors so close to Shambala? Ane wondered.

Ane whispered a thought and Brug immediately called the retreat signal. A high-pitched scream echoed through the canyon. All of the kinnaras broke formation and joined the alarm cry, making a sound so loud and piercing that it briefly paralyzed their enemies. The kinnaras used the precious time to shift to a spreading ascent formation, a move that prevented collisions and avoided clusters that would make easy targets for arrows. Ane and the other dakinis in the deepest part of the descent faced the greatest danger.

Unaffected by the paralyzing kinnara shriek and enraged by the slow response of his forces, Yama brutally whipped the nearest nagu archers with his lasso. The dakinis were already well into their ascent by the time the first arrows were loosed, but a full third of the dakini force remained in the lower portions of the canyon. At least he would have them, Yama thought. He cast out his lasso and caught a kinnara around the neck. Its rider used her sword to hack futilely at the indestructible cord as the loop tightened its grip. Only thick scales and armor prevented the cord from severing the kinnara's head, its wings beat in thunderous strokes, fighting bravely against the demon's pull, but Yama's massive weight planted firmly on the rock ledge was immovable. Yama could have easily jerked the cord and snapped the kinnara's neck, but since his initial plan had faltered, he was in a mood to deal out slow retribution. He drew his catch in like a fish on a line with the intention of pummeling the kinnara and its rider into an unrecognizable mound of flesh.

Ane looked up and was thankful that most of her squadron had lifted to safety, but she had no time to rejoice. Arrows were coming at her from every direction. Brug caught at least two arrows in his flank. Fortunately, they struck an area where his scales were thick enough to protect his vital parts, but if the piercing continued he would eventually succumb. She had already witnessed two of her comrades fall. Some of her dakini archers had managed to take out several of the enemy positions, but there were still more positioned above them. Ane's mind raced to find a solution. Clearly going up would only put them in greater danger. She commanded the nearest comrades to drop into a steep dive and make their way along the canyon floor to find a place beyond the enemy positions where they might ascend safely. The other dakinis quickly mimicked the retreat pattern. Ane stayed behind continuing to dodge arrows as she waited for her remaining forces to get clear of the trap. She was about to join them when she noticed Dolma, her second in command, being pulled to the canyon wall by Yama. Ane shuddered at the thought of facing Yama in battle. Humans rarely survived a direct encounter with a demon-god. Nevertheless, she guided Brug to fly directly for him.

Yama raised his club ready to strike the first satisfying blow to his impudent catch, his purulent sores spewing black pus in anticipation. It had been a long time since he had manifest in his wrathful form and he was planning to enjoy every moment. Having only two eyes, he was at a disadvantage compared to his three-eyed demon brother. A third eye was always useful for keeping watch when occupied with a particularly absorbing task. Consequently, he was caught off guard when an arrow struck his right eye and a sword gashed at his raised club arm. Neither were serious wounds. His sight would recover when he pulled the arrow shaft out, but it required the use his lasso arm since his wounded right arm would also take a few minutes to recover. As soon as he loosed his grip on the lasso in order to pull out the arrow shaft, Brug cried out to Dolma's mount, Nam, to fold and drop. Immediately, the cord ripped from Yama's palm and slipped over the cliff edge. Trusting her kinnara, Dolma gripped Nam's reins as they fell. Only at the last moment did Nam open her wings to alight on the canyon floor. Dolma quickly removed the dreadful lasso and tossed it aside as if were a venomous serpent. Remounting, she spoke a few reassuring words to her mount before joining the retreat through the canyon.

With his sight restored, Yama's only desire was to kill the attacker who denied him his prize. Realizing the success of her strategy, Ane did not wish to test her luck further with Yama. She intended to flee with all speed. However, Brug was less cautious; he made a quick turn and approached Yama from behind taking a swipe with his talons at the demon-god's club dislodging it from his wounded arm.

"Brug, what are you doing?" Ane cried in dismay. Yama bellowed a sound of frustration so loud that it loosed rocks from the canyon wall. Despite the horrendous sound, Brug was impassive. In a prideful display, the kinnara swung around again but this time he faced the wrathful monster, hovering at the cliff edge just beyond the demon's reach and issuing an ear-shattering shriek.

Yama recognized the contemptuous dakini displayed before him. "So, Palden sends her little pet to insult me. Well consider yourself marked for an especially unpleasant death. I will send you to your mistress wrapped in your own entrails."

Before Yama could raise his club to strike, Brug folded his wings and dropped into the canyon with blinding speed. Yama's last words echoed back to him from empty air where the dakini had been only an instant before.

Ane chastised Brug as she guided him to join the retreating dakini. "You're crazy Brug, that last display was totally unnecessary. Your stupid pride is going to get us killed. You were lucky that time. Now, let's see if you can get us through this canyon without getting an arrow in my back."

Carefully moving aside an assortment of tubes and wires, Nurse Holland turned over the comatose body of a dark-haired woman. Despite the hollow cheeks and emaciated musculature, the young woman had once been a stunning beauty. If there was any doubt, the framed photographs standing on the side table evidenced her former glory. One showed a portrait of a teenaged athlete in her prime standing proudly with one foot on a soccer ball. A bush of raven-black hair encircled a face bearing a beaming smile and bright lavender eyes. Another photo showed a young woman dressed in camouflage military fatigues, posing next to an Apache attack helicopter. Though a helmet hid her mass of black hair, the beaming smile was unchanged. Draped over the corners of the photo frame were a rosary and two medals, the Purple Heart and Medal of Honor, awarded to Captain Angela Adrastos. The staff working at the long-term care center knew of the young woman's heroic past and cared for her with a special respect. Nurse Holland had read the yellowed newspaper clippings describing the young captain's extraordinary flying skill in guiding a rocket-damaged helicopter safely to ground. Once grounded, she single handedly held off an enemy advance with cover fire, giving her crew time to extract their wounded. She was the last to run for an evacuation helicopter. As she leapt onto the chopper's deck, a mortar shell blasted her into permanent unconsciousness.

After four years in a veterans care facility, she was suddenly moved to a catholic long-term care center in Marin County. It was unusual to have young patients, but she was catholic and was given priority placement. Oddly, her only regular visitors were head-shaven Buddhist monks in orange robes, who paid for each month's care with a cash-stuffed envelop hand delivered to the business office. After making the payment, the monks went directly to her room and sat in meditation on the floor next to her bed for an hour and sometimes longer. The staff at the center noticed that those visits seemed to calm the young woman, stabilizing her blood pressure and heart rate. Everyone at the care facility thought it strange that Buddhist monks visited a comatose young catholic woman of Greek descent, but the San Francisco area was known for its collision of cultures.

Nurse Holland bathed the young woman's pale, shrapnel-scarred back with a warm washcloth while carrying on a one-sided conversation. "You had a rough night my Sleeping Beauty. Your gown is soaked right through with sweat. The night shift was worried with your heart rate and temp going up like that. That was one of your worst spells yet. Don't you even start thinking about dying on us, not after all the lovin' care we've been givin' you."

While drying her patient's skin, the nurse did a careful search for bedsores. Thankfully, the high-tech foam padding and regular turnings were keeping the dreaded sores at bay. It also helped that the young woman relieved pressure points herself by making involuntary movements, although these were sometimes sudden and violent. The unexpected flailing of arms and legs had left unwary staff with the occasional bruise, but Nurse Holland quickly learned how to avoid injuries. She recognized the first warning sign of an episode: the young woman's eyes would snap open and fix their gaze on some invisible target before her arms and legs began to move, sometimes the spells occurred only rarely and at other times repeatedly over several days. The neurologists ruled out epilepsy, a conclusion that did not surprise Nurse Holland. She had seen enough epileptic seizures to tell that these were different, more like movements of a dreaming cat. At times, the intense unfocused gaze was associated with words spoken in a strange language that passed over dry lips in a breathy hiss. Nurse Holland finished dressing the young woman in a fresh gown and began brushing her hair. "You have such beautiful hair but it needs regular brushing. The day that you wake up I want you to look as beautiful as your picture and maybe then you can tell me about your dreams."

One heard the great horns of Shambala echoing faintly through the canyon. The sound, intended to guide warriors home if disoriented by bad weather or battle wounds, was like the voice of a mother calling her children. Presently, it was more a lift to the spirit than a guiding beacon. The Druk squadron had narrowly escaped complete disaster, their return was long overdue and there were many wounded among their ranks. Just how many sisters were lost would have to be determined when the group reassembled at the palace.

Ane guessed that Lady Palden had ordered the horns sounded. Undoubtedly Palden was keeping watch from her tower. Was she worried? Did a demon-god have the capacity to worry? Ane suddenly realized that her squadron was likely not visible from Palden's tower. They were flying at low altitude in the event that a wounded rider or mount needed rest or assistance. Ane signaled her squadron to rise above the canyon wall so Lady Palden might see them. At the higher elevation, Ane saw that they were near the Shield perimeter and the safety of Shambala's valley.

Not long after passing through the Shield, the welcoming song of hundreds of kinarras joined the sound of Kalapa's horns, signaling that the Druk squadron had been spotted. Ane planned to report directly to Lady Palden as soon as the wounded were attended to. The appearance of Yama and so many nagu warriors within striking distance of Shambala was unexpected. Somehow, the enemy had evaded the eyes of scouts and patrols. If Palden did worry, then this news would be no consolation.

The battle torn dakini warriors assembled on the temple plaza, where groups of healers were waiting to tend to the riders and their mounts. Despite several arrows in his flank, Brug touched down with his usual grace. During the return flight, he kept repeating, "I'm well mistress." Despite his reassurance, Ane was worried. When a healer approached, she anxiously directed him to look at Brug; the tips of nagu arrows were poisoned, but timely treatment could neutralize the effect. After a few moments of inspection, the healer pulled the arrows out.

"Fortunately, this one has a tough hide," the healer commented. "It looks like the arrow heads embedded in the scales and never made it to the flesh, but I'll put on some salve to neutralize poison just to be sure. You can return to your eyrie as soon as I'm done."

Before going, Ane assessed the condition of her squadron and made a final head count. The damage was not as bad as she feared, but they would need a time of healing before returning to the patrols. Sadly, four riders and their mounts were missing. Since bonding caused a rider and mount to become a single entity, a kinnara stayed and defended its rider to the death, just as the dakini would do for her mount. Thankfully, Dolma, her second in command, had survived, although the encounter with Yama severely injured her mount, Nam.

Dolma gushed with gratitude and embraced Ane when she came to her. "Ane, thanks for coming back for us. Your courage is a blessing and teaching to all of us."

"It was mostly Brug's doing." Ane answered. "Nothing gets his scales up like a demon-god on the rampage."

After speaking with each of the surviving Druk dakinis, Ane mounted Brug and made the short flight back to her chamber. The clouds in the west were tinged pink by the setting sun. "It's late; the other warriors will in the eating hall," she thought. Brug entered the eyrie window and gently alighted on his nest. Ane removed and stowed her saddle and gear. As she turned to enter her chamber, she was startled to find Lady Palden waiting for her.

"Was it Yama?" she asked abruptly, dispensing with any formal greeting.

Ane quickly pressed her palms together and bowed before answering. "Yes, Lady Palden. He laid a trap for us, but most of my squadron managed to escape."

"Tell me every detail," Palden ordered.

Ane described the ambush, reliving every harrowing moment.

Pen showed Gesar to his quarters in the Senge tapah barracks, which was one of eight positioned symmetrically around the city to house the eight cavalry units. The barracks' design incorporated an economical use of space while providing a place of privacy for each warrior. The room was simple with only spartan comforts. Clothing and riding gear were neatly stored in a wardrobe that stood next to a simple frame bed. One corner of the room with a mat and floor cushion served as a private meditation area. In the opposite corner, a spiral staircase led down to the stables. Windows and a second entrance with and arched doorway were in a wall facing a balcony overlooking the training field. All of the quarters opened onto the common balcony which formed a semicircular promenade partially enclosing the practice field and allowing panoramic views of training formations. Stairways and paved paths allowed access to baths, meeting halls, and gardens on the upper levels of the fortress city.

Ben waited while Gesar inspected his new quarters. Gesar turned to him and asked, "You called me your newest hindmost. What does that mean?"

"It is your rank. We ride according to rank. You will replace Chiru, who now occupies the rear position of the column. He will become your confidant and teach you of our routines, but you will learn more of this later. Now, you're probably hungry. I'll show you to the mess now."

"Mess? I didn't think you ate solid food. I thought you lived off that flask of amrita you carry around." Gesar said.

"We can for a while. The amrita provides enough sustenance, but sometimes we get an urge to chew," Ben said with a half smile. "Follow me."

A continuous drone of horns echoed in the distance as the two men walked the path to the main eating hall. "The horns, I heard them start up shortly after we arrived, what are they for?" Gesar asked.

"They call for the missing Druk dakini squadron." Ben replied.

"Do you think they're okay?"

Ben looked skyward as he answered. "I suspect they encountered a demon-god, but I'm sure they will return. There is no captain more skilled than Ane."

"I hope your right." Gesar said, surprised by the sincerity of his concern.

"Ah, we're here." Ben said as they approached a large building with an arched roof.

Opening a circular wooden door with an elaborately carved dragon handle, Ben entered with Gesar at his heels. The two men stopped a moment on a landing at the top a broad stair overlooking a massive hall brightly lit by a perimeter of sconce lamps, hanging lanterns and skylights. Hundreds of men and women sat on cushioned floor mats at rows of low tables with servers carrying platters of food among them.

"As you might guess, we don't spend all of our time with just our own units. This is the one of the places where Buddha warriors of different units can meet and socialize," Ben commented.

"They don't seem to be talking much," Gesar noted, thinking that the atmosphere in the hall was rather subdued considering the number of diners present.

"Look there," Ben said, pointing to a section of unoccupied tables. "Those places are left empty for the Druk squadron. The quiet is in respect for them."

Ben and Gesar descended the stair and joined a group of men and women at a table. Ben knew everyone and made introductions. The women were from Kra and Galme dakini squadrons and the men form the Wa and Kang tapah units. Some of the men and women were introduced as couples, indicating that more than professional relationships were permitted between dakini and tapah. After the introductions, there was considerable discussion regarding recent encounters with enemy units, but curiously no one questioned Gesar about his origin nor did anyone speak about their other life. The Buddha warriors were obviously from different cultures, and according to Lama Zhangpo, all had another existence in the Human realm. Even Ben recalled a former life in Montana, but had noted his recollections of that life were fading. Did the warriors eventually forget their pasts? Indeed, Shambala was intoxicating to the senses, thrusting one's awareness into the present and overwhelming thoughts of the past. Gesar felt as if he had to fight to hold on to his memories of San Francisco, although compared to Shambala, that life seemed grey and mundane. To preserve his sanity, he needed to make sense of his bizarre circumstance. He wanted to know more about the other warriors and especially Shambala's enemies. At a lull in the conversation Gesar asked. "The nagu, where do they come from?"

After a lingering silence, Amala, captain of the Kra dakini squadron, answered. "They are incarnates of humans. After death, the core sentience of a human must journey to find a new incarnation. That journey is plagued many dangers and without guidance or appropriate training in life, a sentient can be trapped in the lower realms where they might incarnate as nagu, to be enslaved by Zerden and his minions. The Buddha showed us the way to escape that fate, The Path of Enlightenment. Those living in Shambala are sentient beings of higher consciousness who have found their way to the doorstep of the god realm. As you have learned, even the animals of

Shambala have a higher level of consciousness. Because Shambala threatens Zerden's power, he is bent on destroying it."

Before Gesar could pose another question, the horns that had been droning in the background suddenly stopped and the air filled with the cry of hundreds of soprano voices singing in an eerie harmony that resonated through every corner of the hall. After several minutes, the strangely beautiful song ended and dining warriors throughout the hall broke into a spontaneous cheer. The previously restrained atmosphere in the hall changed; the noise level increased with animated conversations and the occasional eruption of laughter.

"What just happened?" Gesar asked.

"That was the welcoming song of the kinnaras. It means the Druk squadron has returned." Ben said as he signaled a server to bring food to the table.

Noting that Ben's mood remained somber, Gesar asked, "What's wrong, why didn't you cheer with the others?"

"The Senge lost three good warriors during our last sortie and many more men would have been lost if not for the arrival of the phurba bearer. Tomorrow, we will hold the honoring ceremony for them. If the Druk dakini engaged a god demon as we did, I suspect they too may be honoring the fallen. "

Gesar prayed the raven-haired beauty was among the survivors. He had never felt such a strong attraction to a woman before. But was she only a phantom, a product of his unconscious desire? It would be his kind of luck that the woman of his dreams was just that, a dream. Before falling prey to more doubts, a platter of food was set before him. An intense odor of spices seized his awareness, distracting his dark thoughts. Like his enhanced physical strength, his incarnation apparently had heightened senses of sight, smell and taste. Despite his doubts about its reality, the meal was perhaps the most delicious and nourishing of his life.

With his three eyes burning with rage, Mahakala shouted at his fellow demon-god, his voice echoing throughout the massive cavern like thunder. "Yama! Your stupidity is exceeded only by the vast emptiness in your head."

Yama remained defiant despite Mahakala's rebuke, "It was an excellent plan. I would have destroyed the whole squadron if not for Palden's pet."

Mahakala slammed the butt of his tilug against the stone floor. "Excellent plan? Are you serious? You fool, your plan was so excellent that virtually all of the dakinis escaped and by attacking prematurely, you have shown our hand. Why do you think I have been spending my time out on that miserable plain?"

"To draw their forces into the open," Yama answered, purulence dripping from the corners of his mouth.

Mahakala pointed his tilug blade at Yama's head. "Your brains must be leaking out of those boils of yours. Were you even listening when we discussed strategy? The fang warriors on the plain are meant to distract Shambala's forces while we establish garrisons near the Shield perimeter. Have you forgotten the size of the force we will need to defeat Shambala? It will require hundreds of thousands of fang warriors to weaken the Shield, and that may give us only a limited time to cross into Shambala with Zerden's elite captains to destroy the throne. Now, your 'excellent plan' has exposed us. The dakinis that escaped your trap have undoubtedly informed my former consort of the very large contingent of fang warriors that attacked them within less than a day's march of the Shield. Palden will be asking how such a force could slip by her patrols. The eyes of Shambala will now turn away from the plains of Asura. If they discover where we have positioned Zerden's portals, combined units of tapah and dakini can pin us down indefinitely. That is what your excellent plan has achieved."

Yama smashed his spiked club on the cave floor, causing loose rock to fall from the cave roof. "I'm tired of waiting in these rat holes!" he shouted. "You have wasted time breeding your flying pets and diverting forces to dig these tunnels when we could have reduced our enemies by more than half by now."

Mahakala shook his head in disgust and responded. "Perhaps, but our forces would have been reduced by even greater numbers, leaving us still exiled to the Asura outlands without a means to penetrate the Shield. We agreed that breaking the Shield is our primary goal, but that thought seems to have oozed out of that stupid pus-filled head of yours. Now we must attack before we are a fully prepared."

"Who are you to chastise me?" Yama growled.

"I'm the only thing between you and Zerden's wrath. You forget that you don't have the Shield to protect you anymore. Now go back to your armies and await the signal to march!" Mahakala ordered.

When Yama did not move, Mahakala prepared to counter any rash acts of vengeance, gripping his weapons and fixing his eyes on the defiant demon-god. Yama glared back, his eyes full of spite.

Restraining an urge to strike a blow, Yama stomped out of the cave, dragging his lasso behind him. Mahakala did not relax until Yama was completely out of sight. He did not like the fact that disputes among the rebel demon-gods were growing more frequent. Reverting to their demon forms came with all of the complications of ego clashes. Zerden respected the power of the united demon-gods and had promised them an equal share of the spoils as a reward for their defection, but he would quickly capitalize on any fractiousness.

Goba turned sharply and galloped full speed at the next row of targets, each no larger than a hand and swinging pendulum-like from a series of elevated beams. "Yes!" Gesar exclaimed with satisfaction when his arrow struck another target dead on.

"You'd better nock another arrow or I will pass the targets while you congratulate yourself," Goba warned.

Riding Goba on the training field was the high point of Gesar's day. At first, the telepathic connection with his horse was disturbing. Sometimes he was unable to separate his thoughts from those of Goba. Just who was in control was constantly in question. Was he riding Goba or was Goba just carrying him? Eventually, Gesar realized that it was a matter of acceptance, mutual trust and respect. With minds joined, there was no need for spurring, pulling reins, or voicing commands. A rider's intent combined with animal instinct was all that was necessary to achieve amazing feats of 'horse-man-ship'. Only physical and psychological limits restricted their potential. In the first days of training, Gesar and Goba had mastered the basic group formation maneuvers. They likewise easily learned the fighting exercises, a task greatly accelerated by Gesar's experience with weapons and martial arts. Goba also enjoyed the training except for the days committed to practicing various types of mounts and dismounts.

Ben watched Goba complete his last turn and trot pridefully into the finish zone. "I'm impressed," Ben commented. "If all of our tapah learned so quickly our enemies would certainly reconsider challenging the forces of Shambala."

"I knew we would make a good team," Goba voiced in Gesar's mind.

"Thanks for the complement captain," Gesar answered. "But it's mostly Goba. He's been watching the tapah practice on the training field since he was a foal."

Ben smiled and said. "It's one thing to watch and another to execute. Anyhow, my complement was for you both. Soon you and Goba will be ready to patrol with us, but you have yet to learn to perform combined maneuvers with a dakini squadron. It looks like you will have your opportunity to meet Ane again. Tomorrow, we practice with the Druk dakini squadron. They have been resting since their encounter with Yama and are eager for some exercise."

"Then Ane survived the ambush." Gesar said.

"Yes, and she brought important intelligence regarding our enemy that raises the urgency of getting everyone battle ready as quickly as possible. Our defenses may not be prepared for what is to come."

Despite Ben's foreboding words, Gesar hoped this bizarre other existence would last at least another day. During his training, his eyes often looked skyward to watch the silhouettes of the kinnaras with their women riders flying in various formations and he wondered if Ane was among them. He had grown accustom to hearing the song of the kinnaras each day as they welcomed their riders in preparation for their patrols. There was something reassuring about the kinnaras' song, as if it announced that the Path of Enlightenment was still open to humanity.

During meals, there was much talk about the demon-gods and their rebellion, but Gesar had yet to see a demon-god at close proximity. His only contacts were a distant view of Mahakala pursuing the tapah warriors on the plain of Asura and a brief glimpse of Begtse as he rode his warhorse, Lok, past the Senge barracks' gate on his way to his tower refuge. Even from a distance, Begtse was an imposing figure, a tall helmeted warrior riding on the back of a horse that was nearly twice the size of Goba. The notion of demon-gods in angelic forms was as incredible as their demonic forms. Gesar had always thought that the bizarre nightmarish figures displayed in explicit detail on Buddhist temple walls and thangkas were purely the imaginary products of overzealous monks. Rather, he learned that the images were based upon the memories of enlightened monks who had joined with the bodhisattvas during the time of the Taming. After the Taming, the demon-gods adopted angelic forms and for more than two thousand years they were content with their role as guardians of Shambala. Regrettably, some of them had grown tired of their service and now an epic war was impending.

Gesar woke before dawn on the day the Senge tapah were to train with the Druk dakini. He attempted a morning meditation but found it difficult to concentrate. Forgoing the effort, he left his chambers to walk on the balcony promenade, stepping through his door into the chilled morning air. Other than two sentries posted at the field gates, the training field was deserted. The muffled sounds of horses and stable hands at work came from below. Overhead, the pale glow of the Shield shimmered in the predawn half-light. Gesar was glad for the opportunity to clear his head in relative solitude. It had been a night of interrupted sleep and disturbing dreams. For several days, he had not thought about his other life. His experience in Shambala was so vivid that he was beginning to doubt that there ever was another life, yet images of life in San Francisco intruded his dreams. Once, he woke to Dr. Ashki's voice whispering words of encouragement. There were other more menacing images as well. He dreamt of Ane lying in a hospital bed, thin, pale and helpless with a red-eyed demon looming over her. Yet, by the time he was riding Goba out of his stable into the morning sunshine, he was so filled with the anticipation of seeing Ane again that he had largely forgotten about his disturbing night.

After several routine warm up maneuvers, Ben ordered the Senge tapah to assemble at one end of the training field. Moments later, the sky was filled with dakinis, flying in complex interlacing patterns and casting ominous shadows that darted erratically around the open field. The flight display lasted a few minutes and then the dakinis began to descend. Ane was first to touch ground with Brug coming to a high stepping halt just in front of Ben.

Pressing his palms together, Ben bowed his head and offered a formal greeting. "Welcome captain. The Senge tapah are honored to have the opportunity to train with the renowned Druk dakinis. Your squadron's courage facing the demon-god, Yama, is a source of inspiration for all of us."

Ane returned the bow. "Your men are no less inspiring, captain Jigme. I heard about your encounter with Mahakala. Surviving the wrath of a demon-god is not easy, but at least we had the sky the escape to."

Ben smiled. "We would not be here if we didn't have the protection of a phurba to escape to," he said.

Ane laughed and said, "I guess we're both just good runners."

Gesar watched and listened to the meeting of captains from the line of mounted men waiting in silence. Gesar's heart had stepped up its pace when Ane landed only yards away from him. She was indeed as beautiful as he remembered. At that moment, Goba's voice intruded his thoughts, "You like her."

Gesar tried to suppress a response.

"We are soul-bound. You cannot hide your feelings from me, I know you like her," Goba persisted.

"I guess it's pointless trying keep anything from you." Gesar responded.

"You're lucky that I'm not jealous. In fact, I'm going to help you make her your mate. If you want a mare, you have to first get her attention." Goba suddenly reared and whinnied, whipping his long mane back and forth. All eyes turned on the undisciplined tapah.

"Who is that?" Ane asked.

"It's someone that you have already met," Ben said as he turned and ordered, "Remove your helm, tapah."

Embarrassed, Gesar lifted off his helmet. "Forgive me, captain."

Surprised, Ane asked, "Is that you, Gesar?"

"Yes captain," he answered, gratified that she had remembered him.

"I'm not your captain, so you may call me Ane. When did you return to Shambala?"

"I don't know for sure." Gesar said.

Ben injected. "We found him at a choten on the southwest trail to the Plain of Deception ten days ago."

"And you are already one of the Senge tapah. That is an accomplishment. I knew you must be a skilled warrior when I saw you repel that dron scout. It's good to see that you found your way back to us."

"Thanks, and it's good to see you again." Gesar meant it.

Intruding Gesar's mind, Goba said, "I think she likes you, but you had better watch out for her mount. He's the jealous type."

As Chidag turned a corner, late afternoon sunlight flashed through his truck's windshield. Angrily, he pulled down the window visor and adjusted his sunglasses. He hated the yellow sun of this realm; it caused pain his head and aggravated his growing impatience. He had searched for more than a week without success, visiting nearly every hospital and long-term care facility in San Francisco and at least half of those in Oakland. The Sleepers would be easy to kill once located, but they were hidden better than he had anticipated. Among them, Palden's first captain especially had to be eliminated, but until she was found, he would kill every sleeping warrior he could find.

He now regretted killing the watcher without extracting some information. Up to now, he had avoided the watchers, but perhaps that strategy was flawed. Undoubtedly, they harbored his quarry and it was time to change tactics. Finding the watchers would be a simple task as they would be keeping vigil at the house of his human host, hoping for his return. He decided that a new plan would be wise and though it had been more than a week since leaving his host's house, the return route immediately assembled in his consciousness. Filled with a fresh sense of purpose, Chidag pressed the brake pedal and performed a sudden U-turn, a maneuver his host body had performed uncountable times in pursuit of perpetrators. The host flesh seemed eager to return home and for Chidag, it was a relief to have the sun at his back.

Chidag grinned when he noticed the white van parked a half block from the Cutter house. The watchers are as patient as they are predictable, he thought. As he drove by the van, he glowered at its driver. Surprised by Chidag's defiant appearance, the watcher's eyes widened in terror and he spilled a coffee cup while fumbling for a mobile phone. Chidag had confirmed his suspicion and enjoyed the amusing side effect elicited by his gaze. His nostrils caught the scent of fear and his killing reflex briefly surged, forcing him to suppress an impulse to put his truck into reverse and ram the watcher's vehicle. Instead, he turned into Officer Charles Cutter's driveway, parked the truck in the garage and entered the house to await the opportunity to execute his plan.

Brother William ignored the painful burn on his thigh as he keyed his mobile phone. After days of watching an empty house, he had resigned himself to the opinion that Zerden's minion would never risk exposure by returning to his host's domicile. The creature wanted to avoid interference from the Kalacakra. Hadn't he viciously killed Brother Zak in order to elude them? Consequently, when Chidag returned with such sudden brazenness, it profoundly upset William's state of mind. After the incident with Brother Zak, the watchers were instructed to keep at a safe distance and retreat if the creature approached them. William wanted to do more than retreat; every instinct told him to run away as far as possible. He was only a novice monk and not a particularly brave one. A single look from Chidag was quite effective in instilling fear and crushing all hope. Why had the creature returned, blatantly announcing his presence, unconcerned by the Kalacakra surveillance? Considering that this entity was among the first born of Zerden's children, its depths of deceit and cruelty were likely unfathomable. Brother William's knuckles whitened with tension as he gripped the mobile phone waiting for an answer. After four rings, a voice answered.

"You have news, Brother William?"

"Your holiness, he has returned and is in the house," answered William.

A response to this news came after a pause. "It has been decided that the host must be destroyed. It is the only way to exorcise Chidag from this world before he inflicts more harm."

"But I am alone and without weapons."

"Brother William, I would never expect you to attempt such a thing. You will do nothing but continue to watch. We must act quickly while Chidag is in the house. I have already prepared a team for this purpose. They have the weapons required to destroy the creature and will be joining you shortly. Call immediately if the creature leaves the house and remember to flee if he approaches you."

"Yes, your holiness."

Brother William closed the connection and pocketed his phone with a trembling hand. It was now after sunset and the growing darkness did not help to allay his fear. While keeping his attention focused on the Cutter house, he tried to calm himself with breathing exercises and mantra recitations. A half an hour passed and the house remained so quiet that he feared Chidag might have left unseen, but when a crack of artificial light appeared between window curtains, William sighed with relief. Chidag was apparently still in the house.

A few minutes later, another van containing several shaven-headed monks quietly pulled up next to William's van. A brother in the passenger seat rolled down his window and signaled William to roll down his. William obeyed immediately.

"Is the creature still in the house?" asked the brother.

"Yes," answered William.

"Good. We can proceed as planned and Brother William you should leave now."

The vehicle's driver turned off the headlights and slowly rolled the van forward, stopping in front of the Cutter house. Brother William was about to start his engine to leave, but his curiosity caused him to linger a while longer. The arrival of a van full of fellow monks partially quelled his fears and what he witnessed next transfixed his attention. Several shadows darted from the van, positioning themselves at points around the house with one silently climbing to the roof. Several more moments passed and then the silent shadows returned to their vehicle. Assuming the mission had been accomplished, William started his engine and was about to turn into the street when the Cutter house exploded in a flash of white light and was engulfed by an intense inferno. Blinded, William felt his van rock as the shockwave hit. When his eyes readjusted, he noticed that his fellow brothers had already fled the scene. In a partial state of panic, Brother William turned his vehicle around and sped away.

William did not relax until he was several miles away. He took deep breaths as the cool evening air rushed through his open window. "It's over. It's finally over, No more watching." he whispered to himself. He planned to return immediately to the temple. After a simple meal, he would sleep, join his brothers in morning meditation and everything would be back to a quiet routine. William checked his rear view mirror as he merged into the freeway traffic, failing to notice the two red embers glowing in the dark cabin behind his seat.

At dawn, the firefighters packed away their gear at the scene of a fire that had totally incinerated the house of Officer Charles Cutter. It had burned all night and was an obvious case of arson. Shortly after arriving at the scene, the firefighters were dismayed when the fire burned hotter with the addition of water. An alert sergeant realized the cause. "Jesus!" he yelled. "It's a goddamn magnesium fire, stop the water." By the time appropriate chemicals were obtained to combat the blaze, the house was reduced to ash. While the other firefighters boarded their their trucks to leave, one remained among smoking embers raking through the ashes with what appeared to be a metal rod.

A smoke raw voice yelled to him from one of the fire trucks. "Come on. Give it up man! We already looked. That fire was hot enough to incinerate bone."

As the lone firefighter turned to leave, he concealed a long triple-edged blade with an elaborately carved handle under his ash-smudged coat. His brow furrowed with a terrible realization as he walked back to the truck to join the others. Chidag Nagpo had never been in the house; the circle of white fire intended to prevent his escape could not have killed him. His host body should have been found charred and weakened, but the flesh still living. Only a phurba stabbed through the flesh, pinning his body to the earth, could drive Chidag back to the outlands of Asura.

Clouds darkened the sky and an unseasonably cold wind laid siege to the walls of Dagpa Akar lamasery when Jhado left his meditation room. A steady background roar echoed through the corridors as he made his way down the stairs from his apartments. Stopping to look at the garden from a balcony window, he noticed that the prayer flags strung over the courtyard whipped furiously, straining their tethers and whistling in the wind stream. Fallen leaves and petals danced wildly in miniature cyclones. His greatest concern was for the citrus trees and he hoped the weather would pass before any serious damage occurred. For the permanent residents of the lamasery, fresh produce was among their few luxuries and they depended heavily on the gardens to supplement their simple diet. Turning from the balcony, Jhado continued his descent to the dukhang, which also served as the temple's thekpu or ceremonial space. As he passed along a windowless corridor, the flickering flames of butter oil lamps

74

struggled to stay alight in errant drafts, causing a chaotic dance of shadows on the walls. "How long will the flames last?" he thought, and the metaphor for the present state of affairs did not escape him. Taking pause at this pessimistic thought, he realized that he had allowed negativity to gnaw at his spirit. Recognizing the danger, he immediately emptied his mind. It was not good to begin an initiation ceremony with a distracted mind, especially when guiding a group of initiates on a journey that would challenge their grasp of reality.

Nine days earlier, Jhado sat upon his brocade throne and gave audience to a young woman named Kensang who had been elected spokesperson for five new Kalacakra initiates. Her fellow students had revealed their wisdom in selecting her as their representative. She performed the formal request impeccably; her words and gestures were imbued with such sincerity that Jhado had no doubts of her commitment and he accepted the initiation request without hesitation. The students withdrew after receiving his formal blessing, and then Jhado instructed his assistants to prepare the thekpu for the initiation ceremony.

First, they performed the Dance of the Earth and positioned a ring of warding phurbas to prevent potential intrusion by the enemies of enlightenment. Once the space was secure, they collected the items that required blessing by the High Lama. The scent of sandalwood incense permeated the room as the sacred materials and objects were set before Jhado, even the tools used for the making of the sand mandala required cleansing of any negative energy. In Dagpa Akar negative influences were generated mostly unintentionally. The colored sands might have been exposed to the idle gossip of a monk or nun during the many hours of their preparation. The chalk line used to mark out the mandala outlines may have been spun or trimmed without total attention. The metaphysical space and all within it had to be scoured of even the slightest impurity in order to briefly open a portal to the divine palace.

Once the necessary implements and materials were purified, the mandala's construction was begun. For the first three days, Jhado participated directly, snapping the chalk lines, invoking the deities and adding the first colored lines representing the body, word and mind of the Buddha. Over the next five days, monk and nun assistants completed the mandala. They started in the middle and worked outward, using long serrated funnels and wood scrapers to create an image that exploded with color and impossible detail. The completed circle, no more than two meters in diameter, depicted a sacred land with its animals, plants, central palace, and hundreds of divine occupants. To ensure that it be seen only at the proper moment, the completed mandala was concealed behind curtains.

On the tenth day, the mandala was to be revealed to the initiates under Jhado's direction. Rows of adepts and novices in deep orange robes were seated in their respective position according to rank. Their voices filled the thekpu with the drone of chanting as Jhado sat in his brocade throne. The five blindfolded initiates waited near the curtained mandala. In Jhado's judgment, they seemed composed and prepared to begin the journey. The previous day, each was given stalks of kushi grass to place under their bedding; its scent along with the recitation of special mantras was intended to help them gain control of the dream state. This skill was critical to their initiation as well as their eventual service to Shambala. After taking their vows, the blindfolds were removed and each student approached the throne to receive the seven initiations. Jhado's task was to take each initiate through a ritualistic rebirth and rearing, in order to be born as a pure and sacred being. Kensang was the last to approach the throne, demonstrating that humility tempered her strength. When he exchanged glances with the young woman, he sensed a profound wisdom in her steady gaze. There was something special about this young nun. Was this the next leader of the sisters of Dagpa Akar? He wondered.

When the rebirthing ceremony was complete, Jhado signaled assistants to part the curtain and usher the initiates forward to view the mandala. Once they were seated comfortably, he gave them a long period to absorb the mandala's image until it filled every corner of their consciousness. Once satisfied that all of the initiates had reached the proper state of concentration, he spoke the words that would guide them on their first journey to another realm. "As you learned in practice, hold the image in your mind with your eyes closed."

As he spoke, Jhado recalled his own initiation many years before as a highly disciplined and promising young initiate. When he first glimpsed the mandala, it appeared as a two-dimensional image with amazing complexity and seductive colors which drew his eyes progressively into the scene, inviting him to wander among the innumerable paths and symbols. When he had become comfortable with his visual meandering, his master's voice invaded his consciousness. "Close your eyes, abandon fear, release control and let your awareness fall deeper into the mandala."

That was the point of Jhado's greatest challenge. His instinct was to maintain control. How could he simply let go? Discipline and control were the mortar and stone of his very foundation; they had made him a shining and admired student. After an internal struggle that seemed to last an eternity, he finally obeyed his master's instruction and let go, releasing all attachment to passing the test of initiation. If he failed, then so be it. The mandala changed almost instantly. First, the symbols began to move, and then a beautiful three-dimensional palace rose up from the two-dimensional surface. He saw a domed white temple at the summit of a walled city surrounded by a glass smooth lake. Eight spokes stretched out from the central palace to end at the base of eight towers standing on the perimeter of the island city. As the lotus-shaped city acquired more detail, the numerous symbols transformed into miniature people and animals, moving about the island or wandering the surrounding countryside. Jhado recalled his exhilaration when the mandala came to life; it was the sacred land of Shambala and his point of view was nothing less than god-like. Before the seduction of false omnipotence overcame him, his master urged them further, "Do not tarry. Enter the palace while the gate is open to you."

In response, Jhado forced away the spell that held him and he desperately searched for a gateway. So enamored by the overall scene, he had failed to notice anything like an entrance. Scanning the outer walls of the island fortress with his consciousness, he saw a flash of light emerge from an arched portal. The entrance called to him but he did not know how to enter. I see it but my ego is too great to pass through, he thought. As if his thoughts were being overheard, his master said, "Compress your awareness and enter." The command sounded absurd, but somehow Jhado understood and obeyed. By ignoring his desire to possess the whole image and compressing all of his awareness on the gate, the perspective instantly changed, and he found himself standing next to his master at the portal of the island city. No longer the omnipotent watcher, he was now part of the mandala. "We must wait for the others to join us," the master instructed. Eventually, the other initiates assembled and the master instructed them to follow him.

His master led them through a tunnel, across a courtyard, and then up a maze of corridors and stairways. After mounting five levels, they reached the domed temple, which rested upon a great plaza overlooking a tier of beautiful gardens. Their robes whipped noiselessly in the wind as they stood on the island summit, facing massive doors decorated with an elaborate relief of a lotus surrounded by carved figures of gods, demons, warriors and holy men. Strangely, the plaza was empty but for the initiates and their master. The city occupants he had seen from the omnipotent point-of-view seemed to have vanished. Jhado had felt himself growing progressively lighter as his master led them upward. Now at the summit, he feared that the next gust of wind would carry him away like a dry leaf. Again, his master's words came at the appropriate moment. "You have only to hold on a moment longer for the initiation is nearly complete. Behind these doors are both the end and the beginning of your journey. You may now enter." The master pulled open the doors and urged the initiates to follow him. Upon crossing the temple threshold, Jhado became aware of an intense light emanating from core of the temple. He moved toward it, knowing instinctively that he must enter the flame. As he approached, a tongue of light reached out, encircled him in a blinding flash and in that brief moment, Jhado experienced perfect peace, his mind wiped of all fear and filled with true knowledge. When his eyes blinked open, he was back in the thekpu with the two-dimensional mandala and a life path with unwavering purpose set before him.

After many years on that path, Jhado was now a master, guiding initiates through the sacred city just as his teacher had for him, providing them a glimpse of the sacred city they would vow to protect. Upon completing the last stage of the journey, Jhado waited for the initiates to recover; he saw their eyes open wide with new understanding. Clearly, the experience had changed them, but Jhado knew that this was still the beginning. As their training progressed, they would need to project more than their consciousness in order to interact physically with the occupants of Shambala.

While observing the students' reactions, Jhado heard the rustling of robes and a familiar shuffling of feet. Tenzin had entered the room, wearing a concerned expression. The old monk must have been waiting anxiously for the ceremony to reach a point where he could enter with minimal disturbance. He moved to a position within Jhado's view and made eye contact. The look reported unfortunate news, but despite the old monk's apparent anxiety, Jhado did not rush the end of the ceremony. Instead, with a slightest of hand gesture he signaled Tenzin to wait in the tower chamber. Unruffled, Jhado continued the ceremony, giving thanks to the deities for their participation and then performed the ritual destruction of the mandala. His assistants collected the colored sand in urns. Some would go to Shambala while the rest would be scattered according to ritual to bless to earth.

When his part in the ceremony was complete, Jhado returned immediately to his chambers. As he entered the room, Tenzin was sitting on a cushion spinning a prayer wheel and chanting. The old monk completed his mantra before rising to greet the lama with a bow. He did not speak; an exchange of glances was enough to direct Jhado to his computer terminal; Tenzin had already loaded the page with the latest Haiku poem on the display.

Serpent bares its maw
Untouched by the Buddha's light
He hunts in darkness
Kasa

Jhado understood. Chidag had resurfaced, an attempt to destroy him had failed, and he had disappeared again. Though disappointing, there was minor comfort in the words. At least Chidag had not yet located his prey as he was apparently still on the hunt. So far, the strategy of moving the bodies of the known Buddha warriors to safe havens had succeeded in confounding him.

Jhado suddenly remembered the young man he met on the trail overlooking the Asura plain. "Tenzin, have they located Despa yet?" he asked.

"Venerable one, he has an address in San Francisco, but we don't yet know where his body sleeps. Our people have gone to his apartment, but it has been empty for several days. He could be anywhere."

"I doubt that." Jhado said. "He is a new Buddha warrior. He is likely in a medical center. Have Kasa's people been instructed to search hospitals in the region?"

"It is already being done."

Jhado nodded his approval. "My old friend, your forethought is exceeded only by your wisdom. You may return to your other duties. I will take over here."

Tenzin bowed, but before leaving the lama's chamber, he said gravely. "Your holiness, that is not the only poem. There are other messages from Jakarta and Copenhagen."

As he turned to the computer display to search for the code names of his Indonesian and Danish lamas, Jhado prepared himself for the news that Tenzin's expression had already divulged. When he found the haiku poems, he read them quickly.

The one from the Indonesian temple read:

The stone is lifted
And scorpion scurries out
Stinger raised to strike
Monkee

The one from Denmark read:

Just one unfilled crack
Lets mangy rat squeeze through with
Cruel winter hunger
Beowulf

The messages were clear. Two more of Zerden's minions had entered the Human realm. Were others roaming undetected? Jhado applied his discipline to calm a heartbeat that instinctively begged to race in panic. He told himself that the latest demon incarnates were likely beings of lesser power than Chidag, but the situation was growing more difficult faster than he had anticipated. He would have to send phurbas to Jakarta and Copenhagen immediately. In addition to the serpent, his Haiku metaphors would now involve a scorpion and rat. He keyed in a message for all.

Beast stalks in darkness
While the wary white stag leaps
At first leaf's rustle
Dan Poe

Jhado realized that it was not a helpful message. Under the circumstances, all he could offer was common sense advice: be wary and prepare to act quickly. He left the computer on, hoping that the solar cells would hold their charge until the weather cleared. There was a backup manual generator, but he disliked imposing the additional work upon his brothers and sisters. Life at Dagpa Akar was hard enough. With Zerden's minions roaming freely in the Human realm, the haiku site needed regular monitoring. For the moment, the enemy was in control, but Jhado had learned that control could sometimes be a liability.

If nothing else, combined maneuvers with the dakini squadron demonstrated the advantage of close air support during a battle. Similar to any combined air and ground attack, the basic strategy was to first soften enemy positions from the air with repeated barrages of arrows followed by a pincer-type cavalry charge. Once the ground forces had engaged, dakinis continued to harass enemy reinforcements from the air. Most impressive was the dakini's ability to drop and decapitate with blinding speed, a maneuver that Gesar had witnessed at his first meeting with Ane. Shambala's dominance of sky was their greatest tactical advantage; Zerden's nagu army would be hard pressed to advance against such a combined force.

During the training exercise, Goba was eager and fearless, constantly outracing his peers to be the first to meet the lines of spear-bearing mannequins while making sure he was never far from Brug's shadow. Gesar had to concentrate to keep his sword strikes in time with Goba's stride, but his mount's effort to maintain close proximity to Ane did not escape him.

"You're purposely keeping us near her. What are you doing? " Gesar asked.

"You will soon see, my rider," Goba answered.

When virtually every mannequin had been dismembered or trampled, a horn sounded to end the exercise and Ben shouted, "Now, pair off with the nearest dakini and practice with swords! Remember, we don't want to kill each other, use only flat edge strikes!"

Brug's wing draft raised a cloud of dust as he landed. Ane patted Brug's neck and dismounted. Smiling, she walked up to Gesar and said, "I know this pairing was not accidental."

"It was Goba's doing." Gesar said.

"Not many horses could do such a thing while running a battle gauntlet."

"Being the Senge hindmost, I wouldn't know." Gesar responded.

Ane laughed. "I suppose Goba should not be scolded for being skilled. Besides, he's too handsome to be scolded," she said.

Goba's voice intruded Gesar's mind. "I like her."

Behind Ane, Brug kicked up a clod of earth with a taloned foot and emitted a hiss.

Goba intruded again, "I told you he was the jealous type."

"Settle down Brug!" Ane shouted. "You know you will always be my favorite."

Gesar dismounted and said, "I'm not sure how this drill works."

Ane flashed a wry smile. "It's fairly simple. Just draw your sword, step clear of the animals and fight as if your life depended on it."

Gesar's sword rang as he drew it from its sheath. The sword was well balanced and its grip was comfortable in the palm. He had practiced sword fighting with other Senge tapah and had learned their style, which he embellished with his own moves based on his martial arts experience. After taking but three steps away from Goba, he caught the flash of Ane's sword from the corner of his eye. He barely had time to block the blow. She was upon him like a berserker. Strike after strike, she pressed forward forcing Gesar to retreat and feverishly block her blows. Fortunately, he was on open ground with space to maneuver. Had he been against a wall, he would have been in serious trouble. She was highly skilled with the sword, avoiding rhythmic or repetitive patterns of strikes. Despite his Shambala amplified strength and stamina, Gesar realized that he had to change tactics soon, eventually he would make an ineffective block and suffer the embarrassing consequence. Her forward focused advance meant that the only way he could make an offensive blow was to get behind her. He waited for just the right strike to make his move. It came when Ane raised her sword from her right shoulder and swung with a diagonal strike. Instead of his usual block and retreat move, he stepped directly into the blow, catching Ane's blade on the down swing and pushing his sword upward to deflect the strike. Continuing his forward motion, he passed under her raised arm and then spun around quickly with the flat of his blade aimed at her back. There was a loud crack when his sword contacted her armor, but rather than following through with an additional offensive strike, he paused as Ane stumbled. He regretted the mistake. Ane regained her footing faster then he had anticipated. She used her forward momentum to spin and leap, aiming the flat of her blade at Gesar's helmet. The sound of the impact practically split his eardrums. His ears were still ringing as Ane looked down on his sprawled form.

"I believe that would have been a mortal blow," she said extending a hand to help him to his feet. "You could have had me, but you didn't follow through."

"Yeah, my mistake, I guess I was surprised to actually make contact after all that retreating." He said, speaking above the sound of clashing weapons that continued around them.

"Not so surprised as I," she responded. "Other than Lady Palden, you are the first to lay a blade on me."

Picking up his sword to sheath it, Gesar said, "I'm not so sure if I should be proud of that fact."

Ane likewise sheathed her sword and said, "We try to avoid pride around here, so I thank you for teaching me a lesson in humility today."

Brushing the dirt from his uniform, Gesar laughed and said, "Well it must be a lesson by example since I'm the one eating dust today."

Ane smiled and said, "Well, I took advantage of your good nature. I'm sure you won't be so forgiving with a real enemy. I just hope I'll be around long enough to practice with you again."

"What do you mean? Why wouldn't you be around?" Gesar asked.

Ane's expression turned serious. "Shambala's defenders exist as Sleeper and Warrior. Here, we can defend ourselves, but in the Human realm we are vulnerable. We recently learned that our enemies have invaded the Human realm to seek out and kill us. An especially nasty demon is in San Francisco area. There are several of us from the area. My lieutenant and best friend, Dolma, is from there. I think my father owned a restaurant in the wharf district, but that's all pretty foggy now. You may have noticed that the longer you're in Shambala the less you can remember of your other life."

"Can anything be done?" Gesar asked.

"Not really. The Sleepers are pretty helpless. We depend on our allies in the Human realm, the Kalacakra, they're trying to protect us, but they can't protect every Buddha warrior. They don't even know all of our locations. Any day, I might simply vanish in flash. Not my preference, but at least it should be a nice light show."

"I guess I'm in the same boat. I was living in San Francisco, at least I think I was." said Gesar.

Ane smiled and said. "There's no point worrying about it. We have more in common than good swordsmanship, were both Golden Gate brats. Perhaps, we were destined to meet here. The God of Light works in strange ways, but I suppose being in Shambala has already proved that point."

Gesar turned his gaze downward as he said the words, "To tell you the truth, I have my doubts about all of this, including you. It's too much like a crazy dream. Demons, kinnaras and telepathic horses, I keep asking myself when will I wake up."

Ane took Gesar's hand, forcing him to give his full attention. Her grip was strong. "Do you feel this? I'm here and now, and that's all that matters. In my first days here, I had similar doubts, which I expressed to Lady Palden, and she told me that doubt is the first step on the path to enlightenment. Dream or no dream, I'm committed to this path." Ane released Gesar's hand and added, "I know it's hard, but if you need any moral support, you can count on me."

"Thanks," Gesar said. "I have one question. I know San Francisco has its share of bizarre characters, but wouldn't a demon walking the streets of San Francisco sort of stand out? "

Ane laughed and answered. "They have to possess a human body in order to function in the Human realm."

"So dealing with demonic possession is not just the province of the Catholic Church?" Gesar asked.

"I'm afraid not," answered Ane.

"Well how can you recognize a demon-possessed human?"

"I have been told that they abhor bright light and they are very difficult to kill." Ane responded.

"But they can be killed, right?" Gesar inquired.

"Only if you can pin them to the earth with a phurba."

Gesar remembered that an ancient phurba was among the items he had inherited from his grandfather, who had called it a sacred tent stake. "My grandfather had one of those. I never gave much thought to them before, but I'm starting to gain a lot of respect for those tent stakes."

"What do you mean tent stakes?" Ane asked, confused.

Before Gesar could explain, the cacophony of clashing weapons surrounding them was suddenly silenced. A dark shadow swept over the practice grounds and all eyes turned upward. Overhead, a dakini mounted on the back of an especially large kinnara fitted with gold armor circled the practice field. On each banking turn, the plates of polished armor flashed with reflected sunshine. The kinnara's iridescent golden wings accentuated the impressive lighting effect. After a graceful spiraling descent, the dakini landed in a clearing in the middle of the field.

"It's Lady Palden," Ane whispered.

All weapons were stowed and heads bowed in respect as Lady Palden dismounted her kinnara. Unfamiliar with protocol, Gesar was glad that he had already sheathed his sword. Awkwardly, he mimicked the respectful gesture of the others, but not before catching a glimpse of the most striking woman that he had ever seen. Though Palden Lhamo, demon-god, had taken human form, she was obviously not human. No human radiated such divine beauty and bestial power. The experience reminded him of his grandfather's description of the 'terrifying beauty' of a snow leopard that he encountered in the mountains of Tibet. The intensity in her gaze was so piercing that unprepared viewers were forced to avert their eyes to avoid feeling overwhelmed. In addition to her supernatural radiance, her outer attire clearly stated that she was of high rank. Her armor was similar in basic design to that of the other dakinis, but lavishly embellished with intricately embossed silver work and precious stones, and unlike the other dakinis, she bore on her head a golden war-band decorated with blood rubies and she wore a wide belt strung with huge pearls carved in the shape of human skulls. The famed fire sword hung from her belt, its jewel-encrusted pummel protruding from her left hip.

Lady Palden's dark eyes turned immediately in Ane's direction and she called, "First captain of the Druk dakini, come here, I wish to show you something."

Without hesitation, Ane obeyed, stopping in front of the demon-god, pressing her palms together and kneeling to begin a formal prostration bow.

The demon-god extended her hand and gently touched a long finger to Ane's forehead, forestalling the bow. "Dispense with protocol," she said. "You need not bow. It is more important that you see what I have brought."

The Lady turned and retrieved a bulging sack that was bound to her kinnara's saddle. Untying the top, she spilled the contents onto the ground. Everyone nearby emitted a simultaneous gasp. Before them lay a blood encrusted head of a horned and fanged reptile, a beast previously unknown to Shambala or the Asura outlands.

"This was discovered flying near the Shield perimeter by the Kra dakini squadron this morning. It required the effort of six dakinis to subdue and kill it."

"Did you say flying?" Ane said staring at the terrifying visage.

"Yes," Palden answered. "The rest of the carcass is too large to move, but it reportedly had leathery wings and was more than thrice the size of a kinnara. It seems the enemies of Shambala wish to deny us our command of the sky. I suspect this is just one of a much larger brood that our enemies have created."

Ane's mind immediately formulated an action plan, "We must develop training techniques for combating these creatures. How did the Kra kill it?"

"Its weakness is its wings. The Kra discovered that repeated puncturing and slashing at the wings will eventually drive it to ground, but this one did not have a rider to carry out protective countermeasures. In a real battle, they will likely be much more difficult to kill."

"At least we now know what we have to deal with. It's better than being surprised in battle." Ane commented.

"Yes, we have been fortunate to gain this knowledge our enemy's activities, but it also means that we must assume that an attack will come sooner than later. Once they learn that we know about these flying serpents, they will be forced to attack quickly while we are unprepared to defend against them."

"But any attack would be futile. They will die the moment they attempt to cross the Shield." Ane reminded.

Lady Palden's expression darkened. "The Shield is powerful but not infinitely powerful. Our protection is limited by how much our enemy is willing to pay for passage. I know Mahakala too well. He is cunning and merciless. He knows that Shambala suffers with each sentient being that the Shield repels. Zerden has had millennia to expand his nagu armies and Mahakala knows how use them to exploit our weakness. He would not hesitate to sacrifice millions to achieve his purpose."

Stunned by Lady Palden's revelation, Ane asked. "Do you really think they have that many?"

"I suspect it is very possible and you have shown us that the nagu forces are nearer to Shambala than we suspected. After your encounter with Yama, I dispatched the other dakini squadrons to begin a closer inspection of the lesser used passes that cross the inner mountain ring. At least two squadrons noted small groups of dron warriors emerging from cave openings. According to our records, no such caves existed before. This is undoubtedly Mahakala's doing, he has been building garrisons right at our threshold. He must be using Zerden's portals to move forces from the lower realms into Asura. It seems that the enemy troop movements on the Asura plain were intended as a distraction."

Feeling the urge to act, Ane said, "Lady Palden, I suggest that we strike first. We can lay siege to their garrisons. They will be vulnerable in the passes where we can keep them locked up. Those gorges are so narrow that an enemy loses any numerical advantage."

Lady Palden seemed to smile before speaking. "Then, we are of like mind, but we must act quickly, which leads me to the other reason that I have come here." Palden turned to Ben and said, "Captain Jigme of the Senge tapah, it is fortunate that your men work so well with the Druk dakini squadron, for I have asked Begtse to dispatch you to join the Druk at first light tomorrow. Your combined forces will make the first strike against the cave garrison we located yesterday."

Ben nodded in respect and said, "The Senge tapah will do as you wish my Lady."

Lady Palden then returned to her golden kinnara and mounted the saddle. Before taking flight, she looked to Ane and said, 'When you have finished here, come to my tower. I am holding a meeting of all of the dakini captains to discuss this new flying beast. As you rightly point out, we will need an appropriate strategy to defeat them."

"What do you wish done with the beast's head?" Ane asked.

As Palden's kinnara spread its wings and leapt into flight she commanded, "Enlighten it!"

Flying into the distance, Lady Palden and her mount glowed like a miniature sun. When the light vanished beyond the wall, Ane withdrew her pouch of rust-colored powder and sprinkled it upon the ghastly reptilian head. A moment later, it vanished in a blinding flash of light.

"What is that powder?" Gesar asked.

"Sand." Ane responded.

Incredulous, Gesar reacted, "I know that's not just sand."

Ane laughed and said, "Oh, it's definitely sand. It just happens to be from a special sand painting prepared by the demon-god, Hayagriva, and his Kalacakra monks. Nonliving flesh covered and encircled by the sand is banished from this realm."

"Where does it go?"

Ane hesitated a moment before responding, "I'll try to explain, but you should really ask one of the monks. It goes to a sort of soul recycling center. If there is any soul-stuff associated with the flesh, then it will have a chance to incarnate again, hopefully more aware the next time round. With every soul that advances Shambala grows stronger."

"That sounds nice, but be careful not spill any of that sand on me," Gesar jibed.

"I won't have to. The Buddha warriors always go out in a flash."

$\mathbf{D}$r. Ashki had just left his office when his cell phone rang. The ring tone sounded with a traditional song and drumbeat for a Navajo two-step dance. He flipped it open and answered. "Hello."

"Dr. Ashki?"

He recognized the voice of Dr. Chandron, the tired neurosurgical resident he had met several times in the hospital where Gesar Despa was in a drug-induced coma. "Yeah, this is Ashki."

"Chandron here, you said you wanted to be called when we were ready to take Mr. Despa out of coma."

"That's right."

"Well the last scan showed no brain swelling after the steroid taper and no evidence of recurrent bleeding." Chandron explained. "As you know, that's been a problem for us and we've had to keep him in coma longer than we anticipated. Tomorrow morning, we plan to withdraw the barbiturates and wake him up. He should regain consciousness by noon."

"I'll definitely be there." Ashki replied. "He doesn't have family in the area and it will be good for him to see a familiar face when he wakes."

"Okay then, I'll see you tomorrow."

"Thanks for calling and get some rest Chandron." Ashki ended. He flipped his cell phone closed and tucked it into his pocket as he walked the rest of the distance to his car. He was worried about Gesar. A planned five-day drug-induced coma had been stretched to nearly two weeks due to recurrence of subdural bleeding. If Gesar successfully came out of coma, a detailed neurological exam would have to be done in order to be sure no permanent brain damage had occurred. Ashki wanted Gesar to come through unscathed.

Professionally, his concern was more personal than it probably should be. Against his own nature, he had learned to keep some distance from his patients. As a young medical resident, every patient lost was a personal loss. In those days, he took failure as an affront to his ego; cruel fate slighting his abilities, but his involvement in Gesar's case was different. With Gesar, he felt more like a father than a physician.

Ashki didn't know why he felt a special connection with his half-Tibetan patient. Perhaps, he saw some of himself in the young man. They had much in common despite having roots in opposite sides of the world. Both were from cultures with potent spiritual beliefs. Both had once prided themselves on physical skills that were lost to injury or disease. Both had lost parents, and they both loved horses. Photos and paintings of horses covered the walls of Ashki's office. Of all of his patients, Gesar was the only one who could name all of the different breeds on display.

Smiling at the memory, he muttered to himself, "I never asked him how he knows so much about horses."

There was something extraordinary about Gesar and Ashki sensed that the young man needed allies. He had even engaged the services of a hataathli, a Navajo medicine man, to wander the spirit realms on the young man's behalf. After getting into his car, Ashki reached back into his pocket for his cell phone and dialed a number in New Mexico. He hoped he could make a connection. Phone service to Navajo country was sometimes unreliable. After five rings, a deep voice roughened by years of inhaling the smoke of open fires and burning sage answered, "Ya' ateeh,"

"Ya' ateeh shi che," Ashki greeted. After a period of obligatory courtesy conversation, Ashki asked, "What have you learned of that young man I spoke of?"

Brother William started the van as Brother Kai climbed into the passenger seat. Kai, a tall, olive-skinned Hawaiian with serious dark eyes was a Bhikshu, a fully ordained Kalacakra monk. Trained to recognize Zerden's minions, Kai was one of the seniors assigned to watch for those who had breached the divide between realms. He had gained some celebrity among his brothers by being the one to detect the arrival of Chidag Nagpo.

William felt intimidated by Kai and the other seniors trained to recognize demonic incarnates. As a novice Getsül monk, William was not instructed in the depths of Kalacakra esoterica, but he was both fascinated and frightened by the stories he had heard from his seniors. Since the unexpected appearance and disappearance of Chidag Nagpo, novices were paired with senior monks or nuns for protection. There were no guarantees of safety however, memories of the mutilated body of Brother Zak, a fully ordained Bhikshu, were still fresh in the minds of novices and adepts.

William broke the silence as Kai fastened his seat belt. "Tell me again, who we are looking for today?"

Kai loosened his shirt collar. Both men were dressed in plain clothing for the day's clandestine assignment. The bright orange robes of their order were comfortable, but attracted attention in public.

"His name is Despa." Kai answered.

A wrought iron gate closed behind them as the van left the temple grounds. For a short while, their route paralleled a looming flagstone wall that enclosed the monastery before turning onto a main thoroughfare choked with traffic.

"Is it true that our instructions came directly from Dagpa Akar?" William asked.

Kai lightly patted his jacket, confirming he had pocketed his cell phone and other necessities. "Yes it's true. The order came directly

90

from Lama Zhangpo. Despa is a new Buddha warrior of Shambala and we are to find and protect him like the others."

From the little he knew of Dagpa Akar, William realized the implication of Kai's words. Although, the notion that highly trained Kalacakra adepts could move between realms was still difficult to believe. "That means someone actually saw him in Shambala?"

"Yes." Kai answered, staring absently out the windshield and providing no further details.

"I suppose it was hard to locate Despa." William prodded.

After a brief silence, Kai responded. "His name is unusual, so it was easy to find his address in San Francisco, but he has no roommate or family in the area. It was only after many days of delicately dropped questions that we finally located him at the University Hospital."

"Strange, that's where you discovered Chidag."

"Yes." Kai answered curtly, lightly patting his jacket pockets again.

The curt responses were making it clear to William that Kai was not feeling conversational. "Okay, I'll shut up. You might as well use this time to meditate. In this traffic, we won't reach the hospital for at least another forty minutes," William suggested.

Chidag listened to the monks' conversation. He had hidden in back of the van for two days, drawing on the knowledge of his host and straining to control his moments of rage. His host flesh experienced the time as a "stake out", a tedious period of waiting and gathering knowledge of one's enemy. At night he ventured from the van to learn the layout of the monastery, but returned to his hiding place by day. Hiding among the discarded robes of his enemies was not only humiliating but repellent for the first son of Munpa Zerden; the stench of human weakness was unbearable. He was restrained only by the possibility that these tiresome monks might lead him to the Buddha warriors. He hungered to end the insufferable waiting, but to accomplish his mission he had to be patient and measure his violence. He needed these monks alive. His only regret was that he would not witness the dismay in the eyes of the defenders of Shambala as they watched their comrades vanish.

Tightly clutching his weapons, Mahakala warily entered Naraka's main gate. The fortress-city housing Munpa Zerden's nagu armies lay

91

beyond the Plain of Deception in a basin bordered by craggy bluffs. As the city's massive portcullis closed behind him, Mahakala's three eyes scanned the battlements for signs of treachery. The imposing walls were three times the height of the tallest demon-god and gruesomely decorated with bones embedded in a blood-red mortar. Naraka had never been under siege so the walls were intended to contain more than to deter. Mahakala was never at ease during these visits, as his alliance with Zerden was not based on mutual trust. Both parties were taking serious risks. At any time, Zerden might find it more advantageous to eliminate his former enemies, who were now vulnerable without the protection of Shambala. Subjugating an immortal demon-god would cost Zerden dearly, but after many centuries of preparation, the master of Eighty Thousand Negativities had abundant capital to spend. Fortunately, the bulk of the Zerden's forces were in secret mountain garrisons surrounding Shambala making an attack within Naraka unlikely, especially with two other rebel guardians in residence.

Mahakala advanced, maintaining at least the appearance of arrogant indifference. A bizarre assortment of minions, nagu warriors and slaves, quickly cleared a path for his massive form as he strode down the main thoroughfare leading to Naraka's central citadel. There, he intended to meet his fellow rebels. It was at Mahakala's insistence that Changpa and Kubera remain in Naraka, developing tactics to neutralize Shambala's defenders. The strategy had the secondary benefit of allowing the rebel demon-gods to acquire a certain measure of control over Zerden's forces in the event that their new partner might consider betraying them.

After crossing an open space patrolled by nagu dron units, Mahakala reached a high wall of glassy black stone that was topped with a line of jagged points completely enclosing Naraka's central keep. No gate or other portal of entry was apparent. Beyond the wall, a permanent veil of grey smoke carrying the stench of death and rotting waste hung amidst the towers of the citadel. Its source was a vast complex of breeding pens, weapon forges, and battle pits. Mahakala found a section of wall where the upward dripping spikes formed a particular configuration and pressed one of his clawed hands against it. Suddenly, the wall section liquefied, becoming translucent black ooze and emitting an ear-splitting, high-pitched shriek. Mahakala stepped into the wall, unaffected by its eerie greeting. A moment later, he was within the keep and the wall behind him was again solid and silent.

Across a slate-paved plaza, his fellow demon-god, Changpa Karpo emerged from a doorway; his four hands were presently weaponless, but a sword and club hung at his belt. A small retinue of nagu warriors followed behind him. Of the demon-gods, Changpa was the most distracting in his demonic form, having four faces, all looking in different directions and speaking alternately or at times, in concert. In conversation, his neck was constantly twisting back and forth, giving the impression that his huge head was spinning.

"Welcome brother! We heard the wall announce your arrival. It seems to emit an especially happy shriek when you come to visit," greeted Changpa's foreface while his other faces presented broad yellow-fanged grins.

Mahakala muttered a response that reeked of disgust. Changpa was always the cheery one. In the time before the Taming, during the millennia of dealing out mayhem and murder, he always had a smile on a least one of his faces. Frankly, Mahakala was surprised that Changpa, who basked in his popularity at Kalapa palace, had joined the rebellion. He had expected the more aloof Betsge to join his ranks. Changpa and Betsge were both master riders who led divisions of tapah and both had important knowledge regarding tapah battle strategy. Unfortunately, Changpa came with his nauseating cheeriness and constant referral to himself as "we".

Changpa's four mouths spoke in unison, "It's not that your pretty face isn't always a welcome sight brother, but we were not expecting you so soon."

"It was not my preference to come here now, but Yama, our pus-headed brother, has forced a change in our plans. His impatience has alerted Shambala to our cave garrisons."

"Well my handsome brother, that is unfortunate. We suppose that eliminates the element of surprise, but it seems a bit late to propose a new plan. Our forces are already in position."

"Your sounding as empty headed as Yama. Of course, we cannot create a new plan, but we can advance our timetable. Our attack must come before the next full moon"

Changpa's four faces took on different expressions, one surprised, one puzzled, one concerned, and one disinterested. His foreface then spoke, "We thought we needed the naga-ta at full force before the attack. Only about half of the beasts and riders have been trained."

"They will have to do. Our nagu ground forces are in excess and should be able to compensate."

An expression of doubt passed over all of Changpa's faces. "In that case, we cannot guarantee control of the sky. You know very well what the dakini can do in battle. They consistently bested my tapah in practice drills."

"We far outnumber Shambala's defenders. We don't need to control the sky; we simply need to keep the dakini occupied, while our nagu attack. Do you have enough naga-ta for that?"

Changpa's foreface answered. "I think we have enough naga-ta, but that fat sloth, Kubera, has been slow in training skilled riders."

"Where is Kubera?" Mahakala asked.

Changpa pointed two of his four arms at the tallest tower in the keep. "He's up there selecting riders for the naga-ta."

Mahakala kept one eye fixed on Changpa while his others looked upward. Near the top of a looming black tower, he saw the silhouette of a naga-ta perched at a window with a manlike figure mounting its back. Once positioned, the rider pulled a set of reins. The naga-ta let out a shriek, spread its leathery wings and leapt from the tower. After a fast dive, the naga-ta scooped upward, beating its wings in slow powerful strokes that stirred eddies in the smoke-filled air. Then suddenly, it banked sharply to circle around the tower. The force of the sudden turn was apparently too much for the rider who slipped from the saddle and fell from the sky to join a pile of broken bodies stacked at the base of the tower. A moment later, a long pole bearing a dangling piece of meat emerged from the tower window. Eagerly, the naga-ta returned to his perch, tore the flesh offering from the pole and swallowed it in a single gulp.

Mahakala pointed his tilug in the direction of the tower as he spoke. "I hope that is not an example of your best riding talent."

Three of Changpa's faces grinned while his foreface spoke. "No. You have only seen Kubera's method of finding talent. Only those who can stay in the saddle for four turns around the tower are selected to go on to complete their training. So far, that has been about one in fifty."

In the centuries that Mahakala served as a guardian of Shambala, he had never seen a dakini fall from her mount. The telepathic connection of rider and mount was a great advantage. Reins were used rarely, allowing the dakini to give full attention to the use of her weapons. Even a seriously wounded kinnara would never allow its rider to fall. We only have to delay them, Mahakala reassured himself. "Tell Kubera to meet us in the keep-hall. We must begin to dispatch the naga-ta immediately."

Changpas's left face glared at one of his nagu retinue and said, "Do as he said!" The nagu dron saluted with a nod of his helmeted head and then ran in the direction of the tower with his weapons clacking against his black armor.

Mahakala and Changpa waited for Kubera to arrive at the keep sanctuary. Superficially, the domed hall had the appearance of a grotesquely decorated throne room, but on a dais stood a rectangular monolith made of a black stone similar to the liquefying walls that surrounded the citadel. As tall and broad as Mahakala, the monolith reflected no light despite a perfectly smooth surface. Like the mysterious section of citadel wall, the monolith was a portal, but this door was for use only by Zerden's most trusted minions. Rarely, Zerden would make an appearance, emerging from his nether realm in a shadowy form that was impossible to bring into focus. When Mahakala learned that Zerden had other such portals, he immediately realized their tactical potential.

To allay Zerden's mistrust of his demon-god allies, Mahakala always held his planning sessions in the keep-hall in full view of the monolith. Albeit, this was probably unnecessary since a contingent of Zerden's elite guard was assigned to protect the unconscious body of Chidag Nagpo that lay in an open sarcophagus propped up in front of the monolith. Mahakala noticed that two other sarcophagi had joined Chidag's. After the Taming, the bodhisattvas established a barrier between Asura and the Human realm, denying demonic incarnations among humans. However, the sworn Guardians of Shambala knew of methods to circumvent the barrier. Mahakala had sensed Zerden's delight upon learning the secret of passage to the Human realm. It was after that revelation that Zerden gave Mahakala command of all nagu forces and full responsibility for executing the defeat of Shambala. It was almost as if Zerden had lost personal interest in the war. Mahakala had interpreted his advancement as a reward, but he was beginning to wonder if Zerden had another agenda.

"I see that Zerden has wasted no time in sending others to the Human realm," Mahakala commented.

Changpa's faces responded as a chorus, "Yes, two of Chidag's brothers were carried in here one day and placed next to him. To be honest, we don't see the family resemblance, other than being mutually ugly."

"Have you looked in mirror lately?" Mahakala asked with a sarcastic smile of fangs.

The huge iron-strapped doors of the keep stronghold banged open and Kubera arrived moving in his usual unhurried manner.

Unlike the seven other demon-gods, he did not have a wrathful demonic form. Rather he had grown fatter, grossly fat, since leaving Shambala. Adorned in gold armor studded with every sort of precious jewel, he flaunted his love of trinkets. His war gear was purely for show since Kubera would never engage in a physical battle; his power was mental. His enemies were usually eliminated by some inexplicable means before they could think of attacking him. Despite Kubera's audacity, Mahakala was glad to have him among his horde, if only as a counterbalance to Yama's idiotic impulsiveness. Kubera had been working with Changpa to develop a force of flying beasts, the naga-ta, to challenge the dakini squadrons. After some prodding, it was Kubera who found the means to breed the naga-ta from a creature found in Zerden's realms. Though the beasts were not sentient, they were larger and reasonably trainable. Unfortunately, neither Kubera nor Changpa had practical experience in airborne battle maneuvers. Changpa drew upon as much of his horse-warrior technique as possible, while Kubera worked from his memory of dakini battle drills.

"Welcome to Naraka," said Kubera, his voice a squeaky tenor compared to the resonant baritones of his demon-god brothers.

Mahakala answered abruptly. "I've had enough greetings for one day. We have important matters to attend to, and you have kept us waiting overlong."

Kubera shook his head and said. "Hurry, hurry, you are always in such a hurry. You were far more patient when you were in Shambala. You were almost tolerable. I also miss that lovely ruby you used to have on your forehead. Do you still have it? I would be happy to take it off your hands if you don't need it."

Mahakala bristled, his eyes bulging in anger. "Listen Kubera. Don't test my patience with sarcasm!"

"Calm yourself, calm yourself. You'll wake Zerden's children," Kubera said, lazily waving his pudgy ring-laden hand in the direction of the coffin-beds. "We both know your threats are empty, but no matter. If business is what you want, then let's get down to it. What is so urgent that you must pay us this unannounced visit?"

Mahakala grumbled a barely audible curse and then spoke. "As I informed our four-faced brother here, Yama has foolishly revealed our mountain garrisons. Palden will undoubtedly send forces against them. She knows that she can tie us up in the mountain passes. Our only option is to attack Shambala quickly. The dakinis are our greatest threat and naga-ta must be sent out to neutralize them."

Kubera scratched his head, pushing his jeweled crown askew. "I would advise against that plan. It is premature. I'm sure Changpa has told you that our naga-ta have not yet reached the numerical advantage that we planned for and their riders are not exactly skilled."

Mahakala's eyes flared. "I'm beginning to get annoyed by your constant excuses for delay. We must attack now. We only need enough naga-ta to keep the dakini forces occupied."

"Very well, you shall have your naga-ta." Kubera said. "In fact, I have already sent a reconnaissance group several days ago. I thought it would be wise to train them at our mountain strongholds, so they will be better adapted to atmospheric conditions. After being in this place, I doubt they can tolerate fresh air. Now would you like something to eat? I'm famished and my midday meal is waiting. I apologize that I have nothing prepared for you, but a freshly killed stack of nagu at the base of the north tower might interest you."

Mahakala glared angrily at his rotund confederate.

"The column of Senge tapah crossed the Vishvamata ice bridge before dawn. Riding in paired formation, Gesar was next to his riding partner, Chiru, a wiry man descended from a people who roamed the Eurasian Steppe. Like Gesar, he was an excellent rider and a recent recruit to Shambala's defenders. Gesar's coming had relieved him of his title as "Hindmost". The column followed the Kalapa road until it became an unpaved horse trail, barely discernable in the predawn darkness. After crossing several shallow streams, the column ascended foothills and a series of cutbacks, finally reaching the southeast pass and the boundary of Shambala. Invisible during the climb, the pass appeared abruptly as a steeply walled gap winding between towering mountains. In the early morning light, the pass shimmered when viewed through the Shield barrier.

In accord with their rank, Gesar and Chiru were at end of the column. Gesar was the last to go through the barrier. He tensed, expecting to experience another trial by fire, but was surprised to feel only a brief tingling sensation. When he commented on this difference, Chiru explained. "The Shield tests us only when we enter Shambala."

The Senge had ridden for more than four hours and were approaching the place where they were to rendezvous with the Druk dakini. During the journey, Goba was silent as was often the case in the morning. Usually preoccupied with eating and digesting, he rarely invaded Gesar's thoughts before midday. The horses also respected the early morning as a time for their riders to meditate. Gesar searched the sky for the dakini squadron, but only stars twinkled in an expanse of cold cerulean blue brushed with wispy cirrus clouds.

Goba interrupted Gesar's thoughts. "Don't waste your time looking for them. Those lazy kinnaras sleep all morning."

"They will be here soon." Gesar replied. Even as he finished his words, the faint song of kinnaras echoed from the direction of the palace.

"I told you. They are only just leaving the palace." Goba chided.

When the Senge column reached the snowy summit of the pass, a formation of dakinis appeared overhead. Gesar recognized Ane in the lead position with her sword arm raised in salute and her wreath of black hair whipping in the wind. The sight reminded him of their first meeting. While the main part of the dakini squadron slowed to match the pace of the cavalry below, a group of four dakini scouts was dispatched to fly ahead. According to the report of the Kra dakini captain, a nagu cave stronghold was located south of Mount Shiwa only a half-day's ride from the Shield border, so they expected to engage enemy forces about midday. Nevertheless, since the nagu stronghold was only the first discovered, the mountains could be riddled with such hideaways. Despite dakini scouts, ambush was a real possibility, so all remained silent and alert. Strategically placed padding prevented the rattling of armor and weapons. Even telepathic communication between riders and their mounts was kept to a minimum in order to minimize distraction.

As midday drew near, the trail showed signs of enemy activity, a partial boot print obscured by runoff, a discarded arrow, the remnant of a gruesome meal and a damaged choten. Not long after the discovery of the vandalized choten, one of the dakini scouts returned, approaching at a hurried pace. The kinnara's silhouette appeared suddenly from the south and landed at the front of the horse column near Ben. A moment later, Ane landed, dismounted Brug, and joined in an animated conversation with her scout and the Senge captain.

Suddenly, the two dakinis returned to their mounts and took to the air as Ben turned to face his column. "Draw swords! The enemy comes to us!" He cried. The air resonated with the ring of steel as the Senge tapah drew their weapons. Overhead, Ane waved a signal to her dakini squadron. In response, they pulled bows from saddle packs and nocked arrows. The orders came not a moment too soon. At once, the sound of war cries preceded a raging river of black armor that rushed toward them along the canyon floor. Above, four shrieking winged serpents mounted by nagu riders flew erratically as three dakini scouts harried them. Dwarfed by the massive flying serpents, the kinnaras darted back and forth attempting to slash leathery wings while avoiding snapping jaws and enemy arrows.

Plainly, the enemy had anticipated Shambala's attack. To avoid entrapment, they had left their garrison and went on the offensive.

Though outnumbered, the tapah had a strategic defensive advantage in a confined space. Ben ordered his men to fall back to the most defensible position in the canyon and waving his sword, he signaled the battle formation.

Gesar recognized the signal. Ben ordered them to prepare a defensive maneuver called 'The Path of Enlightenment'.

Immediately, the column split into halves with horses moving to opposite sides of the canyon and opening a path through their middle. In the air above, Ane directed two groups of dakinis to assist in battling the flying serpents while the remainder fixed arrows on the most forward phalanx of nagu.

Dakini arrows rained down with deadly accuracy, first taking out enemy archers then systematically slowing and thinning the oncoming wave. Ane raised a hand and the shower of dakini arrows abruptly ceased. Without hesitation, the surviving nagu regrouped and surged toward the Senge tapah. The horse warriors held position and waited.

"Let them seek the path!" Ben shouted.

In response, the leader of the nagu attack raised a barbed spear and his followers let out an eerie battle cry consisting of a mixture of shrieks and howls. A moment later, the fang warriors were rushing into the midst of the waiting tapah.

"Let them find the path" Ben cried.

On that order, the tapah closed ranks and their warhorses squeezed the nagu into a narrow strip where they were cut down from both sides. When the tapah closed ranks, the dakini renewed their rain of arrows keeping nagu reinforcements at bay until Ben yelled, "Let them seek the path!" The tapah column separated and waited for the next wave, leaving the path littered with black armored bodies.

Gesar and Goba joined the fray with flawless technique. Goba pressed, dodged, and spun, constantly keeping his rider in position to make perfect sword strikes while avoiding enemy blows. Compressing the enemy in to a narrow space made spears useless. Having only experienced the 'Path' maneuver in practice drills, Gesar was surprised by how effectively the nagu attack was neutralized, since real battle conditions often thwart even the best practiced maneuvers.

Waiting for the dakinis' rain of arrows to stop, Gesar prepared for the next attack, but was suddenly struck by a spell of dizziness and violent trembling.

Sensing Gesar's distress, Goba asked, "Rider, what is wrong?"

"No! Not now, this can't be a dream."

"How can I help rider?"

"Goba, something's happening to me," Gesar replied. "I felt this way before, just before waking up in my apartment. I think I need to find a choten."

"I understand rider," answered Goba as he broke away from the tapah ranks and galloped back up the canyon. Gesar's partner, Chiru, had but an instant to notice Gesar's departure before the next wave of nagu was upon them. "Gesar! Come back!" he cried.

Overhead, Ane watched the battle, acutely aware of movements on the ground and in the air. The coordinated maneuvers of dakinis and tapah required her full attention. Brug followed her thoughts, flying precisely to where she needed to be to signal changes in formations. The huge flying serpents were complicating execution, but the dakinis she had sent to engage them had downed one of the beasts. She was grateful that there were only four of them. Any more and the tapah would be exposed with no air support.

As her squadron allowed the second wave of nagu to enter the "path", she noticed a horse break from the tapah ranks. "Goba?" she wondered, recognizing the flowing blonde mane. Quickly scanning the sky, she searched for her lieutenant, Dolma. She spotted Dolma on her mount, Nam, circling overhead. She was holding back from the main battle having not fully recovered from the encounter with Yama. Brug beat his wings to gain altitude while Ane anxiously signaled Dolma to take over battle direction. When Dolma waved her sword in acknowledgment, Ane directed Brug to dive in pursuit of the fleeing rider.

Gliding into the canyon's shadow, she saw Goba galloping at full speed, in an apparent retreat. "Brug, something's wrong. Goba would never run from battle and Gesar is no coward."

"They ride into the enemy." Brug's voice invaded Ane's mind.

Brug's better vision had spotted the new danger. Focusing her eyes beyond a vandalized choten, Ane saw the threat. Rounding a bend in the gorge was the lead edge of another nagu army. Among them, towered a monster that could be nothing but a demon. The sight filled her with a sickening realization. The Senge tapah were pinned against an anvil and a dreadful hammer was about to fall upon them. Unaware of their danger, Gesar and Goba ran recklessly toward an enemy that would slaughter them with ease. Ane's mind raced, torn between helping Gesar and the need to warn the main cavalry unit. Desperately she sought a solution that would include saving Gesar, but there was only one logical choice. She had to warn the Senge

101

tapah immediately, they needed every moment she could give them to prepare.

"May the Light of Illumination protect them," she said with tears streaming down her cheeks. "Brug, go to the Senge with all speed."

Brug banked sharply and returned to the main battle. Ahead, a bank of dark clouds was congealing in the distance over the Plain of Deception. Below, the clash of weapons sounding through the canyon suddenly stopped. The Senge "path" opened again to receive the next attack, but the nagu army facing them failed to advance when the dakini halted their rain of arrows. A dron captain in a spiked helmet raised a spear to signal a halt to the attack. The Senge appeared to relax, thinking the enemy was defeated and about to retreat, but Ane knew the truth. The enemy only waited for the hammer to fall. The enemy strategy seemed flawless; with no route of escape the Senge would be crushed. The dakini could retreat to safety but their code would not allow them leave the Senge tapah to be slaughtered.

As Brug landed next to Ben and Dawa, her cheeks stung with tears. "Another nagu force is approaching your rear and they have the demon, Gnyan, with them!" she shouted.

Without answering, Ben signaled his men to assume a retreat formation. Though confused, the men obeyed without question.

"What are you doing?" Ane asked.

"Exercising our only option, we have to fight our way back to Shambala."

"There are too many of them."

Ben pointed to the nagu army that faced them. "If the dakinis can slow them down, the Senge tapah will deal with what's between us and Shambala."

As Brug spread his wings to lift off, Ane said, "Very well, the Druk will cover your retreat and I will send a messenger to Kalapa palace to request reinforcements."

The latter was a false hope. They both knew the battle would be long over before reinforcements could arrive. At least Lady Palden would learn how they had come to their end.

Ane heard the thundering retreat of the Senge tapah echo from the canyon as she directed her dakinis to resume their rain of arrows.

Curled horns protruded from the sides of Gnyan's ovine-like head, but any resemblance to a ram ended there. Red ember eyes, fanged maw, purple-black hide, and clawed hands clearly marked him as a demon-god. Though he was less powerful than the demon-gods of Shambala, he had never betrayed his true nature. As the former supreme commander of the nagu hordes, he railed in protest when Zerden appointed Mahakala as his new master. He was not convinced that the former Guardians of Shambala could be trusted after those centuries as the tamed pets of Sangpo Bumtri. Despite his efforts to prove otherwise, none of his spies reported any suspicious activity that would shed doubt on the loyalty of the rebel demon-gods, but he still refused to trust them. Only grudgingly would he admit that the alliance with them had advanced Zerden's effort to defeat Shambala.

Towering over the dron warriors marching around him, Gnyan had a full view of the way ahead. A hideous grin formed on his maw when he noticed the lone tapah riding toward his army, but his smile quickly turned into a grimace when he saw the dakini banking away in the sky overhead. Prodding the nearest dron warriors with a barbed tilug he yelled. "Step up the pace! We've been spotted."

When the approaching horse suddenly stopped and reared, Gnyan viciously shoved his dron warriors aside and advanced in pursuit of the lone rider. "Make way, the rider is mine!" He ordered. Once clear of his troops, he broke into a trot, his huge strides rapidly closing the distance between him and his quarry.

Goba had reached the choten when he caught the scent of the approaching enemy and reared in surprise. "The enemy comes," he warned, but Gesar was in no condition to understand or respond. His vision was blurred. Waves of nausea assaulted him. Goba's sudden rear nearly threw him from the saddle. Awkwardly, he dismounted and stumbled toward the choten, stripping the armor off his searing skin. After a few unsteady steps, he reached his goal. The little shrine though damaged and sharply askew, still harbored an intact Buddha statue. He put one hand on the figure as Ane had showed him. Forcing his eyes into focus, Gesar searched and found the golden eyes. As he did, he heard a defiant whinny. Turning his head, he glimpsed Goba enveloped in the shadow of a ghastly demon-god and the scene vanished.

Dr. Ashki entered the intensive care unit shortly before noon. Dr. Chandron, the neurosurgical resident, was at Gesar's bedside performing an examination while a nurse hovered nearby adjusting rates of intravenous fluid and keeping watch on the various devices monitoring heart and lung function. The room was devoid of windows except for a glass partition that provided a view from a central nursing station.

"How's he doing?" Ashki asked.

Startled, the resident turned around and looked up at the hulking Navajo. Nervously fingering his stethoscope, he answered. "Oh! Hello Dr. Ashki, I'm glad you could make it. He's been pretty restless since we stopped the barbiturates. I needed to order restraints to keep him from ripping his lines out. I suspect he will be waking up soon."

Frowning, the nurse turned to Chandron and announced. "His heart rate and temp have shot up in the past couple of minutes but he's still asleep. He seems to be fighting the stimulants."

"That's strange, but as long as his blood pressure looks good and his rhythm is okay, I think he'll be fine. We just have to keep a close eye on him as he wakes up."

Ashki watched in silence as the resident performed a series of routine neurological tests. From Gesar's responses, Ashki could tell the young man was coming out of coma, but not easily.

"Do you mind if I speak to him?" Ashki asked.

"No, go right ahead. It will probably help to hear a familiar voice."

Dr. Ashki stepped to head of the bed and bent to whisper in Gesar's ear. "It's okay son. This is Dr. Ashki. You were badly hurt and you've been asleep for quite awhile. It's time for you wake now."

Gesar's eyes suddenly snapped wide open. The image of Goba rearing before a towering horned demon-god with a fanged maw still burned in his mind. He pulled against his restraints and yelled. "Goba!"

"It's okay son. You're back now." Ashki comforted.

Glancing at the monitors, Chandron said, "His vitals are good. He's just disoriented. It's a common reaction when waking from coma."

The image of Goba faded to be replaced by Dr. Ashki's concerned expression. Gesar then became aware of a hospital room, tubes, wires, electronic displays, and two other people. Shambala was gone. "No! Not now! Goba needs me. I have to go back."

Dr. Ashki placed a hand on Gesar's restrained arm. "Who is Goba?"

"My horse!"

Chandron interrupted. "Mr. Despa, you've been in a coma and you are confused. It's a normal reaction. I'm Dr. Chandron. I've been taking care of you for the past couple of weeks. You're at the San Francisco General Hospital Medical Center. You suffered a head injury with some bleeding on the brain. You will be confused for a while, but you're going to be okay."

Gesar jerked at his wrist restraints. "Take these off!"

"Of course, but you must be careful with the I.V. line, we will take it out when we're sure your okay." The resident turned and nodded to the nurse standing behind him, who scurried to the bed and unfastened the wrist and leg restraints.

With a distraught expression and watery eyes, Gesar looked up at Ashki and said, "I was in a battle and they need me. I've must go back and warn them. I saw a demon-god. Please, put me back to sleep." Reaching out his hand, he gripped Ashki's arm. "It wasn't a dream. Let me go back."

"Yes, I believe you son." Ashki gestured to Chandron and nurse to leave.

Chandron nodded and said. "His vitals are stable. We can monitor him from the nursing station."

When Chandron and the nurse left the room, Ashki gently placed his palm over Gesar's hand. Gesar relaxed, releasing his grip and leaving a wheal on Ashki's forearm.

Looking directly into Gesar's eyes, Ashki said, "I do believe you. I spoke with a hataathli. He is one of my peoples' most respected medicine men. He can enter a trance and journey to the spirit world. He's invisible there, but he sees and hears. He told me about the Blessing Way warriors and he believes that you are one of them. He spoke about the war between the Blessing Way Warriors and the chindi ghost armies. For the Navajo, chindi are evil spirits, like bad kharma that can hang around after you die. That is why the Navajo stay away from the recently deceased."

As Gesar listened, his vivid memories of Shambala were fraying at the edges, slipping away into the place of lost dreams. He struggled to hold them, rejecting the reality of doctors, intravenous tubes and glowing display monitors. Unconsciously clenching his fists he said, "I am a warrior with the Senge tapah. I must go back. I'm needed."

"I don't know if that's possible. The hataathli said that if you are called back to this world then it is because the need is greater here."

Recalling the impending danger to Shambala's forces, he was about to protest, but his mind refused to accept two realities simultaneously. Despite his efforts, Ane, Goba and the tapah were dissolving into mist and he could do nothing for them. In order not to completely lose Shambala, he pushed the memories into a back corner of his consciousness. Relying on his discipline, he took control of his breath, calmed his mind and slowly allowed the hospital room to become his new reality.

Dr. Ashki stayed at Gesar's bedside, talking and providing details regarding the recent accident and the progression of his medical condition. Gesar absorbed little of Ashki's words, but the rhythmic pattern of his voice was grounding and provided a foothold for a mind caught between worlds. By the time Ashki left, Gesar had provisionally accepted his present reality. Ashki's last words were, "I will come to visit again tomorrow. And remember, you are not insane."

Concentrating on his breathing, Gesar assembled memories of his old identity with its job, apartment and potentially terminal illness. As he lay on his back staring blankly at a lichen-green ceiling, an orderly quietly entered the room pushing a cart of cleaning equipment. Gesar turned his head and said, "Is there any food coming? I'm suddenly feeling very hungry."

"You're conscious!" The orderly answered in surprise.

"Yes, unfortunately I am."

After a furtive glance over his shoulder, the orderly whispered, "Is your name Despa? Gesar Despa?"

"That's what it says on my wrist band."

Taking a mop from his cart, the orderly said, "I have been sent to find you, but I was expecting that you would be unconscious."

"Who are you?" Gesar asked suspiciously.

Avoiding direct eye contact, the orderly began to mop the floor and answered. "Please speak softly and don't look at me directly. I must not draw attention; I'm not actually employed by this hospital. My name is Kai, a monk of the Kalacakra. We are protectors of the sleeping Buddha warriors. I came here to protect you. Excuse my reaction; I am not used to having conversations with my charges. As I said, they are usually unresponsive. I cannot tell you more since I'm not permitted to speak of our work, but I can tell you that you are in danger."

In a sudden flash, Gesar recalled his conversation with Ane on the Senge tapah training field. She spoke of Kalacakra allies, her other incarnation, and a demon on the loose in the San Francisco area. "You know of Shambala?" Gesar asked.

Kai rinsed the mop and wrung out the excess water. "Yes, it is one of several realms. Some in my order have the ability to enter other realms at will. That is how we learned of you. But now that you're awake, it changes everything."

Gesar experienced another flash of memory. "I remember a monk. His name was Jhado Zhangpo. He asked questions about me. He told you about me, didn't he?"

Having completed the floor, Kai was now cleaning surfaces with a disinfectant spray and cloth. "Perhaps, but as I said, I am not permitted to speak of our work. If you did meet Rinpoche Zhangpo, then consider yourself blessed, very few have had that privilege. Now, before I leave I must give you instructions. Since you're awake, you are less of a threat to our enemy. He is looking for Sleepers."

"Just who is looking?" Gesar asked.

"An enemy of Shambala who has entered the Human realm, his demon name is Chidag Nagpo."

The monk's story matched what Ane had told him. Perhaps, he was not delusional and if not, then Ane might really exist. "There was a warrior in Shambala, her name was Ane. Is she under your protection?"

Packing the last of the cleaning items onto his cart, Kai ignored the question and said, "On your table, there is a piece of paper with a phone number. Call me when you are released from here. We will pick you up and arrange a means to monitor your whereabouts."

Mildly offended by Kai's presumption, Gesar responded, "You're assuming that I want you to know my whereabouts."

For the first time since entering the room, Kai looked directly at Gesar and said, "You must trust me Mr. Despa. You are in no condition to survive an encounter with the demon Chidag Nagpo." He then left, keeping to his masquerade, pushing the cleaning cart before himself and moving to another unit.

Not long after the monk had left, Gesar noticed a powerfully built man in dark glasses standing near the nursing station flashing a police badge. After a short exchange, the man turned toward Gesar's room. He walked to the room partition, briefly removed his sunglasses and peered through the glass. Gesar caught a glimpse of the man's pitiless expression and a red glow behind his pupils. Bolting upright, Gesar swung his legs off the bed to stand up, but his legs refused to support his weight and he collapsed. The floor, still damp from the monk's mop, was cold against his cheek. His arm bled and stung with pain where his I.V. line had ripped away. Alarms sounded at the nursing station.

Chidag recognized the telltale turquoise glow in the eyes when he peered into the young man's face, but unexpectedly, he was awake and had triggered an alarm. Chidag restrained his instincts and refitted his sunglasses. Two nurses with worried expressions rushed by him to go to Gesar's aid. This one will be for later, he thought as he turned to leave.

Brother William perused a gourmet food magazine and sipped a fruit drink while he waited in the hospital lobby. Engrossed in an article discussing novel truffle recipes, he failed to see Officer Cutter pass by him and return to his hiding place in the back of the monastery van. Several minutes later, Kai appeared, having changed out of his hospital housekeeper's uniform.

Kai tapped William on the shoulder. "Brother William, you were supposed to be keeping watch, not reading magazines."

"I'm sorry, I got bored. You were gone a long time. I guess you had to clean every room on the floor. Did you find Despa?" asked William.

Bearing a serious expression, Kai answered while removing a cell phone from his pocket. "Yes, I found him, but he's awake. I told him to contact us as soon as he's discharged from here. I must report this to our lama, immediately."

"So now where do we go?"

"Back to the temple," answered Kai.

The faithful demon-gods of Shambala gathered in the pinnacle chamber of Palden Lhamo's watchtower. Eight windows surrounded them and provided a panoramic view of the snow-capped mountain ranged encircling the valley. Brightly lit by late afternoon sunshine, the idyllic valley seemed oblivious to the danger that lurked at its border. Herd animals grazed peacefully upon sunny hills and flocks of waterfowl paddled silently upon the snowy peaks mirrored in Lake Shambala. Overhead, young kinnaras practiced flying maneuvers in an azure sky that was marred only by a dark bank of clouds slowly consuming the horizon in the southeast.

Compared to her living quarters at the base of the tower, Palden's eyrie was sparsely furnished. Eight benches formed an octagon around a centrally placed carpet decorated with an elaborate eight-petaled lotus mandala. When alone, Palden would sit upon a bench facing a window, but during a group meeting such as this, the demon-gods sat facing each other. All were seated except Betsge, who stood at the southeast window, his eyes fixed upon the threatening band of clouds.

Betsge turned to face his fellows, his armor rattling with the sudden movement. "Surely, you understand what Mahakala means to do!" he said.

Yamantaka struck his staff on the floor. "Of course we understand, but it's hard to believe Zerden would allow Mahakala to make such an enormous sacrifice of his forces. Penetration of the Shield by force will profoundly deplete the nagu armies. Even if Mahakala could position such numbers within striking distance of Shambala, it would take Zerden another thousand years to recover his strength if Mahakala fails."

Palden interrupted. "I know Mahakala better than all of you and failure is not part of his consciousness. Now that he and the others have reverted to their ancient forms, they will not be constrained by reason. I agree with Betsge, Mahakala will strike ruthlessly with all of his forces and soon."

Hayagriva's monk's robes rustled when he stood to speak. "If that is the case, then it seems that our immediate concern should be defense of the Shield. I would suggest a combined strategy to achieve this. We must plant as many phurbas as possible along our border trails and passes to impede their advance so as to give us an opportunity to attack them before they can take up positions at the Shield barrier."

"You know that phurbas are in short supply among our Kalacakra allies," Betsge challenged.

"That is why they must be strategically placed. If we can slow the advance of only portions of the nagu armies, it will give the Buddha warriors time to deplete their numbers." Hayagriva countered, reseating himself.

Yamantaka's gnarled hand tightly clenched his staff as he pointed at his fellows, "If Mahakala's force is greater than we surmise, then we must consider the possibility that the Shield will be breached. You all know what I am thinking. We all made an oath, but if we are forced to revert to wrathful form, can we keep it?"

Palden's eyes slowly scanned the group before responding. "Yes, we swore an oath to protect the throne of Illumination. In the end, we may have to revert to our original forms, which will no doubt ignite old desires, but those of us who remained loyal to Shambala had the discipline to resist Mahakala's coercion and I'm sure we will hold to our promise."

Her fellow demon-gods did not respond. She could sense their doubts. Were they strong enough? Perhaps her words were only an attempt to fend off her own doubts regarding her self-control. There was no way to predict what would happen when they reverted to their demonic forms. Although she had rejected her old existence, she remembered the seduction of bloodlust and unbridled power. Once tasted, it was highly addictive. Perhaps, Mahakala was right; the demon-gods would never achieve the pure emptiness required to step into the flame of Bumtri's throne and enter the highest Sura realm.

Sensing the discomfort among the demon-gods, Hayagriva broke the silence. "It may not need to come to that if we act to protect the Shield now."

Palden rose from her seat, her jeweled circlet flashing as it passed through a beam of afternoon sunlight. "Then let us act quickly. I have already instructed the dakini to focus their search efforts on the near passes. We know our enemy has hidden strongholds nearby, but we don't know how many. Presently, the Druk and Senge are on a mission to engage one of the strongholds."

"And I have sent the remaining tapah units to patrol the Shield perimeter at the most likely fronts of attack." Betsge added.

Using his staff for support, Yamantaka pushed himself to standing position and said, "I will work with the Seers and make preparations to move those living in the valley within the walls of Kalapa,"

Hayagriva was the last to stand, adjusting his orange robes as he spoke, "I will send a messenger to request more phurbas, but we must not forget that the Shield is not our only battlefront. Zerden's minions are entering the Human realm. Roaming freely, they can inflict great harm to our Buddha warriors. Lama Zhangpo will need phurbas to banish the interlopers."

"Our need is the greater," Palden responded. "If Shambala falls, we lose all."

The demon-gods nodded their heads in agreement and adjourned to attend to their assignments, leaving by way of the stairs that wound through the tower's interior. Palden remained in her eyrie keeping watch at the window. Scanning the southeast gap, she spotted a lone dakini crossing the Shield barrier. A few minutes later, horns sounded from the rampart, announcing the sighting. When the dakini messenger alighted, Palden was waiting on the palace plaza, standing beside her golden kinnara, Skarma.

The dakini dismounted, ran to Palden and bowed. Palden recognized Dolma, the Druk squadron's second in command.

"Speak." Palden ordered.

"We were drawn into a trap my lady. When I left the battle, the Senge were in a canyon caught between two nagu armies with the demon, Gnyan, leading one of them. The Druk are with them and they will stay until the last warrior falls. I came with all speed, but I fear the battle may be over before reinforcements can reach them."

Palden's left hand clenched the pummel of the sword hanging at her side. She strained to control the surge of anger that sprang up from a dark ancient place lingering within her. She could feel her eyes filling with demon fire. How many bearers of bad news had she killed in a sudden rage during her time as a demon? She could not recall, but no matter, those days were long behind her. Now she had learned to restrain, regret and repent.

"Lady Palden, if you will permit, I wish to rejoin my squadron," Dolma added, her eyes no longer averted, but fixed bravely against Palden's soul piercing gaze.

Palden's expression immediately softened, her rage quenched by Dolma's tear filled eyes, bottomless pools of courage. She was thankful to be among these humans. They strengthened her will to hold her demon-self at bay. Their readiness to shorten their already brief lives and their total faith in hope never ceased to surprise and humble. "You will not return alone," Palden responded. "The Dorje squadron is patrolling the south perimeter of the Shield. They are the nearest reinforcements. Go now, find them and lead them to the battle."

"I will, my Lady." Dolma pressed her palms together, bowed and ran to her mount,

As Dolma disappeared beyond the walls, Palden resisted a sudden impulse to dash to her mount and follow. Before the rebellion, she gave no thought to time, but now the idle hours of waiting within the confines of the Shield were unbearable. She was a creature of action; her nature was to fight, to be in the midst of the storm. No, she was the storm, but after the Taming, she had learned to temper her nature for the sake of Shambala and The Path. The bodhisattvas, in their wisdom, had given her the secret prayer that would bar demon-gods passage through the Shield, but what Mahakala did not know was that neither she nor any of the other demon-gods could venture beyond the Shield for it would also bar their return. Presently, the Shield defined the walls of her prison.

Deep beneath Dagpa Akar, Tenzin listened at the door of the meditation chamber bearing the sign of The Endless Knot. A dull echoing thud, thud, thud answered his three knocks. Expecting two strikes for three, the old monk briefly hesitated in confusion before shouldering the stone door open. When he pushed his lamp into the pitch-black chamber, a pair of eyes in hollow sockets squinted in response.

"Brother Jamyang. Are you well?" asked Tenzin. "We did not expect your return so soon."

His throat parched, Jamyang answered in a raspy whisper, "I must speak with the Rinpoche at once. I have a message for him."

"You should drink and eat first."

Jamyang squeezed through the doorway. "There is too little time. Complete your rounds and bring tea to the Rinpoche's chambers. I must hurry."

"As you wish," Tenzin said with a bow as he watched Jamyang's back disappear up the stairwell.

Jhado was meditating when Jamyang's knock fell upon his door. He was disturbed during meditation only in a dire emergency. Despite knowing this, he maintained a relaxed and regular breath pattern. "Enter." he said calmly.

The door swung open and a haggard, unshaven Brother Jamyang entered the room and knelt before Jhado, who sat upright upon a raised rectangular meditation cushion.

Jhado spoke first. "Brother Jamyang, from the look of you I take it that you bring unpleasant news."

"Unfortunately that is true, your holiness," Jamyang said, his dry mouth straining to form the words.

Jhado reached for a nearby teapot, poured the remnants of his early morning tea into a cup, and offered it to Jamyang. "Drink this. You can barely speak, brother. You have not given yourself time to recover from your journey."

Jamyang took the liquid in several focused sips before speaking, "Forgive me your holiness, but there is urgency, Hayagriva himself asked me to carry a message to you."

Jhado nodded, giving consent for Jamyang to proceed.

Cradling the teacup in his palms, Jamyang ordered his thoughts. Slowly and clearly he delivered his words. "Enemy forces are massing around Shambala. An attack is imminent. The Council of Guardians believes that Mahakala intends to overwhelm the Shield's power by sacrificing great numbers of nagu. Hayagriva requests phurbas as soon as possible to help defend the Shield. He also wishes to know the status of Chidag. He believes Chidag's incarnation must be destroyed with all haste to discourage the passage of more of Zerden's children. With Shambala under siege, the dakini can no longer defend the chotens."

Jhado listened while looking through the east window that was behind Jamyang. It was well after dawn and light should have been beaming into his chamber, but an unseasonable cloud cover continued to shroud the sun. Oil lamps provided most of the room's illumination. For several days, the batteries had been below optimal charge and a bicycle driven generator was required to supplement the solar panels in order for Jhado to use the temple computer.

"How many phurbas does Hayagriva request?" Jhado asked.

"He would like enough to block every way into Shambala."

Jhado sighed. "I fear you have come too late. I am also sad to report that Chidag remains at large and we have received word that other minions of Zerden have incarnated in this realm. I've sent our phurbas to temples caring for Buddha warriors. Presently, we have only three phurbas remaining that were about to be shipped. As you know, we can make only one demon-banisher per moon cycle."

Jamyang returned the teacup to the tray next to Jhado. "Then we can offer no help to Shambala?"

"There may be another way, but it will risk exposure of Dagpa Akar. We were not the only temple with the knowledge to make phurbas. In the ancient days others made the demon-banishers. I will ask our allies among the Sun Tribe to send emissaries to monasteries throughout the plateau to request phurbas. The mountains provide many places to hide sacred objects and it is unlikely that the Chinese confiscated everything of value."

"Your holiness, but Shambala has no time to spare."

Before Jhado could respond, there was a gentle knock on the doorframe. Tenzin stood in the open doorway bearing a tray.

Jhado rose from his cushion, "Come in Tenzin, Jamyang must restore his strength."

Jhado directed Jamyang to sit at a low wooden table with legs carved into likenesses of clawed dragon feet and a top elaborately inlaid with ivory and rosewood. Tenzin offered him a steamed towel. Jamyang accepted it and bathed his hands and face, while Tenzin filled a cup with hot ghee tea and spread out a light meal.

"Refresh your self, Brother," Jhado instructed. "After such a long time in the chambers you will need some time to recover and then you may return to Shambala with the phurbas that we have. If we find more phurbas, we will find others to carry them. Now eat and I will see what news there is of Chidag Nagpo."

Jhado went to his office in a adjacent room and was surprised that the computer display came to life immediately. Despite the overcast day, the batteries were charged. He wondered which unfortunate monk or nun had spent the last several hours on a fixed bicycle charging the temple batteries. In minutes, he was scanning through the most recently posted haiku poems. Since Chidag's disappearance, he had checked the haiku website for news of Chidag twice daily, but nothing had been posted for many days, so he was relieved when a poem appeared on just the second page he had opened.

Hungry field mice wait
For golden seed to ripen
Hidden serpent smiles
Kasa

114

Chidag, the "serpent", was still in hiding and Kasa's monks, the "mice," were waiting for him to reveal himself. Knowing the nature of such creatures, Chidag had to be exerting great restraint, Jhado thought. He would undoubtedly reveal himself soon, but Jhado was loath to imagine how that might manifest; he could only hope that Kasa's people would get some warning. Jhado quickly composed a reply.

Hungry wolves circle
White stag in forest's embrace
A moonless night comes
Dan Poe

The metaphor was simple. Kasa would learn that Shambala, the 'white stag', was under immediate threat by enemy forces, "hungry wolves', and realize this added urgency to cast Chidag from the Human realm before he could do harm to the Sleepers. Jhado was about to close the session when another haiku from Kasa appeared on his screen.

The Ling kingdom's first
Walks among the mortal ones
His eyes wide open
Kasa

Jhado pondered a moment to comprehend the message. The "Ling kingdom" referred to ancient Tibetan mythology. Suddenly, the meaning was obvious. The first king of Ling was Gesar. In the foothills overlooking the plains of Asura, he had encountered a Buddha warrior named Gesar Despa from San Francisco. Kasa had been instructed to locate and protect the young man's unconscious body. Jhado's initial puzzlement was because he had only given Kasa the young man's surname, Despa, which meant 'brave' in Tibetan had simplified his original cryptic instruction to Kasa, which read:

There is one called Brave
In the highest of kingdoms
Who sleeps among you
Dan Poe

Apparently, Kasa's people had succeeded in finding the one whose name meant "brave" in the "highest of kingdoms", Tibet, but apparently he had regained consciousness. It was one of those rare cases, in which an untrained sentient moves back and forth between realms. Even for a highly trained Kalacakra adept, the journey between realms was a tremendous stress.

Jhado whispered to himself. "Despa must think he's losing his sanity. I pray he has the strength to persevere."

"Your holiness, do you have other instructions?"

Startled, Jhado looked up. He had not noticed Tenzin approach his desk. "Yes Tenzin. Shambala needs phurbas, as many as can be gathered."

"But we have only three and one is still in the making."

"That is why we must send word quickly to our allies among the Sun Tribe. They can visit temples throughout the plateau and tell them of our need. Some may have ancient phurbas hidden away."

"Your holiness, those temples will be watched by Chinese police."

"We have no choice but to take the risk. If Shambala falls, the discovery of Dagpa Akar will be of no consequence. Now please excuse me, I must speak with Brother Jamyang before we send him back to Shambala."

The vast Zhaxika grasslands of Kham were normally two days ride from Temple Dagpa Akar, but urgency forced brother Chongtul to travel throughout the night despite the danger to himself and his horse. Fortunately, he had negotiated the rocky switch back trail that descended to the grassland during the last hours of daylight. It was late morning when he spotted the white maikhan tents dotting the rust-tinged plain like a fresh crop of mushrooms. A late summer festival gathering was underway. Brightly colored pennants and prayer flags strung on guy-lines danced in the wind. People in colorful costumes wandered among an assortment of yak, sheep, and goats, but the largest group was assembled around a makeshift racing field where riders tended their horses in preparation for the contest. Brother Chongtul regretted having to intrude during this traditional time of respite.

The people of Zhaxika were nomads, living most of year in the cold and all of the year at high altitude, their festivals were brief precious times of celebration and warmth. The Khampas were often thought of as living fossils, since their way of life had remained largely unchanged for thousands of years. Like a mountain, they had stood out of time watching the world transform around them. A world ignorant of the role they had played in protecting The Path of Enlightenment and freedom of humanity. During the time of the Taming, the Sun Tribe provided warriors to aid the great avatar, Lord Shenrab, who fought Lagring, the last of demons incarnate in the Human realm. Embattled on a mountain glacier, the demon triggered an avalanche that buried Shenrab in an ice cave. In order to survive, the avatar entered a state of deep meditation and appeared among the Zhaxika nomads as a vision of a holy man encircled by a bright aura. The holy man requested their aid and pointed to the mountain. Without hesitation, both men and women answered the call to climb the mountain and challenge Lagring. Archers distracted the demon, while others dug Lord Shenrab from his frozen prison. Once in the light, Lord Shenrab awoke from his trance armed with new powers. He called his allies to stand near him and called the sun's heat upon the mountain. The glacier melted and swept Lagring down the mountain in a torrent of water. The demon's broken body lay at the base of the mountain on the bank of a new river. There, with a touch of a finger, Shenrab cast the demon spirit back to the lower realms and resurrected his physical form as a devout monk. Since that time, the people of Zhaxika were known as the Sun Tribe, faithfully serving the Path of Enlightenment and protecting the secret of Dagpa Akar. By encouraging the notion that they were ruthless marauders, few outsiders dared to venture in the land of the Khampas or the vicinity of Dagpa Akar.

As brother Chongtul dismounted his exhausted horse, a group of smiling men approached, pressing their palms together and bowing to him. These were the legendary men of Kham. All were wearing khaki robes and riding boots. Unlike the stocky western Tibetans, these men were at least two meters tall with large fierce eyes aside sharp noses. Each wore a single turquoise earring, accenting long black hair plaited into a hero's braid tied with a red ribbon or leather thong. One of them offered Chongtul a steadying hand until he found his legs, while the others took his horse to be fed and watered.

Soon a throng of curious, dirt-smudged children joined the welcoming party, the older ones bowed while the younger erupted with shy giggles. Chongtul smiled graciously and returned their greetings, but he was feeling anxious to deliver his message. "I need to speak with Lozang Gyatso," he said to the two men nearest to him. Sensing the monk's distress, the taller of the two men shouted, "Clear the way children!"

The man introduced himself as Gawa and led the monk into the core of the tent village, negotiating a spider web of guy-lines and animal pens. From the smell of animals and the well-worn footpaths among the tents, it was obvious the gathering had been going on for several days. Gawa soon directed Chongtul to a large tent decorated with black trim, colorful brocade and paintings of the eight auspicious Buddhist symbols.

Standing at the tent flap, Gawa announced, "Chief Gyatso, a monk is here to speak with you."

A powerful voice responded, "Please, please enter brother and bless our dwelling with your presence."

Chongtul pulled the flap aside and entered. A striking young woman in a thick brocade dress and an elder man in a yak hide robe were standing with hands pressed together offering welcoming bows. Chongtul returned the bow.

The young woman stepped forward, extending to the monk the traditional symbol of welcome, a white scarf, and said, "Good fortune to you venerable brother."

"Thank you for your kind welcome, Lozang. I am Brother Chongtul from Dagpa Akar."

Lozang was an older version of the young men who had greeted Chongtul upon his arrival. His braided hair was mostly grey, but when his weathered face smiled, the years fell away. "The brothers and sisters of Dagpa Akar are always welcome among us."

Chongtul tucked the white scarf in his robe and waited for the formal introductions.

"This is my youngest daughter, Monlam. She still cares for her old father, while she waits for a husband who can match her riding talent."

Monlam blushed. "I will serve tea and momo," she said, bowing and making her way to a glowing brazier.

Lozang gestured to a low table surrounded by an assortment of comfortable brocade cushions. "Brother Chongtul, come, come, please sit."

Chongtul seated himself at one end of the table. It was a relief to be cross-legged on solid ground after being in the saddle all night; however, he also was suddenly aware of his own exhaustion.

Lozang sat opposite the monk. "You've met one of my sons-in-law, Gawa. It is fortunate that you arrived before the afternoon races. An hour later and we would all have been at the field and there would have been no one to welcome you."

Before Chongtul could reply, Monlam arrived with a tray and set out cups of tea and plates of warm dumplings.

Recognizing his guest's fatigue, Lozang urged, "I see that you have had ridden hard so you must carry important news from Dagpa Akar, but please eat and drink, at least rest a little. You look tired, holy brother."

Chongtul complied, taking a few sips of tea and swallowing a dumpling, but his appetite was constrained by the urgency of his charge. "Again, I thank you for your kind hospitality. Dagpa Akar deeply values our friendship with your people. The Sun Tribe has long protected and provided us, and I regret that I have been charged to ask another service of you."

Lozang set down his cup. "You know we are pledged to preserve The Path of Enlightenment in any way we can. Please, tell me what do you need?"

"Rinpoche Zhangpo has received an urgent request from Shambala. That is why I rode through the night to reach you."

Lozang's eyes widened and Monlam turned from the brazier to listen to the monk's words.

"The Path is under grave threat. Four of Shambala's demon-gods have joined forces with the Master of Eighty-thousand negativities. They hope to restore their power as it was in the days before the Taming. Fortunately, Lady Palden was able to banish them beyond the Shield, but the Council of Guardians suspects the rebels intend to break Shambala's defenses by using an overwhelming attack. The Council of Guardians fears that the sacrifice of an enormous number of sentient beings could possibly quench the sacred flame and open the way for Zerden to dominate the middle realms. For over two thousand years, he has swollen his armies with lost sentients that wandered into his realm. The Buddha warriors will likely not be able to stop a massive attack so they are requesting demon banishers to help them protect the Shield. We have only three remaining at Dagpa Akar, far too few to protect the vast border of Shambala."

Staring down at the steaming cup cradled his in his hand, Lozang replied, "But holy brother, surely you know my people do not possess the knowledge to make such powerful talismans."

"Yes, yes, Rinpoche Zhangpo knows this, but he believes that there may be demon banishers that were hidden by other Temples across the plateau. I have come to ask you to send people to collect and deliver them to Dagpa Akar. It will mean sending couriers in all directions immediately."

Lozang looked up, "My people will be happy to help, but secrecy will be difficult to maintain, especially during the festival season. Kham horsemen wandering among the cities and towns at this time will raise suspicions. As you know, our reputation has left us with a measure of freedom, but the Chinese think of us as no more than biting flies. They tolerate us as long as we keep to ourselves and behave reasonably. If they sense any threat they will not hesitate to send in exterminators"

Chongtul took another swallow of his tea before responding, "We realize the danger and that is why I am so reluctant to ask this of you, but there is no alternative. If Shambala falls, humanity may not get another opportunity for freedom. At the time of the Taming, Zerden was weak and the demon-gods were divided. They will not make the same mistake. As a united force, the balance of power shifts to their side. Without the Path of Enlightenment, Zerden will become reaper of all sentients."

Stroking his weathered forehead, Lozang paused to consider, then he asked, "How soon do you need the phurbas?"

"The Council suspects an attack is imminent."

"We will need at least seven days. There are many temples to visit." Lozang replied.

"Rinpoche believes only the oldest temples would likely have demon banishers. That may help limit your search."

Slapping his thigh, Lozang replied, "Very well then. I will send my best people after today's race. My sons will be among them. Dagpa Akar can expect to hear from my people in eight days."

"Thank you Lozang. Blessings upon you and the Sun Tribe."

Monlam brought fresh tea and a plate stacked with dried yak and goat cheese. "Please eat and rest a little before the race," she said.

Chongtul noticed Monlam's callused hands. She too was a rider and like most Kham women, as tough in a fight as any man. It was no wonder the Chinese government eventually decided that complete subjugation of these people was not worth the trouble.

Dolma's anxiety intensified as she searched the southern sector in ever widening circles. Scanning the sky and scouring canyons, she saw no sign of the Dorje dakini. Even Nam, her mount, with eagle-like vision saw nothing but the occasional discarded weapon. The search was taking too long. The Senge tapah and her dakini sisters were falling in battle while she sought the Dorje reinforcements. A horrifying thought struck her. Perhaps, the Dorje had been victims of a trap. Suddenly, Dolma faced a terrible dilemma. Should she return to Shambala and report the missing Dorje squadron or join her Druk sisters in battle? Recalling Ane's brave challenge of Yama, her loyalty to her Druk dakini sisters won out. Abandoning her search, she directed Nam to the southeast. After rounding a mountainside, she had full view of the southeast where a dark cloudbank portended bad weather. "Nam, I hope we can reach them before the storm."

Nam beat her wings to gain altitude and Dolma heard Nam's voice enter in her mind, "Look below, mistress." Dolma looked down and the sight caused her to gasp. On the canyon trail below, a seemingly endless river of black armor flowed steadily toward

121

Shambala. Groups of dron warriors carried mutilated bodies of kinnaras still bearing the crossed lightning bolt symbol of the Dorje squadron. "Buddha protect us. Nam, we must warn Shambala."

Gnyan rushed forward, his rage fixed on the dismounted rider kneeling next to the broken choten. Blocking Gnyan's path, Goba held his ground and caused the demon to slow his pace. Gnyan spat a dismissive curse and raised his tilug to sweep the impudent animal away. As the whistling blade descended, the choten suddenly emitted an intense flash of light and Goba did the unexpected. He charged directly at Gnyan with all speed, throwing his weight into the demon's legs. The flash-blinded demon stumbled backward, driving his tilug into the earth to regain his balance. When his eyes readjusted, the war horse had galloped beyond reach of his weapon and an entire tapah unit was riding directly toward him.

As the Senge tapah rode toward Gnyan, Ane did her best to direct the rear defense. Despite showers of arrows interspersed with repeated diving attacks, the nagu army steadily advanced in pursuit of the retreating tapah. When the Senge tapah had sounded their retreat, the enemy captain signaled his army to raise shields and pursue. Covered by their shields, the dron warriors were difficult to hit with arrows from above. The flying serpents were a further complication, tying up dakinis that should be attacking enemy ground forces. Only one of the four serpents had been downed; its huge carcass lay at the bottom of the canyon with nagu warriors skirting around it. Suddenly, Ane saw a solution. Directing Brug into a wide banking turn, she shouted a command to her squadron, "Everyone, break off and attack the serpents! Closing Lotus formation!"

Moments later, the three remaining naga-ta were enclosed within a sphere of dakini. Using hand signals, Ane provided final instructions. In an impressive display of speed and coordination, the dakinis performed a flurry of repeated attacks slashing at leathery wings while steadily herding the naga-ta directly over advancing ground force. As the 'lotus closed', the serpents were forced into a tight cluster. Hobbled by numerous slashes, two of the naga-ta collided, entangled wings and dropped into the canyon, crushing at least ten dron warriors. Soon the other followed, plunging into the chasm and forming a dam of twisted flesh that blocked the enemy advance.

Leading the tapah retreat, Captain Jigme, formerly Ben Wilson of rough stock rodeo fame was the first to see Goba running from the demon who barred the trail ahead. Seeing Goba's empty saddle, Ben assumed Gesar had been slain. The demon was definitely Gnyan, his fanged ovine profile and purple hide were unmistakable. Surprisingly, the creature was separated from his main army and was jogging forward to engage the oncoming cavalry, seemingly unaware that his army trailed a considerable distance behind. Ben quickly recognized the tactical advantage; it was much easier to distract a demon unaccompanied by an army of nagu dron warriors. His men had only to slip by the demon and then plow a furrow through the enemy force.

Ben cried out a simple command that was relayed down the line of tapah. "Crow and spear!"

Ben raised his bow and nocked an arrow as he approached the demon. Before coming within reach of the demon's weapon, Ben loosed his arrow and Dawa suddenly turned sharply to the left while the following tapah loosed an arrow and turned sharply right. The alternating pattern continued with each horse making a clockwise or counter clockwise turn around the demon loosing a steady barrage of arrows at the demon's eyes. After completing a round, each horse warrior rode at full gallop toward the nagu army, substituting their bows for charging spears.

Gnyan's howls of frustration echoed through the canyon as he batted away the incessant stream of arrows. Only when the last of the Senge riders approached did the barrage of arrows diminish. Gnyan fixed his aim on the last pair of riders, ready to cut them down with a single blow. Before he could strike, a cloud of dakinis fell from a dark sky with bright swords biting his exposed flesh.

With Gnyan pinned down, the Senge rode unmolested into the nagu army. Surprised and confused, the nagu frontline broke under the piercing momentum of the tapah warhorses. Like breaking through a dam, the resistance collapsed after penetrating the frontline. Unprepared, the enemy warriors to the rear were swept away by the torrent of riders. Maintaining an unbroken column, the tapah spears deflected nagu warriors to the right and left, clearing a path through a sea of black armor. Goba fell into the charge, adding his momentum to the thrust of man and horse. By the time the Senge emerged on the far side of the black sea, the impending storm struck in full force.

Not knowing if the battle had been won or lost, a baffled nagu rear guard watched the tapah disappear into a downpour of snow and sleet. When the tapah were clear, Ane ordered her squadron to break off and join the retreat.

Clouds of powdery snow exploded with each footfall as Mahakala ran through the starlit mountain pass. It was a bitterly frigid night, but he was oblivious to cold and even if he had had the sensations of a mortal, he would not have noticed physical discomfort. He was too preoccupied trying to keep pace with the naga-ta that flew above him while suffering the idle chit-chat of his companion, Changpa Karpo. While his middle eye kept watch overhead, the others were forced to view Changpa, who ran on the trail just ahead of him. Changpa was always the faster runner. Unfortunately, the distance between them was not enough that he could ignore the incessant chatter discharging from Changpa's four faces.

"We're looking forward to a good fight. Naraka was getting quite boring," said Changpa's rear face.

Changpa's left face turned to Mahakala. "Don't you find running invigorating? It reminds me of the old days when we roamed wherever and whenever we wished."

Then Changpa's right face turned to Mahakala. "Look at Kubera up there, riding with his fat head in the air like he was Palden's equal. We know he's a coward and wouldn't risk a fingernail in a real fight. Frankly, we were surprised he agreed to come along."

Changpa's foreface spun around. "You're being rather quiet my three-eyed brother. At least Kubera can converse. You're not having trouble keeping up with us are you?"

Infuriated, Mahakala answered, "Just shut your mouths up and keep running! I only regret that you weren't light enough to be up there riding with Kubera, and then he could listen to your constant prattle."

Three of Changpa's faces laughed in unison while the hind face spoke. "We forgot just how short tempered you were. Very well, you shall have your silence, at least until we join Yama. Can you tell me when that will be?"

"We should reach the cave by sunrise."

"Will Yama have our forces in place for the attack?" asked Changpa's right face.

"You're prattling again." Mahakala growled.

On the day of his discharge from the hospital, Gesar's mood hit a new low. His spirit sank when the physical therapist handed him a walker and said, "You're going to need this, at least for awhile. Keep doing the exercises that I taught you. In a week or two as you get stronger, you might only need a cane. A cab will be coming to pick you up and take you home today. We set up a follow up appointment for you in two weeks. If that's a problem, call us to change the date."

Gesar watched as the cab driver remove the walker from the trunk. So this is how it is going to be, he thought. I get disabled bit by bit until I'm completely helpless. After paying the driver, he used the walker to make his way to his apartment and opened the front door, pushing aside a pile of unopened mail. Silent and musty, his rooms felt more like a tomb than a home. Nothing had been moved since the morning he left for work several weeks ago. Dead houseplants were covered with a layer of dust and unwashed dishes remained stacked in the kitchen sink. The only detectable life was the small flashing light on his telephone indicating voice mail.

Shaking his head, he muttered, "What a mess. I guess I have to start somewhere." He parked his walker, sat in a chair and started listening to telephone messages. The first calls were from administrators at the college, inquiring if he would be able to return to his teaching duties. Eventually, he came to a message, which had been recorded that morning.

"Hello, Gesar, this is Dr. Ashki. I called the hospital and found out you were set free today. Sorry, I couldn't make it there to take you home. Call me when you're ready to talk. I know this is all pretty tough for you."

The next call he had missed by less than an hour. It was from the mysterious monk, Kai, who claimed to be his protector.

125

"Mr. Despa, this is Kai, you did not call today as I instructed you to do. I only just learned of your discharge. You are in grave danger and it is important that we know your whereabouts. Call me as soon as you get home. In any case, I will be coming to speak with you at your apartment. It would be convenient if you would consider coming to live at our temple, where we could provide better protection."

Gesar reached into his pocket and retrieved the crumpled note with the phone number that Kai had left him and tossed it on the side table. He had intentionally not called; he simply was not ready to have a Buddhist monk as a baby sitter, especially after seeing the red-eyed creature appear only minutes after meeting the monk. He suspected Brother Kai could not provide much protection, but at least the monk affirmed that his experience in Shambala was more than just a dream or delusion. Yet delusion provided the most sensible explanation. The seeds of such a delusion were part of him. He first heard of other realms of existence as a child. During horseback rides in the Sierra Nevada Mountains, his grandfather would sometimes talk of his beliefs.

"There are six realms of existence," he said. "They are the Hell, Hungry-ghost, Animal, Human, Asura and Deva realms."

"I know about hell," the child Gesar replied. "That is where bad people are burned and punished by devils forever after they die."

His grandfather chuckled at the comment, "No, that is not quite true. The lower realms are places where souls keep returning until they have cleaned away the dirt of their bad actions. We live many lifetimes and each one is an opportunity to cleanse ourselves so that we can eventually advance to the deva realm."

"How do you know this, Grandfather?"

"The Buddha taught this and showed us the way to escape the lower realms and perpetual reincarnation. It is called the Path of Enlightenment."

"Are there devils in the hell realm?" Gesar asked.

His grandfather's expression turned serious. "There are enemies of the Path trapped in all of the lower realms who use souls to fulfill their own desires, but when the Buddha opened the Path, some demons were convinced to become his allies. They serve in Shambala."

"What's Shambala?"

"It is a shining land in the Asura realm where the gate to the Deva realm is held open and protected from the enemies of the Path."

The trail they were riding on reached an overlook, revealing a broad valley with a beautiful lake reflecting mountains and clouds. "Shambala can't be much better than this!" Gesar yelled as he spurred his pony into a gallop.

If his experience were not a product of a delusional mind harvesting childhood stories, then Ane should exist as a Sleeper in this reality. She said she was from San Francisco and he remembered her name, Angela. If she existed, then he was not crazy and his consciousness did incarnate in another realm while in a coma.

Gesar picked up the telephone and then hesitated. Staring at the telephone keypad, he wondered what Dr. Ashki's response would be. Finally, he keyed in the numbers. After four rings a voice answered, "Hello."

"Hi Dr. Ashki, this is Gesar. I'm sorry to bother you."

"Hey, it's no bother, I told you to call me. I'm not just your doctor, I'm your friend."

"Thanks. I really appreciate what you've done for me."

"So how are you doing?"

"I've had better times," Gesar replied. "But I'm calling because there's a favor I want to ask of you."

"If it's in my power and it's legal, then consider it done."

Gesar hesitated.

"Do you remember in the hospital, when I was waking up, you said that you believed me about being in another place?"

"Yeah, I remember. The medicine man spoke of you being there, your story is not bizarre in my culture."

"Well, I'm still trying to pull it together for myself. When I was in that place, I met a woman. She said that she was from San Francisco. I think she might be in a hospital unconscious, probably in a coma. If I could find her, then I would know that I wasn't crazy."

Ashki interrupted. "Gesar, you're not crazy. You've been given a gift. Isn't your own experience enough proof?"

"It would still help if I knew she really existed. Being a doctor, I thought you might be able to find her. She's probably in a medical facility in the area."

"Do you know her name?"

"Her name is Angela, Angela Adrastos. I think. And it might help to know that she's a pilot or at least was a pilot."

"Okay, I'll make some calls and let you know what I find out, but in the meantime, you just focus on daily tasks and get your life back together. Perhaps, the reason you were called back to this world is to find this girl. And remember to call me whenever you need any moral support."

Gesar said goodbye and hung up, knowing that he had not given any details of his experiences in Shambala, nor mentioned the meeting with Kai or seeing the red-eyed creature in the intensive care unit. He thought it better not to expose another to potential danger, real or not.

Grabbing his walker, Gesar crossed the room to an intricately carved wooden chest. The hinges creaked as he raised the heavy door to reveal a neatly arranged collection of Tibetan Buddhist religious items. According to his grandfather, they were very old and had been carried over the Himalayas by donkey caravan. Nearly all were gifts from the monks that his grandfather had helped to escape from Tibet. Among the prayer wheels, dzi beads, rolled thangkas, vajra scepters, and singing bells was the item he sought. He lifted it from the chest and removed its silk wrapping. Its tapered, three-edged blade was sharp and untarnished. Gesar was skeptical when his grandfather claimed the blade was made from a meteorite, but seeing the pristine state of the blade, it was clear that it was made of some unusual alloy. The intricately worked handle was half the length of the blade and bore two faces, looking in opposite directions much like the two-faced Roman god, Janus. One face was in a serene sleep while the other bore the wide-awake expression of an angry warrior.

Holding the blade upright, Kesar looked over his shoulder at the large pile of unopened mail on the floor by his apartment door and said, "I suppose you'd be a better tent stake than a letter opener."

Chidag had noticed a change come over the monastery. Hectic comings and goings interrupted the monastery's usual quiet daily routines. When he roamed the temple grounds at night disguised in discarded robes, groups of monks would suddenly rush off in vehicles smelling of fear. Something had disturbed them. He was certain no one had recognized him nor discovered the body of the one who had chanced upon his hiding place. He had carefully concealed the body beyond the temple grounds in a dense forest where even scavengers would have to work to enjoy it. Perhaps, the assault of Shambala had begun and its defenders were suffering defeats. This thought spurred his resolve to fulfill his appointed task, but so far, his efforts to locate the Sleepers had been frustrated. From the back of the van, he listened to the two monks and waited for his fortunes to improve.

"Isn't Despa coming with us?" asked Brother William as Kai climbed into the passenger seat.

"No. I tried to convince him to come, but he refused."

"Does he understand the situation?"

Kai fastened his seat belt. "He claims he can take care of himself, but I think he's deluding himself. The man can barely walk. Still, we can't force him to come with us. We can only hope that Chidag has no interest in him."

Brother William started the van and turned into traffic. "I'm surprised he didn't take our offer. We could have supported him with a lot of his daily needs."

Kai's forehead frowned more deeply than usual. "He did say something disturbing before I left. He said that we should be careful, because we were probably being watched."

William nervously looked into the rear view mirror for any trailing vehicles. "What did you tell him?"

"I assured him that we were always careful."

The two monks were silent during the remainder of the drive back to the temple. During the journey, William continued to glance at his mirrors looking for suspicious trailing vehicles. When they arrived at the temple, Chidag fortunes changed.

Before leaving the vehicle, Kai said, "Don't forget. Next week it is our turn to check on the Sleepers. Do you know the route?"

"Yes, I did it once before with Brother Lodro." answered William.

"By the way, has Lodro showed up yet?" Kai asked.

"I don't think so, but you know Lodro. He's probably on one of his hiking trips."

Chidag grinned hungrily, saliva pooling in his mouth. His fortunes had improved.

A singing bell resonated as Jhado peered through a spy-hole. A group of monks and nuns sat in meditation around a single phurba mounted upright upon a crystal stand. Regrettably, the phurba would not be ready until the next full moon, likely not soon enough to be of any help to Shambala. Phurba making was time intensive and energy consuming. Of the several types of phurbas, the demon banishers were the most difficult to make. Every stage of construction and preparation required flawless execution and only a few of the temple adepts knew the details of each stage. The blade's metallic alloy was composed of precise proportions of precious metals and meteoric iron mixed with the ashes of an enlightened saint. Blacksmithing was done at night to prevent furnace smoke from being detected by Chinese patrols. Inlaid with select jewels, its handle bore the faces of The Sleeper and The Warrior carved from bodhi wood obtained from a direct descendant of the tree that shaded the Buddha at time of his awakening. Once constructed, the physical weapon was nothing but an impotent artifact until the next, and more difficult, stage was completed. Jhado presently witnessed that stage, a continuous vigil of meditation with the combined intent of eight highly disciplined minds focused on awakening the phurba. It was exhausting for the participants who were relieved only once every eight hours. Throughout the meditation, a bell sounded every three minutes, maintaining a continuous resonance in the circular chamber. Only two dim butter-lamps illuminated the room since signs of the phurba's awakening could only be recognized in darkness.

While Jhado watched through the spy-hole, Tenzin silently approached and bowed before speaking. "Excuse my intrusion your holiness. I have come to inform you that the Sun Tribe emissaries have been dispatched."

Jhado turned to face the old monk. "Very good, let's hope they return with more phurbas."

Tenzin stroked his age-spotted pate. "I fear they might return with the Chinese army behind them."

"I understand your worries, my old friend. I may be younger than you, but I too remember the bloodshed of those days. Many of our best were killed or imprisoned to save Dagpa Akar. Now, we must be prepared to give all to save Shambala."

"Yes, your holiness, but we are so few."

Jhado felt the despair in Tenzin's voice. "Tenzin, you know very well that when we take despair into battle we give our enemy an ally in our camp. We must abandon despair and be like the ever hopeful gambler and confidently place our small bet on the table though the odds are against us."

Tenzin gave a half smile. "Of course your holiness, as always you speak truly. It is just that I have never been lucky at games of chance. Excuse me holiness; it is time that I make my rounds in the chambers."

"How many are in the chambers?" Jhado asked.

"Five."

"When the phurbas arrive, we will need every available adept to carry them."

"Arrangements have already been made, your holiness"

"Excellent. Now return to your duties my friend."

Tenzin bowed, turned away, and carried his ancient bones down the hall. Jhado resumed viewing the phurba preparation. At the next sounding of the bell, he saw the phurba blade release a brief flash of blue light.

"At last, it begins to awake," he whispered to himself.

On the third day after his discharge, Gesar unceremoniously tossed the walker into the back of his largest closet. After discharge from the hospital, he had focused on regaining strength and piecing his life back together. His apartment was clean, but he had not yet replaced the dead houseplants. He was in the midst of qigong meditation pose when the phone rang. Grabbing his cane, he hobbled across the room, picked up the phone and sat down.

"Hello."

"Hey Gesar. It's Dr. Ashki. How are you doing?"

"Well, I dumped the walker today."

"That's great. Like I said, motivation makes all the difference."

"I hope your right, because that's about all I got."

"Perhaps this will cheer you up. After a little detective work and a lot of string pulling, I can prove that you're definitely not crazy. I found Angela Adrastos."

Gesar felt his pulse quicken. "Really? Where is she?"

"So knowing that she exists isn't enough for you."

"I would like to see her."

"Technically, I'm seriously violating medical privacy policy, but since you seem to be a close friend of hers, I think I can stretch the rules for a visit. You might be surprised to learn that she's not in San Francisco. That's why it took some effort to locate her. She's in Marin County at a catholic retirement and long term care facility."

Perplexed, Gesar asked. "Retirement community, isn't that for old people?"

"Normally, yes, but someone managed to have her transferred there. It's not where you would expect to find a young military vet in a coma."

"The monks." Gesar whispered.

"What was that?"

"Nothing, I was just thinking aloud. Do you have an address?"

"Yeah. Got a pen and paper handy?

Gesar unconsciously touched the tender spot on his scalp where his skull had been drilled. "No need. I have a hole in my head but I think my memory is still okay."

Oten's small motorbike strained and puttered as it climbed the steep hill up to the Kathok monastery. Having little trust in machinery, he regretted having to leave his horse behind, but his mission required haste and stealth. Some of the more remote temples were accessible only by horse or donkey trail, but a Khampa on horseback in larger towns and villages would draw unwanted attention.

After his winning ride at the horse festival, the celebration had been cut short when his father, Lozang, unexpectedly called a meeting of the Sun Tribe's hardiest young men and women. In a crowded tent, they sat and listened to a monk bearing a message from Dagpa Akar. Such messages from Dagpa Akar were rare, but were usually important requests for aid; this one was particularly urgent. The monk had provided very specific instructions. He taught them a phrase and gave each of them a scroll of paper bearing an elaborately painted symbol.

"Request an audience with the abbot," he instructed, "use the words I taught you and offer the scroll when you gain access to the abbot. If he is an ally, he will understand and give you audience and say. 'How can I serve Dagpa Akar and those that guard the gates between realms?' Only then should you present our request. Otherwise, simply ask for a blessing and leave."

As he approached the temple, Aten remembered the monk's instructions and wondered what kind of reception he would receive. The Kathok monastery was over a thousand years old and a famed holy site. Its main temple was at the uppermost part of a town that consisted of a dramatic complex of red-roofed buildings constructed in multiple tiers on the side of a green mountain. Monks, town residents, pilgrims and the occasional tourist moved about the narrow streets. Aten parked his motorbike against a courtyard wall and walked the remaining distance up to the temple. Two red-robed monks at the temple door greeted him with bows. He returned the bow and spoke. "Holy brothers, I beg audience with your abbot."

The shorter of the red-robed monks replied, "The abbot is in residence, but he cannot see every visitor."

"My name is Aten and I carry an important message and a gift for him."

The monk hesitated, looking at Aten with greater scrutiny. "I will deliver your message and gift. You can be certain that I will request that he offer a blessing for you."

Aten expected that his first request to see the abbot would be denied, but he maintained his composure and bowed again before speaking, "Holy brother, I thank you and I will take your kind offer to deliver my words, but I must deliver the gift myself."

"Very well, what is your message?"

"Simply tell him this, 'The Guardians of The Sacred Lotus are in need.' I think he will understand."

The monk was puzzled, but courteous enough to leave without asking for more explanation. While Aten waited, he recited prayers as he spun the large prayer wheel in the temple's vestibule. About twenty minutes later, the short monk returned.

"The abbot will see you. Follow me."

In silence, Aten followed the monk through the temple passages until they reached a beautifully decorated room. Huge elaborately painted thangkas hung from the walls. Overhead, a ceiling mural depicted hundreds of images of the Buddha in his past and future manifestations. Opposite the entryway, an elderly man in red and orange robes sat upon a cushioned dais. Despite his spectacles, a bright and intense gaze was noticeable from across the room. Both Aten and his monk guide bowed to the abbot.

"This is the messenger, your holiness."

"Send him forward and return to your duties." The abbot spoke with an unexpectedly strong voice for his age.

Aten advanced to the dais and bowed again, but did not speak until his monk guide had left the room. "Your holiness, I thank you for this audience. My name is Aten Gyatso."

"I understand that you have something to give me?"

"Yes, your holiness." Aten withdrew the scroll from his coat and placed it the abbot's ancient palm.

The abbot untied the ribbon and slowly unrolled the scroll. His eyes widened at the image on the paper. "I never expected to see this symbol in this lifetime," he said and then added, "How can I serve Dagpa Akar and those that guard the gates between realms?"

Aten relaxed and presented the request.

When Aten finished his story, the old abbot said, "Circumstances must be truly dire if Dagpa Akar needs to call upon us. It has been so long that some have begun to doubt that Dagpa Akar still existed, but we who are still faithful continue to pass on the secret words to our successors. I am happy to know that Dagpa Akar endures and I am gratified to say that we can offer help. We have eight demon banishers that were hidden before the invasion. I will retrieve these for you."

Aten pressed his palms together and bowed deeply. "Thank you, your holiness."

Second lieutenant Peng of the People's Liberation Army watched intently as the Kham tribesman entered the monastery. The young man may have arrived on a motorbike, but the facial features, braided hair and clothing were unmistakably those of a Khampa. It was unusual for their kind to be on a pilgrimage at this time. The dung-footed bumpkins never liked to be far from their horses. They were nothing more than the sons of brigands and bandits. He suspected the Khampa was up to something, probably smuggling artifacts. He considered arresting the man immediately, but decided it would be better to make the arrest after the Khampa left the temple with incriminating contraband.

The Druk dakini flew ahead to Kalapa palace once the Senge tapah were safely within confines of the Shield. The great horns echoed across Shambala valley as the battle worn dakini approached the island fortress. Despite the tranquil elegance of slender moonlit towers reflected in Lake Shambala, the scene on the palace ramparts was far from serene. Aglow with the light of a thousand torches, the fortress bustled with preparations for a coming siege. Ane's squadron flew directly to the broad plaza surrounding the temple dome where attendants were treating wounded dakini and their mounts, most of whom bore the crossed lightning bolt emblem of the Dorje squadron. As Brug touched down, Ane saw Lady Palden speaking with a group of dakini captains assembled on the temple steps. After giving Brug a loving stroke on the head, she quickly dismounted to join the conference of captains.

Before Ane could offer a formal bow, Palden bounded down the steps and took Ane by both hands. "Thank the Thousand Buddhas. I was relieved when I heard the horns sound the return of your squadron. Dolma brought word of your dire situation and as you can see, it has not been a good day for the Dorje squadron."

Lady Palden's emotional greeting surprised Ane. The demon-god had never before touched her. Her skin felt oddly warm and electric, but more surprising was her greeting, spoken as if from a worried friend rather than an immortal being.

Ane had instinctively averted her eyes when Palden approached, but in response to Palden's touch and words, she could not help but look up to meet the demon-god's gaze. She expected pools of demon-fire that could burn into the marrow of the soul, but instead she saw warm hazel eyes glistening with tears of relief.

Temporarily dumbstruck, Ane did not speak until Palden released her and then her words were halting. "Yes… my…my lady, we were fortunate to fend off the demon, Gnyan, and manage to escape…we suffered mostly minor injuries and…" She found it especially hard to say the next words, "and the Senge lost at least one." She looked at the other captains gathered on the temple steps and noticed that Kara, the Dorje captain, was not among them. "Where is Kara?" Ane asked.

Palden's tone changed, her voice tightened with anger and her dark pupils briefly flashed with demon-fire. "They were led into a trap. The Dorje patrol came upon a group of the enemy flying beasts. We have learned that they are called naga-ta, no doubt that is Kubera's doing. Kara ordered an attack and her squadron pursued the beasts into a canyon where Yama was waiting with archers much like your previous encounter with him. Kara and nine others were lost in battle. We have gravely underestimated the enemy. Their numbers are far greater than we thought. The mountains could have hundreds of Mahakala's cave garrisons. I am gathering the captains to discuss strategies. We await the arrival of the last of the tapah units. Join us in the south council chamber after you have assessed your wounded and refreshed yourself."

Ane bowed and returned to take stock of her squadron. When Ane reached her squadron, the ever-efficient Dolma was already making the rounds. Her lieutenant was a strong warrior, competent leader and friend. Ane was confident she would make a fine captain should fate deem it necessary.

Dolma greeted her with a tight hug. "Ane, forgive me for not returning to you. I had to bring warning of the approaching nagu armies."

When they separated, Ane responded. "You did what you were supposed to do. I instructed you to report our situation to Lady Palden. I never intended that you come back, at least not alone."

"The waiting has been terrible. I couldn't stand the idea of my sisters falling in battle while I was safe in Shambala."

"You made the right decision. Besides, you know me; I can get out of just about any tough situation."

Dolma smiled. "Yes, I heard how you dammed up the canyon with naga-ta carcasses."

"It was just an inspiration." Ane then changed the subject. "I see you've already started looking at our wounded. How does it look?"

"Mostly superficial wounds. Considering you were facing Gnyan, it's a miracle we didn't lose anyone."

"We discovered his weakness."

"What's that?" Dolma asked.

"Besides being ugly and purple, he's easily distracted."

"What about the Senge? They were on the ground facing him directly."

"Miraculously, I believe they lost only one."

"Do you know who it was?"

"Yes. Gesar, the new one. He was a San Franciscan, like us."

Dolma sensed Ane was holding back. "I'm sorry Ane. I know he was more than just a comrade to you. He liked you; I saw the way he looked at you and stayed near you during our combined maneuvers with the Senge. And you let him strike you during the sword drill. I've never seen anyone but Lady Palden put a sword on you. I thought you might be considering him as a consort."

Ane let her temper flare. "I don't choose consorts and I did not let him strike me! He's... I mean he was a good swordsman."

"Ane, you may be my captain, but you are also my friend." Dolma responded. "I can see you are hurting. That Gesar was so skilled only makes the loss greater. He was truly worthy of you. I'm truly sorry."

Ane fought back tears. "He's gone, just like any of us may go, without warning. That's why I don't have a tapah consort. I don't want to talk about it anymore. Now, let's finish assessing our battle readiness. I must attend a meeting of the captains."

Dolma silently bowed to her captain and the two separated to finish their inspection. Considering the fate of the Dorje, the Druk had been fortunate. Many of their kinnaras had suffered arrow wounds or slashes from Gnyan's tilug, but they had all survived and would be fit for battle after treatment and rest.

As Lady Palden waited for the captains to assemble, each stopped at the council room entrance to bow to her. Although she wore only a simple black gown with a silver belt embossed with her signature skull design, her presence dominated the council chamber. Her shining hair seemed to sparkle, reflecting light from the myriad of jewels set in a domed ceiling to simulate stars in a night sky. Her skin glowed, competing with the golden light emanating from lamps mounted between the tapestries that covered every wall. The tapestries depicting heroes and avatars defeating the minions of Munpa Zerden were intended to inspire, but neither Palden's angelic composure nor romantic images could lift the subdued mood among those who had learned of the fate of Dorje captain and nine of her squadron.

As the captains found their respective places at a massive round table inlaid with the various unit emblems, there was a smoldering solemnity among them. Before taking their seats, each captain stopped to pay their respects to the Dorje lieutenant, Cespa, who had replaced her former captain at the crossed lightning emblem.

Ane was the last of the dakini captains to arrive, but did not hurry to her seat on Palden's right. Rather, she went to embrace Cespa and lingered to shed tears together.

When the captains were finally seated, Palden tallied the group. Noticing one empty seat, she said. "Welcome captains! It seems only Captain Jigme of the Senge has not yet arrived,"

As she spoke, the wooden chamber doors swung open and Ben entered still wearing his mud spattered armor. Only his helmet and sword belt had been discarded. He pressed his palms together and bowed before speaking, "Forgive my appearance Lady Palden. My men and I have only just returned to barracks. I came as soon as I received word of your summons."

"There is no need to apologize. We are all aware of your circumstance. Please take your place captain."

Doing his best to minimize the clatter of his armor, Ben sat down at the emblem of the snow lion.

Palden continued. "Before we begin discussing strategies, we must first remember our fallen comrades with a moment of meditation."

Picking up an elaborately carved hardwood rod, she struck a large bowl-shaped bell that sat upon the table. The room filled with a tone that penetrated the body. She sounded the bell ten times. When the last vibration faded into silence, the group prayed for the fallen warriors. In unison they recited, "May their minds know the Path of Illumination. May their essence seek the Source of Illumination. May their souls find the Peace of Illumination. May their selflessness brighten the Light of Illumination. Namo Amida Buddha."

During the ceremony, Ane noticed Palden had sounded the bell only ten times. She had not recognized that Gesar of the Senge had also fallen in battle. The Senge would have to hold a ceremony later. Ane made a mental note to attend. She felt responsible for Gesar's loss; the image of him riding into the jaws of Gnyan's army gnawed at her. Why did he run from the battle? Certainly, he was no coward. She had wanted desperately to warn him, but saving a whole tapah unit was the correct tactical decision. Still, it did not lessen her pain nor hide her shameful realization that she had nearly abandoned the Senge to save Gesar. She tried to convince herself that her feelings would have been the same for whoever it might have been, yet her reaction to Dolma's comments worried her. She felt some guilt losing her temper with her friend. Perhaps, there was some truth in what she said. Could there be more? Affection? Love? No, she was first captain of the dakini; attachments were out of the question. Palden's voice jolted Ane back to the present.

"I have called this meeting to bring word from the Council of Guardians. It is clear that the worst suspicions of the Council have been confirmed and we must discuss adjustments to our defense strategy." Palden paused to assess reactions and could not help but be moved by the undaunted expressions.

"Until now, the enemy has not considered challenging the Shield, but our betrayers have shown our enemy the way to weaken this defense. By sacrificing the greater part of his force in a simultaneous attack, Zerden can cause a collapse of the Shield, providing enough time to allow his invasion force into the valley. It is an enormous gamble since failure will cripple his forces for another thousand years. The secret garrisons that we discovered encircling Shambala make it clear that Zerden has decided to take this risk. The Guardians propose that we pursue the obvious counter strategy. We must disrupt any coordinated enemy strike and reduce their numbers to a harmless level. Do you agree?"

Cespa was first to respond. "Lady Palden, what is a harmless level? I have seen just a small part of the nagu army and their numbers were many. Our forces are mainly excursionary keeping the mountain passes and trails clear of enemy companies. We have never been so significantly outnumbered nor have we ever been challenged for dominion of the sky."

Palden raised a palm. "I fear I cannot give you a specific answer, we suspect that enemy will need to sacrifice hundreds of thousands."

Even the highly disciplined ranks of captains released their breath in shock.

"The Guardians understand that we cannot engage the enemy in sustained battles. Our basic tactic must be tarry and harry. We have requested phurbas from our Kalacakra allies to be planted along trails and passes. The dakini and tapah forces will take up positions around the Shield perimeter and perform coordinated attack and retreat maneuvers. If any of you have suggestions offer them up now."

Ben stood up and addressed his fellow tapah captains as he spoke. "You will possibly be facing one of the demons as we did earlier today. The Crow maneuver proved very effective in distracting them, but you must keep aiming for their eyes."

When Ben finished, Ane spoke, directing comments to her sister dakini captains, "Dakini squadrons should go ahead of the tapah units to deal with flying naga-ta so we can better support the tapah ground force. The beasts can be stopped using a Closing Lotus maneuver."

Tashi, captain of the Kalapa palace guard spoke next, "I will ask the Seers concentrate efforts on the passes. They should be able to detect enemy movements and survey battles from the palace to help coordinate our forces."

Other captains contributed suggestions based on their personal experiences, but no one objected to the basic strategy proposed by the Council of Guardians. The plan utilized Shambala's strengths to best advantage. While the enemy was superior in numbers, the forces of Shambala had greater speed, a better knowledge of the terrain and the ability to retreat behind the safety of the Shield while it remained intact. Before the meeting adjourned, tapah and dakini units were assigned to each other. The Senge and Druk remained together, having proved their effectiveness as coordinated fighting units.

When the meeting adjourned, the captains bowed and waited for Lady Palden to exit the room before leaving. Ben waved to Ane as she started to leave. When he made eye contact, he called out, "Ane, meet me in the corridor."

Ane made her way through the crowd and found Ben waiting in the corridor looking out of a window facing the eastern ramparts and lake. In the distance, a waxing gibbous moon hung over mount Jetsunmu, its light catching the ghostly mist rising from Trinity Falls before laying a silver path across Lake Shambala. There were very few views from Kalapa palace that were not breathtaking.

"Ben!" Ane called.

Ben's armor rattled as he turned to face Ane. He looked as tired as she felt. It had been a long day for both of them.

Ane bowed and said. "Tell me you don't want to discuss details of combined maneuvers."

Ben attempted a half smile before responding. "No, perhaps tomorrow. I wanted to thank you for that brilliant move in making the naga-ta dam. I've heard about your strategic skills in the heat of battle, but now I have had the honor of getting first hand experience. Not only did you save our rearguard, I'm sure it added to the surprise we gave Gnyan's army. They definitely were not expecting a direct frontal assault. They must have thought we had already wiped out the first army and were starting on them."

Ane was in no mood to bask in praise. "I'm just glad it worked out. We may not be so lucky next time."

Ben countered. "That was not luck. That was pure brilliant thinking."

"I wasn't brilliant enough to save Gesar."

Puzzled, Ben asked, "What do you mean?"

Ane forced back tears. "You must know that Gesar is dead, I watched him and Goba ride straight into Gnyan's army. I couldn't stop them. There just wasn't..."

Ben interrupted. "Gesar is gone, but I don't believe he's dead. Goba returned to barracks with us. I cannot commune with Goba directly but Dawa tells me he's waiting for Gesar's return. Gnyan was near a choten when we engaged him. The chorten was damaged but its Buddha was intact. It seems Gesar escaped by returning to the Human realm."

Ane felt a weight lift from her heart and the joy that replaced it took her by surprise. Impulse overcame her. Ignoring his battle soiled armor, she threw her arms around Ben with tears of joy pooling on her cheeks. "Thank you. Thank you, Ben."

141

Flummoxed, Ben waited for Ane to release him and said, "I thought I was here to thank you."

Ghastly shadows danced on the walls of the torch lit cavern where four hideous shapes huddled around a map of Shambala valley carved as a relief in the stone floor. Replicating Shambala's protective inner and outer mountain ranges, a jagged range of scaled-down peaks surrounded the dwarf-sized valley. Water dripped from the ceiling filling a miniature version of the Shenla River and Lake Shambala before seeping into a myriad of invisible cracks and fractures. In the midst of the lake was a toy-like replica of Kalapa fortress with its summit dome surrounded by eight white towers. A circular white line painted across the geography defined the perimeter of the Shield.

Kubera pointed a partially eaten haunch at the map. "Look there, you even got Mount Rewa in the right place. I'm impressed. I didn't know we had such talent among our ranks. Who did this?"

Mahakala hissed, his third eye making a disturbing scan of Kubera's flabby face for hints of mockery. "It was constructed with my direction."

Kubera chuckled. "Commissioned under threat of a slow death, eh?"

"Motivation is the whetstone of talent," Changpa's foreface piped up cheerily, his four faces vying for a view of the map, making his head seem to spin.

"Let me see," demanded his left face.

"Be silent! The one leading us into battle should have the best view," cried his foreface.

"We should take turns or I will never get to see it and I'm the smart one," complained his hind face."

"Pstt," spat his right face. "You can see it when we leave."

"Silence!" howled Yama with a spurt of black pus leaping from his grotesque face and landing into the tiny Lake Shambala with a puff of vapor. Yama, like Mahakala, had little tolerance for Changpa's vacuous chatter.

"You can all shut up and listen!" Mahakala ordered, pounding the hilt of his tilug into the floor, dislodging a shower of loose gravel from the cavern roof. "If we are to succeed then we must all understand our parts and coordinate the attack." Using his tilug as a pointer, Mahakala continued. "You all know Shambala valley has

142

only three points of entry, the northeast, southeast and southwest passes. The Council of Guardians will be expecting us to move our forces through these passes and they will no doubt concentrate their defense at those passes. We will be sure not to disappoint them. You will each lead a part of our army through these passes."

Kubera pulled the haunch from his mouth, bits of partially chewed meat spattered upon the map as he spoke, "Stop there! I agreed to help with logistics but I am not leading any army in to a nest of tapah and dakini. I don't mind watching from a safe distance, but keep me away from those nasty stinging arrows."

Using two of his six arms, Mahakala rearranged his belt with its array of dreadful weapons while his third eye remained fixed on Kubera. "I didn't mean you. Yama, Changpa and Gnyan will direct the ground assaults. You can return to Naraka and continue training naga-ta riders to keep the dakini squadrons occupied."

"And just what will you be doing, General?" Yama asked derisively, pointing his lasso at Mahakala.

"I will be directing the bulk of our force through the northern pass."

"There is no northern pass." Changpa's hind face commented.

A hideous grin congealed on Mahakala's face, exposing his yellowed fangs. "That's because it has been overlooked. It is true that the north gap only crosses the inner range and penetration through the outer range at that point is impossible, but we discovered a path from the north base of Mount Rewa, which runs northeast between the inner and outer ranges. While Shambala was preoccupied with my diversions on the Asura plain, I have been using the trail to establish garrisons in the north. These forces will enter the valley before the Seers can warn the palace defense. By the time they realize their mistake, we will have occupied the north borderlands and west end of the valley where the Shield does not reach."

Yama snapped his razor wire lasso and sliced off the top of the child-sized version of Mount Shiwa, which bordered the southeast pass. "It still seems that we are going to be down here in the south taking on the brunt of the fighting, while you stroll into Shambala valley without resistance."

Mahakala flashed Yama an annoyed glare. "Only temporarily you fool. When they notice my force advancing, they will send defenders to protect the northern border spreading their defenses thin enough to allow your armies to march over the passes. At that point, you must press forward and let all of your reserves into the valley just beyond the Shield perimeter. Instruct your forces to hold at a distance of one hundred paces from the Shield, until I signal the advance."

"Why should we wait for your signal?" Yama asked. "Every hunter knows that when your prey stumbles you strike immediately. I promised to get my lasso around the neck of Palden's pet captain and I will not let her slip through my fingers again."

Mahakala growled and slammed his tilug hilt into the floor again, dislodging another shower of gravel. "How many times must I explain this? We can only break the Shield barrier with a well-timed simultaneous charge. One army cannot do it alone. We will sacrifice a large part of our army in a first coordinated assault, but when the Shield fails, the rest can enter Shambala."

"How will we know when to attack?" Changpa's faces asked in unison.

"A bright flash will light the valley. Look for it and send your forces into the Shield without hesitation or distraction."

"How can you possibly light the whole valley?" Yama asked.

"That knowledge is best kept to as few as possible. I can only say that it will require a sacrifice."

"I will not be denied my revenge." Yama declared.

Mahakala's eyes flared with demon fire, daring anyone to oppose him. "I don't care what you do after the Shield is breached, but you must advance your forces into the Shield when you see the signal. If your timing is off, the Shield will hold and we will not be able to enter the valley."

Mahakala felt he was spending too much effort maintaining discipline among his fellows. Since reverting to demonic form, they were becoming progressively more difficult to control. Demon-nature, motivated by brutality, blood lust, and self-indulgence was not conducive to cooperation and discipline. In the centuries after the treaty with the bodhisattvas, he had forgotten how bestial they had once been and was surprised at how quickly the reversion had progressed. He had only to rein them in until Shambala was defeated.

Kubera tossed the meat-stripped bone over his shoulder and then wiped his greasy hand on the front of his shirt. "I don't mean to offend my three-eyed brother," he said, "but once you get into the valley how do you plan on crossing Lake Shambala?"

"Once we are in the valley, we will have abundant material for bridge building." Mahakala answered, jabbing his tilug into the map in a space north of the miniature Shenla River.

Changpa's foreface let out a cheery laugh and said, "Oh yes, the ancient forest."

Aten followed the abbot through a series of courtyards and narrow alleys, sometimes zigzagging among closely spaced whitewashed buildings. Over the centuries, Dorje Den Kathok monastery had become a complex warren of structures and paths whose number and location were known to only to its oldest residents. Aten had lost his bearings almost immediately and could only discern that the abbot was leading him steadily upward. Finally, the abbot guided him through a wooden door at the end of a shaded alley. The roar of rushing water filled the air and a refreshing spray tickled Aten's cheeks, waking him from the semi-trance he had fallen into during the confusing meander through the monastery. The abbot waited on the bank of an icy stream that cascaded down a dangerously steep fall of slick rocks. When Aten caught up to the monk, they seemed to have reached an impasse.

The abbot turned to Aten and said, "We are outside of the monastery and must cross the stream here. It is as dangerous as it looks, but if you follow my steps exactly, you'll be safe."

The abbot stepped to edge of the waterfall where spray and furious eddies of foam obscured any view of the rocks. With surprisingly agility, the old abbot leapt into the stream and crossed to the other side in three wide steps. He stood on the opposite shore with the hem of his robes dripping with icy water. "Now, it's your turn."

Suppressing his doubts, Aten moved to the edge of stream. Remembering who he was, he made a leap of faith for the honor of the Sun Tribe. He was surprised when his feet came down on a broad flat stone hidden by water and mist.

"There are two more of those stones positioned a wide step apart. Move without hesitation and you will not get quite so wet," the abbot instructed.

Thankful that he had remembered to oil his riding boots, Aten followed the abbot's instruction and shortly joined him on the opposite shore. When he looked back across the stream, the door in the monastery wall was invisible, hidden by rock and mist.

"It is not far now," said the abbot.

Now they were well beyond the monastery perimeter following a steep path that looked to be a trail used mostly by goats and mountain sheep, which ended at a wall of tall boulders. The abbot disappeared behind one of the rocks. Aten followed in time to see the abbot squeeze sideways through a crack little more than two hand widths apart.

The old abbot grunted as he forced himself through. "I'm afraid this is a task for the ascetic Buddha. I'm not as thin as I was in my youth," he said.

Aten removed his coat and exhaled all of his breath in order to get through the narrow opening. He took a deep inhalation when he reached the inner chamber, where the abbot had already located and lit an oil lamp. Around him were stacks of crates covered with heavy quilted blankets.

After experiencing the narrow opening, Aten asked the obvious question. "Excuse my curiosity venerable one but how were these brought into here?"

The old abbot smiled and answered. "I supposed that would seem puzzling, but there was no magic involved. A group of monks working together can move the boulders. This chamber was carved into Do-Nian Mountain as instructed by of our founder, Tampa Deshek. With his holy foresight, he knew we would need a place to preserve our most sacred objects and writings during times of external aggression. Your people know well that our land has suffered many wars and despots. In the past thousand years, the chamber has hidden many brothers and sisters escaping brutal kings and regimes."

"I am deeply humbled to be permitted to see such a sacred place," said Aten.

"Young man, it is I who is humbled that Dorje Den monastery can help Shambala in it its time of need. Tampa Deshek may have foreseen it. Now, let us find those demon banishers."

The abbot held his lamp aloft, his glowing face turning back and forth, as he scanned the chamber. He then walked to a stack of boxes against the nearest wall. He yanked away the covering blanket, creating a nimbus of dust around the lamp. "Ah yes! That is the one. See, it is dated nineteen-fifty-one. These ones were hidden just before the Chinese invaded. I will hold the lamp while you open the crate."

Aten lifted the crate down from the stack. Using the curved blade of his short knife, he pried the lid off the crate. Within the crate there was a beautifully inlaid rosewood chest carefully packed in woolen wadding.

"If my memory serves me, the demon banishers should be in there. Take a look."

Aten removed the chest and set it on the chamber floor. He brushed away the wadding fragments, revealing the image of the serene Buddha surrounded by the Eight Wisdom Bodhisattvas, known as the 'demon tamers'. He attempted to lift the hinged top but it resisted. "It seems to be locked."

"Oh yes," the abbot responded. "Just give me a moment."

The abbot held his lamp over the chest and thought a moment. "Ah, I remember now." He then pressed the foreheads of each of the eight bodhisattvas in a designated order, naming them as he did so, "Chana Dorje, Kuntu-zangpo, Sai Nyingpo, Chenresi, Jampa, Namkai Nyingpo, Sarva, and Jampelyang." Finally, the abbot touched the forehead of the Buddha and there was a barely audible click. "There, now try it," he said.

The chest lid lifted without resistance, eight elongate lacquered wood boxes lay within stacked upon a bed of red silk, each inscribed with the name of one of the Eight Wisdom Bodhisattvas.

"Go ahead slide them open," urged the abbot. "I must see if they still hold their power. It has been many years and I will need to test them."

One by one, Aten slid open the draws of the eight lacquered boxes, withdrew the untarnished triple-edged daggers and handed them to the abbot. Other than etched symbols and designs on the blades, the phurbas were similar, bearing the relief images of the Sleeper and Warrior facing opposite directions. With point down and Sleeper facing west, the abbot held each dagger at arm length and began to throat chant. For several minutes, his voice echoed through the chamber and then suddenly, the first blade flashed with blue-white light. Aten's eyes widened with amazement. By the time the eighth blade was tested, he had become accustomed to miracles.

A broad smile crossed the abbot's round face. "We are fortunate. All of the demon banishers have held their power. Take them to Dagpa Akar with my blessing. To conserve space in your pack you won't need the boxes, we can wrap the blades in silk."

Jamyang calmly watched the light vanish as the door to the meditation chamber rolled shut. In pitch black, he sat upon a cushion with a jade hammer in one hand and Dagpa Akar's last three phurbas in a cloth bag upon his lap. They were too few to be of much help to Shambala. He could only hope that others would follow. When the stone door came to rest, three dull knocks reverberated through the tiny chamber. Jamyang answered with two strikes of his hammer, signaling that he was ready to begin. Setting the hammer aside, he waited several minutes to accommodate the complete silence and darkness and then he started the Kalacakra ritual that would open the door to another realm. Resting his hands upon his thighs in the gesture of the Dhyana mudra, he imagined the choten located on the southeast rampart of Kalapa palace. He pictured it bathed in light for it would be daytime in Shambala. Keeping his eyes open, he focused on the mental image and chanted repetitively, "Om Mani Peme Hung, Om Mani Peme Hung, Om Mani Peme Hung." When the rhythm of the mantra and his breath were in synchrony, he steadily slowed his breath and heartbeat. Eventually, the syllables of the mantra became a thin whisper of breath so faint that a physician would have deemed his body dead. His awareness of the meditation chamber fell into a deep crack of consciousness where only an ember of life remained in the Human realm. The image of the choten began to fill with detail, now in bright sunlight and set against a background of cloud-enshrouded mountaintops. Shadows of whipping prayer flags danced upon it. A crisp breeze struck his left cheek and a stone bench held his weight. Finally, he heard a voice carried by wind. "Brother Jamyang has returned."

Looking in the direction of the voice, he saw the demon-gods, Yamantaka and Hayagriva, on the rampart surrounded by a group of palace guards and a semi-transparent Seer. Two of the guards separated from the others. Both wore light armor covered with tabards bearing the palace insignia of the Dharma Wheel. One guard ran off at a run toward the palace, undoubtedly a messenger sent to Lady Palden. The other approached Jamyang to offer himself as escort. Jamyang recognized the man, Tashi, a captain of the palace guard, a broad shouldered man who usually carried a wide smile to match, but at present, his expression was tempered with concern.

Tashi stopped to bow and then offered a greeting. "Welcome back venerable one. Can I assist you?"

Jamyang raised himself from the bench. "Thank you Tashi, I would be grateful if you could carry this," he said, stretching out a hand with the bag of phurbas. "It is fortunate that Yamantaka and Hayagriva are here. I must speak with them."

Tashi walked next to Jamyang as he made his way to the group of men and demon-gods. A steady north wind whipped Yamantaka's long beard against his shoulder and flapped Hayagriva's orange robes like a flag. Even from a distance, Jamyang sensed uneasiness among them. When he reached the group, he pressed his palms together, bowed and waited to be recognized by the demon-gods.

"Greetings, Brother Jamyang. I hope you bring good news, because our Seer has just detected a large enemy force moving toward the southeast pass. We have just sent a runner to inform Palden."

"That is indeed unwelcome news and I'm sorry to report that I have only three phurbas from Dagpa Akar." Jamyang pointed to the bag.

"Only three?" Hayagriva asked.

"Rinpoche Jhado Zhangpo sends his deepest apologies. More of Zerden's children have entered the Human realm and demon banishers were issued to protect the Sleepers. Attempts are being made to acquire more phurbas, but as to when and how many will be found, I cannot say."

"Three will not be enough." Hayagriva protested.

"They will have to do for now," Yamantaka, countered. The ancient hermit raised his staff and pointed beyond the wall to the southeast. "It is a question of where to best use the ones that we have. Perhaps, the Seer can help us."

The Seers were among the most mysterious of Kalapa's visitors; they were shamans from various human aboriginal cultures. Ironically, in Chinese, *sha men* means Buddhist monk and like the monks of Dagpa Akar, they had the ability to journey between realms at will, but unlike the monks they could not fully incarnate nor could they move sacred objects between realms. They remained in Shambala only transiently. There were never enough Seers. Those that chose to serve Shambala floated ghostlike on the ramparts with their intense shining eyes fixed on the landscape, visualizing events occurring nearly a hundred kilometers away. Similar to the tapah and dakini mounts, they did not speak directly but rather projected their thoughts into the minds of others, transcending language barriers. Unfortunately, until recently, the Seers had wasted their efforts searching for enemy units on the distant Plain of Deception.

Yamantaka posed his question to the Seer, "We have only three demon banishers. How can we best use them to counter the enemy advance?"

Jamyang watched the Seer's semi-transparent body slowly turn, his distant gaze passing over the group. His long straight hair, unmoved by the stiff north wind, was spread over bare chest and arms decorated with an intricate pattern of tattoos. The tattoo markings were more substantial than the flesh, remaining solid as the body flickered in an out of visibility.

A voice, sounding like his own, suddenly entered Jamyang's mind. It was always unsettling to hear a thought that was not your own, yet it was an experience that was routine to dakini and tapah. "The enemy has not yet reached the summit of the pass. Three banishers set upon the valley side of the pass will not stop them, but a clever placement could narrow their approach. This may slow the advance and keep the enemy from flanking defenders."

"Yes, of course," Yamantaka agreed. "The nagu could be concentrated onto a narrow line of defense."

"They will not be that concentrated," argued Hayagriva. Do not forget, we must post defenders at the other passes. If we are to protect the Shield, Mahakala must pay dearly for every piece of ground. We simply need more phurbas."

Yamantaka was about to respond when the Seer interrupted everyone's thoughts. "Do not tarry. The enemy presses hard."

"He is right. We cannot worry about the other passes now. The enemy is at our doorstep."

Jamyang spoke. "I will place the demon banishers. If I leave immediately, I can reach the pass…"

Hayagriva stopped Jamyang with a raised palm. "Your offer is appreciated Brother, but this placement will require a military strategist. I ask you to return to Dagpa Akar and obtain more demon banishers."

"Tashi, these phurbas must be taken to Palden immediately," ordered Yamantaka. "She and Begtse should be mustering dakini and tapah units by now."

Yamantaka had barely finished speaking when the great horns mounted on the plaza sounded the muster. Hundreds of kinnaras answered with a war cry so loud that it momentarily stopped the north wind.

One felt dreadfully unprepared. The final confrontation was beginning and events were unfolding too quickly. There was not time to locate all of the nagu garrisons or anticipate enemy subterfuge. There was only time to react. Luckily, strained discipline and confusion among enemy ranks delayed the regrouping of Gnyan's army south of Mount Shiwa, but the respite was too brief. Less than three days after the encounter with Gnyan, a Seer detected a larger enemy force marching for the southeast pass and Shambala's defenders had been deployed immediately. With a steady north wind at their back, three dakini squadrons flew in standard triangle formation, Druk in point position, Kra on right and Dragpo on left flank. Below, a column of three tapah units, Senge, Kang and Dom, followed on the Kalapa road to the southeast pass. Ane knew the pass well; it was the widest and the most difficult to defend. Strategically, invasion by the southeast pass was predictable, perhaps too predictable. Mahakala had already shown his skill at deception by covertly establishing cave garrisons at Shambala's doorstep.

When the dakini crossed the Shield barrier, Ane signaled the three squadrons to separate; each carried a phurba from Dagpa Akar. After a hasty conference among the dakini captains, they agreed to fly ahead of the tapah units and fix the phurbas along a diagonal line on the east side of the pass forcing the enemy against the steeper slope of Mount Shiwa. If all went according to plan, the enemy frontline would narrow to half a kilometer and with good timing also suffer significant losses. As point squadron, the Druk headed deep into the gap intending to place the first phurba near the summit of the pass. Late afternoon shadows already obscured the ground below. Ane took a draught of amrita and ordered the rest of her squadron to do the same. Visibility was critical and they would need every possible advantage, especially when the night battle started. Fortunately in a few hours, a moon would illuminate the pass, assuming the weather cooperated.

While scanning for enemy scouts, Ane heard Dolma suddenly cry out. "Naga-ta!"

Where Dolma pointed, a group of four dark figures appeared in the sky over the top of the pass.

"Looks like it's going to be a race for the top, Brug."

Brug beat his wings to gain altitude. "They cannot match my speed, mistress," his voice sounded in Ane's mind, full of its usual self assurance.

As Brug broke formation Ane called out to Dolma, "You're in command, you know what to do."

Dolma nodded, raised her sword and waved the squadron forward with a battle cry. "For Shambala and the Path!" In response, the kinnaras let out an earsplitting call, creating a shockwave of sound that blasted through the pass, dislodging snow from nearby slopes.

"That will get their attention." Ane said as the Druk squadron passed below her.

The group of naga-ta immediately separated.

"Well Brug, it looks like they learned from our last encounter. The Closing Lotus may not work anymore. They're not going to let themselves get bunched up this time. No matter, my sisters just have to keep them busy." Ane leaned forward, tightened her grip on Brug's rein and commanded. "Let's go."

Brug tucked his wings in and dove. In moments, they had reached near terminal velocity, angling downward toward the pass summit. Forcing her eyes open against the rush of cold air, she glimpsed black armored legions nearing the top of pass, flowing like dark blood against the white snow. Suppressing her dread, Ane turned her attention to her mission. "Brug, we have to reach the summit before them."

"Hold on tightly mistress, we are nearly there."

Brug plunged for his goal, the rock-jutted snowfield approached with alarming speed. Suddenly, his wings snapped open, tail feathers fanned and the ground exploded in a cloud of icy powder. As Brug trotted to a stop, Ane heard the thunder of war drums and dakini battle cries. Overhead, the naga-ta were under attack by a swarm of dakinis who darted back and forth slashing at their huge leathery wings and shooting arrows at their black-armored riders. The scene was a violent airborne roundup as the dakinis attempted to herd the naga-ta together while avoiding talons and impaling blows from their barbed tails. Armed with standard poisoned arrows, the heavily armored naga-ta riders were obviously poorly trained at shooting in flight, failing to compensate for their momentum. Despite their lack of skill, they were dangerous enough to keep the dakini fury directed away from the ground force.

"Okay Brug, now go find a place to keep an eye on me. I have to wait for the nagu to come over the pass. It shouldn't be long, the drums are near and I can already smell the stench of cave rot."

"Mistress, I cannot leave you during a battle."

Ane patted Brug's neck. "Don't worry, I have a phurba and you will know when I'm in trouble. I just want you to keep out of sight. If it was possible to hide you I would let you stay, but if the enemy notices you, they will be wary."

Brug spread his wings and leapt from the ground. As he took flight, he sent his parting words. "I obey under protest."

Brug vanished into the mist-covered slopes overlooking the pass while Ane hid behind a boulder to wait for the bulk of the nagu army to fill the pass. The war-drums of the advancing nagu force grew louder and stepped up their beat. Overhead, the dakinis' attempt to cluster the naga-ta was progressing slowly. The naga-ta riders understood the dakini strategy and made every effort to break out of the closing sphere of dakini. One naga-ta challenged a perimeter position where three secondary dakinis began a combined attack to drive it back. The beast let out a guttural roar and performed a sudden spin, sweeping its massive tail into two of the dakinis' mounts. The stunned kinnaras tumbled and briefly lost altitude. Seizing the opportunity, the naga-ta escaped the Closing Lotus formation and was free to harry the dakini outer defense, but instead of assisting his comrades, the rider fixed his attention on Ane and started into a dive.

Ane felt a bolt of malice directed at her. He knows, she thought. Mahakala was certainly aware that phurbas could impede his forces and he must have specifically ordered the naga-ta riders to seek and destroy anyone on the ground who might be planting them. Ane looked in the direction of the drumbeat. She estimated that about half of the nagu force had passed over the summit. She needed more time. The three phurbas needed to be placed at the right moment for maximum effect, but the attacking naga-ta would reach her first.

Brug's voice entered her mind. "I am coming mistress."

Brug bolted from his roost on the mountain slope, but was too far away to reach Ane in time.

Brother William's stomach growled as he turned the ignition key. He was feeling inappropriately cranky for a Buddhist monk. His sandaled feet were wet from walking across rain soaked grass and he had missed breakfast after morning meditation because Brother Kai wished to leave especially early in hopes of getting back to the temple before evening meditation. Brother William had discovered there were drawbacks to having a bhikshu monk as a partner, Kai seemed impervious to discomfort and for him meals were optional. It was going to be a long day.

"How do you want to do the rounds?" William asked curtly.

"Drive out to Marin first then we can work our way back into town. That way we'll miss most of the heavy traffic."

"I know a nice place in Sausalito where we could have breakfast," William ventured.

"So, you're hungry again. Have you considered asking to be permanently assigned to the temple kitchens?" Kai jabbed.

"Sorry, it's just that I missed breakfast this morning."

Kai cracked a rare smile. "I was joking. I won't be responsible for starving a novice monk. Drop me off at our first stop and you can go find a place to graze and then come back and pick me up."

It was still early as they approached the fog-shrouded Golden Gate Bridge, its huge towers emerging out of the clouds like ironclad giants, but Brother William did not notice as his mind was elsewhere. Kai was not one for idle chatter so Brother William daydreamed about meandering north for a side trip to a quaint restaurant overlooking Bodega Bay or going inland to sample a bit of wine and cheese in Sonoma, but he knew he would most likely have to settle for a veggie sandwich in San Rafael.

Traffic thinned and the mist cleared a few miles north of the bridge. They made good time reaching their first stop, a medical care facility nestled in the Marin county highlands. Brother William stopped the van at the building's main entrance. At this point, his stomach was growling regularly and the cattle dotting the hills along the highway were challenging his commitment to vegetarianism.

Kai unbuckled his seat belt and got out. Before closing the door, Kai shook his head, smiled at William and said, "Go get some food. The way your stomach was growling, I was beginning to worry that you might take a bite out of me. I should be done in about an hour."

William waited for Kai enter the building before negotiating the circular driveway that led back into the main road. As he turned onto the main road, he looked in his rear view mirror and noticed that the van's rear door had swung open.

Stopping the van, he muttered, "The latch must be broken."

He got out, walked to the back of the van and slammed the door shut. He yanked on the handle and the door held tightly. He opened it again and inspected the latch, noticing the nest of ochre robes in the back. "I've got to remember to drop those at the temple laundry," he thought as he closed the door.

Leaning lightly on his cane, Gesar waited on the wet pavement for Dr. Ashki to arrive. It was cool and misty after a night of rain. A remnant of the night's runoff trickled across the sidewalk into the gutter. Gesar wore his leather jacket, not so much for comfort, but rather for its deep inner pocket, which presently held his grandfather's phurba. If an incarnate demon was hunting him, then he was not going out without a fight, but encountering a demon was not uppermost on his list of concerns. After Dr. Ashki had told him of Angela Andrastos' existence, he knew that he had to see her if only to convince himself that it was the woman he had met in Shambala and not just a stranger with the same name, but he was apprehensive. What would he discover? How would he react? He desperately wanted her to be as he remembered her, strong, daring and beautiful, but he knew that was not realistic. She had been in a coma for years and he knew what happened to the comatose; he was still feeling the effects of his own coma experience after only two weeks of unconsciousness. His greatest fear was that his reaction would be pity mixed with abhorrence. Ashki had tried to talk him out of going, but finally relented on the condition that he came along for support.

Ashki tapped his horn as he pulled his car next to the curb. The passenger-side power window opened. Ashki's broad face leaned toward the opening. "G'morning, do you need any help getting in?"

"No, I can handle it. The cane is mostly for show." Gesar lied. After briefly wrestling with the car door, Gesar settled into the passenger seat and positioned his cane.

Dr. Ashki kept the car in park. "Are you sure you're ready to do this?" he asked.

"Yes, I have to do it."

"Okay, but I'm going to have to charge you a day's pay and I don't come cheap." Ashki joked.

Gesar smiled.

Ashki laughed as he turned into the road. "That's better. You were looking a bit tense."

"I guess I've been feeling sorry for myself lately," Gesar admitted.

"Well, it's a natural reaction, but I know you'll get through it. By the way, I don't mean to be rude, but can I ask what that bulge is under your jacket?"

Gesar drew the phurba out and set it on his lap.

Ashki's glanced at the object. "Whoa! That's one intimidating knife. I'm not sure it's legal to walk around with something like that. I believe there's a limit on pocket knife blade length. May I ask what you planning on doing with it?"

Gesar ran his fingers over the elaborately decorated handle. "It's called a phurba. It belonged to my grandfather. There are different kinds of them, but this one is called a demon killer and the blade is supposedly made from the metal of a falling star. This is going to sound weird, but when I was in coma, Ane... or Angela told me there was a demon in San Francisco and I think I saw him in the hospital after you left me. I could possibly be just crazy and if I'm not, I don't even know if this thing will work."

Ashki's dark eyes remained fixed on the road. After a thoughtful silence, he responded. "Perhaps it's not so crazy. The Navajo also have demons; they are called 'anaye'. In our legends, there is a story about two hero brothers who defeated anaye with magic knives made of black flint from the morning star. I suppose a little metaphysical protection won't hurt, but you better keep that thing hidden. An arrest would not help my career."

Gesar slipped the phurba back under his jacket and said. "There's something else you should know."

"What's that?"

"The demon is a cop."

From a shadowed corner of the courtyard, Lieutenant Peng and a small contingent of police watched the entrance of Dorje Den Kathok monastery. Peng had instructed the local police to arrest the Kham tribesman as soon as he emerged. Unless the bumpkin was planning to join the order, he had been in the monastery an unusually long time. When the horse lover finally appeared, he was practically running to his motorbike carrying a bag that he did not have when he entered the monastery. A smile of self-satisfaction crossed Peng's face. His intuition and attention to detail had again served him well. No doubt, the tribesman was dealing in valuable artifacts for sale on the black market.

Aten was about to start his motorbike when he was arrested. A firm hand was placed on his shoulder and he was ordered to get off the bike. He protested and resisted handing over his bag until one of the police officers threatened him with a club. The look in the policeman's eyes was terrifyingly businesslike. His expression said I can beat you to a pulp as impeccably as I shine my boots. Accepting that escape was not an option, Aten went peacefully. The three police officers escorted him back to the main road and roughly shoved him into the backseat of a car. A few moments later, a man dressed in plain clothes climbed in next to him.

"Well horse-lover, I hope you're not in a hurry. I'm Lieutenant Peng of the Peoples Republic Army and you have been arrested for suspicion of crimes against the people."

Aten remained silent.

Ane stepped out from behind a boulder to show herself to the advancing nagu army. "For Shambala and the Path!" she cried waving her sword over her head. The nearest part of the enemy line noticed her, let out a guttural cry and charged. Overhead, a naga-ta's silhouette blackened the sky as it fell upon her position. Brug's voice sounded in her mind, "Run, mistress!" Responding as if her own thought, she sprinted down a snow covered rock fall, sheathing her sword in mid stride. The naga-ta's shadow weighed on her as its rider released his arrows. She darted back and forth, barely keeping her footing as arrows skipped over the ground around her. Glancing over her shoulder, she saw that no more than fifty nagu warriors had broken rank to pursue her. Her plan to attract the bulk of the flank had failed.

"Skata!" The Greek expletive, spontaneously erupting from her unconscious, surprised her. She had not heard the word since childhood. Turning sharply left, she ran directly at the main enemy column. Her sudden swerve took the naga-ta rider by surprise, forcing him to make a wide banking turn. The flaw in her new plan became immediately apparent; her nagu pursuers now had less distance to close.

As it turned to make its second attack, the naga-ta let out an ear-piercing shriek and the main nagu column took notice of the events happening on the ground. The war drums went silent, orders shouted, and suddenly Ane was running at a thousand spear points. Above the enemy line, a dark shape fell from the sky. The earth shook followed by cries of dismay and the nagu flank surged forward. The Druk had managed to down one of the naga-ta into the midst of the nagu column, but Ane remained the focus of their wrath. She estimated she had but seconds before being impaled.

She stopped, pulled the phurba from the sheath strapped to her thigh, dropped to her knees and raised the blade over her head.

Taking a breath, she began counting off the seconds. Before reaching five, she was lifted and thrown, tumbling head over heels, sharp rocks scraping her armor before coming to crushing halt on her back. When her eyes came into focus, huge taloned feet spread like open maws of death loomed over her.

Her right hand still gripped the phurba handle. Instinctively, she pointed the blade at her attacker. Bracing herself for the worst, she heard Brug's cry and the menacing talons suddenly swerved away. Leathery wings the size of mainsails beat wildly, encircling Ane in a blinding snow blizzard. Above, Brug sunk his talons into the naga-ta's neck. The massive creature twisted and flailed, whipping about the smaller kinnara that hung on tenaciously. In its desperation, the naga-ta threw its rider who lay broken on a jutting rock formation. Brug strained and held on.

Without hesitation, Ane plunged the phurba into the ground, its blade cutting through rock like soft clay. Releasing her grip, the blade exploded with light, its power burning through her like the first time she crossed the Shield barrier. The dome of light spread out for a hundred meters in every direction. Overhead, the naga-ta vanished from Brug's grip and every nagu warrior within its range flashed into incorporate sentience, leaving behind clouds of ash.

Brug landed next to Ane, who was still on her knees reeling from the rush of burning power. "Am I still here Brug?"

"Yes, mistress."

"I think I'll need a little help getting on."

Brug tossed his rein to Ane with a flick of his beak and then stooped. Ane used the rein to pull herself onto the saddle. "Thanks Brug. Let's see what we've done."

Brug spread his wings, trotted a few steps and lifted into the air. Once airborne, Ane regained enough of her wits to take stock of the situation. She had roughly positioned the phurba in the right location effectively slowing the enemy advance but despite transmuting nearly a thousand warriors, it had not significantly reduced their numbers. Drums started up again and the black river continued its flow toward the valley. Overhead, the Druk were attempting to down the last naga-ta, but the beast was getting assistance from archers on the ground.

As Ane flew over the enemy host to join her squadron, Dolma signaled a group of dakini to neutralize the ground archers. By the time Ane reached her squadron, the last of the four naga-ta was lying in a heap on a rocky slope, but the nagu host continued its relentless march, moving faster on the downward slope. The pass was in deep shadow when the Druk squadron regrouped. Enemy torches began to dot the broad trail below.

"Sisters look!" Ane yelled. "They're giving us light shoot by on the way back!"

Druk arrows began to snipe nagu-warriors near torches. Ahead, a dome of light exploded on the east side of the pass and the nagu torches surged to the west. The war drums halted and the Druk cheered, but the incessant dirge resumed by the time they joined the Kra squadron.

Dragpo squadron was to plant the last phurba that would squeeze the nagu column to the far west side of the pass. The Druk and Kra waited for the next dome of light to bloom in the pass, but to their dismay it did not appear.

"Something's wrong." Ane waved a hand signal and the dakini squadrons started into a dive to reach the Dragpo position. Below, enemy torches were rushing forward and closing together to form a circle above which Dragpo dakinis darted back and forth. Ane gasped at what she saw within the clearing. The demon-god, Yama, pressed his clawed foot upon the writhing body of a Dragpo dakini while holding his tilug aloft bearing the severed head of her kinnara. The phurba was still strapped to the dakini's thigh when she suddenly flashed out of existence.

"Skata!" Ane exclaimed. "Dolma, tell them to get out of there and fall back to the rendezvous point. I will fly ahead and warn the tapah units."

We are not ready, she thought as Dolma broke formation. Mahakala was expecting the phurbas. Not only did he send naga-ta to look for them, but he sent Yama ahead to make sure the mouth of the pass would remain clear.

In a windowless room, Aten sat at a wooden table opposite lieutenant Peng of the Peoples Republic Army. Banners, hung on the packed-earth brick walls, bore Chinese calligraphy shouting propaganda in bright red ink.

"Enslaved people of Tibet! The Great People of the Chinese Republic come to free you from the shackles of religious ignorance."

"Enslaved people of Tibet! Expose the corrupt lamas who would steal your wealth and defile your minds."

The room was part of old "re-education center" built in the time of the Cultural Revolution. At its entrance, two guards stood between Aten and any attempt to escape. Peng tapped the eraser end of a pencil on the table as he questioned his prisoner.

"What is your name Khampa?" Peng asked.

Aten spoke proudly. "My name is Aten Gyatso, third son of Lozang Gyatso."

Peng shook his head in disgust. "You people breed like goats, don't you know there are rules limiting family size."

"Perhaps in China, your rules don't apply to my people. We are part of the Tibetan Autonomous Region."

Annoyed, Peng threw his pencil on the table, breaking its recently sharpened point. "This is China! Your so-called Autonomous Region is nothing more than a farce to placate visiting Westerners."

Aten smiled. "It is good to see that the Chinese army employs honest men."

"Sarcasm is no way to buy favor, horse lover." Peng warned.

"I assure you, I was speaking from my heart. We Khampas are a simple people."

"Then I will ask simple questions. What were you doing at the temple?"

"I was acquiring religious items made by the monks for my family to use for prayer and meditation."

Peng laughed, then picked up Aten's bag from the floor and placed in on the table. "You do realize that if these religious items have any value on the black market, you will be working for many years at a prison work camp far away from your pretty horses."

Without responding, Aten kept his proud gaze fixed on the lieutenant.

Peng untied the bag, turned it over and let its contents role out. "Let's see what religious items you were in such a hurry to take away,"

Eight cloth wrapped cylinders tumbled across the table. Peng tore off the wrappings and stared with an expression of disbelief at eight bundles of incense.

Yeshi had climbed the side of the mountain on foot to reach the outer wall of the monastery where he sat waiting for his brother's signal to scale the wall. From the beginning, Aten had decided that the only way to get phurbas past Chinese spies was to pass them over

161

the monastery wall to his brother Yeshi, who had remained outside of town. Yeshi was certain that he had made the climb undetected and was alarmed when he heard footsteps come around a corner of the wall. To his relief, his smiling brother, Aten, appeared.

"Many tashi deleks, brother!" Aten greeted.

"You gave me a fright." Yeshi complained, as he stood upright. "How did you get over the wall?"

"There's a hidden door up there. Only the abbot and a few trusted monks know about it."

"It's too bad we didn't know about that earlier."

Aten slapped his brother on the back, "More bad for me than you. I'm the one who's going to be arrested."

"I take it then, you have the phurbas?" Yeshi asked.

Aten slipped the bag from his shoulder and offered it to his brother. "Yes, we have done well brother, here are eight demon banishers."

Yeshi accepted the bag with reverence.

"Make sure they get to Dagpa Akar safely and tell Gawa to take good care of my horse," Aten instructed.

"I will brother. Gawa will be waiting for you as planned."

"Hopefully, he won't need to wait too long. Now, I must go get arrested."

"Zha-xi-de-le," Yeshi offered a traditional good luck blessing as he watched his brother disappear around the corner. Slinging the bag across his shoulder, he started his descent, keeping as inconspicuous as possible.

Jhado read the title on the pecha's label and then withdrew it from one of the innumerable cubbyholes that lined the walls of Dagpa Akar's library. Many of the pechas were hundreds of years old and some were copies of manuscripts more than a thousand years old. Each was stored carefully between wooden plates, wrapped in cloth and labeled. The pecha that Jhado selected was a copy of an ancient text titled, *Gift of the Eight Bodhisattvas*, supposedly written by one of his previous incarnations. He sought the book because of a nagging sensation that he had forgotten an important piece of information that could be used to protect the Buddha warriors. For centuries, the Kalacakra had sought out and cared for the Buddha warriors, whose material bodies were split between realms, one vulnerable, unconscious or catatonic in the Human realm, the other a powerful warrior in the Asura realm.

When the eight Wisdom Bodhisattvas banished demons to the Asura and Hell realms they created a barrier to keep them from returning to the Human realm, which until recently, had remained impermeable. Mahakala had shown Zerden's minions a means to enter the Human realm, but not without sacrifice; the act required the use of borrowed mortal flesh for incarnation. Though mortal, the possessed human body was difficult to destroy and in order to sever the demon's connection with the Human realm the body or its remains had to be pinned to the earth with a demon banisher. Jhado was aware if these facts, but he was certain there was something else; a critical element he had failed to recall.

Jhado set the pecha on a reading table and sat cross-legged before it. He carefully unwrapped the cloth and lifted the top wooden board from the stack of unbound rectangular sheets of paper. When he lifted the first sheet, he was surprised that the fragile paper threatened to crumble; it was the original manuscript not a copy. More surprising was the ancient scribe's calligraphy, which though faded, was identical to his own in every detail, even down to the extra long down strokes on the letters, 'ta' and 'ha'. Though he fully accepted the notion of reincarnation, it was always startling to see the physical evidence confirming his Tulku title. A thousand years ago, at least a part of his sentience had lived another life in the halls of Dagpa Akar.

His fingers sensed a familiarity in the paper's texture; suddenly they desired to act independently. Surrendering to the impulse, he let his hands turn through the pages until they halted on a page in the middle of the stack. Jhado read the words.

"The Path of Enlightenment was opened to all of humanity by the eight Wisdom Bodhisattvas. They defeated the demons that once roamed freely between the realms enslaving spirit and flesh. The eight Wisdom Bodhisattvas then constructed protections for the sacred places. The Human realm was protected by the Kharma Shield, the land of Po by a Ring of Gompas and Holy sites, and Shambala by the Dharma Shield."

Jhado's fingers moved again, turning over more pages, stopping again near the bottom of the stack. He read the page.

"To traverse the Kharma Shield, there must be two, Sleeper and Warrior. The Sleeper is as vulnerable as a lotus petal, the Warrior as strong as a diamond. Only a human may hold flesh in Sura and Asura. Demon flesh is excluded from the Human Realm. It may sleep in one realm, but will wake to the Tulku's prayer."

The words, "wake to the Tulku's prayer," echoed in his mind, filling the silent void that had plagued him for so many days. He had found the vulnerability that he sought. The minions of Zerden had learned to insert their will into the Human realm by using borrowed flesh, but their power to control it depended completely on their sleeping flesh in another realm. A simple chant, sung by a Tulku in the presence of a sleeping demon, would force them to awake in their own realm. There was no need to seek the interlopers in the Human realm, he need only to find their sleeping forms in the Asura realm. Disconcertingly, there was only one place that they could be, Naraka, the most terrifying place in the Asura realm and to Jhado's further dismay, his was the only name on the short list of available Tulkus.

At the sound of rustling robes, Jhado looked up from his text. Old Tenzin stepped forward and bowed. "Your holiness, riders have been sited on the trail below the temple."

"Has someone been sent to meet them?"

"Chongtul is on his way. He will know if they are our friends."

"If they are friends, then it will be Sun Tribesmen with phurbas."

"Your holiness, there is more news."

Jhado waited, one hand still holding the page of the ancient manuscript.

"Brother Jamyang has returned from Shambala."

he tapah units were at the rendezvous point in the foothills overlooking the mouth of the southeastern pass when the first dakini squadrons arrived. Night had fallen in earnest and a full moon peeked over the mountains to the east. Brug landed near a warrior of the Senge unit.

"Where is your captain?" She asked.

The man pointed to a hill on his left. "He's up there surveying our position."

Ane leapt from Brug's back and ran up the hill as Ben dismounted to meet her. She stopped to catch her breath then said. "Ben...I...I mean captain Jigme. We have to change our plan."

Ben removed his helmet. "I suspected there were complications when I didn't see a phurba bloom in the lower pass."

Ane explained quickly. "We placed the first two phurbas in the upper pass, but the Dragpo squadron was intercepted by Yama in the lower pass. The tapah units won't be able to use the phurba positions as we planned. The enemy front can spread out and cut you off. They were expecting us to place phurbas. They had naga-ta scouts looking for us."

Ben's eyes scanned the tapah units in silence before speaking. "We don't have many options left. Are we as outnumbered as the Seer reported?"

"I'm afraid so. The phurbas eliminated about two thousand nagu, but that was just a fraction of them."

"Then we cannot hold them, we can use swift rolling attacks to diminish their numbers and contain their front as long as possible until we are pushed back to the Shield. The Senge will attack from the east, Dom from the west and Kang at their center, in that order. We will need dakini cover during the retreat phases, and especially if Yama is in the vicinity."

Ane pressed her palms together, bowed, and said, "You will have it. We will wait in the east hills until we hear your horns."

Ben returned the bow and said, "It seems your mount has saved you a run."

Ane turned, Brug was behind her stooping, waiting to be mounted.

Kai closely examined the comatose young woman until he was satisfied that she was being well cared for. Feeding tube and intravenous lines were properly maintained. There were no signs of injury or illness. Her pulse was rapid, but strong. Though her face was relaxed, trembling eyelids revealed that she was in an active dream state. Kai knew those eyes were gazing upon another realm. Bending over, he whispered into her ear, "Warrior of Shambala, I will stay a short while and give you a little strength." He then removed a small figurine of the Buddha from the bedside table drawer and placed it on the floor. He sat before the little statue and entered a deep state of meditation, chanting a Kalacakra prayer that would send life-sustaining energy into the body of the unconscious woman.

While in his trance, Kai did not notice the figure appear at the door behind him. Nor did he sense the creature's presence until the instant before the pistol grip struck his skull.

Chidag slipped the gun back into the holster at his hip as he stepped over the monk's body to reach the unconscious woman's bedside. Placing his fingers on her quivering eyelids, he stretched them open to look into her pupils where he saw a blue glow deep in her eyes. A smile crossed his face as his hand slid to her throat and began to squeeze.

After replenishing their arrows from the tapah supply wagons, the dakini squadrons roosted in the moon shadowed foothills on the east side of the pass. In stoic silence, the women warriors listened to the echo of enemy war drums as thousands of torches flowed steadily toward the moonlit Shambala valley. The dakinis had used the time to refresh themselves with amrita and rest their mounts until the enemy frontline was below the snowline. At any moment, the tapah horns would sound and a cloud of kinnaras would pour out of the hills, blocking out the moon as they descended upon the nagu army.

Having finished discussing details of battle formations, Ane and Dolma waited together on a rock outcropping. Brug opened and closed his talons in anticipation. Dolma's mount, Nam, rustled her wing feathers as she crouched into ready position. The two women touched palms and nodded a silent message of support to each other.

Dolma broke the silence. "Ane, what's wrong? You look strange."

"What do you mean?"

Dolma's expression suddenly turned to one of fear and her voice strained with terror. "You're fading, I can't see you."

Nam suddenly shrieked, the tapah horns sounded and Dolma flashed out of existence.

Yeshi was wary as his horse negotiated the rocky trail. A single misstep would send him and his horse sliding off the edge into the icy river that rushed though the gorge fifty meters below. He much preferred the rolling Zhaxika grassland with its slow meandering streams. He and the two other men selected to deliver phurbas to Dagpa Akar had followed the sketchy directions provided by his father, which curiously did not include finding a monastery gate. The men were given simple instructions, find the trail and ride for half a day. His father explained that the directions were purposely incomplete so that if they were arrested by the Chinese, they could not reveal Dagpa Akar's location.

The three horses slowly picked along the trail. Yeshi was certain they had come the correct distance, but there was no sign of an ancient monastery and fewer signs of human activity. He was beginning to suspect that they were on the wrong trail, when a figure in monk's robes leaning on a wooden staff appeared in front of them. Yeshi recognized the monk. "Brother Chongtul?"

"Welcome to Dagpa Akar, fourth son of Lozang Gyatso."

Yeshi and the other two riders dropped their reins, pressed their palms together and bowed.

Chongtul returned the bow and instructed, "Dismount and follow me." He then led the men off the main trail to what amounted to not more than a goat path. Eventually, the path transitioned into a distinct footpath that paralleled a steep rise of rock. The path curved and went steadily upward until suddenly they stood before a massive wooden gate reinforced with ornamented metal straps. Chongtul

167

rapped the door in an odd rhythm and moments later, it opened. Two tall monks in heavily padded robes stood on the other side. Yeshi recognized the giant monks as dhob-dhob, a class of guardian monks trained in defensive fighting arts. Beyond the two guards, the path continued until it reached a main gate in the wall of the monastery, in front of which had been constructed a mani wall of prayer stones.

Chongtul knocked again and another pair of dhob-dhob monks admitted the party into the main complex. The big monks unloaded the packs from the horses, handed them to the riders and then took the animals to stable. Within the monastery walls was a complex amalgam of buildings that were almost impossible to discern from the mountainside. As he followed Brother Chongtul, Yeshi marveled at how such a huge structure could remain hidden for so many centuries. Chongtul led the men to a room in where an old monk was preparing refreshment for them.

"Tenzin, I leave them in your hands." Chongtul said. He then bowed to the group and left.

Tenzin turned to the young men, his bright eyes glinting under wispy white haired brows. "Please, please, put down your bags and sit. Eat and drink. The tea is hot and the tsampa is warm."

"I thank you venerable brother, but my father instructed us to deliver our charge to Dagpa Akar with all speed."

Tenzin opened a gap-toothed smile and said, "And you have done so. I will inform his holiness, the Tulku, immediately. How many phurbas were you able to gather?"

"I fear only eight." Yeshi answered. "Not all of our tribesmen have returned and there may be more, but father said to deliver what we had."

"Your father is wise. There is indeed urgency and I will go to the lama, while you refresh yourselves." Tenzin bowed and shuffled from the room.

Tenzin informed Jhado of the arrival of the Khampas as the lama was about to his leave chambers, "Your holiness, men of the Sun Tribe have arrived with eight phurbas. I have given them refreshment in the south guest rooms."

"That is good news Tenzin. I shall go immediately and thank them."

Meeting and thanking the young Khampas took longer than Jhado had anticipated. These brave, honest men of the earth with their wind-burned faces and calloused hands were faithful allies, deserving more than a terse encounter. They seemed deeply privileged to have had audience with the famed tulku lama of Dagpa Akar and Jhado parted feeling honored to have met them.

Before leaving the guest room, Jhado bowed and said, "My brothers, you may stay with us until you are ready to return. I give my blessing to you and your people."

Jhado walked directly to the reception hall where Brother Jamyang was waiting. Jhado did not like making subordinates wait for him, but Tenzin's interruption had been welcome and justified. Jamyang bowed as Jhado took his seat on the elevated dais with the tapestry backdrop of the Buddha and the eight Wisdom Bodhisattvas. The ever-present scent of sandalwood incense hung in the air.

Jhado sensed anxiety in Jamyang's movements. "Brother Jamyang, please forgive me for keeping you waiting. What word from Shambala?"

Jamyang took a calming breath before speaking, "Your holiness, the siege of Shambala has begun in earnest. A massive nagu force was marching on the southeast border when I left. The phurbas that I delivered were to be used to slow the advance, but they will be of little help. Hayagriva again sends an appeal for more phurbas."

"I have good news in that regard. Our allies among the Sun Tribe have acquired eight more demon banishers." Jhado responded.

"That is welcome news but eight will still not be enough to stop Zerden's host."

"Is the enemy in sufficient numbers to threaten the Shield?" Jhado asked.

"Not at present, but the Council of Guardians believes that this is only the first group. Mahakala knows the Shield's power and he would not mount an attack unless he was certain of success."

"Are you strong enough to carry the new phurbas to Shambala today?" Jhado asked.

Jamyang hesitated. "Yes, my recent journey was brief, but as you know, I cannot carry eight phurbas by myself."

"You won't have to. Tenzin has identified three others who are prepared to make the journey. For one, this will be a first crossing between realms."

"Who is it?" asked Jamyang.

"Sister Kensang." Jhado answered.

"Your holiness is that wise? She is but a new initiate. Most fail their first attempt to make the crossing. Could you not go in her stead?"

"I have observed Sister Kensang. She is highly advanced for her years. I believe she can make the crossing with minimal instruction from you. I too will be making the crossing, but not to Shambala."

Jamyang's eyes widened with surprise. "Your holiness, what are you intending?"

"I must go to Naraka."

Jamyang's eyes widened again, this time in shock. "For what purpose would you take such a risk? Dagpa Akar cannot afford to lose you."

Jhado laughed and said. "Dagpa Akar has lost me several times, but I always seem to find my way back."

Feeling much better with a full stomach, Brother William waited in the van in front of the long-term care facility. He had found a decent vegetarian restaurant called *Grandma Alice's Restaurant*, established by hippies turned yuppies. The motto on the menu said, '*You can get anything you want, as long as its local, organic and meat free.*' He ordered veggie chimichangas with extra sour cream and a Very-berry smoothie to go. As he slurped down the last of his smoothie, it occurred to him that perhaps he should have ordered one for Brother Kai, but on second thought dismissed the notion. "Too rich for Kai's taste," he said to himself.

It was more than an hour since he had left on his excursion and he was surprised that the ever-punctual Brother Kai was not waiting to scold him for being late. He turned off the engine and started reading a local newspaper he had purchased in town. He finished section A and was about to start on section B when the passenger door swung open.

"You're late." William said, folding his paper. When his eyes turned to his passenger, his face drained of blood and he fought to keep his lunch down. He remembered that malicious face leering at him from a passing truck while he watched the Cutter house. Terrified, William's eyes fixed on the dark shaft of a gun barrel pointing at his chest. "Wha...Wha...What do you want?" he stammered.

The cruel mouth finally spoke, "Where are the rest of them?"

"Wha...What do you mean?"

William winced as Chidag pushed the gun barrel against his breastbone. "My host tells me that this weapon is called a three-fifty-seven and has a large and fast bullet. At this range, your heart will explode as it passes through you. Now where are the other Sleepers?"

William felt his bladder wanting to release it contents. "Brother Kai knows, I just drive the van and wait."

"Then you will drive to your next stop. There are no other Sleepers here."

"But where's Brother Kai?"

Chidag could smell that fear was heavy on this one; he would obey. "Drive!"

Brother William knew that he should do something brave, but instead he started the van and drove.

One cried out, "Dolma!", but her friend and second-in-command was gone. Only Dolma's mount, Nam, remained, her head turning wildly from side to side desperately looking for her mistress, her mind suddenly empty of human thoughts. On the pass below, the advancing nagu army halted when the defiant sound of tapah horns rolled against them. There was no time for mourning or consoling, Nam would have to find her own way.

"Fly!" she cried and Brug leapt from his perch to join the great flock of kinnaras descending into the throes of battle.

Riding in moonlight, the Senge armor shot toward the nagu east flank like an arrow of shining stars, the dakinis reaching them just as the first weapons clashed. While the dakini squadrons harried the enemy's center, the Senge struck and rolled off, biting a gouge from their flank. Horns sounded again and the Dom tapah gouged the west flank and disappeared. Before the nagu center could shift to support its flank, the Kang unit fell upon them and retreated, leaving another wound in the frontline, but moments later, the enemy recovered, drums resumed and the nagu line marched over the remains of their comrades. Soon, the tapah horns sounded again followed by another series gouge and retreat attacks. Again, the hit and run strategy briefly halted the enemy advance.

The dakinis formed three spiral columns over the enemy frontline; each assigned to support a tapah unit with arrow cover. Ane circled in formation with the rest of her squadron waiting for the next Senge attack. In the heat of battle, she had pushed aside her grief for Dolma's loss, focusing on keeping the attacks coordinated. As she reached the crest of the spiral, she searched again for the demon-god, Yama, who had been strangely absent from the fray. Though they were only biting the tip of the enemy host that poured through the pass, she was sure the attacks would get Yama's attention. She was beginning the downturn of the spiral when she

172

heard the Senge horn sound an alarm from the shadowed hills. Ane responded immediately. "Break and follow!"

The Druk spiral collapsed into triangle formation and sped to the sound of the horn. The Senge were supposed to be in the nearest foothills setting up for the next attack, but were absent when the Druk reached the position. The low wail of the horn called again, Ane followed. Passing over the next hill, she found the Senge ambushed by Yama, trapped on a steep narrow twisting gulley trail. The demon whipped his razor lasso back and forth, cutting his way along the line of cavalry that desperately attempted to retreat. Headless horses tumbled to ground while their riders flashed out of existence.

Instantly, Brug cried the kinnara attack call. Ane's sword flashed in the moonlight and as one, they dove for the Lord of Death, falling upon him like a bolt of lightning. Ane's sword slashed the demon's lasso arm with all the momentum of the dive. Yama recoiled, black pus spurting from his boil-covered face, spattering Brug's breastplate and sizzling like acid. Brug turned sharply, briefly hovering near the demon and readying for another strike. Ane's eyes fixed on the demon's deeply gashed arm, realizing that another well-aimed strike would sever it completely. As she raised her sword, she suddenly lurched forward in her saddle. With demon speed, Yama had grabbed Brug's leg with his remaining intact arm and jerked. Brug beat his wings wildly while trying to rake the demon with his sharp beak, but Yama held his catch firmly at arm's length.

Gripping her saddle's knee wells, Ane stared into a hideous fanged grin. "I was hoping to find you. I told you I would have my revenge," it said.

"Traitor!" Ane cried, her sword taking futile swings at the disgusting skull-crowned head just beyond her reach.

Yama emitted something approximating a laugh, but failed to deliver the deathblow she was expecting. Needing one hand to hold the struggling kinnara, he was unable to use the other; his lasso lay limp upon his dangling hand. The near severing gash was still healing, offering precious moments for Ane to leap to safety but she refused to abandon Brug to face the demon's wrath alone. At least, she had given the Senge enough breathing space to retreat. Arrows began humming through the air as her sisters assembled overhead attempting to distract the demon, but Yama cleverly used his catch to shield himself.

The clawed fingers on Yama's wounded arm flexed taking grip of his lasso handle. His wound had nearly healed. The demon-god grinned and performed a practice swing with his favorite weapon.

His red ember eyes glowed with delight. "Palden has trained her pet well, but not well enough," he said, holding his lasso aloft and swinging its handle to open a loop for his victims. "Dakini and kinnara are one, did she not teach you? Now, you will die as one, bound together one last time before I take you apart."

As Ane raised her sword, preparing to defend to the last, the ear-splitting cry of a kinnara froze the air. In a flash, Yama was thrown backward in a flurry of feathers. Suddenly Brug was free, lifting away from his captor. Blinded, Yama stumbled and tore madly at the kinnara sinking its talons in his face, but Dolma's mount, Nam, held on tenaciously even as her wings were separated from her torso. As Brug flew up to join the rest of the Druk, Ane recited the prayer of the fallen warrior. "May their minds know the Path of Illumination. May their essence seek the Source of Illumination. May their souls find the Peace of Illumination. May their selflessness brighten the Light of Illumination. Namo Amida Buddha."

In the dakini tradition, Nam had bravely joined her rider in death.

Without captives to shield him, Yama was an open target. As the moon left its azimuth and started to descend into the western sky, Dakini arrows harried him until he finally relented and lumbered back to his army. Once the demon-god was well out of sight, Ane instructed the Druk to rejoin the other dakini squadrons while she sought out what remained of the Senge. She found them regrouping in a basin nestled in the hills above the ambush site and was relieved to see Captain Jigme busy issuing orders.

"Ben, how are your men?" she asked as she dismounted Brug.

Ben's expression shifted from surprise to joy. "Ane! Thank the Buddha you got away. We thought you were lost. We were about to sing a prayer to your sacrifice."

"You can sing a prayer, but not to me. Sing for Dolma and Nam. They were lost tonight." The words were painful and she longed to mourn for her friend, but it was not yet the time. Most distressingly, Dolma had not been killed in the Asura realm; the Guardians would need to be informed. "But you too have suffered losses. I saw your men falling under Yama's lasso tonight," she added.

"We lost four and it would have been many more had you not answered our call. Again, we are indebted to your courage. We are reduced to fifty-six riders with some wounded, but we will be ready for the next attack."

Ane watched the remaining Senge as they mounted their horses, preparing for another battle. "You have made four attacks against the nagu and been ambushed by a god demon. Your men are in no condition for another raid."

Ben said responded defiantly. "We have no choice. I don't need to tell you that we are fighting for Shambala's existence. The Shield is its last protection and must not fall. The only way to prevent that is to reduce Zerden's forces for as long as possible despite our losses."

Before Ane could argue, a dakini appeared overhead and landed nearby. Her kinarra bore the Jalus emblem. She quickly dismounted, approached the captains and performed the formal blessing bow. Ane recognized Chandra, the Jalus second-in-command, a beautiful woman with straight black hair and features suggesting that she was from the Indian subcontinent.

"Thank the Buddha, I found you," she started, breathlessly. "When I found the other units, the Druk were just returning to join them, but they could only point me in the general direction of where to find you."

Clearly, Chandra was agitated. Ane suspected it was the message she carried. "Calm yourself Chandra. I take it you have unpleasant news from Shambala?"

Chandra took a breath before speaking. "Yes, not long after you deployed for the southeast pass, nagu armies were seen marching on the other passes as we expected. The demon Changpa is leading the southwest offensive and Gnyan, the northeast. Fortunately, dakini and tapah units were already en route to defend them. The Jalus were engaged in the southwest pass, when the message came from the palace."

Chandra paused to compose herself, a sign that Ane and Ben took as a warning to prepare themselves for the actual bad news.

Chandra continued. "The northwest valley is breached. A vast nagu army led by Mahakala has entered through the northern range and is taking positions along the Shield perimeter."

Ane was astonished. Her fears and intuition had been right. Mahakala was too clever to be predictable. "How could that happen? There is no way to get an army over those mountains."

"No one is sure how, but they must have been amassing in secret for a long time. The Seers were focusing on the major passes. No one looked to the northwest until a few hours ago."

"What are our orders?" Ben asked.

"We are to retreat and make repeated forays against the enemy from the Shield perimeter. We are to wear them away like drops of water cutting through rock. That is at least how the Lord Guardian, Yamantaka described it."

Ane listened to the metaphor, poetic and possibly inspirational, but obviously misplaced. It took many years for a steady drip to cut through rock; they had only hours and the equivalent of a mountain to cut through, but she kept her reservations to herself. It was not the time to quash optimism.

"Where are we to take up positions?" Ane asked.

"Lady Palden wishes the Druk to return to the palace, The Senge must join Dom and Kang units along the southern rim of the Shield."

Ane responded with shocked disbelief. "Return to the palace! You must be mistaken; every available warrior is needed on the Shield perimeter."

"The Lady Palden wants to reserve at least one dakini squadron to defend the palace."

The implication was clear, Palden was preparing for the worst, perhaps expecting it. So much for not quashing optimism, she thought.

Jhado entered the Asura realm by way of the choten where he had had first encountered Gesar Despa, the unfortunate Buddha warrior torn between realms. For his present mission, the choten had two advantages, it was nearest to his destination and the image of it was fresh in his mind. It was a simple matter to visualize the solitary choten overlooking the barren Plain of Deception and when he appeared, other than the phase of the moon, the scene was remarkably similar to that first night. Time had passed in the Asura, but strangely out of synchrony with that in the Human realm. Time stretched as one passed into upper realms until one reached Nirvana and moved beyond the realms of time. Jhado only hoped for enough time to fulfill his mission.

Without hesitation, he bounded down the trail to the plain, stopping briefly where he had planted the phurba that had saved the Senge tapah unit. The demon banisher was untouched, still barring enemies from approaching the trailhead. For this journey too, he carried another phurba, one recently fashioned in Dagpa Akar. After a trying deliberation, he concluded that the single phurba would be of greater value to his mission.

After securing the blade beneath his robe, he set off across the unfriendly landscape, moving with incredible speed, seeming to fly over barren hillocks and treacherous crevasses. Though the road to

Naraka appeared devoid of nagu warriors, he avoided it, keeping to shadows as much as possible. Other than a group of ominous shapes flying in the distance toward Shambala, he encountered no enemies. Even the immediate outlands of Naraka were empty of dron scouts, indicating that Mahakala had enlisted virtually the whole of Zerden's reserve army of enslaved sentients for the siege of Shambala.

The moon was low over a western ridge when Jhado reached the bone-embedded outer wall of Naraka. There, the road ended at a massive iron portcullis cast in a design of writhing serpents. Although there were no sentries posted on the walls, he was certain the gate was guarded. He concealed himself not far from the gate behind a twisted pile of debris to consider his next move. His options were limited. He could temporarily discorporate and pass through the portcullis like one of the incorporeal Seers but that would require leaving the phurba behind, which unlike him would remain fully materialized in Asura. Alternatively, he could simply jump over the wall, relying on the elements of luck and surprise when he landed in the midst of a dron guard unit. He favored the latter choice if only as a test of his faith, but in the end he thought it best to add an element of prudence.

Stepping back, he crouched and leapt for the top of the wall, melting quickly into shadow to survey the yard behind the gate. As he had guessed, dron archers were posted in a series of niches surrounding the yard. Like the classic castle cities of the Human realm, Naraka's first ward served as its primary killing ground for invaders but Jhado doubted this one was for defense. Beyond the first ward, a broad avenue lined by a hodgepodge of buildings led to the inner fortress and keep. Macabre shapes, silhouetted by firelight, moved on the avenue and among the buildings. Even if he managed to get by the first ward, the avenue was too long and too populated to pass through unnoticed. With the avenue out of the question, he chose the high road.

In two bounds, he crossed the distance between himself and the first roof, and then silently made his way among chimneys spewing acrid smoke until he reached the last building along Naraka's main avenue. Before him was an open space, a no man's land, that stretched between the public dwellings and a high, spiked fortress wall as smooth and black as onyx. Like a belt of missing reality, the gateless wall enclosed the central keep, whose high towers were visible jutting here and there through drifting layers of moonlit mist. Jhado was familiar with stories of the gateless wall of Naraka, which was more of a malevolent living creature rather than an inanimate barrier. It reportedly could change its shape, grow razor-sharp spikes and raise a shrieking alarm when an enemy attempted to breach it.

Jhado jumped from his roof perch, made a last survey to be sure there were no dron patrols nearby, and then started walking cautiously toward the gateless wall. As he passed the halfway point, he noticed the wall change. The jagged teeth along its top began to stretch upward and sharpen. The wall had sensed his presence, but he had no choice but to continue and find a way into Naraka's keep.

ঽঽ

Dr. Ashki steered his car along a curved drive decorated on each side with artistically composed rock gardens and colorful beds of flowers. "This is supposed to be the place," he announced.

Gesar had read the sign at the entrance, *Saint Mary's Center for Assisted Living and Long Term Care.* It was a complex of buildings surrounded by park-like grounds with groomed paths and pergola shaded benches. In his experience, such places projected an upbeat exterior, but were depressing as hell when you actually visited the interior. The smell of chronic incontinence was the first thing to hit you, followed by a scene of arthritic bodies scattered about in wheel chairs or sagging sofas, with chins upon chest waiting for death.

"So Angela is in this place?" Gesar asked, uneasily.

"I doubt if she's in the assisted living center," Ashki answered. "She's in a coma, so she's probable in a medical care wing under professional nursing care. This is a big place so we need to ask at the desk in the office wing."

A puffy-faced, middle-aged woman at the reception desk looked up at Ashki's enormous hulk and was suspicious when he inquired about the whereabouts of Angela Andrastos, but after applying a dose of charm and assuring her of his credentials, she eagerly provided the information. "She doesn't get many visitors, but you can find her in Building C. Just continue along the drive. You can't miss it, there's a sign on the building."

Ashki stopped the car in front of Building C. "This is your last chance to forget about this whole thing," he said.

Gesar paused to assess his feelings, and then said, "No. I have to do this. Maybe, I'll regret it. Whatever I find, I'll live with it."

"Do you want me to come with you?"

As Gesar grabbed his cane and climbed out of the car he answered, "No, but thanks for all your help, I really do appreciate everything you've done."

179

Ashki offered a broad Navajo smile. "Remember, you haven't got my bill yet. I'll wait for you out here and take your time, I'm on the clock."

Gesar managed a brief smile before he entered Building C.

There was a hint of twilight in the eastern sky when the Druk dakinis approached the torch dotted ramparts of Kalapa palace. It had been a mournful return, they felt as if they had deserted their sisters in battle and the empty space in their formation was a constant reminder of Dolma. When Brug landed on the temple plaza, Ane was a seething vat of emotion. She was heartbroken at losing Dolma, furious at losing control of the battle and terrified at the possibility of losing Shambala. In hindsight, it was obvious that Mahakala had used distraction to foil Shambala's defenders, but more discouraging was that they had not anticipated such a ploy. It had been his tactic from the beginning, distracting them with decoy raids against the outlands while surreptitiously establishing garrisons virtually at Shambala's doorstep. By placing assassins in the Human realm, he kept their Kalacakra allies distracted. Though futile and likely suicidal, she wanted immediately to fly to the western end of the valley and rain arrows on the three-eyed demon-god.

Brug's resonant voice suddenly invaded her mental turmoil. "Beware mistress, Mahakala blinds you."

Brug's simple statement, intended to express concern, struck her with its deep wisdom. She again had unwittingly fallen into Mahakala's trap of distraction. "You're right Brug. I forgot the Buddha warrior's oath. We defend without pride. We fight without hate. We die without fear. We come without karma." She recited.

Ane signaled her squadron to dismount as healers and handlers ran out to assist them. She patted Brug's neck and instructed him to let the healers treat his wounded legs where the demon-god Yama had held a crushing grip. "Wait here until I return, I must speak with Lady Palden."

After a brief search of the plaza, she found Tashi, a captain of the palace guard. The two captains bowed to each other and Ane asked, "Tashi, where is Lady Palden?"

"She is with the other Guardians in the east council chamber. I think she is expecting you. I already sent word to her that the Druk have returned."

"Thanks," she said and was about to turn away, but was restrained by Tashi's hand placed on her arm.

"Dolma is not with you. Where is she?" He asked in a voice strained with angst.

Ane suddenly realized her haste had led to an awful blunder. Tashi had been Dolma's consort. They had been lovers for at least a year and were recently bonded. She should have told him immediately. She reached out and took his hands. Her eyes welled with battle-frozen tears. "She's gone. We lost her and Nam."

"How?" Tashi asked.

Ane was unsure if she should provide details. "That's what I must tell the Guardians."

A knowing expression crossed Tashi's face. "She did not die in the Asura realm."

"How did you know?"

"You would have told me if she had died in battle."

Ane felt a pang of guilt for not being completely open. "I'm so sorry Tashi. She vanished right before me while we waited to attack the enemy on the southeast pass."

"Dolma's not the only one," Tashi reported somberly. "Just after you deployed with the Senge, I lost one of my guards in the same way."

"The Council knows then?" Ane asked.

"Only about my guard, there may be others, but we have not yet received word from the units at the Shield perimeter. Forgive me, I delay you. Go, you must report to the council, later we will sing the song of the fallen warrior together."

Before parting, Ane embraced Tashi and they shed tears together.

Unlike the south council chamber, the east was for more intimate meetings. Instead of inspiring battle scenes, the tapestries hanging in the east chamber depicted the Eight Wisdom Bodhisattvas in quiet meditation. A restful glow from a perimeter of oil lamps illuminated a domed white ceiling and marble floor inlaid with a dharma wheel design. Its furnishings consisted of a semicircle of eight chairs, individually carved for each of the demon-god guardians, which faced a row of simple benches for other attendees. When Ane opened the chamber door, Lady Palden, Betsge, Yamantaka and Hayagriva were seated with three Kalacakra monks and a nun in attendance. Palden wore her bejeweled golden armor and her sheathed fire sword leaned against her chair. That she wore battle gear in a council meeting emphasized the gravity of Shambala's circumstance.

Standing at the entrance, Ane bowed to the group and waited. Palden gestured to her to come forward. As Ane approached, she noticed eight phurbas on the floor neatly arranged upon strips of silk cloth and spread out in front of the seated demon-gods. Ane joined the line of Kalacakra facing the demon-gods..

"Welcome, captain. We've been expecting you." Palden started. "Let me introduce our friends, Brothers Jamyang, Geshe and Nawang, and Sister Kensang. They have shortly arrived from Dagpa Akar bearing the phurbas that you see before us. We have been discussing options for the best use of these precious weapons."

After a brief round of formal introductory bows, Ane turned to the seated demon-gods and said, "There is something that I have to report."

"Speak." Palden said.

Ane fought back her emotions as she spoke. "My lieutenant, Dolma, was lost tonight, but she did not fall in battle. She died in the Human realm."

Yamatanka interrupted, "That is the second in less than a day. It can only mean that Zerden's hunters are finding their prey in the Human realm."

Hayagriva turned his eyes on the Kalacakra and asked, "Can any of you tell us anything regarding efforts to protect our Buddha warriors?"

Brother Jamyang spoke for the group. "As I said, our watchers have detected at least three of Zerden's minions in the Human realm. Whenever possible, the Sleepers have been moved to safer locations and our agents have attempted to monitor the movements of the hunters, but they have proved elusive and difficult to defeat. They are clever, strong and ruthless. Our most senior monks have proved to be no match for them. When I left Dagpa Akar, Chidag Nagpo had escaped surveillance and now there may be others at large."

"Are you saying that our Kalacakra allies are powerless against them?" Palden asked.

"No, not completely," Jamyang answered. "A well delivered phurba will banish them from the Human realm, but there is possibly another way to defeat them."

There was a moment of silence as all waited for Jamyang's next words. "Tulku Lama Zhangpo believes that the flesh of Zerden's minions sleeps in Naraka. As we speak, he journeys there to attempt to wake them. If he succeeds, it will force them back to the Asura realm."

Yamantaka tapped his staff on the floor. "It is a very dangerous strategy. Naraka does not repel its enemies. It swallows them. Even if he is successful, he will be facing some of Zerden's worst issue and we are in no position to assist him."

"I fear we can only pray for him." Hayagriva added.

Palden added. "Yes, for the moment that is all we can do. Clearly, our Kalacakra allies are doing everything possible to protect the Sleepers in the Human realm. We must focus our attention on the defense of Shambala."

Lord Betsge finally broke his pensive silence. "I think you mean defense of this palace. We are vastly outnumbered and we cannot defend the whole Shield perimeter. Mahakala will act swiftly. We can be certain that the Shield will be breached. It is only a matter of time. We should pull our forces back to a defensible position as soon as possible."

"I think you underestimate the Shield," Hayagriva countered. "Destruction of the Shield will require a perfectly timed assault. Mahakala's nagu armies are as spread out as our own. A perfectly coordinated assault is virtually impossible."

At the mention of Mahakala, a wave of nostalgia briefly softened Palden's determined expression. When she was Mahakala's lover, she had admired his keen intelligence, but sometimes feared his ruthless single mindedness at attaining goals. Mahakala did not waste effort on poorly designed strategies. There was no doubt that he would attend to every strategic detail. "Betsge is right," she defended. "Mahakala would not invest so much without an effective plan of execution. He has already proved himself cleverer than us. We must prepare for the Shield to be breached. Betsge, organize the regrouping of our forces if the Shield fails."

Betsge's rose from his chair. "I already have messengers prepared to ride. I will see that they are dispatched immediately."

Betsge left the room, armor clattering with each broad step.

Palden set her dark eyes on the assembled group of mortals, her golden armor reflecting the light of a hundred oil lamps. "Now, to the matter at hand, we have eight phurbas, how do we best use them defend the palace against four rebel demon-gods?"

Though clearly designed to be defended, Ane had never thought about defending Kalapa palace before. The Shield was supposed to preclude the need. It was hard to imagine the Shield could possibly fail.

183

After a silence that nearly stretched to the point of discomfort, Sister Kensang asked with her eyes averted. "Lord and Lady Guardians, may I speak?"

"Of course," Palden answered, amazed at the confidence in the young sister's voice.

Respectful yet determined, Kensang spoke, "Sacred Guardians, perhaps I speak out of turn for I am but a Kalacakra initiate. Only recently have I ascended the levels of Shambala's jeweled palace in pure consciousness with my master's guidance. I have seen its many paths and avenues, gardens and plazas. It is a place of divine beauty and must not be defiled. In my studies, I have had the honor to read the ancient termas stored at Dagpa Akar. The sacred texts left by the great bodhisattvas tell of many things. One of those texts describes the taming a demon. I believe we could use the same method."

"Continue sister," Palden urged.

Sister Kensang explained.

After his humiliation in the battle of Mount Rewa, the demon Gnyan was feeling especially vengeful. Mahakala's scathing abuse and belittling accusations of ineptitude were still wedged in his craw, refusing digestion.

"You're worse than pus-headed, Yama." Mahakala railed. "You had a whole tapah unit in your grasp, how could they possibly slip by you? I can't believe Zerden made you prime general. I'm surprised he didn't have you flayed open at birth."

"Like you, I was never born and you can't speak to me like one of your underlings." Gnyan protested.

"You *are* one of my underlings! Have you forgotten that Zerden appointed me prime general? I should send you back to Naraka to face Zerden's wrath, but I will give you an opportunity to redeem yourself. You will regroup your army and invade Shambala valley by way of the northeast pass."

"The southeast pass would be much closer." Gnyan said.

Mahakala laughed derisively. "I want you to have a few days march to think about your incompetence. Kubera will give you details of the attack plan. Be sure to follow them precisely!"

Seething in his own vitriol for the whole trek, Gnyan had marched his army to Shambala's northeast pass while under the constant watch of a squad of Kubera's naga-ta riders. He despised

Kubera almost as much as Mahakala. He especially did not trust the devious fat interloper or his flying beasts.

Fueled by his anger, Gnyan pushed his army hard; they had mounted the summit of the pass and were already descending toward the valley before encountering any resistance. Shambala's defenders did manage to halt the advance and reduce his force by a half legion, until he personally intervened to drive them off. The wretched dakinis tried distracting him again but this time he stayed within a protective ring of his own archers. He could have used the help of Kubera's naga-ta, but the miserable cowards always kept to the rear. Why were they holding back? Yet to his satisfaction, Shambala's forces were eventually defeated and forced to run to the safety of their Shield without assistance from Kubera's useless naga-ta.

When Shambala's defenders had retreated and the way into the valley was clear, he followed the next part of Mahakala's instruction. He moved his forces into position along the Shield perimeter and ordered his captains to rush their units forward when they saw a flash of light over the valley. He still did not know how Mahakala would achieve that trick. Even Zerden had not found a way to penetrate Shambala's Shield after thousands of years. His final task was simply to watch the siege from a promontory overlooking the valley, which Mahakala had described in some detail and he found without difficulty. There he waited, viewing a panorama of the valley. Now that the moon had set behind the western range, the valley was blanketed in darkness except for the insulting spot of light in the midst of Lake Shambala. Soon, he would be stomping out the last embers of that light, and in the mayhem he would find a way to restore his standing with Zerden. Palden would undoubtedly be a prize his master would appreciate.

While Gnyan gazed upon the valley plotting his future, he heard a naga-ta's shriek. He scanned the sky for the source of the sound. Above and behind him, a group of the flying beasts was coming toward his position. Delivering a message, he thought. He turned away, failing to notice the rigging of chains and grappling hooks hanging from their legs. He remained oblivious until the hooks sank into his flesh and he was suddenly dangling in midair, wildly thrashing his arms and legs. It took four naga-ta to lift his massive weight high over the valley and above the upper limit of the Shield, where they released him.

Tangled in chains, Gnyan fell toward that insulting spot of light floating on Lake Shambala, but he never reached it. Between him and Kalapa palace was the Shield of Shambala, the one thing that could incinerate his flesh and separate him from immortality. As it did so, an intensely bright light flashed over the entire valley providing the armies of Munpa Zerden the signal to charge into the Shield.

$$\text{{\Large ৰৱ}}$$

A wary nurse with a gut-piercing glare interrogated Gesar when he asked to see Angela Andrastos. "Just who are you?" she asked.

"I'm a friend. I was cleared by the receptionist in the main building."

"I've never seen you before. Only the monks from the temple in San Francisco come to see her."

Gesar recognized an opportunity and took a chance with name-dropping. "I'm a friend of Brother Kai at the monastery."

The nurse's glare softened. "He's a nice man. Always prays for her, you know. She always seems better after his visits."

"Yes, I know." Gesar echoed. So Kai has been here, he thought.

"She's in room eight."

Catching a glimpse of the nurse's nametag he said, "Thanks, Nurse Holland, I'm glad Angela has you looking out for her."

Nurse Holland smiled and returned to her rounds, pushing a medication cart.

Room number eight was a short hobble down the hall. Gesar hesitated at the door, leaning on his cane as he mustered the nerve to enter the room. "For Shambala and the Path," he whispered sarcastically, as he crossed the threshold.

His breath stopped at his first sight of Angela Andrastos. Bathed in a pool of light cast from the room's one window was the woman from his dream, thin and pale, but most certainly Ane, captain of the Druk dakini. A photo at the bedside draped with military medals only confirmed his impression; it showed the woman he had met in another realm, young, strong and full of life as he remembered her. The contrast with the current image of the frail and vulnerable, bedridden woman was heart rending. Yet, her beauty was preserved. A wreath of shining black hair encircled a perfectly symmetrical face with full lips, slightly chapped, trembling as if trying to speak.

Gesar reached out and took her hand, cradling it tenderly in his own. In Shambala, that hand wielded a sword. Here, it was limp with thin fingers bent by contracture. Tears welled in his eyes as he realized the truth. He had not come to prove his sanity; he had come because he loved her. Part of him wanted to wail at the injustice of being separated from her by disease and dimension.

As he lingered at her bedside, watching her fluttering eyelids and trembling lips, he wondered what those eyes gazed upon. He imagined being with her in Shambala, strolling the water gardens of Kalapa palace. The minutes passed and eventually he remembered that Dr. Ashki was waiting for him. Gently, he released her hand, kissed her forehead and whispered a farewell. He then turned to leave only to be startled by two men standing in the doorway. The nearest had a boyish face with a terrified expression and was dressed in a Buddhist monk's robes. Behind him was a tall, broad-chested man with a cruel mouth and eyes hidden by sunglasses. A shining police badge glowed on his dark shirt. Recognition struck Gesar like a bolt of lightning and his free hand went for the phurba in his jacket.

Before Gnyan's blazing sacrifice, the order to retreat had arrived from the Council of Guardians. As the tapah and dakini units made there way to new defensive positions, a miniature sun briefly appeared over Shambala, bathing the valley in blinding light and then vanishing as quickly as it appeared. The warriors blinked and rubbed their flash-blinded eyes, while trying to calm their startled mounts. Ignoring the ominous event, captains waved their units onward and then suddenly, the Shield was ablaze with wild dancing lights. Soundless bolts of lightning flashed overhead, erupting from the outer Shield perimeter, snaking upward and finally descending on the temple summit of Kalapa palace.

Goaded by their demon commanders, thousands of nagu warriors charged into the Shield perimeter, their physical incarnations instantly vaporized leaving nothing but discorporate sentience imbued with malice. Waves of corruption fell upon Shambala, like stinking offal discharged into a fountain of purity. For a long while, the wild dance of lightning continued as the Shield attempted to cleanse itself of defiled consciousness, but the pollution proved overwhelming. The dancing lights dimmed and finally expired, leaving a miasmic shroud reeking of seared flesh, which hung over the valley, denying the promise of dawn.

When the Shield collapsed, a third of the Zerden's army remained, but it still far outnumbered Shambala's defenders. Converging from all directions, nagu forces poured into the valley, while tapah and dakini units rushed to defend the major routes to Kalapa palace.

A menacing row of spikes along the upper edge of the Naraka keep wall lengthened wherever Jhado approached. Attempting a jump was out of the question, and by the look of its light devouring substance, he suspected it could devour anything that dared to touch it.

"So, you're alive," Jhado whispered, and as he said the words, an inspiration came to him.

The phurba's blade glowed as he withdrew it from his robe. Slowly, he advanced its point toward the wall. The area of wall nearest the point melted and dimpled inward like an animal cringing from a firebrand. As he advanced the blade further, the wall retreated, growing thinner until a hole the width of his hand formed. The black flesh around the opening trembled, straining to close the wound, but the phurba's power kept the wall at bay, providing a porthole view of the keep within. The keep was a warren of barracks, steaming refuse pits and smoking forges bordering an open plaza that Jhado guessed must be accessible by whatever served as the usual portal of entry. Beyond the plaza was the keep's dominant structure, an imposing windowless cube topped with a beehive dome and surrounded by four pinnacled towers.

Chidag will be there, Jhado thought as he removed the phurba blade from the wall, whose black flesh resealed with an intimidating snap, reminding him that he could not enter despite his surreptitious glance within. Slipping the phurba back into his robe, he cautiously made his way along the perimeter of the wall looking for some sign of the keep's entrance, but he stopped dead at the sound of rattling armor and stomping boots. A nagu guard unit was returning to the keep. With no place to hide, Jhado could only pray that silence and shadow would provide sufficient camouflage. He watched the patrol march directly up to the gateless wall, where their leader briefly hesitated before vanishing into its blackness. He was followed shortly by a single file of comrades. As they passed through the wall, a soul-crushing shriek pierced the night air.

189

Jhado suddenly understood the wall's secret and acted without hesitation. Snatching the phurba from his robe, he plunged it with full force into the wall's black flesh, its dreadful wail intensified as it recoiled from the glowing blade. The stench of the Naraka's keep gushed out of a hole that splayed open to the size of a barrel. Before the opening narrowed, Jhado dove through, dashed into the nearest refuse pit and quickly returned the glowing phurba to his robe. Jhado's speed was such that even the most alert sentry would have seen but a flash of light in the shadows. The affronted wall prolonged its warning cry, attempting to expose the intruder, but still smarting from the phurba's searing touch, it sounded more like a whipped dog than an alarm.

When the wall's howl finally stopped, Jhado peeked over the edge of the refuse pit, ignoring the stench and trying not to think about the oozing mass he was standing on. To his relief, the wall's prolonged outcry had attracted no attention. Apparently, the sentries patrolling the inner plaza had expected the arrival of the guard unit and failed to notice any change from the wall's usual alarm.

Jhado's objective was on the far side of the wide, well-patrolled plaza. He reached a hand into his robe and gripped the phurba handle. He had hoped to save it to make his escape, but he could see no alternative solution. Leaping out of the pit, he started a purposeful but unhurried walk across the plaza. With one hand on the phurba hidden beneath the folds of his robe, he did his best to become just another nagu silhouette going to his next duty assignment. Behaving as if you simply belonged was often the best means to go unnoticed, and the strategy worked well for most of the crossing. The great beehive dome of Naraka's stronghold was looming over him when the guards finally challenged him.

"Halt!" a voice ordered, sounding like gravel filling a dry well. "Only demon generals and the master's children may approach the sanctuary."

Glancing over his shoulder, Jhado stopped in response to the order and tightened his grip on the phurba's handle. An elite dron warrior followed by a nagu foot patrol jogged toward him. They had nearly reached Jhado when he suddenly bolted for the stronghold, shocking the nagu patrol by his burst of superhuman speed. The alarm was raised and other patrols joined the pursuit of the intruder. As he neared the sanctuary, Jhado plunged the phurba into the stone path, vaporizing the pursuing nagu patrols as well as the sentries guarding the keep entrance. In seconds, he was mounting the stairs to the sanctuary's huge iron-strapped door. When he reached the uppermost landing, he shouldered the door with all of his strength. The door was unlocked, relying purely on its sheer mass to bar entry of anything less than an immortal. Although he was no match for a demon-god, Jhado's enhanced strength as a lung-gom-pa was enough to open a crack wide enough to admit one scrawny monk. When the door closed behind him, the howls of nagu patrols colliding with the phurba barrier were replaced by an eerie silence.

The pungent scent of burning tar licked Jhado's nostrils as his eyes adjusted to the strange light within the sanctuary. The source of the stench was a row of smoking sconce lamps mounted on columns lining the perimeter of the outer walls, which cast a feeble orange light that died in the oppressive black space of the dome vault overhead. The architect's assignment had been clear, create a structure where light was imprisoned and constantly beat it into submission. The columns and walls were decorated with bizarre symbols painted in a monochrome blood-rust red. Jhado guessed they were warning signs, written in the ancient tongue of the demons, most likely not very subtle references to the flaying and dismemberment of intruders.

Opposite the entrance, the column-lined hall pointed to the sanctuary's focal point. At the far end, standing upon a dais was a light swallowing, rectangular monolith resembling a section of the gateless wall. Nearby, three sarcophagi were propped at angles facing the monolith. Oversized benches, tables and chairs were stored against the walls, indicating the room was more than a mausoleum or sanctum dedicated to the worship of chaos. Here is where Mahakala and the other rebels likely sat with Zerden's commanders to devise their plan to conquer Shambala.

When Jhado stepped off the entrance landing he felt a sharp pain in his foot. In the dim light he had not noticed the floor. It was black mortar inlayed with sharp fragments of teeth and bone, creating a macabre mosaic depicting the various manifestations of the Eighty-thousand Negativities. It was, in essence, Munpa Zerden's family album filling the length and breadth of the room, providing no place to step without touching a symbol of defilement.

Other than getting his feet tenderized by the shard-embedded floor, Jhado reached the dais unmolested. Climbing onto the dais, he looked at the occupant of the largest casket. He had never seen Chidag Nagpo, but the unconscious creature fit the descriptions given in the ancient pechas of the one called the Life-Stealing Fiend. He was twice the height of a man and hideous. His bulging eyes were covered with a nictating membrane, fangs jutted from a lipless slit of a mouth, and cords of blood-matted hair surrounded his head. His tree-like arms and legs were bare, but his broad torso was dressed in metal-studded black leather and his clawed hand gripped the infamous four-pointed Crux of Evil, a multipurpose weapon, useful for throwing or slashing. The other caskets held Chidag's notorious companions, Dang Ba, recognizable by his jeweled cap made from a skull, and Na Tsha by his reptilian features. Both gripped weapons in a gnarled bundle of fingers.

Jhado shuddered at what he was about to do—wake these creatures with no good escape plan. Taking calming breaths, he sat on the edge of the dais and recalled the words of the bodhisattva's song, failing to notice the ripple in the black monolith that loomed behind him. A spear and a hand emerged, then an arm and leg. A boot thudded on the dais floor and Jhado turned his head.

Battles raged as dawn strained to penetrate the thick haze over Shambala valley. With instructions to slow the enemy advance, Shambala's forces had taken defensive positions after the Shield failed. On the Emerald Bridge they forced enemy columns into the river gorge to be swept onto the rocks at the bottom of Trinity Falls. Along the upper Shenla, they charged out of tall savannah grasses, attacking enemy flanks as they marched along the riverbank and forcing them into the icy rapids. On the southern pass roads where there was less tactical advantage, the tapah and dakini defenders continued repeated hit and run attacks. Only in the north was the enemy unchallenged, where Mahakala's troops marched through the forests along the Shenla River, aiming for the ford in the shallows at the western end of Lake Shambala.

When the palace horns sounded the call for Shambala's forces to retreat to Kalapa palace, the Druk and Senge units prepared to defend the shallows. Several tapah units were expected to return from the west along the Shenla road. The Druk and Senge were tasked with ensuring that Mahakala's forces did not cut off their retreat. Perched high on Kalapa's western rampart, the Druk dakini watched the ford while Senge archers took positions on the south bank of the river.

As she waited with her squadron, Ane recalled her meeting with Lady Palden in the east council chamber, where the demon-god had privately confided answers to questions that were circulating among the Buddha warriors.

Fearing that she might give offense, Ane was reluctant to raise the question, but considering the dire nature of their situation, she had to speak. "Lady Palden, with the enemy now in the valley, some of the captains have asked, when will the Guardians challenge the rebels?"

"I fear the Buddha warriors must defeat Mahakala and the other rebels without the direct aid of the Guardians," she said.

"Forgive me Lady Palden, I don't understand." Ane replied.

Palden paused a moment before explaining. "For two thousand years, we have been shedding the sins of our past. If the faithful Guardians engage the rebels in battle, we must revert to our wrathful forms. We cannot predict what will happen when we again experience old lusts."

"Surely you are different than you were in those days." Ane protested.

A flash of red appeared in Palden's eyes. "You don't understand the temptation. I used those same words to reassure the other faithful Guardians, but they doubt that we have changed enough and they are wise to have doubts. Since the Taming, we have existed in a delicate balance. Look at how easily Mahakala and the others have regressed into beasts. Trust me. You would not like my demon form. I have stripped flesh from human bones as you would peel a fruit and I enjoyed doing it!"

"But we are vastly outnumbered. What would you have us do?" Ane asked.

"We must gather what remains of our defenders to Kalapa Palace and pray that Sister Kensang's plan will succeed. At least we might purchase some time."

"And what orders do you have for the Druk?"

Palden's expression softened. "After such a night you are still eager for battle. I do have orders for you. The Seers have told us that Mahakala's army marches for the Shenla ford. He will attempt to stop our retreating ground forces from reaching the safety of the palace. I have spoken with Lord Begtse and you are to join the Senge in defending the ford until the remaining tapah units are safely within the walls of Kalapa. The horns will sound twice. The first will recall our forces; the second will recall your squadron and the Senge."

"Lady Palden, there is another question which is on the minds of all of us."

"Yes, speak."

"Can the Shield be restored?"

"We do not know. Perhaps the strength of Sangpo will return if we can protect the throne from Mahakala. The Council is certain that

Mahakala's true goal is to utterly destroy the throne to ensure the Shield cannot be restored. Even now, there is only a flicker of light on the throne. We have no idea if it will die or be healed, but you can be assured that the Guardians will defend the throne for as long as we can hold on to our reason."

"I will pray that it will be reborn soon," Ane said.

"We are all praying that Sangpo's strength will return."

Ane pressed her palms together and bowed to Palden before leaving to carry out her orders.

As she gazed across the lake from Kalapa's ramparts, the dawn cast a blood red glow across the valley. Unconsciously, Ane turned to speak with Dolma and was painfully reminded of her loss. The Buddha warriors were a limited commodity; while superior to the enemy in strength and speed, tapah, dakini and palace guards units comprised less than two thousand. Every lost warrior was a severe wound to Shambala's defense. The vision of Gesar riding alone into a nagu army flashed into her consciousness. Would he return? Since leaving Lady Palden, thoughts of him kept invading her mind to the point that Brug had noticed.

"Mistress misses the horse warrior," he said.

"He's gone, Brug. He may never return."

"The horse warrior will come to you." Brug replied, preening his right wing.

Strangely, Ane understood, she did sense Gesar's presence.

Gesar froze, suddenly reminded of the adage not to bring a knife to a gunfight. A malicious smile appeared on the face of the man pointing the pistol at him. Wary of the phurba growing heavier by the moment in Gesar's hand, the demon weighed his options. The icy silence stretched until the demon finally laughed and said. "I will kill you in self-defense. She will die in the crossfire."

It was then that the trembling Brother William decided it was time to do something brave. Suddenly, he grabbed the gun, wrenching it from the demon's right hand. Chidag backhanded the monk. The powerful blow sent William tumbling to the floor unconscious and the gun skidding under the bed.

Enraged, Chidag kicked the monk's body sending it flying to the other side of the room and when he turned, Gesar was charging at him with a shining phurba blade. Compromised by his muscle weakness, Gesar's speed was slower then his mental intent and he was no match for the reflexes of an incarnate demon. Chidag easily dodged the strike and slammed Gesar into the wall. Though stunned, Gesar forced himself to stay on his feet. Before he could raise the phurba for another strike, Chidag's fist connected with his jaw. Gesar's head hit the doorframe with a crack. The world went black and the phurba dropped from his hand, hitting the floor with a metallic ring.

Chidag emitted a sickening chuckle of satisfaction and turned his attention to the sleeping woman.

Shingdong opened the stable door and let Goba free. Only rarely did the old stable master free a riderless horse, usually man and horse died together in battle. A horse separated from its soul-bound rider eventually experienced an overwhelming urge to seek its rider or join him in death. Goba's time had come. After the collapse of the Shield, the horse had created such a commotion that it was impossible to ignore him. Long before the kicking started, Shingdong had noticed Goba's agitation. He had barely finished fitting the tack and armor pieces, when the horse kicked open his stall and trotted to the stable door. Shingdong adeptly hooked Gesar's armor kit to the saddle horn before Goba bolted from the stable.

When Goba reached the Vishvamata ice bridge, the first of the recalled tapah units was returning to the palace. Splinters of ice flew up from his hooves as he galloped by them. A riderless horse running in the opposite direction surprised the tired column of tapah, but no one questioned the action of a horse bearing the Senge emblem.

With her attention focused on the north bank of the Shenla river, Ane did not notice Goba cross the ice bridge and run for the Shenla Road. Instead, she saw the first sign that Mahakala's army was approaching; flames and great billows of thick smoke were rising from forests and grasslands north of the river. A northwest breeze carried a massive shroud of smoke toward the river.

"Skata!" Ane cried. "He's trying to blind the Senge archers."

There was no reason to wait any longer. Mahakala's army would attempt the river crossing as soon as the smoke reached the ford. Ane raised her sword and signaled the Druk to attack. In perfect unison, the Druk squadron leapt from the ramparts and made for the Shenla shallows. Ane shuddered at the possibility that Mahakala would be hiding in the smoke and prayed Lady Palden's prediction was correct. She had said, "Once Mahakala is in the valley he will be reluctant to expose himself. He is expecting a challenge from the faithful demon-gods and he knows Lord Begtse is faster with a blade. It takes time to regrow six arms and a leg. No, he won't risk joining the fray unless his army fails to make the crossing."

As the Druk squadron glided over the Shenla marshes, a wall of grey smoke rolled across the ford denying Senge archers a view of the opposite bank. The initial plan to pin the enemy on the north bank had evaporated. Now, it was to be a close quarter battle on the river. In order to avoid collisions in the dense smoke, Ane signaled the Druk to use the Dharma Wheel maneuver. In response, the squadron formed a rotating Ferris wheel over the river creating a steady stream of dakinis that would cut through the enemy like a circular saw. It was up to the Senge archers to stop anything that slipped by them.

From the south bank, when Ben saw the Druk dakini take up the Dharma Wheel formation and disappear into the cloud of smoke, he understood what his men had to do. Following his rider's thought, Dawa galloped along riverbank as Ben shouted new orders to the Senge archers hidden in the trees. "Let no enemy touch this bank!"

When Gesar regained consciousness, he looked at his empty hand and knew that he had failed. The phurba was gone as was the hospital room. He sat with his back against a choten, facing a collection of neatly kept buildings bathed in an eerie red light. He stood up to get his bearings. The choten was in the midst of a village surrounded by rolling hills with a line of cloud-enshrouded mountains in the distance. "Shambala," he whispered in recognition, but everything was wrong. The village was deserted and an ominous mist overhead pressed on his spirit like a jackboot.

"Damn it!" he yelled in anguish. He did not want to be here, Ane needed him in the Human realm. A demon was going to kill her in her hospital bed. Here, he could do nothing to stop it. And then he realized that he should not be here, not in the valley. Only Kalacakra entered Shambala by way of chotens within Shambala valley. The Shield excluded all others. Something was terribly wrong.

He jogged along a road to the edge of the village to get a better view. His one consolation was that here in the Asura realm, his body was whole again, free of disease. His legs moved with ease as he ran past an orchard and climbed to an overlook. He was definitely in Shambala. In the northeast, the great dome of Kalapa palace was visible on the lake. Estimating the distance, he guessed that he was in Nyrima, a small village that according to Ben was where amrita was prepared. Presently, the village and surrounding orchards were abandoned. More disconcerting was the wall of grey-black smoke in the north, billowing up to reinforce the oppressive layer of mist clinging to the valley. "The Shield has fallen," he gasped. The sudden realization plunged like a firebrand into a fresh wound. He started to run, hoping Asura's temporal shift would give him the time to reach the palace for help before Ane was lost.

The road from Nyrima ran north to meet the Shenla River road, directly to where the ominous wall of smoke swallowed the sky.

Gesar had run only a kilometer when a familiar voice entered his mind.

"I come to you."

"Goba!"

When Gesar topped the next hill, he heard the pounding hooves and saw a dark horse with a flowing blond mane trailed by a line of dust. The joy of reunion between a soul-bound horse and rider is difficult to temper even under tragic circumstances. Both horse and rider stepped up their paces and the two practically collided in a swirling cloud of road dust.

Goba nuzzled Gesar's face. "I knew you would return, rider."

Gesar patted Goba's neck. "I missed you Goba. I thought you were only a dream."

"All is dream." Goba answered.

"Perhaps, but there's no time to argue, we must return to Kalapa, Ane, the dakini captain is in danger."

"Yes, she fights to defend the river." As Goba's words entered Gesar's mind, he saw an image of a dakini squadron flying away from the Kalapa ramparts; it was a glimpse of Goba's recent memory as he galloped from the palace.

Gesar's response came without thought. "We must go to them."

Goba made a sudden shake and the kit bag fell from the saddle horn and hit the ground with a clang. "Prepare for battle. I will carry you."

Gesar put on his armor and inspected Goba's tack. Head and chest foreplates had been fitted well. Sword and bow were in place and the quiver full of arrows. Grabbing the reins, he jumped into the saddle. Goba reared and galloped northward.

Jhado dove. The spear gouged a chunk of stone from the edge of the dais before skittering half the length of the keep hall. Jhado rolled to his feet and spun around to face an elite nagu dron warrior. The distinctive fanged helmet hid his face, but Jhado fixed his eyes on the two swords, a long curved katana in the right and a short double-edged blade in the left hand. Realizing that he had underestimated Jhado's agility, the dron warrior approached cautiously sizing up his prey and positioning himself to protect the resting demons.

Anticipating the nagu's move, Jhado leapt onto the dais. The long sword whistled by his ear as he put the nearest casket between himself and the dron warrior. Jhado waited for the next move. The dron warrior held his position, keeping both swords pointed at Jhado and occasionally glancing at the portal. A leg and arm started to emerge from its rippling surface. The dron was waiting for reinforcements. Jhado realized that short of a miracle, his mission was about to end dismally. He had been naive to think Zerden would leave his children unguarded. The sleeping demons were obviously propped near the nursery door to allow their attendants swift access in the event of a threat.

In a sudden flash of brilliance, Jhado dashed under the largest casket, which held Chidag's body. As Jhado hoped, the sword-wielding dron warrior did not pursue. Confident that he and his comrades would soon kill this intruder, the dron only turned to track the monk like a cat watching a mouse.

In the Asura realm, the lung-gom-pa's greatest physical power is in the legs. Jhado squatted, tightened his back against the casket's underside and sprung upward with all of his strength. The huge box and its occupant tipped over and crashed to the floor at the portal threshold, crushing the unwary dron warrior who had just appeared. His sword-wielding comrade looked on in disbelief at the half-exposed broken body with one arm still grasping a spear shaft.

Unlike the dron warrior, Jhado did not hesitate. With Chidag's massive sarcophagus blocking passage through the portal, he had evened his odds. He jumped, rolled, and snatched the spear from the hand of the crushed dron warrior. In a blink, he was on his feet with a nagu spear in hand. Astonished by the sudden turn of events, the nagu swordsman watched Jhado move to an open area on the dais.

"I should warn you, I mastered the staff when I was a boy," Jhado said, but failed to add that that boy had been in a previous incarnation. He was relying on urgency to restore his skill.

Jhado's defiant words shattered the dron warrior's stupor and he charged at him in a whir of spinning blades. Clearly one of Zerden's more highly trained warriors, the dron pressed forward while Jhado used all of his concentration to block and retreat. Knowing the basic tenant not to be backed against a wall, Jhado turned as he retreated. As the contest continued, skills acquired in another lifetime started to surface like bamboo shoots piercing hard clay. Here and there, Jhado managed to get a blow in between blocks. Then, with a sudden body change he spun and struck a solid blow on his attackers left wrist, sending the short sword clanging to the floor.

Defending against a single sword was much easier than dealing with two. Jhado's movements became smoother. The feel of the shaft is his hand felt more familiar though its balance was off. He almost laughed when a lost memory of a defensive move suddenly surfaced. In another life, he had invented the move after watching a shrew avoid a hawk strike by diving into the snow only to emerge unharmed a short distance away. He had named the move, 'Shrew Seeks-the-Earth', and he doubted the dron warrior had ever encountered it.

When the dron warrior angled a sword strike to the upper body, Jhado did not attempt a block. Instead, he dropped into a deep squat with one leg extended, letting the sword pass over his head. Meanwhile, his spear tip spiraled down in a steep arc over the floor before biting cleaning through the dron warrior's left knee. The warrior immediately collapsed in a heap of black armor. As Jhado approached, the heap raised a sword and swung wildly, but Jhado quickly disarmed the nagu and pointed a spear blade at his throat.

"I do not wish to kill you." Jhado said.

"That's too bad." The sanctuary suddenly echoed with a squeaky tenor.

It was not the voice of a nagu warrior, which was usually no more than a low-pitched growl. Jhado turned around. The demon-god, Kubera, emerged from the shadows behind a set of columns.

"That's too bad," Kubera repeated. "I doubt the creature would have the same consideration for you, especially, that one. He is one of Zerden's hand picked baby sitters and doesn't take kindly to those who disturb his charges."

The nagu dron attempted to roll over and let out a howl.

"Such a loyal servant should not be allowed to suffer." Kubera said as he walked over to the dron and placed a foot on his head. Slowly, he applied his massive weight, the helmeted head cracked and collapsed like an overripe melon.

Jhado winced in horror and asked, "How did you get in here? I sealed the entrance with a phurba."

Kubera clicked his teeth disdainfully before speaking. "You are brave to put questions to a demon-god in the heart of Naraka. Some would consider it the height of insolence for you just to set foot in this place, but fortunately, for you, I am quite forgiving. To answer your question, I have made it my business to learn all the ins and outs of Naraka's keep. I came as soon as the yard patrols raised the alarm. I've been watching you for some time now."

"What do you intend?" Jhado asked, keeping the spear pointed at the demon-god, though he knew it was a futile gesture.

"That is a good question. What shall I do with you? You have certainly got yourself noticed, here and in the lower realms."

Mahakala grew impatient as he watched the bodies of his nagu shock troops float down the river toward the marshes. He had charred half of the forest north of the Shenla to provide a sufficient smoke screen for his army yet Shambala's defenders had managed to find a way hold the shallows. The dakinis continued to be a thorn in his side. He needed to neutralize them with naga-ta, but due to incompetent handling their numbers were limited and those remaining were with Yama and Changpa, both of whom were exasperatingly overdue. By now, Changpa should have taken the Shenla road and routed the irritating tapah unit that was defending the south shore.

He was sick of this bottleneck; it was time that he ended it. He had held back, deterred by the possibility that Betsge was among tapah on the opposite shore, but Betsge's bravado would have driven him to reveal himself by now. "Enough of this!" Mahakala growled as he drew his weapons and stepped into the river.

At that moment, Goba had reached the south bank of the Shenla River. It had been a hard ride and his flanks glistened with sweat as he negotiated the trees and underbrush. Gesar strained to see through the haze of smoke, searching for the Senge. Among a stand trees overlooking the river, he recognized his riding mate and called out to him, "Chiru!"

Chiru was mounted on his horse and holding a bow. He turned to the familiar voice with an expression of joyful recognition. "Gesar! Your back! We missed you. Are you okay?"

"Yeah, pretty much."

"I knew you would make it back. Goba never gave up on you. You're just in time for some action. Unfortunately, things haven't been going too well for us." Chiru added as he nocked a fresh arrow.

"I noticed, but I'm looking for captain Jigme. I have to see him right away."

Chiru jutted a chin to his right and answered. "I think he's that way, just upstream from here."

"Thanks, and it's good to see you again."

"You're welcome my Senge brother. When we're done here, I'll meet you for tea." Chiru replied with a grin and then he added. "And thanks for coming back. At least I'm not hindmost anymore."

Under other circumstances, Gesar would have laughed, but he only could manage a fleeting smile as he turned away to find captain Jigme. Not far upstream, Gesar saw the bright red of a captain's helmet tassel and rode for it.

"Ben! I mean, Captain Jigme," Gesar called as Goba trotted through the underbrush.

Ben glanced over his shoulder and shouted. "Gesar! Welcome back! I hoped you would return. I would offer you a formal greeting, but as you can see we are somewhat occupied."

"The Shield is gone, what happened?" Gesar asked.

The captain answered, drawing his bow and keeping his attention on the river bank. "Mahakala succeeded. It was sickening. We saw the Shield falter and collapse. A hundred thousand sentients must have been sacrificed in the blink of an eye. They entered the valley from every pass and Mahakala found a way in from the north and he force-marched his army here to the ford. We figured he's attempting to cut off the tapah units retreating to the palace. Luckily, we anticipated his move and positioned a defense here, but Mahakala is clever; he set fires to blind our archers. Nevertheless, we are to hold them at the ford until the valley is evacuated and all tapah units have returned to the palace. Your bow is welcome."

"I can't. I came to ask your help. I've got to find Ane. She is in danger in the Human realm. Where is she?"

An arrow whistled off Ben's bow and hurtled for a shadow emerging from the smoke, hitting its target with a thud followed by a splash. "She and the rest of the Druk are in that haze," Ben answered. "There's nothing you can do for her, not here. If she survives, you will see her when we are called back to Kalapa."

"I could ride to the palace and speak with the Kalacakra monks. They might be able to help or at least they could show me how to get back to Human realm." Gesar suggested.

"Shambala is more important than any one of us." Ben replied sternly. "Ane knows that applies to her."

"But, I know where she sleeps, someone could help her." Gesar appealed.

"In this realm you are Senge and I am your captain. Nock your bow and take a position." Ben ordered, never taking his eyes off the shoreline.

"Yes captain," Gesar relented, realizing that Ben was right. However maddening, he had to accept the reality of the moment. He could do nothing. His body lay as unconscious and as vulnerable as the young woman he had tried to defend in the nursing home. Dejected, he rode away letting Goba find a defensive position overlooking the shoreline. Goba found a place on high ground hidden by a wall of dense underbrush. "Rider, the air is heavy with tree death, but I can still smell the enemy. Prepare your bow."

Gesar drew his bow and waited.

Brug completed a perfect roll and entered the downward sweep of the Dharma Wheel formation. The smoke-filled air stung Ane's eyes, her throat was raw and her lungs begged to cough, but the dakini strategy depended on silence and speed. Blinded by smoke, she trusted Brug to locate the water's surface. He dove and glided so low over the surface that reeds brushed at his talons. Despite the physical discomfort, the dakinis had turned the obscuring smoke to their advantage. As they attempted to ford the Shenla shallows, the unwary nagu warrior's last vision was that of a dark shape surging out of the grey and the flash of a deadly sword. Sweep after sweep of silent dakinis thinned the ranks of Mahakala's army while the Senge disposed of any leaking dregs.

Having grown accustomed to the rhythm of the formation, the unexpected shriek of a kinnara struck Ane with a jolt. The next shock came when she glided over a headless kinnara and a severed wing floating lifeless in river.

"Mahakala," the name issued from her lips as a whispered curse.

Reacting with the speed of thought, Brug sounded the retreat, his warning cry cutting through the acrid murk. Brug lifted and banked away just as Mahakala's huge bulk emerged from the gloom. The demon's red eyes flared as he swung his tilug, the air ringing metallic as the blade passed through Brug's tail feathers.

"That was too close."

"Forgive my slowness mistress." Brug apologized.

"Forgiven. Now, we must regroup and provide cover for the Senge. Mahakala will now cross the river to clear the south bank."

Brug ascended, breaking through the ceiling of smoke. The remaining Druk squadron circled in standard formation, awaiting orders. Ane inhaled a cleansing lungful of fresh air and then did a brief head count. Mercifully, most of the Druk had survived. Only one was missing; it was Rinchen. Her name meant "precious jewel" and so appropriate. Loved by all, she was a shining personality always raising the spirits of her sisters. Her mount, Torma, was a young kinnara with a bent for playful aerial maneuvers. The loss would be a serious blow to the Druk morale.

With no time to shed tears, Ane suppressed her grief and signaled her orders. As the Druk formed attack groups, the horns of Kalapa sounded the final call to return to the palace. Now they had to run with demon-gods and four nagu armies biting at their heels.

Dr. Ashki ignored the ache in his hip as he jogged down the hallway searching rooms. Something was horribly wrong; there should have been at least one nurse on duty. When he spotted the phurba lying on the floor in an open doorway, he ran to it. He stopped at the entrance. The room was a shambles. Gesar was slumped against the wall; the plaster was cracked and smeared with blood where his head had smashed against it. An orange-robed monk and a nurse lay unconscious on the floor. A large man wearing sunglasses pulled a syringe from his neck and reached menacingly for a comatose woman lying in a hospital bed. The scene spoke for itself. The man at the bedside had battered Gesar and the others unconscious. The nurse was apparently his most recent victim. She had fought with her only weapon, a syringe and needle.

Ashki yelled. "Anaye! Get away from her!"

Chidag turned, flashed a disturbing grin and said, "I haven't heard that name in a long time."

"Get away from that woman!" Ashki commanded again.

Chidag laughed derisively. Ignoring the command, he placed his hand on the woman's throat.

Though he had not played football since college, Ashki had not forgotten how to tackle. In four strides, he crossed the room and slammed his full bulk into his target, throwing the demon over his shoulder. Angela Andrastos' photos and medals went flying as Chidag's face cracked squarely against the bedside table. Dazed and light-blinded, Chidag picked himself up and turned around with blood dripping from the corner of his mouth and shattered sunglasses dangling from one ear. The attack had surprised and stunned him; whatever drug had been in that syringe was dulling his host's body. Brushing the broken sunglasses away, Chidag forced his eyes into focus, searching for the impertinent human. When he saw Ashki's shape bent over the unconscious nurse and monk, he unleashed his fury. His eyes flared with demon fire and he charged.

Ashki sprang to his feet. Fearing the demon might cause further harm to the unconscious victims, his body instinctively took a defensive lineman's stance. In his day, he had stopped bigger men on the gridiron. Tucking his head low, he aimed his shoulder for Chidag's lower chest. A lung full of air exploded from the demon's mouth with sickening hiss when the two men collided, but Chidag did not relent. For several moments, Ashki held his own, managing to wrestle the demon away from the unconscious victims. Driven by rage, Chidag fought off the effects of the chemical that weakened him. With a sudden surge of force, he elbowed Ashki across the neck, causing him to stumble backward and trip over Gesar's legs. Flat on his back, Ashki gasped for air through a spastic trachea. When he rolled onto his hands and knees, Chidag kicked him in the side. Ashki's body lifted and landed in the open doorway with a thud. The hard fought for air left him with a disgusting wheeze. Having suffering many violent hits in his football career, Ashki did not succumb to attacks easily. Instead, he had learned to use adrenaline to heighten the senses, slow down time and speed the mind. In his moment of adrenaline-stretched time, he felt the hard shape of the phurba pressed against his chest. The demon had kicked him onto the place where Gesar had dropped it. He saw the room it minute detail, a crack in the tile, the trickle of blood on the wall behind Gesar's head, the gun under the bed, the discarded syringe and the malicious foot preparing to make a fatal kick. His stretched moment of time was only half over when the foot started its path toward his head. It seemed a simple matter to twist his torso, snatch the phurba, and aim for the planted back foot.

The blade penetrated surprisingly easily, passing through boot and bone before findings its way into the concrete floor. The blade then exploded into a sphere of intense white light. The demon's kick halted in midair. His face twisted into an expression of shock while the demon fire in his eyes flickered into darkness. When officer Cutter's body collapsed to the floor, the phurba had crumbled into harmless ash.

Gesar's was unprepared for what stepped out of the smoke and onto the south bank. He had seen Mahakala only once before, a three-eyed, six-armed horror chasing the Senge tapah across the Plain of Deception. Now here he was less than fifty paces away. The demon-god hesitated, his eyes scanning the bank for a victim while the horns of Kalapa palace echoed through the valley. Hidden in dense vegetation, Gesar was unnoticed at first, but then the demon-god seemed to draw on another sense and his ember eyes bore down on his position.

Gesar's bow was already fully drawn and his target selected. He loosed the arrow at the moment Mahakala's spiteful glare fixed upon him. The arrow shot to its mark, burying deep into the demon's third eye. Mahakala let out a dreadful howl, the sound erupted from the earth, shaking boulders and trees. Black fluid gushed from the wound as he ripped the arrow from his eye and tossed it into the river. Salvaging his composure, Mahakala focused his malice on the offending horse warrior and started climbing the steep bank, brushing aside small trees as if they were blades of grass.

"Run!"

Before the word escaped Gesar's mouth, Goba spun around and sprinted for the Shenla road,

When Gesar emerged from the forest, Ben and the other Senge were already assembled, organizing the retreat in response to the palace horns.

"Mahakala is coming!" Gesar yelled as he rode toward his comrades.

Before Gesar could join the group, Mahakala burst out of the forest behind him, his three pairs of arms blooming with an assortment of weapons.

Organized chaos ensued.

"Make for the palace!" Ben ordered. The Senge took to the road at full gallop.

With only the first of his nagu warriors reaching the south bank, Mahakala pursued the tapah alone. Infuriated and desperate for retribution, he pressed forward, steadily closing the gap between himself and his target, the dark horse with the blonde mane lagging at the rear.

Sensing the demon's approach, Goba sprinted forward out of weapons' reach. Looking over his shoulder, Gesar saw Mahakala grimace in frustration and cast his tilug, its curved blade arching overhead, spinning end over end in a deadly blur. Linked to Gesar's mind, Goba saw the same image and turned sharply. The tilug cut directly through the place where Goba had been and shattered a wall at the edge of the road. Ignoring his miss, Mahakala accelerated, cracking paving stones beneath his pounding mass. In moments, he had put the horse and rider within reach of his spiked club. He raised his weapon to crush Goba's flank, when suddenly a downpour of arrows peppered his arms and chest. With his third eye blinded, he failed to notice the Druk squadron appear overhead. Forced to abandon his single-minded pursuit, he halted desperately slapping away the arrows that rained down from a red sky filled with a swarm of dakinis. Finally he relented, defiantly shook his weapons at the dakinis, and then turned around to rejoin his army.

Goba's voice invaded Gesar's mind, "She is above."

Gesar understood and was suddenly relieved. "Someone must have stopped the demon hunter. Ashki, it must have been Dr. Ashki. He must have come looking for me. She's alive. She's safe."

Goba interrupted Gesar's celebratory moment. "Look ahead, rider," he warned.

Ahead in the distance, silhouettes of flying naga-ta hovered over dark bands of nagu brigades oozing from the hills to the east and southeast, all flowing toward Lake Shambala where a retreating unit of tapah crossed the Vishvamata ice bridge under the protection of a dakini squadron. The enemy was fast approaching and it was unlikely the Senge could reach the Tara quay before it was overtaken.

Goba's pace slowed. Gesar sensed weakness building in his horse's stride. "Goba, you've had no rest. Can you still run?"

"Your strength is my strength."

Gesar suddenly remembered that his body could be dying in the Human realm. He was probably broken and bleeding in a Marin County long-term care facility. At least, he could make the best of what time he had left in Shambala. Reaching for a source of inner strength he cried, "For Shambala and the Path!" Goba's steps lengthened and they caught up with the Senge column.

Overhead, the Druk dakinis, satisfied that Mahakala was not an immediate threat, changed formation and banked away to intercept the nagu advancing on Tara quay. It was up to the dakini squadrons to buy the precious time the Senge needed to reach the ice bridge.

Chidag's overturned sarcophagus shuddered. Both Jhado and Kubera turned their heads to the sound.

"Well, it appears Zerden's first born has awakened from his long sleep. I suspect he's not a morning person." Kubera giggled at his own joke. "I learned that phrase from one of the Buddha warriors." He added.

Jhado was certain that he had not woken Chidag, which meant that someone with better luck than his had successfully delivered a demon banisher in the Human realm. However, Chidag's siblings were still at large. Jhado's mind raced for a solution to his predicament, but every scenario ended badly. "It seems I have failed," Jhado admitted.

Kubera's flabby face formed a smile, and then he walked to Chidag's sarcophagus and sat upon it. "No, I beg to differ. I am here to ensure your success. I assume you have some means to wake the others. If so, I recommend that you do so now. I'm not sure how long I can restrain this one."

Jhado was stunned, but suddenly understood. Kubera was a secret ally. That was why he had kept in the shadows and failed to aid the dron warrior. "You, you were never one of the rebels."

"I must admit, I have been deceptive. When Mahakala convinced Yama and Changpo to join him, I thought it was best that someone should go along and keep an eye on them. I tried to delay Mahakala's siege as long as possible, but he can be irritatingly single-minded. I must say that your coming was quite unexpected. You may be the first Kalacakra to make it this far and that was quite a clever idea to use the sarcophagus to block the portal. Zerden uses his door to keep watch on this room, so I have been unable to do much about Chidag and his chums by myself. It's nice not being watched for a change. Now, you must do your part while I improvise an escape." The box beneath Kubera's mass quaked again.

Jhado did not hesitate. He sat in meditation pose, controlled his breath and repeated a sequence Bodhisattva mantras. The mantras were ancient sounds designed to purify the soul and everything with hearing range.

Om mani padme hum
Om ah ra pa tsa na dhih
Om maitri mahamaitri maitriye svaha
Om vajrapani hum

The sacred sounds filled the room and flowed through the foul space like a cleansing rain. With each repetition, Jhado's voice grew louder until the sanctuary of Naraka keep shook with revulsion and its rim of dispirited lamps brightened, pushing back the crushing darkness. Suddenly, Dang Ba's casket erupted with a tortured howl while Na Tsha hissed as his scaly arms reached out swinging violently at unseen attackers.

"They seem to waking. I believe this would be the appropriate time to leave." Kubera interrupted, lurching back and forth, as Chidag struggled to lift the sarcophagus.

When Jhado stopped singing, the sanctuary lamps dimmed again. Wondering what to do now, he turned to Kubera, who pointed a stubby finger between two columns at the side of dais. "There you will find a way out," the demon-god said, his rolls of fat rippling with each jolt of the casket. "I suggest that you hurry, I will deal with this."

"Will you be alright?" Jhado asked.

"I've already devised a plan. Now, go!"

Jhado ran and disappeared into the deep shadows between the columns. There, he found a hidden door leading to an unlit passage. Blinded by total darkness, he felt his way along a wall, stepping carefully and hoping not to fall into some hidden abyss. Other than a crash that briefly reverberated from the keep chamber, silence filled the darkness, leaving only the senses of touch and smell to guide him. The corridor turned sharply left then continued straight onward. From his rough memory of Naraka's layout, he surmised that he was going toward the inner keep apartments, not his preferred destination. To his relief, he reached an intersection. Opening all of his senses, he stopped and waited. A slight waft of air brushed his right cheek carrying the stench of Naraka's waste pits. Following the odor, he took a right turn and the corridor ran steeply downward. As he went deeper, the wall grew clammy to the touch and Naraka's distinctive stench intensified. When he reached bottom, his foot plunged into the source of the odor. After crossing a shallow stream of vile liquid, he started a steady upward climb on slippery cobblestones. He continued, having no idea how long he had been in Naraka's underground passages. In the darkness, he had lost all sense of time and distance. Finally, after seeming endless darkness, a glint of light beckoned. He followed it until Naraka's bowel disgorged him beyond its walls into blinding morning light.

When Jhado disappeared into the passage, Kubera wasted no time. He shuttled his huge bulk into the shadows with surprising speed. With Kubera's mass removed from his sarcophagus, Chidag hurled it away, sending it crashing down among his bewildered brothers, both incensed as they picked themselves up from the rubble of their own shattered caskets. The three baffled demons stared at each other warily, each wondering who was responsible for the affront. Who would dare wake them and desecrate their sleeping place?

A distressed Kubera suddenly appeared, rushing into the sanctuary from the hidden passage. "Comrades! Comrades!" He cried. "An enemy is in Naraka. He has violated the sanctuary and I see he has disturbed your rest. Thank Zerden! You are unharmed. Did you see him? It is fortunate that I arrived before he harmed you. He carries demon banishers. He blocked the sanctuary entrance and I had to use the underground passage from the keep. You were obviously his target. He must be hiding nearby. Until we find him, you should go to Zerden for guidance."

Chidag looked suspiciously at Kubera, his eyes burning with anger. While trapped under the sarcophagus, he was certain that he had heard the fat one's annoying voice. He started kicking through the rubble looking for some evidence that Kubera was lying, but his foot still smarted from the recent touch of a demon banisher and the thought that there could be more of them within the walls of Naraka keep was troubling. Relenting, he retrieved his four-bladed crux from the rubble and growled something incomprehensible to his brothers. A moment later, the three of them disappeared into the light swallowing portal.

"I doubt Zerden will to be happy to see them," Kubera whispered to himself as he turned away.

Dr. Ashki phoned for help and began treating the victims. To his relief, everyone was breathing except the attacker, a fact that surprised Ashki, since he had only wounded one foot and there was no bleeding. Ashki suspected that a cause of death would not be determined when the coroner performed an autopsy. Fortunately, the nurse and monk were regaining consciousness. Both suffered concussions, but would recover. Gesar was in the worst shape, likely having bled into his skull again. His breathing was shallow and pulse irregular.

"This is a damn medical facility. There's got to be some meds here." Ashki thought. Searching the halls, he found an abandoned medication cart and pushed it back to the room. Locating a syringe and a vial of prednisone, he administered a dose to Gesar to help stave off brain damage. He then started an intravenous line and hung a bag of saline. By the time the emergency response team arrived Gesar's vital signs had stabilized.

Ashki spent the remainder of his day in a police station, answering an endless string of questions. The sudden resurrection of Officer Cutter, who presumably died in a house fire, was no less a mystery then why he suddenly went on rampages in two Marin county long-term care facilities, killing at least two and attempting to kill four others. Despite every effort, the investigating detective could find no connection between Officer Cutter and Angela Adrastos or any of the other victims for that matter.

Ashki did not volunteer his other knowledge of the situation. Police detectives did not like metaphysical explanations for criminal acts. It was likely that when they questioned the young monk, he had also avoided mentioning anything paranormal. Fortunately, the case was so full of mysteries that the police overlooked more probing questions like, what were he and Gesar doing at the facility. Rather, they were particularly obsessed about the missing weapon that had pierced Officer Cutter's foot. Ashki bent the truth on that point.

The investigating detective scanned over the preliminary report as he spoke. "All Cutter had showing was a split lip and perfectly clean hole through his left shoe and foot. Just what did you stab him with?"

"I don't know exactly." Ashki lied. "It just was something on the floor where he knocked me down. After he knocked me down. I was stunned and just grabbed whatever it was that I fell on. I had to act quickly, he was about to kick me in the head."

"How do you suppose the weapon just vanished?" The detective asked suspiciously.

"I don't know. There was broken glass around, perhaps I used a shard of glass and it shattered."

"Maybe, we did find some glassy material on his boot. The forensic lab is testing it. It still doesn't explain why there was no blood around the wound."

Ashki offered a diverting explanation. "If his heart suddenly stopped before I stabbed him, there would be no bleeding would there?"

The detective's voice dripped with doubt. "Being a doctor, you would know better than I, but we'll wait and see if the coroner agrees with you."

Eventually the detective tired of the interview and released Ashki, who went to the hospital to check on Gesar. Attached to a web of wires and tubing, Gesar was in a deep coma, this time not artificially maintained. A head bandage covered a skull fracture and new trephine holes had been bored to drain blood from his brain.

Ashki reached into his pocket, removed a small Buddha figurine and set it on the bedside table. "I bought this on the way over. Funny what you can get in a twenty-four hour box store. I thought you could use someone to watch over you when I'm not here."

Silent, Gesar's chest rose and fell with steady breaths.

"Well my young friend, I really didn't think you'd be back in here so soon, but then you're probably not here are you?"

Gesar's closed eyelids quivered.

Ashki sat a short while watching Gesar dream. Before leaving, he took Gesar's hand, gently squeezed and said, "Warrior I will be back, I hope you find Angela and that horse of yours."

Exhausted, Ashki limped back to his car, his shoulder and hip burning with pain after the day's events. As soon as he got into his car, he reached into the glove compartment for a bottle of analgesic tablets. He swallowed them dry and then punched in a number with a New Mexico area code into his cell phone.

After several rings a familiar voice answered in the Dineh language, "Ya' ateeh."

"Ya' ateeh shi che," Ashki greeted.

"Shash, is that you?" The old voice used one of Ashki's nicknames, meaning bear, a not so subtle reference to his stature. At least it was better then his earlier childhood name, Tsiishch'ili, meaning curly locks.

"Aoo' Sani, it's me."

"Callin' kinda late heh? You're lucky I'm awake. Just came out of the hogan. Had a healin' tonight. Practically the whole clan up here."

"I'm really sorry to call so late, but I have a favor to ask."

"You know I'll do anything for you as long as you're not goin' to ask for money."

Ashki laughed. "No, but I'll gladly send you some."

"No, never touch the stuff. They don't take cash or visa in the spirit world, but I could use a new truck."

"I can probably help with that." Ashki offered.

"Just kiddin' Shash, I'd probably just wreck it. How can I help you?"

"Remember that young man I talked to you about?"

"Aoo', the spirit warrior."

"Yeah, well I think he's returned to the spirit world."

"You want me to check on him?"

"If you can,"Ashkii answered.

The old voice grew solemn. "Shash, there's trouble in that world. There's a cloud of lost spirits blindin' our vision. We believe a great war has begun. It has been in the dreams of all the hataathli."

Ashki paused then said, "Then it is too much to ask?"

"No. I will sing the song and try to find that one, but if I don't see him, it don't mean he's not there."

"Ahhee shi che," Ashki thanked and hung up.

As Mahakala's army congregated on the Shenla road, Changpa arrived with his force from the southwest pass. Mahakala was in no mood for pleasantries when Changpa jogged up with a grinning foreface.

"Take that moronic grin off your face. Your tardiness cost a third of my army. You were supposed to march to the Shenla road without delay." Mahakala accused.

Changpa's right face twisted forward and defended, "We planned to ignore the tapah and make straight for the road, but we couldn't resist, could we?"

"They drove our best spear unit into the Shenla rapids. They had to be punished," Changpa's left face joined in angrily.

"We chased them west and lost them in the canyons," spouted Changpa's rear face. "Somehow, they slipped by us. We saw them retreating for the palace, but unfortunately too far ahead to pursue."

"Such insolence, to think we trained some of those tapah," said foreface. "They must be punished when we take the palace."

"What happened to your eye?" interrupted Changpa's right face, noticing Mahakala's wound.

Mahakala ignored the question and howled in frustration. "Why didn't you use the naga-ta I gave you? You had naga-ta to be your eyes from above."

"They were occupied with dakinis," Changpa's rear face defended.

"All six of them?" Mahakala queried.

Changpa's left face grew sheepish. "Actually, three of them."

Mahakala howled again. "How could you lose three naga-ta?"

Right face answered, "Dakinis killed them over the pass."

"Kubera was right. We don't have enough naga-ta." Foreface added.

Mahakala looked up and saw a group of three blurs moving overhead. His third eye was beginning to regain its sight. Changpa's remaining naga-ta were attempting a crude flying formation.

"Look at them. They can't even form a simple spearhead. If that fat lout had trained the riders better, they would have been more than enough." He complained.

"Compared to kinnaras, they do tend to lumber," Changpa's right face observed.

"Though you must admit, they are quite sturdy," replied rear face.

"Enough!" spat Mahakala, shaking his spiked club. "There's no time for your inane commentary. Did you at least build the siege barges?"

"Of course," foreface replied. "A construction detail was dispatched as soon as we entered the valley as planned. They should be on the river not far behind us."

Mahakala relaxed. "Good, you're not a complete fool. And speaking of fools, it appears that Yama is nearing the quay."

Changpa's right face twisted foreword, "It's disappointing that neither Palden nor the other Guardians have challenged us. I was looking forward to a good earth shaking fight like in the old days."

"You should be more suspicious than disappointed." Mahakala chided. "I expected Betsge to be on this side of the river, but he and the others are keeping to the palace. I am beginning to suspect they are afraid to take their demon forms, perhaps they fear the transformation will weaken their faith. If so, this could be to our advantage. We need only to force them to revert to their original forms."

Changpa's left face turned forward with a grotesquely quizzical expression and asked, "How do we do that?"

"We use their weaknesses. After two thousand years, you must have assessed your fellow Guardians for weaknesses. I certainly know Palden's."

"You always were the mistrusting and conniving one." Changpa's rear face mumbled.

"Foresight and planning have always served me well," countered Mahakala. "Now gather your army, we must join Yama at the quay. If you hurry, you will have the satisfaction of destroying at least one tapah unit."

The Senge met Yama's army at the crossroad where the Shenla River and Emerald roads converged with the Kalapa road from the southeast pass. In the center of the wide crossroad, Shambala's great golden Buddha statue sat on a massive stone pedestal. Bearing a serene expression, the Enlightened One held up an open palm, both welcoming and warding with a single gesture. His serenity starkly contrasted with the frenzied battle that raged around his pedestal. On the paved avenue, Senge spears collided with enemy shields with a deafening crash amidst a cacophony of clanging swords and crushing clubs. In the rear of the enemy line, the demon-god, Yama, whipped reluctant stragglers with his razor lasso, urging his nagu legions forward onto tapah spear points. In the sky, swarms of dakinis darted back and forth attempting to drive away a flock of naga-ta, providing cover for the enemy front line.

Despite a desperate effort to cut a path through the nagu horde, a wall of half-living flesh halted the Senge advance. They fought to prise open even the narrowest crack through the northwest corner of the crossroad to give access to the Tara quay, but the enemy pressed in from both north and south, blocking the way.

Exposing a grisly expanse of teeth, Yama's pus-dripping face grinned in satisfaction as he watched the Senge advance grind to a halt, trapped between the high walls bordering the Shenla road. His army pressed their front while the forces of Mahakala and Changpa marched on their rear. He was pleased that Palden and the others would witness the Senge tapah exterminated on their doorstep.

Gesar could hear the drums of Mahakala's advancing force as Goba trotted to a stop at the rear of the Senge column. The column of warhorses jostled with frustration, unable to advance to assist their comrades battling at the front. Gesar looked behind, searching for a alternative route of retreat but Goba quenched his hopes. "It is too late. They have reached the Nyrima road."

"Then, it looks like it ends here," Gesar said.

"I cannot know the end until it comes." Goba replied.

Gesar patted Goba's neck then looked overhead to watch the wild dance of dakinis locked in a ferocious aerial battle to reclaim the air space over the crossroad. He could only hope that Ane was among them and regretted that he would not see her again. Knowing that the demon hunter in the Human realm had failed provided some solace. At least, she was spared a meaningless death.

Lady Palden surveyed the battle from the Kalapa ramparts; her spirit was heavy with doubt after seeing the pitiful flicker of light struggling to stay alive on the throne of Sangpo Bumtri. Having never suffered such an assault since its creation, the once formidable pillar of light that protected Shambala might never regain its power. To add to her burden, the Senge tapah were fighting for survival because she delayed sounding the final retreat until the return of the Drizai tapah, who had been delayed eluding the four-faced rebel demon-god, Changpa, in the canyons of the west valley.

Palden closed her eyes and felt a wave of emotion. She was deeply saddened at the thought of Mahakala and the other rebel demon-gods, drunk on blood lust and bestial egotism. Again, she was surprised by the strange feelings and realized that the centuries in service as a Guardian of Shambala must indeed have changed her. She no longer hated nor denied the enemies of the path. They were simply misguided sentients trapped in the lower realms. The rebel demon-gods had chosen to step backward into a world of perpetual, but familiar ignorance.

The situation reminded her of a story she had once learned from a Kalacakra lama. It told of two monks who lived like brothers and when they died were reincarnated, one as a heavenly being and the other as a lowly dung worm. When the heavenly brother tried to help his friend into heaven, the worm brother irately refused, preferring the familiarity of his warm dark dung heap. In the same way, the traitorous demon-gods had rejected the opportunity to be more than a dung worm, but these demon dung worms wanted to keep all sentient beings in the dung heap with them. Ironically, they wished to subjugate the very humans who had offered them a path to freedom. If the rebels succeeded, they would set back the advance of consciousness and prolong the suffering of humankind for yet more millennia.

Palden opened her eyes, tears blurring the swarm of dakinis that struggled to save the Senge tapah trapped at the crossroad. "It is up to you," she whispered.

A spiked tail nearly impaled Ane as she slashed an arm length hole in the naga-ta's leathery wing. She looked over her shoulder hoping for some effect, but the huge beast's course was unchanged. The dark mass of scales twisted, spread its wings like a giant broom and swept down upon a dakini archer group. The naga-ta were getting progressively more difficult to defeat. They and their nagu riders had improved their tactics, learning to protect each other, while effectively harrying dakini archers.

When Brug banked away for another attack, Ane gained a panoramic view of the battle. The demon-god Yama stood on a nagu-blackened hill, cracking his razor whip and driving his army into the crossroad. Above, most of Kalapa's eight exhausted dakini squadrons fought naga-ta while groups of dakini archers attempted to slip below the aerial fray to take shots at the nagu frontline, but their efforts were ineffective. Only a steady shower of arrows could help the trapped Senge column. On the Shenla road, Mahakala's nagu army approached the rear of the Senge column with alarming speed and beyond them, an ominous armada of barges floated downriver.

Ane signaled her squadron that she was breaking off. "Sweep in Brug," she directed. "We have to find a way."

"Yes mistress." Brug answered in his usual unflappable tone.

Brug turned and dove, then leveled off in a flight path toward the crossroad. Passing over the massive Buddha, Brug's talons grazed the statue's head, which let out low-pitched ring. Though barely audible over the clash of weapons and war cries, the sound was enough to awaken a possibility in Ane's mind. Then, as Brug turned away from the crossroad, Ane caught a glimpse of a dark horse with a blonde mane at the very end of the Senge column.

"That's Gesar," she said, startled by the joy she felt.

"Yes, mistress."

"He's at the rear. Mahakala will reach him first."

218

"That is a truth, mistress."

"Brug, we have to help. I have a plan. Do you understand my intention?"

"As always, mistress."

"I need a big spiteful one, Brug."

"As you wish, mistress."

Brug beat his wings to gain altitude. Flying well above the aerial battle, he circled to scan the pack of naga-ta. Among the larger beasts, was an especially aggressive one, who chased his attackers, snapping at them with his jaws or thrashing with his spiked tail.

"Can you handle that one?" Ane asked.

"Of course, mistress."

"Brug, don't be overconfident. This won't be easy and it's going to test us to the limit. We might not survive, and either way, I just hope we'll be forgiven for what were about to do."

"I'm never brash, mistress," Brug answered.

"Brug, sometimes you're impossible. I have a long list of experiences to counter that claim, but I don't have the time. Now go!"

Brug closed his wings and dove for the vicious naga-ta, which snapped at a nearby dakini while its nagu rider followed with a volley of arrows. In freefall, Ane's steadied her sword arm against the rush of air. Her strategy depended on blinding speed and perfectly timed sword strike. Though it was a common dakini maneuver, she had never tried the dive and strike on a flying target. As she approached, the naga-ta loomed like a small island in the sky, with its nagu rider a tiny figure sitting in a saddle. With a thunderous clap, Brug's wings snapped opened and his talons spread, ripping deep gouges in the flank of the naga-ta while Ane separated a hand from its rider with a clean cut through the wrist. Both beast and rider shrieked.

"He can't ignore that one. Now move it, Brug!" Ane cried.

On Ane's command, Brug banked away just as a spiked tail swept by him like a sadistic flyswatter. Brug turned and hovered a moment in full view of the naga-ta and its rider. Then, after offering a defiant screech, he folded his wings and plunged away. The outraged naga-ta shrieked and dove in pursuit.

Sheathing her sword, Ane tightened both hands on Brug's rein. "Okay Brug. That was the easy part."

Brug controlled his dive, keeping just beyond the reach of the naga-ta's snapping jaws while carefully directing his pursuer in a flight path from southwest to northeast toward the crossroad. Brug accelerated as the crossroad drew closer. Driven by blind wrath, the naga-ta shrieked and followed with mad abandon.

The great golden Buddha waited calmly with one palm raised. Three men, standing one upon the other would barely span the length of that single golden hand welcoming seekers of the Path while warding its enemies. Suddenly, the giant palm was there, gleaming brightly in spite of the smoke dimmed sky. Brug exploded every wing and tail feather, creating a cushion of breaking air. Deftly, he rode that cushion and passed safely over the top of the statue, his tail feathers gently brushing the Buddha's smooth forehead. With ten times more momentum and far less agility, the pursuing naga-ta's fate was sealed. With immense force, it slammed into the giant Buddha, lifting the huge statue off its pedestal and sending it crashing onto the nagu army with an earthshaking clang. The massive statue filled the entire northeast corner of the crossroad, while the naga-ta fell into an unmoving heap in the southwest corner, its neck broken on the edge of the golden Buddha's palm. Its ejected rider was cast onto a carpet of raised spears. For a moment, the battle halted as both armies looked on in shocked amazement. Realizing what Ane had done, Ben sounded his horn to rally the Senge. With Yama's reserves cut off, the horse warriors pressed forward and quickly cleared a path to the quay road.

The sight of the naga-ta colliding with the massive Buddha statue and sending it tumbling from its pedestal temporarily mesmerized Gesar and the other Senge. Fortunately, their horses remained composed and followed their instinct to run the moment the way ahead was open. Goba carried Gesar forward not a moment too soon, for enemy arrows began to fall where they had been. They were the last to reach the Vishvamata ice bridge. Not far behind, nagu-forces were in pursuit, pouring through a demolished a section of the wall that bordered the lake roads. Without losing stride, Goba's hooves struck the mysterious ice, so thin that fish were visible beneath it, yet so strong that it could hold the weight of a thousand mounted warriors at full gallop. Ahead, the Senge column was disappearing into the Vishvamata passage. Behind, dakini squadrons harassed the nagu frontline, slowing their advance. To the west, Gesar saw the first of the huge siege barges appear out of the marshes, each poled and paddled by at least a hundred nagu warriors. Mahakala had planned well. He had devised a means to overcome Kalapa's defensive water barrier.

As Gesar passed beneath the bejeweled Vishvamata mandala, the ice-bridge melted and horns sounded from the palace ramparts calling the dakini squadrons to retreat. After going from fry pan to fire, the quiet climb through the Vishvamata passage to the Diamond courtyard was a relief, but the tunnel was darker than Gesar remembered. The sky's dismal rust-red overcast had dimmed the light that normally illuminated the tunnel, another defense lost.

The Senge assembled beneath the mirrored wall of the Diamond courtyard, where Ben consulted with an officer bearing the Dharma Wheel insignia on his tunic. After counting heads, Ben issued orders. "The enemy is at our threshold, so we will have to honor our lost brothers later. Presently, we are to stable our mounts and report immediately to the south ramparts. During the siege, we under command of the palace guard."

Gesar looked to the sky where dakini formations flew in silence to their assembly points on the temple mount plaza. Goba's voice interrupted his thoughts. "Do not worry. She is among them."

The rebel demon-gods stood amongst the devastation at the crossroad as the massive naga-ta carcass was slowly dragged away by a company of nagu warriors. Mahakala had ordered the crossroad cleared to accommodate the nagu legions waiting to march to Tara quay. Meanwhile, on the waters of Lake Shambala, other nagu companies positioned and lashed together siege barges to form a broad floating bridge.

"Twice now Palden's pet has used Kubera's naga-ta against us. The beasts are more trouble than their worth." Yama grumbled.

"They are unpredictable in battle," added Changpa's foreface.

Mahakala considered Yama's complaint. It was true that the naga-ta had been a disappointment, but despite their failings, he had taken the valley. Of more concern was that clever captain of the Druk dakini who Yama called 'Palden's pet'. He was surprised that she was still alive. Chidag Nagpo should have destroyed her and others in the Human realm. That mission was apparently less than successful. "No matter," he countered. "We control the quay with much of our force intact and Zerden will send more through the portals. Soon the bridge will be complete and we can begin the siege."

Changpa's left face piped in. "Just what do you have in mind? The bridge will get our armies across the lake, but you well know that the Vishvamata passage can be defended almost indefinitely."

"Perhaps against nagu, but not against us," Mahakala scoffed.

"Excellent!" cried Changpa's foreface. "Finally, we get to lead the attack. I was getting quite bored hanging around in the rear."

"I thought you wanted us to remain in the rear. Why the sudden change?" Yama asked suspiciously.

One of Mahakala's eyes monitored the progress of the floating bridge while the other two glared at Yama. "Have you noticed that Palden and the other guardians have not challenged us since we entered the valley?"

"I took them for cowards." Yama answered.

"Don't be a fool. They're not afraid of us. They're afraid of becoming like us. I am convinced that they fear to revert to their original forms because it might kindle desires that they cannot resist. We need only to provoke them and they will join us."

Yama snapped his whip to hasten the nagu clean up crew. "How can you be so certain? They might be setting an elaborate trap."

"Perhaps, but there's nothing they can do to stop us now. The Shield has fallen and they've wasted their phurbas on the plains and in the passes. Even if they try to block us with more phurbas, we will take the walls of Kalapa apart stone by stone." Mahakala said, emphasizing his point by kicking a huge block of stone from the shattered pedestal.

Changpa drew his sword and his foreface spoke, "Enough talk, let's get started and to think that you call us chatty."

Black pus dripped impatiently from Yama's deformed face "Remember, Palden's pet is mine," he added.

When Tenzin rolled the meditation chamber door aside, Jhado stumbled out of the dark opening. He reached for Tenzin's shoulder and asked, "How long?"

"Your holiness, it has been one day."

"Just a day?" Jhado whispered in disbelief. For him, it felt like a week had passed. He had expended a lot of energy in a short time. He had crossed the Plain of Deception twice, surreptitiously entered Naraka keep, fought off an elite dron warrior, and narrowly escaped Zerden's hell spawn. In all honesty, he never expected to see Dagpa Akar again, at least not in this lifetime.

Jhado felt his legs start to buckle and leaned on Tenzin for support. The old monk asked, "Your holiness, are you well?"

"I'm just weary, my friend."

"Did you succeed in your task?" Tenzin queried as he shouldered Jhado's weight.

"Yes."

The old monk's worry-furrowed forehead relaxed a little. "Then that is our first good news."

As they passed the other meditation chambers, Jhado noticed that they were still sealed. "Has there been any news from Kalapa?" Jhado asked.

"Yes, Brother Nawang returned briefly with a report from Lady Palden."

The two men started up the spiral staircase. Jhado's legs ached with each step. "What was Lady Palden's message?" He asked.

"Your holiness, I hoped to tell you after you've rested a little." Tenzin answered.

"There is no need. Tell me brother Nawang's report?"

Tenzin paused, as if reluctant to answer. Staring into the flickering flame of his oil lamp, he mustered the courage to speak. "Our greatest fear has come to pass. The Shield has fallen and the flame of Shambala is nearly extinguished. The valley is overrun and Shambala's defenders are preparing for the siege of Kalapa."

"Have you informed the other temples?"

"Yes, your holiness. I posted a message shortly after brother Nawang's return."

"Then it seems the phurbas delivered by the Sun Tribesmen were too few and too late." Jhado replied.

"Yes, but Brother Nawang reports that Sister Kensang has proposed a plan to use the phurbas that the great Lady Palden believes has merit."

The details would come later, but Jhado's intuition regarding Sister Kensang was proving valuable. She was wise beyond her years. Jhado was breathless upon reaching the upper level. Tenzin pushed the final door open and the two emerged from behind the great Buddha tapestry and stepped into the empty dukhang. As usual, the scent of incense hung in the air.

Jhado tripped and caught hold of the tapestry for support. "Tenzin, I think you are right. I will rest a little. The fall of the Shield is grave news. Whatever Sister Kensang's has planned, no number of phurbas can replace it. Without the Shield, the siege will continue until Zerden's armies have defiled the valley and raised Kalapa palace."

$hingdong, the Senge stable master, offered a subdued but warm greeting when Gesar and Goba trotted into the stable. "Welcome back young tapah, I am happy that Goba has again found his rider. That one never faltered in waiting for you."

"I missed him too and it is good to see you again, Shingdong," Gesar said as he dismounted. He helped Shingdong remove Goba's forelock and chest armor, but left the saddle on in case the unit had to mobilize during the siege.

Parting from Goba was painful. "I'm sorry Goba, we've been called to the ramparts. I must leave you with Shingdong. There's no room for horses up there, besides you and the other mounts need rest."

"You must not die without me, rider." Goba's voice rang in Gesar's mind with a hint of desperation.

"I promise. I won't." Gesar said, patting Goba's withers.

"Then I will wait." Goba answered.

After stroking Goba's muzzle, Gesar joined a group of Senge tapah, mounting seemingly endless flights of steps up to the ramparts. When they reached the top, officers of the palace guard directed the men to take up long bows and join the line of archers on the crenulated parapet. Urns of burning pitch were spaced at intervals along with sheaves of arrows, ready for lighting. Gesar found an open crenellation and took his position.

The high ramparts were usually constantly wind swept, but presently only a faint breeze stirred the air. Overhead, the sky turned blood red as a haze-obscured sun descended in the west. On the Tara quay, fresh nagu troops gathered in phalanxes and waited in the shadows of their demon-god generals. Below on the lake, the enemy positioned and lashed together huge siege barges. Flaming arrows rained down upon them from the ramparts but the waterlogged decks refused to catch fire. Shambala's defenders had already fought through a night and a day fueled only by draughts of amrita. Now, they faced yet another night of battle. The most they could do was to slow construction of the floating bridge by reducing the numbers of paddling and lashing nagu.

As Gesar surveyed the huge barges in search of a suitable target, a voice surprised him. "Don't wait too long. It will soon be too dark to find a target."

Gesar turned to face a captain of the palace guard, a tall man with broad chest and arms nearly as thick as his thighs. He carried a pike more than twice his height and his face bore a resolute expression, but his eyes betrayed a hidden sadness. Gesar was about to offer a formal greeting, when the man raised a staying hand.

"No need for formalities," he said. "I'm Tashi, captain of the Shar-log guard. I don't believe we have met."

Gesar recognized Shar-log, the Tibetan word for southeast. Like the tapah and dakini, the palace guard consisted of eight units named for the cardinal and noncardinal directions of the section of wall they were assigned to defend. Unlike, the tapah and dakinis, the palace guard was not segregated by sex and all wore the same Dharma Wheel insignia.

Gesar nodded, giving deference to his superior and then answered, "I'm Gesar Despa, hindmost of the Senge tapah."

An understanding half smile broke on Tashi's face. Every tapah held the title of 'hindmost' at the beginning of their service. The hindmost was often the 'butt' of jokes as a lesson in humility.

"Welcome to ranks of Shambala's defenders, but I fear our service may be coming to an end. Mahakala has proved to be as clever as he is ruthless."

Gesar was uncomfortable with Tashi's fatalistic tone, but he had to admit that Mahakala was a remarkable strategist. It was hard to believe that a creature with such a horrid form could be intelligent. Demon-gods adopted grotesque forms to invoke fear as a means to intimidate and paralyze enemies. Apparently, the transformation left their wits relatively intact, compromised only by exaggerated emotions and impulsive behavior.

"He certainly timed the attack well." Gesar agreed. "Now he will have darkness to protect his force against our arrows."

"And he has those." Tashi said, pointing a finger across the lake where dark shapes of naga-ta circled in the sky.

"They're carrying something." Gesar observed.

"Some sort of rigging. No doubt, a weapon meant to be used against us."

"What do we have to use against them?" asked Gesar.

"We have ballistae, but they are not ideal for moving targets and we might accidentally hit our own dakinis in a melee. Our best hope..."

A blast of horns interrupted Tashi's words and the steady shower of fire arrows suddenly halted. A flock of dakinis lifted from the temple plaza and dove toward the floating bridge, which was nearing completion. Each kinnara grasp in its talons a rope tied to a tapered plummet stone. Taking up formation high over the siege bridge, the kinnaras released their burdens. Mayhem ensued as logs splintered and nagu warriors tumbled into the icy lake. For a brief time, the bridge rocked violently, threatening to break apart, yet when the waters calmed it remained, battered but intact. The surviving nagu scrambled to make repairs and lash the final barge in place.

Not willing to have his bridge tested again, Mahakala ordered the siege to begin. A thunder of drums mixed with guttural war cries arose from the direction of the quay. The huge bulks of Mahakala, Yama, and Changpa stepped onto the bridge, trailed by their armies. Above them, the remaining groups of naga-ta flew ahead carrying massive boulders cradled in chain rigging.

"By the Buddha's hand!" Tashi exclaimed. "The demon-gods are leading the siege."

Gesar was confused by Tashi's reaction. "Was that not expected?"

"No. Until now, they have stayed in the rear, sending their nagu forces in first. Three units of the palace guard are defending the Vishvamata passage. They are going to be slaughtered."

As Tashi spoke, the naga-ta were fast approaching while several squadrons of dakinis closed to engage them. On the ramparts, a thousand torches were set ablaze to challenge the growing darkness. Enemy drums grew louder and torch flames vibrated with each thunderous beat. In response, a chorus of kinnara voices split the air with their battle cry, causing the enemy drumbeat to falter.

Lady Palden's pupils glowed like twin embers as she spoke. "Ane, this war stirs strange feelings in me. I want to hate them, but I cannot. They were sworn defenders of Shambala, my confidants, and Mahakala, my consort. For once, our wretched immortal existence had meaning but they would rather be monsters. Their betrayal should ignite my desire for revenge, but instead I feel pain and sadness. I have changed, but what has happened to them? How could they choose to go back to being mindless beasts?"

Ane was shocked when Palden addressed her by her first name and never had the leader of the faithful guardians expressed such emotional conflict, at least not to a mortal. Palden had seemed composed throughout the crisis, but presently she was like a confused friend, desperately searching for answers. An immortal demon-god seeking emotional support from a mortal was a difficult notion to accept.

Ane ventured a response. "I suppose it is hard to be a servant after being the master for so long."

It was the wrong response. Palden's ember eyes flared. "We were never masters! We were slaves to our perversions, attempting to satisfy insatiable hungers. Mahakala and the others are simply serving their lust for domination. I know their minds. Like a pack of hungry wolves, they will come without mercy. They have scented our weakness and wetted their sordid appetites. We cannot count on Sangpo Bumtri to save us; his flame is nearly extinguished. We must rely on courage and cleverness to buy us time. Sister Kensang's plan is our only hope to delay them. Do you understand what you must do?"

Ane forced herself to look back into those glowing eyes. "Yes, Lady Palden."

"Then, I leave it to you to choose who will assist you. Now go, quickly. I hear the enemy drums. The siege has begun."

Ane bowed before taking her leave and then ran to where Brug waited on the plaza. She leapt onto Brug's back and was airborne before settling into the saddle's knee wells. From the temple steps, Palden raised a palm in blessing. Ane sensed sadness in the gesture. She's lonely, Ane suddenly realized. She was trying to cope with a crisis with no one to talk to, at least no other woman. Ane had had Dolma to share her fears and triumphs, but Palden had no one. I will do better next time, Ane thought, but for now she had to fight for that next time.

"Brug, we will need a tapah with a fast mount."

"Yes mistress, he is on the southern wall."

"What do you mean? Who is on the wall?" Ann challenged.

"The one who lingers in your mind," Brug countered.

"Gesar," she admitted. "I guess it's pointless to deny it."

"Your thoughts are my thoughts, mistress."

227

She thought of what would be required of the tapah that she selected and said, "But he's new, the hindmost of the Senge. I should choose a senior or a captain."

"He defeated you mistress," Brug reminded.

Her argument with Brug was selfish resistance; she knew what she had to do. "Very well, go to him."

"I will mistress, but the enemy may reach him first."

Ane looked ahead and as Brug warned, a naga-ta had broken through the dakini battle line and was bearing down on the south rampart.

Kalapa's ancient wall trembled. Instinctively, Gesar covered his face as a section of wall exploded sending a shower of stone plunging into the lake below. The naga-ta 'wrecking ball' hit less than fifty paces from Gesar. The palace guard positioned on that section of wall vanished in flash of light. For a moment, the light illuminated the naga-ta's mammoth shape before it disappeared into the deepening darkness.

"Prepare yourself!" Tashi cried. "It will come again."

As if on cue, the naga-ta's terrible shriek cut through the air. Ignoring the dakinis attempting to slash its wings, the beast swung around, taking a path that would drag its wrecking ball through the line of defenders posted on the wall.

"Move back!" Tashi ordered.

In response, both palace guard and tapah reinforcements retreated from their positions, but not Tashi. Instead, he leapt onto the wall and angled his long pike toward the incoming naga-ta. Balanced on a parapet hundreds of feet over the lake, he braced the butt of his pike against a crenellation and waited, his jaw fixed with stony resolve. Again, the wall shuddered as the boulder hit and was dragged toward Tashi's position, smashing ballistae and toppling buckets of burning pitch in its path. Tashi remained impassive, his thickly muscled arms bulging as he tightened his grip on his barbed pike.

The beast met the pike with a jolt. The naga-ta shrieked and drew back its wings, extinguishing nearby flames in a sudden storm of turbulent air. The pike sunk deep in the beast's underbelly just in front of its harness, but the wound was not mortal. Beating its wings, the naga-ta lifted from the wall carrying away Tashi, who held fast, his left arm gripping the pike shaft as he drew his sword with his right. For a time, the beast disappeared over the lake with only the sound of its shrieks piercing the dark and then suddenly, it appeared in the light of Kalapa's torches without its rider. Flying erratically, it writhed back and forth, frantically trying to tear Tashi off with its fangs. Just out of reach of its snapping jaws, Tashi hung on, hacking at the beast's legs. He had already severed one leg, leaving the "wrecking ball" rigging dangling askew. Relentlessly, he chopped at the remaining leg, steadily cleaving through flesh and bone. In a final act of desperation, the beast whipped its spiked tail beneath its underbelly, impaling Tashi and sending him tumbling into darkness, but in doing so, it ripped away its remaining leg and chain rigging. Before the wounded beast could retreat, the dakinis, who had held back in fear of harming their comrade, closed in and slashed until the beast followed Tashi into the lake's black water.

One of the dakinis separated from the others, landed on the wall, and walked to where Kalapa's defenders still reeled after witnessing Tashi's dramatic sacrifice. Gesar was among them, standing on a piece of shattered parapet, staring down into the dark lake with an expression of confused expectation as if Tashi would miraculously reappear.

"Gesar, are you all right?"

Ane's voice shook him from his daze. He turned to the voice, eyes widening in sudden recognition. She's alive. A sudden wave of joy dashed against his wall of grief. Under other circumstances, he might have succumbed to an urge to jump from his perch and embrace her. Instead, he offered a formal salute and apology. "Forgive me, captain. I wasn't paying attention. It's just that Tashi.... I only just met him."

"There's nothing to forgive. I understand and call me Ane," she said, reaching up and offering a hand.

Letting her hand guide him, he stepped off the block of stone. Sensing the warmth of her hand, he suddenly remembered cradling that same hand with its thin contracted fingers in the Marin County nursing facility. Here, in Asura, her hand was strong and callused by sword practice. Despite her physical strength, her lips and eyelids trembled, struggling to hold back her own grief.

"He could have tried another way. He didn't have to sacrifice himself like that," Gesar lamented.

Ane looked into Gesar's eyes as she spoke. "It was his wish. He chose to follow his consort. Her name was Dolma. She was my friend and lieutenant. Yesterday, she was taken from us. Tashi loved her very much and her loss wounded him deeply. Now, they journey the bardos together. They both fell bravely, defending Shambala and the Path. Though their loss fills us all with sorrow, we must grieve for them later. As we speak, the rebel demon-gods are in the Vishvamata passage."

"Is that why you're here?" Gesar asked.

Ane released Gesar's hand, surprised by her desire to not let go. She desperately wanted to release the feelings that her discipline held at bay. War intensified emotions and the appreciation of life. Since her appearance in Shambala, she had never felt such an attraction, such a distraction. She fantasized shedding her emotional armor and relaxing into his embrace. But she could not risk distractions, not now. Regaining her composure, she answered. "There is a plan. Lady Palden has requested that I assemble a team to execute it. I need a skilled tapah with a fast mount. I saw you on the field with the Senge. There is none faster than Goba."

Watching from his roost on the wall, Brug suddenly invaded Ane's mind. "That is not the whole truth, he also defeated you mistress."

She ignored Brug's internal commentary. "It going to be dangerous, are you willing?"

"Of course, but I am hindmost of the Senge. Are you sure you want me?" Gesar asked.

"You may be hindmost, but you are the only tapah who has bested me in sword combat and Goba is the only horse who can keep pace with Brug. Now, go to Goba and join me at the west gate of the Diamond courtyard, immediately. I will ask Captain Jigme to release you."

"But you haven't told me the plan."

"I will explain everything in the courtyard. Now hurry! The defenders in the Vishvamata passage cannot hold off three demon-gods for long."

Gesar bowed and ran for the Senge stables, never telling her how happy he was to see her again nor how he had been ready to die to protect her.

Two of Mahakala's six arms beat the flames dripping down his chest while his others deflected a volley of well-aimed spears. His gang of demon-gods was making slow progress through the Vishvamata passage. He had not reckoned on the mindless behavior of his fellow rebels, who in their enthusiasm to inflict carnage were constantly getting in each other's way. The tunnel was simply too narrow to accommodate three demon-gods fighting shoulder-to-shoulder. He had also underestimated the resistance put up by Kalapa's defenders. They had devised an effective defense, alternating volleys of burning pitch with spear and arrow attacks, forcing them to beat out flames and pull barbed pikes from their flesh. In spite of his miscalculation, Mahakala was not overly concerned. They were advancing steadily up the incline toward the Diamond courtyard. Soon they would have plenty of shoulder room to establish a beachhead for their nagu armies to begin the sacking of Kalapa.

ooking from a high monastery window with his teacher-guardian at his side, Jhado's eyes were wide with wonder as thousands of lamps wrapped the town in a sphere of golden light. He was a child, his small hands grasping the windowsill as he stood on tip-toe to get a better view. It was the Butter Lamp Festival, a celebration performed at the climax of the New Year festival. His teacher gently placed an age-spotted hand on his shoulder. "Little Bodhisattva, do you know why the people give light on this day?"

The answer came easily to the child Jhado. "They give the light of pure consciousness to honor the Enlightened One."

"You are partly correct. They give light not just to honor the Enlightened One, but also to add their light to his. Every enlightened being brightens the future of humanity."

Jhado woke in darkness with his teacher's words echoing in his mind. The exhaustion he had felt upon his return from Asura was mostly gone. After emerging from the meditation cell, Tenzin had helped him to his chambers, prepared a meal and warmed his bed with a hot iron. The latter was a luxury that Jhado felt some guilt about, but Tenzin insisted on pampering. Admittedly, the warm bed had helped him rest, but more importantly, the sleep had fostered a dream that sparked understanding.

"Tenzin!" Jhado called into the dark.

A crack of light appeared as the chamber door opened and Tenzin entered carrying a lamp. "I am here, your holiness."

"What is the time?"

"It is nearly midnight your holiness." Tenzin answered.

"I need to use the computer. Are the batteries charged?"

"Yes, there should be some power remaining, there was some sunshine today."

"Good. I must contact the other temples immediately. There may be a way for us to assist Shambala."

As Jhado turned to go to his adjoining office, Tenzin said, "I will light the lamps and bring tea."

"Thank you Tenzin. Hot tea would be welcome."

After washing and putting on a fresh robe, Jhado went to his office, where a fresh pot of tea waited on his desk and the room was aglow in warm lamplight. Tenzin's efficiency was nothing less than miraculous. Jhado turned on the computer and poured a cup of tea. It was a relief when the display came to life, but more so when the Haiku posting site appeared. He first looked for messages posted by his fellow lamas who headed Kalacakra temples throughout the world. After a brief search, he found several new poems. The most recent was Tenzin's communication regarding the fall of the Shield. There was little room for hope in Tenzin's words.

The ancient roof falls
On starless night cruel rain seeks
Our hearth's last embers
Dan Poe

The other messages were from the Kalacakra temples reporting on the incarnate demons they had detected. They had been posted before Tenzin's report of the breaching of the Shield and offered more welcome news.

Wounded beast retreats
From white stag with broken tine
While fawn sleeps in peace
Kasa

A hungry bird dives
As scorpion lifts stinger
Never to touch prey
Monkee

The old grey cat sleeps
With full belly in winter
Undisturbed by rats
Beowulf

The poems confirmed that the incarnated demons were no longer an immediate threat to the Sleepers in the Human realm. Regrettably, Kasa's reference to a stag with a "broken tine" indicated that his group had suffered more losses in dealing with Chidag Nagpo. Kasa's people had managed to banish the creature with a phurba, a dangerous act even for the most advanced Kalacakra adept. It was not surprising they had paid dearly to protect the Sleepers under their care, but their victory was only a reprieve. Without the Shield, Kalapa palace would eventually fall and Zerden would certainly send more of his offspring to Human realm. The fate of humanity might depend on a dream. The dream-teacher's words, "every enlightened being brightens the future of humanity," offered a spark of hope. Jhado struggled to compress his instructions into a three-line, twenty-two syllable poem.

Enlightened children
Embrace the dying ember
And hope is reborn
Dan Poe

He prayed his agents would understand the words as an instruction to act. They should know that "enlightened children" referred to the Kalacakra initiates and adepts. In order to "embrace the dying ember," they must recapitulate the Kalacakra initiation journey when they first freely offered themselves to the throne of Sangpo Bumtri. Jhado's dream had been a revelation. He had always thought that the power of Shambala emanated from the throne, but that was a misconception. The throne was a beacon fueled by the pure consciousness of thousands of Kalacakra who had merged with it throughout the ages. For Jhado's plan to work, every living Kalacakra in the Human realm had to be mobilized.

"Tenzin," Jhado called.

The old monk appeared almost instantly, "What is your will, your holiness?"

"Wake Dagpa Akar. Call everyone to the dukhang and prepare for an initiation ceremony. We have no more than two days. "

"Yes your holiness." Tenzin answered with a puzzled expression. Preparations for such a ceremony usually required weeks.

As Tenzin left, Jhado posted another poem so there would be no question as to urgency.

The novice asks when?
The Bodhisattva replies,
There is only now.
Dan Poe

Kalapa's defenders were losing the battle for the Vishvamata portal as Ane handed the phurba to Gesar. "This is the last one," she said. "The rest are held by others who will plant them the moment that you block the portal. Hide it well beneath your cloak. Mahakala must not suspect our intention. When the rebel demons emerge from the portal, we will mount a feint attack against them. In the confusion, you make for the tunnel with all speed. If Mahakala guesses our plan, he will not let anything near the portal gate."

As Gesar secured the phurba under his riding cloak, he said, "I take it this will be pretty much a suicide mission. In addition to demon-gods, the courtyard will be swarming with nagu warriors by the time I reach the passage."

"Not if everything goes as planned," Ane countered. "And it's my job to make sure you get through. The Druk will be overhead, providing cover. I know it won't be easy and I would plant the phurba myself, but a dakini attempting to near the portal would immediately alert Mahakala attention. He will be watching our every move."

Gesar fitted his helmet and said, "Okay I got it. It's simple enough. Ride into the mouth of the tunnel, plant the phurba, and then ride out as if a hell demon were chasing me."

Ane cracked a brief smile. "That's basically it, but the phurba dome will protect you. If the plan works there will be no need to run."

Gesar returned the smile. Ane's large, dark eyes were edged with worry. He sensed she would risk everything to make sure he and Goba survived. "I'm glad you'll be at my back," he said, "but don't do anything silly like trying to pull me from a demon's grip, I'm expendable."

"Not to me," Ane said, surprised by her candidness.

Before Gesar could respond, a horn sounded. A contingent of Kalapa's defenders spilled from the Vishvamata passage and sprinted for the Diamond courtyard gates. Goba snorted and stamped his hooves in anticipation

"Go!" Ane ordered. "Those guards really are running from hell demons."

Gesar galloped away to join a mixed contingent of tapah, while Ane ran to Brug who waited near the courtyard's west gate. In moments, she was airborne circling with the Druk squadron over the Diamond courtyard lit by torches and urns of burning pitch positioned in rows around its perimeter. The Diamond courtyard was a large circular plaza, looking like a huge game board with playing pieces set in motion. When the last of the retreating palace guard slipped to safety, a wall of tapah slowly advanced to meet the three demon-gods who discharged from the Vishvamata tunnel like hellish excrement. Behind them followed a vile river of nagu spearmen.

---

ahakala's deformed face cracked with a semblance of a grin when he stepped into the Diamond courtyard. He had penetrated the walls of the palace and his exile was over, but he was ever cautious. Raising his tilug, he called a warning to his fellows who were about to charge the advancing tapah line. "Stop!"

"Why stop now? We have them on the run." Yama challenged.

"Because, you would walk into a bottomless pit, if I didn't stop you." Mahakala answered as his three eyes darted about, appraising the situation. Other than a handful of defenders posted at the perimeter, the palace guard had retreated and been replaced by tapah. His attention dwelled mainly on the dakinis circling overhead preparing to attack. They were his greatest concern. He was disappointed that there were no naga-ta to challenge the annoying witches. Apparently, the remaining few of Kubera's beasts were being held at bay by dakini defenders. The wall of advancing horse warriors was a lesser concern. He and his comrades could cut through them in minutes.

"Is there a problem?" Changpa's foreface asked.

"It's not what I expected." Mahakala replied, his eyes still scanning for signs of a trap. "I thought that at least Begtse would challenge us here. He must know that we will easily destroy his precious horse warriors."

Yama snapped his razor lasso, impatiently. "Consider it a bonus. Maybe he's come to his senses. Now let's get to it."

"Don't be a fool. You can be certain that Palden will do us no favors." Mahakala countered.

"Well, are we just going to stand here?" Changpa's hind face jibed.

Mahakala's three eyes made a final scan of the courtyard before answering, "Very well, let's finish this."

The three god-demons spread apart and marched forward to meet the line of advancing tapah.

Drug called the attack. As his wail echoed within the walls of the courtyard, half of the dakinis separated from the main group and dove toward the urns of burning pitch. The remainder reached to their quivers and nocked bows. Moments later, a tapah horn sounded and the advancing line of cavalry suddenly halted. Baffled, Yama and Changpa looked to Mahakala for an explanation.

Mahakala simply pointed his tilug at the sky and said, "Did you think this was going to be easy? Prepare yourselves."

The sky over the courtyard was on fire. Urns of flaming pitch rained down among the three god-demons, exploding on the pavement and bathing them in burning chaos. A rain of arrows followed the firestorm. The roars of the assailed demon-gods shook the Diamond courtyard's ancient pavement under foot and hoof. The sight of their leaders madly beating flames and swatting arrows struck trepidation in the nagu frontline, slowing the surge from the Vishvamata portal. A horn sounded again and the tapah resumed its advance.

Gesar leaned low in his saddle. "It's time Goba."

"I know rider. I run for the passage."

Goba bolted ahead of the advancing line reaching full gallop in a few strides. He followed a straight path for the passage, safely skirting by Yama, who was engulfed in flames and busy deflecting arrows. However, the real obstacle lay ahead. The spew of nagu spearman emerging from the passage could not be avoided.

Gesar drew his sword. "There are a lot of them, Goba. I am going to need your eyes as well as mine."

"Rider, we fight as one and we die as one."

"Let's delay the last part, at least until I get the phurba in place."

Distracted by the plight of their demon-god generals, the nagu spearmen failed to notice the lone tapah angling toward them until it was too late. Goba's chest armor smashed through the front line of invaders before they could redirect spears. Nagu warriors toppled onto each other like scythed sheaves of wheat. Meanwhile, Gesar's sword was a blur as it chopped anything threatening Goba's flanks. His main concern was that somewhere in that sea of nagu might be an archer. If Goba's advance started to slow, they would become an easy target.

Ane watched Gesar's charge from above. She realized she had put him in great peril. She had struggled with her decision and nearly selected another tapah, but in the end she forced herself to overcome her attachment. In spite of her feelings for him, she made the correct strategic choice. Goba was the fastest horse and Gesar the most naturally skilled fighter she had ever seen during her time in Shambala. She prayed that Gesar would not be added to the list of those she had to mourn because of strategic decisions.

Hayagriva entered the great temple hall, his robes rustling as he strode to the throne and bowed. Overhead, the massive dome was studded like a starlit night by hundreds of lamps. By comparison, their light overwhelmed the pitiful flicker struggling for life on the altar throne, which once burned as brightly as a miniature sun. Nearby, Palden, Yamantaka and Betsge stood in meditation with eyes fixed upon the throne. Yamantaka's simple hermit rags contrasted sharply with the shining armor worn by Palden and Betsge.

Hayagriva turned to face his fellows. "So we stand guard at the dying light until the end," he said.

"It has not changed since the Shield collapsed," Betsge reported.

"And it is not likely to change for some time. Zerden spent enormously for his admission to Shambala." Hayagriva added.

"If it is any consolation, he will not recover those sacrificed sentients for his use again. Their essences were touched by the light of Bodhisattvas and they will never again wander into the lower realms." Yamantaka explained.

Palden could not contain herself. "Stop being so naïve! Do you really think that matters to Zerden? If this palace falls, he will not only control the Asura realm, but Mahakala has given him a means to pour corruption into the Human realm. The price he paid is nothing compared to his gain."

Yamantaka leaned on his gnarled staff and turned his wrinkled face to Palden. "My sister, despair does not suit you. There is still hope. We have not yet failed."

"You mean the Buddha warriors have not yet failed. We have put everything on them and we are supposed to be the sacred Guardians." Palden countered.

Hayagriva's eyes narrowed as he questioned, "Have you changed your mind? Are you suggesting that we revert to our wrathful forms and fight the rebels?"

"I'm ready. I have been ready from the start." Betsge interjected. "It has been a great frustration to send my tapah against Mahakala, while I brood in my tower. Mahakala knows my skills. He will certainly lose a few of his limbs if he crosses weapons with me."

"No!" Palden snapped. "I have not changed my mind. The risk is too great. If we return to our original forms, we might succumb to the ancient blood lust. We already carry the weight of too many sins."

Betsge shook his head in disgust. "Then we wait here and do nothing, while our rebellious brothers make a ruin of this palace."

"We do as we agreed," Palden responded. "We fight only when they come to destroy the throne."

"It may not come to that. Sister Kensang's plan is a good one and may yet succeed." Yamantaka reminded.

Palden suppressed another outburst. She knew that her accusation of naivety was unfair and untrue. Yamantaka was no doubt the wisest among them. He knew as well as she that even if the Buddha warriors succeeded in delaying Mahakala they would be doing Zerden a favor. Whatever reward Mahakala had bargained out of his new ally, it would not be paid. Zerden had got what he wanted, Shambala without its Shield. Sooner or later they would be forced to defend the temple even if sister Kensang's plan was successful. Yet, under the circumstances, Yamantaka was right to offer some encouragement, however empty. Despite Yamantaka's optimism, the sight of the dying flame was simply too dispiriting, she had to get away. "Remain on guard," she instructed. "I wish to assess the battle. I will return when it is time to defend the throne."

Reaffirming her oath, she bowed to the altar and said, "I give myself to the Path and protect it with my Wrath," then she turned and strode away. The huge temple doors flew open in response to her angry push. A rush of night air bearing the sounds of battle and the smell of burning pitch struck her face. A glance at the eastern sky showed only the faintest light, morning was still hours away. As she walked across the plaza to her kinnara, her golden armor flashed with reflected torchlight. Skarma stooped to let his mistress mount.

"Let us show Mahakala that I'm keeping watch."

Skarma answered with a battle shriek, spread his wings and lifted from the plaza.

The rubies in Palden's war band flared as she drew her fire sword from its sheath.

While his other three faces were responding to the dakini rain of fire with cries of rage and alarm, Changpa's hind face spotted the solitary tapah slashing his way through the sea of nagu warriors pouring from the Vishvamata passage. "That's an eager one," he commented casually.

Nearby, Mahakala was likewise occupied with Shambala's defenders, yet as always, he sequestered a part of his awareness to monitor the battle for signs of a trap, probing for the unexpected. If he had learned anything during his former service as a Guardian of Shambala it was that humans were resourceful and cunning. Vigilance was crucial in order to avoid surprises. That sequestered portion of his consciousness took immediate notice of Changpa's seemingly inapt commentary.

Mahakala glanced in Changpa's direction and asked. "What did you say?"

Changpa's left face responded. "Don't bother us now! Can't you see we're busy?"

"Not you!" Mahakala yelled. "Your backside just said something."

"Don't call us that!" Changpa's hind face objected.

"What was that you just said?" Mahakala demanded, as he deflected a tapah spear.

"Look for yourself," hind face answered. "That foolish tapah back there thinks he can defeat our whole army by himself."

Mahakala jerked his massive head around and saw the lone tapah cutting a path to the passage opening. Somehow, the rider had slipped by Yama. The significance struck Mahakala instantly. "Yama!" he shouted, pointing his tilug at the passage. "Stop that one, he has a phurba!"

"Where?" Yama asked, yanking a fist full of flaming arrows from his shoulder.

240

"He's behind you! You're the nearest. Kill him!"

Yama spun about, locked his gaze on Gesar and ran, heaving a club and swinging his razor lasso in a wide circle over his head.

The instant she saw Yama turn to pursue Gesar, Ane drew her sword and Brug tucked his wings to begin a dive. Mahakala knows, Ane thought as acrid curls of smoke whipped through her wild locks.

"It seems so, mistress," Brug replied.

Gesar looked ahead to his goal. The opening of the Vishvamata passage gaped and torches cast looming shadows of nagu warriors on its walls. Goba's initial charge had easily purchased twenty meters, but he had another thirty meters yet to cross and the enemy had quickly closed ranks, slowing Goba's momentum.

"Push Goba, we're nearly there," Gesar hissed through clenched teeth as his sword cleaved off a nagu spear blade. Goba pressed forward unaware of Yama's lasso speeding toward his rider.

Yama felt confident he had cast his favorite weapon well. In a moment, the loop would encircle the horseman. He relaxed his outstretched arm, waiting for the instant to yank the torso from his victim. Human flesh would yield easily to his razor lasso. Black pus dripped from his ghastly face in anticipation. Suddenly, his eyes flared with shock as his lasso hand separated from his arm at the wrist. Amidst a flurry of feathers, he recognized the defiant expression of Palden's pet. He exploded with rage. Twice now, that dakini had denied him his prey. As the insolent kinnara spread its wings to begin to lift away, Yama swung his club bearing arm, eyes fixed squarely on his target.

The blow came without warning. Ane felt the air forced from her lungs. Her sword flew from her grip as she was torn from her saddle. After a tumbling flight over the courtyard, she hit the cold pavement gasping for air. The taste of warm blood bathed her tongue. She forced her eyes open. A spinning blur slowly congealed into three glowing red eyes peering out of a background of jet. Mahakala, she recognized instantly.

"Remember, that one is mine!" Yama called from a distance.

In response, a double row of fangs appeared in the blackness beneath the glowing eyes. "You fool! This one is nearly dead. Stop that horseman!" Mahakala ordered. "I will finish her."

241

Ane panicked. She had always imagined she would accept death fearlessly, yet some ancient part of her psyche wanted to live. She was helpless, unable to move and in the place in her consciousness where Brug's voice should have been there was silence. She closed her eyes, desperately searching for some sense of her kinnara companion. Instead, visions of a hospital room flashed into her mind and then all went black.

When Jhado entered the dukhang, he again was impressed by Tenzin's efficiency. It was barely dawn and the hall was filled with monks and nuns, working in diligent silence. The centerpiece, the Kalacakra sand painting, was nearly complete. The usual weeks of preparation had to be compressed into a matter of days. Hopefully, other Kalacakra temples around the world had understood his message and were similarly engaged. All depended upon haste, a notion contrary to his Buddhist training. Haste implied desire fraught with distraction and therefore plagued by potential pitfalls. To avoid error, they needed deliberate haste tempered by discipline and detachment.

As Jhado completed his prostrations before the image of the Buddha, Tenzin appeared from behind the great thangka depicting the eight Bodhisattvas. He carried a jade hammer and a recently doused oil lamp with a residual curl of smoke winding from its wick. Does the man never rest? Jhado thought. Immediately behind Tenzin, Brother Jamyang appeared, looking exhausted. Both walked immediately to Jhado and bowed.

Jhado spared formalities. "Brother Jamyang, what have you to report."

"Your holiness," Jamyang panted. "I am happy to see you. When I learned you had journeyed to Naraka, I feared you would never return."

"Yes, by the breath of the Buddha I survived, but tell me of Shambala?"

"The Shield was still lost and Kalapa palace under siege when I left." Jamyang answered.

"What of Sister Kensang's plan?"

"I cannot say. The rebel demon-gods were leading the siege when I was recalled, but only Mahakala, Yama and Changpa were seen. There has been no sign of Kubera. " Jamyang replied.

Jhado placed a hand on Jamyang's shoulder. "On that point, I have good news."

Jamyang's tired eyes opened with puzzlement.

"Kubera remains faithful. Without his help I would have been trapped in Naraka. He positioned himself among the rebels to help restrain them."

"But can he stop the siege?" Jamyang asked.

"Unfortunately, he cannot. To avoid arousing suspicion he must remain in Naraka under the eye of Zerden, but he is clever and I'm certain he will return to Shambala when an opportunity arises."

Jamyang had been recalled unexpectedly from Shambala, but so far without explanation. He took notice of the preparations taking place in the dukhang, an initiation ceremony, now? This was not the time, Kalapa was under siege. It was madness to order this ceremony now. Every master and adept was needed to assist in the defense of Shambala. Jamyang rarely questioned the wisdom of his Lama, but this had to be challenged. "Your holiness, what is happening here? Is this really appropriate?"

"Not only appropriate, but a necessity." Jhado answered.

"I don't understand." Jamyang said, dismayed.

Jhado bent forward and looked directly into Jamyang's eyes. "My brother, if we succeed, all will become clear, but now I need your faith and trust."

Seeing the light of a bodhisattva in his lama's eyes, Jamyang nodded and his doubts melted.

"I am requesting that every adept and advanced novice perform the initiation ceremony. All of our brothers and sisters presently in Shambala must be recalled."

"But our people are bravely assisting in the defense of Kalapa; they may not wish to abandon Shambala in its time of great need." Jamyang commented.

"That is why I'm requesting that you briefly return to Kalapa palace and give a message to Lady Palden."

"As you wish, your holiness, what is your message?"

"Tell her that the Kalacakra must leave in order to give our strength to Sangpo Bumtri. She will understand and allay the concerns of our brothers and sisters. She must defend the throne as long as possible to give us time to prepare. You are to deliver this message as soon as you refresh yourself."

Jamyang bowed and was ushered away by old Tenzin.

Mahakala raised his foot to crush Ane's chest and then hesitated, noticing that the annoying rain of flaming arrows had stopped when the dakini captain was cast into his midst. No doubt the shower would resume as soon as he crushed the remaining life out of her. Let them resume, he thought. Before he could shift his weight to squeeze the final hint of life out of the dakini, a golden vajra hammer slammed squarely into his chest. He stumbled back under the force of the blow and heard a voice laced with a loathing that he had not heard in millennia.

"Gonpo!" Palden cried.

Mahakala recovered his footing and suppressed a grin as he looked at his approaching challenger. It was Palden, reverted to her wrathful form. Thick snakelike locks of black hair writhed around a sharply angulated face with a mouth lined by rows of pointed teeth. She stood nearly equal to his height, her fierce demon eyes glaring at him from above flaring nostrils. A necklace of bones lay above a pair of jutting breasts covered only by an elaborate pattern of gruesome tattoos. A skirt of golden mail was tied about her waist by a belt decorated with human skulls. Her right hand held a sword engulfed in flames.

It was the ancient, untamed Palden. The partner with whom he had wreaked havoc in the middle realms. But why had she used my guardian title, *Gonpo, Lord Protector*? She wishes to remind me of my broken vow, he realized.

"So you have finally come to me as your original self." Mahakala sneered.

Palden raised her sword. "I believe it is you who has come to me and I am prepared to give you the lesson that you came for." As she said the words, she knew he would fail to grasp their meaning.

"You think you can punish me for breaking that foolish vow?"

Palden tightened the grip on her jeweled sword handle and the flames brightened. "That's not the lesson that I bring, but you will learn that you were a fool to break a holy vow. Prepare yourself to feel the touch of my fire sword!"

Mahakala raised his tilug and said, "Of anyone, you should know it is pointless to fight with me. You cannot destroy me."

"And you cannot destroy me." Palden snapped back.

Mahakala's face wrenched, erupting into a rumbling laugh and he said, "I seem to remember the last time we fought each other like this it led to our mating."

Suddenly, Palden's fire sword slashed through air, shattering Mahakala's tilug into harmless fragments. "You're spending too much time with Changpa. Your mouth is starting to spew foolish prattle," she goaded.

Mahakala's eyes flared and his arms spread into a blossom of weapons. "Very well, but by the time we're finished you will join us. Even now, I can see that you enjoy the ancient lust."

Indeed, Palden felt the pleasurable surge of power bursting from her core, like water gushing from a broken dam, refilling a water-starved riverbed. It flowed unconstrained, with neither obligation nor discipline, seductive and addictive. For a moment she weakened, nearly succumbing to the lust and then her eyes fell upon Ane's broken body. Palden raised her sword and said, "It is time for your lesson."

"What could you possibly teach me?"

Palden answered as her sword slashed diagonally, splitting Mahakala's spiked club. "That power is meaningless without compassion."

Nagu warriors scurried out of Yama's path as he rushed to intercept the lone tapah pressing for the Vishvamata portal. He had temporarily lost his lasso hand, but his club bearing arm was still whole and deadly.

With Gesar protecting his flanks, Goba struggled through the press of nagu. As he twisted to his left to deflect a spear thrust, Gesar saw Yama's lasso fall among a tangle of nagu spearmen. He turned to look behind and noticed the approaching demon. "Goba, do you see that?"

"Yes, rider"

"Damn, he's fast. We're not going to make it. We're moving too slow." Gesar observed.

"Hold on!" Goba commanded.

As if another mind controlled his body, Gesar's hand gripped the rein and his thighs tightened against his saddle. He suddenly realized that his connection with Goba was truly two-sided. Goba could control his reactions when necessary.

Exploding in a burst of animal ferocity, Goba kicked wildly and spun, his heavy war shoes battering any nagu in range of his whirlwind of fury. The press of nagu retreated from the storm,

245

clearing a space for Goba to charge. Lowering his head, he sprinted forward ramming through the nagu line with sufficient momentum to reach the portal only moments before Yama.

Only a few strides from his target, Yama raised his club to strike. Overhead, Brug suddenly appeared out of a cloud of smoke with talons spread and eyes trained upon the demon who had struck down his mistress. Before Yama could reach the protection of the stone canopy over the Vishvamata portal, Brug's talons were sinking into his deformed head. Yama swung his club repeatedly to beat off the attacker as sizzling spatters of acidic black pus etched Brug's breast armor.

Seeing Brug was without his mistress, Gesar cried out in dismay, "Ane! Where's Ane?"

Nearby, toppled nagu spearmen had recovered their footing. "Rider, you must act now." Goba ordered.

Instantly, Gesar's body reacted to Goba's intent. His hand reached into the folds of his cloak as he leapt from the saddle. A circle of spears bore down on him as he plunged the phurba into the pavement. The phurba's dome of light bloomed at the portal entrance, scouring the passage of nagu and shoving Yama's hideous bulk into the middle of the Diamond courtyard where Changpa fended off a swarm of dakinis. Nearby, Mahakala and Palden were locked in a furious battle. A heartbeat later, seven more phurba blooms appeared around the perimeter of the courtyard, overlapping and encircling the rebel demon-gods. Horns sounded a retreat and tapah units fell back under the safe perimeter of phurba domes.

Realizing he had been trapped, Mahakala roared and charged Palden. She leapt aside narrowly avoiding a flurry of blades. "Now you're trapped here with time to think on the lesson I've given," she said calmly.

Mahakala stopped and lowered his weapons. "Fighting you is pointless," he said. "At least I have the satisfaction of knowing that you're trapped here with me."

Palden did not respond, but quickly sheathed her sword and walked to where Ane's body lay sprawled on the courtyard. She carefully lifted Ane, a tiny rag doll in her arms, and stepped directly into the glow of the phurba dome. As she carried Ane away, she looked over her shoulder and spoke to the rebel demon-gods, who gaped at her in amazement. "This one has more strength than all of you combined. Never forget that it was these mortals who created the prison that holds you."

Mahakala called after her. "We will not be here long. You don't have Kubera and the Shield is gone. Zerden's armies will reduce Kalapa to rubble and free us."

Palden then turned around to face the trapped rebels, her demon eye's flaring. "Do you really think Zerden will waste effort trying to free you? All of you are nothing more than dim-witted tools who have served their purpose. We have done Zerden a favor by trapping you." Let them choke on that thought, but she had had enough of these fools. At the moment, her concern was for the broken body cradled in her arms, which like the throne of Sangpo Bumtri, held desperately to a flicker of life.

Ϙ resuscitation team rushed into Angela Andrastos' hospital room. The nurse on duty had triggered the alarm when her patient suddenly gasped and stopped breathing. Fortunately, the comatose young woman had been moved to an observation unit after the recent violent events in the extended care center, otherwise her sudden deterioration may have gone unnoticed. Blood tinged froth bubbled from the young woman's nose and mouth as manual bag ventilation was started.

A team nurse lubricated the defibrillator paddles and called out. "Ready! Clear!"

"Wait, stop!" answered a doctor. "She's got a pulse. It's weak but it's there."

As if in confirmation, the heart monitor converted from flat line to an irregular rhythm of beeps.

"I want a ventilator machine in here now, and call for a bedside chest x-ray." The doctor ordered.

"The oximeter readings are improving a little," said the nurse compressing the ventilator bag.

Dusky blue fingers and toes started to turn pink. "Good, keep bagging her. We need that ventilator. She'll die without respiratory support."

The heart monitor continued its intermittent pattern of beeps.

Gesar blinked to clear his vision after the blinding flash. A fine dust and the metallic scent of ozone was all that remained of the host of nagu in the Vishvamata portal. Howls of dismay, echoed through the passage as nagu deep in the portal collided with the perimeter of the phurba's dome. Gesar scanned the courtyard for any sign of Ane. Forty meters from the portal within the protective dome of the phurba lay a crumpled mound of feathers. Gesar leapt onto Goba's back and galloped for it. Throwing himself from the saddle, he ran and knelt to examine the wounded kinnara. It was definitely Brug, who had purchased the seconds Gesar needed to reach the portal. Yama's club had battered him into unconsciousness. The huge raptor lay with wings spread askew, panting and oozing blood onto the ancient paving stones. Despite a frantic search, Ane was nowhere nearby, Gesar feared the worst.

"He dies." Goba coldly observed.

"He can't die." Gesar countered, refusing the ease with which Goba accepted death.

"But he must join his mistress."

Again Gesar searched for any sign of Ane, nothing. Had she flashed into discorporate sentience?

Three dakinis who had been circling above the Diamond courtyard landed near Gesar and ran to his side. Gesar recognized one of them as Amala, captain of the Kra dakini, who he had met on his first visit to the eating hall.

"Gesar, you need not stay. We will see that he is comforted." Amala said, as her companions rushed to reposition Brug and bind his wounds.

"Ane, what happened to Ane?" Gesar asked, struggling to contain his grief.

Amala placed a hand on Gesar's shoulder has she knelt next to him. "She's mortally wounded. The Lady Palden has taken her to the palace infirmary."

"Then she's alive?"

"Yes, but barely." Amala answered.

"I must see her. Where's the infirmary?" Gesar asked, grateful for a glimmer of hope.

Recognizing Gesar's distress, Amala answered. "That wouldn't be wise. I see that you love her and want to be with her, but you must let the healers do what they can. Because of you and your mount we have trapped the rebels." Her chin gestured to the three demon-gods pacing within their circular prison of overlapping phurba domes. "But, the war is not over; your service is still needed. We are still under siege. The rebel demon-gods are biding their time, waiting for their armies to free them. You must rejoin the Senge and help defend the palace."

"But...' Gesar started to protest.

Amala interrupted, "I think you know that Ane would agree with me. She is a dakini captain. Like you, she is sworn to defend Shambala."

Reluctantly accepting Amala's words, Gesar returned to Goba and climbed into his saddle.

Amala called to him, "Gesar! If it is any consolation, she missed you when you were gone. She keeps her feelings hidden, even from herself, but her sisters know of her fondness for you. I believe she would have accepted you as her consort."

Gesar did not answer. "Would have," those were not consoling words. He was well aware of the uncertainties. He remembered Angela Andrastos, the frail woman in the hospital bed. What was happening to her? Could she possibly survive? And depending on the outcome of this war, was there any point to living? The thought of losing Ane, so soon after finding her, opened a hole in Gesar's heart. The Buddha taught that life was a series of unavoidable losses. What greater motivation was there than that to live in the moment? He only wished that he had had more moments with Ane.

Unspurred, Goba trotted toward the Diamond courtyard's west gate, where tapah units were regrouping beneath a phurba dome for dispatch. As they approached the gate, Goba's words filled Gesar's emptiness, "After winter, the first grass of spring is the sweetest."

Dr. Ashki left the hospital with mixed feelings. Gesar had remained in a coma since the blow to his head in the long term care facility. This time the coma was not drug-induced and there was no predicting as to when or if Gesar would wake. From a purely medical point of view, it seemed a waste of a promising life, yet the Navajo in Ashki knew his young patient had another life. His daily visits were usually about half an hour spent mostly in silence, observing and simply being with his young patient. Gesar's vital signs had remained strong and stable, interrupted only by occasional periods of agitation. Ashki had been present during one of those agitated episodes. When the young man's eyes opened, there was no doubt in Ashki's mind that Gesar was "seeing" a different realm.

Ashki was happy to learn that he was not Gesar's only visitor. Monks from the Buddhist temple also kept regular vigils in Gesar's room. Ashki's brief conversations with the monks skirted the subject, but it was clear that they too recognized a metaphysical importance to his comatose patient, as they apparently had with Angela Andrastos. He never told the monks that it was he who had used the phurba to stop the demon-possessed Officer Cutter. He didn't need to, they knew. One monk had commented, "We have been blessed by your courage, doctor Ashki."

Ashki's cell phone sounded the Navajo two-step ringtone. Ashki answered. "Hello."

An old voice replied. "Shash, is that you?"

Ashki recognized the voice immediately. "Aoo' Sani, yes it's me. It's good to hear your voice. How are you doing?"

"Not bad for an old sheep patty, but I'm callin' because I got some news about that young spirit warrior you were askin' about. How's he doin'?"

"Yeah, I was just in the hospital visiting him, he's still unconscious."

"In hospital, hey? I don't know how you can hang around those places. Folks die in there. Good place to get haunted."

Ashki laughed and said, "You know me, Sani. I don't mind ghosts, but tell me what you have learned about our sprit warrior.

"I heard from one of the other hataathli. He is a seer in the realm where your young man travels. The young warrior is there, but things are not good. The ch'iidiitah spirits are invadin' that world. As we thought, there's a great battle and that young spirit warrior is being tested."

Ashki felt a gut spasm and his heart stepped up a pace. He first heard the Navajo word for hell, "ch'iidiitah", in frightening childhood stories. Even now the word elicited a visceral response. "I guessed as much. I had to deal with a possessed one myself." He answered.

"Ooo' Shash, you are a brave one! You should give up that hospital and come be my student. You could do some real healin' with me."

"Thanks for the offer, Sani. It means a lot to me, but at the moment, I'm sort of committed to what I'm doing, perhaps later."

"I can't promise I'll be around, but the invitation is open until I move on."

"Thanks again and I appreciate you gettin' back to me about that young warrior. I will keep a close eye on him and do a lot of praying."

"So long Shash and try an' come up for a visit. It's not good to be away from a hogan for too long, but make sure you leave those ghosts behind."

Ashki laughed again. "Okay I will do that."

"Hágooné."

"And good bye to you, Sani."

When the first light of a red dawn stretched across the mist patched hills beyond Lake Shambala, Kalapa's defenders grasped the full magnitude of the siege. As Palden had suspected, Zerden did not reveal the full extent of his reserves to Mahakala. Throughout the night, more nagu and their demon handlers had poured into the Asura realm by way of the monolith portals hidden in the mountains. Columns of smoke rose from hundreds of fires marking nagu encampments, which marred the land like eschar encrusted wounds on a once verdant landscape. Between them, a ghostly layer of grey smoke clung to the earth obscuring roads and troop movements. A particularly large column of smoke fingered to the sky from the foothills where Nyrima was located; presumably the village had been raised during the night. At least the sky was free of naga-ta. The Kra dakini had downed the last of them just before dawn, but they had paid for the victory, only two thirds of the squad had returned.

Lake Shambala's surface was covered with intact and partially shattered siege barges seething with nagu warriors. During the night the enemy had focused on constructing chains of siege barges and reinforcing the main link from Tara quay, ensuring a corridor for nagu attack units, but the palace wall's integrity was the greater concern. After the Vishvamata passage was blocked, the enemy had begun tunneling. Dakini reconnaissance indicated that the enemy was undermining a wide portion of the south wall, slowly eating at the rampart's foundation like a host of termites. Shambala's defenders had depleted their stores of boulders used to drop upon the nagu miners, who were quickly replaced by reserves when crushed or injured. Unfortunately, in the time it took to carry more boulders up to ramparts, the enemy miners had dug into the safety of their tunnels. Something had to be done. The wall was tall and heavy, if its foundation was sufficiently weakened, it would collapse meaning certain death for all of the nagu miners, but that was an insignificant sacrifice compared to the price paid by Zerden to destroy the Shield.

Ben Wilson, captain of the Senge, stood on the south wall taking stock of the scene. He turned to address his men, who looked exhausted and no doubt felt somewhat uneasy without their mounts. They were cavalry, uncomfortable being out of the saddle and in static defense positions.

"The enemy's intention is obvious," Ben started. "If this section of wall collapses it will form a ramp up to the outer ring. That's what they're waiting for." He pointed to Zerden's lesser demon commanders grouped on Tara quay with nagu companies assembling on the fields and hills behind them With Mahakala and the other rebel god-demons trapped in the Diamond courtyard, subcommanders had assumed direction of the siege and they were likely executing the god-demon's backup plan.

"As soon as the wall falls," Ben continued, "all of those nagu companies out there are going to be charging up that ramp. We need to find a way to save the wall."

Gesar was among the men listening. Without Goba as his emotional counterbalance, he was distracted by worry and doubt. Ane had been struck full force by Yama's club, how could she possibly survive? Damn, what am I doing here? I should be with her, he thought. Then he remembered something his grandfather had said on the day of his first sparring contest. "Listen grandson, worry is a great waste of energy. It's exhausting and leads to nothing but more worry. It is better to do something, anything."

"We should attack!" Gesar blurted.

Gesar's words struck a chord with the men, but their "hindmost" was obviously reacting from irrational impulsion. The reality was that they were under siege and confined to Kalapa palace.

Ben did not let it pass. "We don't need foolish comments. Are you serious or just reacting out of frustration? None of us likes being pinned down, but we need strategy not thoughtless reactions."

"Captain, I'm serious," Gesar defended. "When you're in a defensive position you take on a siege mentality. It's easy to fall into the trap of self-imposed limits. We don't have to sit here and wait for the wall to collapse. We have control of the Vishvamata passage. We just have to freeze the lake. I propose that we send every tapah unit out there. Being mounted, we have superiority. We can clear the wall base and the barges. Once we break up the barges, enemy reinforcements will be confined to the shore since the lake won't freeze for them."

A brief silence ensued as the Senge digested Gesar's plan, then shouts of support erupted from among them. Of course, why didn't we think of that? It was strange how solutions become obvious after being revealed.

Ben laughed as he shook his head in disbelief. Using Gesar's formal title he said, "Hindmost of the Senge, you have shown us that gems sometimes come from our hind end." Laughter broke out among the men. "I will speak with the other tapah captains immediately. I think all of them will be glad for an excuse to get back into the saddle. Senge tapah, take breakfast, then go to the stables and assemble on the training field. We ride in an hour."

The mood among the men lifted as did their exhaustion. A hot drink and bit of solid food after a night of quick swallows of amrita would certainly further buoy their spirits.

ℓalden's restoration to angelic form was not as painful as after the Taming when she had resisted the change, but this time she welcomed it. The Bodhisattvas had selected her angelic form and she was surprised by how much she had come to accept and enjoy it. In the century after her first transfiguration, the human-like image reflected by mirrors was strangely fascinating, but eventually she had become accustomed to the form. After the encounter with Mahakala, she easily restored it from molecular memory. Transfiguration was the nearest thing to death that an immortal god-demon could experience. It meant letting go of everything in order to be born anew from a searing self-induced conflagration. It was a sacrifice she would gladly repeat a thousand times if it meant she could save her dakini captain.

She knelt beside Ane's infirmary bed with an open palm on the young woman's forehead; her long fingers entwined in thick black locks. Stripped of armor and pale from blood loss, Ane seemed more spirit than flesh. Such irony Palden thought. Humans were so frail and ephemeral, yet they had the potential to create miracles. Despite her many powers, Palden could do no miracles. Her immortal palm, though placed lovingly, could do nothing to heal the broken body that now struggled for each breath.

"Lady Palden," a quiet feminine voice called from behind the curtain surrounding Ane's bed.

Palden lifted her palm from Ane's forehead and turned to the sound. "Enter," she answered.

A finely featured young woman with green eyes and blonde hair tied back with an embroidered cloth, pushed the curtain aside and bowed. She was one of the healers who were tirelessly administering to the wounded. "Forgive the intrusion Lady, but a Kalacakra brother, Jamyang, has arrived with a message for you," she announced.

"Where is he?"

"He's waiting in the outer hall. Shall I call him in?"

"No, I will go to him," Palden said, rising to her feet. She wore an ochre sari accented by a burnt sienna scarf loosely wrapped about her neck and slung over one shoulder. In the lamplight she resembled a tongue of flame. Her majestic height towered over the healer, who demurely stepped aside to let her pass.

As Palden walked through the infirmary, the odor of herbal ointments permeated the air and oil lamps cast shadows on curtains where healers attended to the wounded. Occasionally, a curtain would blaze with flash of light, indicating a warrior had been lost. No moans or cries of pain disturbed the regular sounding of bells, whose pitch and frequency acted as both soporific and analgesic for the wounded.

When Palden stepped into the hall, Jamyang stood trancelike between two sconce lamps, his face drawn with exhaustion. His normally shaven head bore a downy coat of silver hair. He had made too many journeys between realms without sufficient rest.

"Brother Jamyang."

Jamyang jerked from his reverie. "Lady Palden," he said, bowing.

"You have a message for me?" Palden asked.

Jamyang answered with averted eyes. "Yes. His holiness, Rinpoche Zhangpo, instructed that I inform you that all Kalacakra must be withdrawn from Shambala immediately."

Palden's eyes narrowed with bewilderment. "May I ask why? The Kalacakra brothers and sisters have been invaluable in helping to coordinate the defense of the palace. Their absence will only weaken us."

"His holiness knows this, but he has a plan to restore the Shield and it will require the participation of every Kalacakra adept."

Palden's eyes widened with surprise. "Can this really be done?"

"There is no certainty, but his holiness believes this is our only opportunity."

"Then it must be done. I will have your brothers and sisters notified. I give you my leave, but how will I know when the Kalacakra are ready to act?"

"His holiness requested that you keep vigil at the throne and defend it as long as possible. If his plan succeeds, you will know when we come."

Palden was torn. Her time comforting the wounded would need to be cut short. "Very well, we will wait and pray."

"There is another message, my Lady." Jamyang said. His eyes still averted.

"Yes," Palden said warily, fearing more bad tidings.

"His holiness said that on his recent journey to Naraka, he learned that Kubera remains faithful, but he is under close scrutiny by Zerden."

Palden was momentarily dumbstruck. This news came as a complete if not unwelcome surprise. If this were true, she had totally misjudged Kubera. Of the demon-gods, Kubera was the youngest and had not participated in the blood frenzies of ancient times, but she had always taken him to be no less depraved. Had he truly remained among the faithful or was he playing a more sophisticated game? He knew the strengths and weaknesses of both sides. Was he playing two sides to emerge as the middle victor? Palden's response was tempered.

"That is welcome news which I hope is true, but Kubera is likely the most cunning among us, I will need more convincing?"

Jamyang let his eyes briefly meet Palden's gaze. "I can only say that his holiness was convinced of Kubera's position and seemed to think the demon-god was in danger."

"That seems quite out of character." Palden answered. "I give you my leave brother."

Jamyang bowed and left.

255

As Palden watched the weary monk leave, doubts stirred within her. Could it be that Kubera had been affected by his many years of service as she had?

The first wave of tapah emerged from the Vishvamata gate under a sky heavy with billowing grey clouds. Nagu companies on the shoreline and siege barges were stunned when a broad expanse of Lake Shambala suddenly froze. Any nagu warrior foolish enough to attempt to venture onto the sacred ice was quickly swallowed by cold water which froze again, sealing them in deep water. The tapah quickly overtook the nearest barge without dakini air support. Speed and surprise compensated for the dakinis, whose mounts were taking a long overdue rest after two days of air battles. While the other tapah units focused on siege barges, the Senge were dispatched to ferret out the nagu undermining the south wall. When the wall came into view, the Senge gaped in shock.

A voice from the front of the Senge column cried, "Great Buddha! Look at that."

A wide crack cut through the lower half of the wall between the south and southwest Guardian towers. Collapse was imminent unless the mining was stopped. Rubble from the dig was piled along the base of the wall, protecting the enemy miners from direct attack. It was shocking how much had been accomplished despite attempts to harry them throughout the night. Clearly, the nagu had developed skillful mining techniques while carving cave fortresses in the mountains around Shambala.

The Senge column halted in front of the wall of rubble.

"We can't get to them," said Chiru, Gesar's riding partner.

"Captain Jigme will have to order us to dismount. In the end it always comes down to boots on the ground." Gesar responded.

As if on cue, Captain Jigme pointed to the rear half of his unit with his sword and cried out, "You, dismount with bows. Follow me and take positions on that wall. The rest provide cover and protect the mounts."

Moments later, Gesar and Chiru were scrambling up a steep hill of scree with bows in hand. They nocked arrows and cautiously glimpsed over the top to view the excavation. Multiple gaping holes had been tunneled into the wall's foundation. Brigades of nagu miners, working in rhythm to the sound of hammer and pick, passed buckets of stone shards and added the contents to the growing wall of rubble.

"Shoot at will!" Jigme ordered.

Surprised, the nagu dropped their buckets and scattered, many falling on each other in the confusion. Those that survived the barrage of Senge arrows retreated into the holes, only to reappear with crossbows, returning fire from behind a hastily assembled wall of shields. Despite the Senge challenge, the steady chipping of stone continued in the background.

"Draw swords!" captain Jigme cried. "We will have to root them out." The order to charge followed.

The Senge performed a feint maneuver to draw a volley of nagu arrows and then charged crying, "For Shambala and the Path!"

As Senge swords met the nagu shields, there was a thundering crash, the ground shook and a shower of stone and dust rained from above. Tapah mounts whinnied and reared. Thoughts of alarm suddenly erupted in the minds of Senge riders.

Horsemen cried from the other side of the scree barrier, "Trebuchet!"

Gesar and the other men suddenly realized they were too late. The deep crack in the Kalapa's southeast rampart was all that the enemy had needed to accomplish. Boulders catapulted from Tara quay were finishing the job. The nagu miners had only to deter any attempt to shore up the wall's foundation.

"Fall back! Everyone to your mounts!" ordered the captain.

Coated in dust, Gesar and Chiru scrambled back over the scree wall and ran for their horses. The Senge who had remained on guard were staring in the direction of Tara quay, where five huge trebuchets had been hauled into position. As Gesar jumped into Goba's saddle, the south wall shook again with another explosion of stone. When the dust cleared a ragged web of small fractures extended the main crack.

"The wall can't take many more of those," observed Chiru.

"We need dakini support now," Gesar answered. "Those trebuchets have to be destroyed."

"The kinnaras have to rest." Chiru said. "They can't fly forever."

Gesar pointed in the direction of the quay and said, "We don't have a choice. Look, they're concentrating forces on the quay.

They're getting ready to attack as soon as the wall collapses. There's not enough time."

Where Gesar pointed, nagu units were massing on the quay, preparing to charge across the barges as soon as Kalapa's wall collapsed. The tapah were still far from the quay, having reached only the second barge in the chain extending to the shore. As the battle raged, two more boulders flew overhead and smashed against the wall, gouging another ugly scar.

The palace guard watching the battle from the ramparts had reached the same conclusion that Gesar had because horns sounded the call to mobilize dakini squadrons. In response, a rag tag mix of dakini squadrons lifted from the palace ramparts. Those kinnaras with enough remaining strength carried urns of burning pitch while the remainder took up support positions.

Palden looked over the balustrade bordering the perimeter of Kalapa's upper level temple plaza. The rust-red sky of the previous day had been replaced by ominous billows that gnawed at the snowy peaks of Shambala's inner ring and sucked the life from the light attempting to penetrate them. Below in the Diamond courtyard, the three trapped rebel demon-gods paced impatiently, probing the phurba barrier with the tips of their weapons evoking showers of defiant sparks. For the time being, Palden was satisfied that they were constrained. It was the sound of boulders crashing against the south rampart that was her immediate concern. Fortunately, when the first boulder struck, all the dakini eyries within the south wall had already been evacuated. Since then she had lost count of the number of impacts the wall had suffered. The wall was their last defense. If it collapsed, defeat by attrition was inevitable unless the Shield could be restored. There were simply too few palace defenders to hold the palace indefinitely against a steady stream of nagu warriors.

When the weary group of dakinis mustered in response to the horns, she offered what words of encouragement she could before they lifted from the plaza to attack the enemy siege engines. After two days of battle, their kinnaras were badly overstretched. Exhaustion was apparent in the deep dips of their flight line caused by a weak down stroke of the wings. Despite their weariness, not one dakini complained or objected to being sent on yet another mission. These mortals deserve victory, she thought, and those querulous fools prowling in their phurba cage deserve defeat and a suitable punishment. It was simple justice, but millennia of experience had taught her that Fate was totally disdainful of Justice. The deserving rarely got their due.

In a cruel accent to her thought, another impact shook the air and a series of parapets on the southwest wall crumbled away. Sickened by the sight, Palden turned away to take her place among the Guardians keeping vigil in the temple. If Zerden's minions reached the temple, they would pay dearly for a victory.

Jhado watched the falling snow from his chamber window. Snow squalls sometimes came in late summer on the high plateau. Snow was a natural teacher of meditation, especially the quiet storms with large lumbering snowflakes. Body and mind easily succumbed to their hypnotic dance; hours could pass away unnoticed while watching their gentle tumbling. Like humans, every snowflake was perfectly unique. Fixing one's awareness on a single snowflake was the greatest teaching, as it followed its path from sky to earth, where the absolute individual joined the pure oneness of snow. It was a poetic metaphor for the Path of Enlightenment.

Shaking himself from his musings, Jhado turned to his desk computer. Under the snow laden clouds, solar cells would be useless and the batteries likely weak. Expecting disappointment, he pushed the power button. To his surprise, the display and computer came to life. Again, he was thankful for the effort of some selfless brother or sister, who had spent hours charging the batteries that morning.

A few minutes later, Jhado was sifting through the latest poems posted on the Haiku web site. Had his message been received and understood? If it had, there would be some kind of response. The first glimpse of hope came in the following words.

As dark clouds gather
Cattle choose a sitting place
And dream of bright days
Beowulf

The poem was written by the Danish lama, who oversaw the European Kalacakra temples. "Thank the Buddha!" Jhado exclaimed. The poem was well constructed and communicated all. "Cattle pick a

260

sitting place" meant they were preparing the meditation ceremony. To "sit" was often used as a synonym for meditation. The phrase, "dream of bright days", referred to Shambala's burning throne. Jhado continued his search for other messages. He next found a poem posted by the California lama, who oversaw Kalacakra temples in the western hemisphere.

On cold moonless night
Moths seek the flickering flame
To join with the light
Kasa

Excellent, Jhado thought, Kasa had understood. He had provided a poem encapsulating the essence of Kalacakra initiation ceremony. Kasa would mobilize all the temples in North and South America, but for the plan to have any chance of effectiveness every Kalacakra community had to participate and there was still no response from Indonesia. For another hour Jhado scrolled through hundreds of poems but to no avail.

A cold draft disturbed the oil lamps and Jhado looked up. Snow had started to blow against the window completely obscuring the view of the plateau. The late summer squall was rapidly becoming a blizzard. Returning his attention to the computer, he noticed that the image on the display was beginning to break up. "Great Buddha, not now," Jhado hissed. Weakening batteries and storm interference were causing his computer to falter.

Jhado performed a page refresh. A somewhat dimmed version of the Haiku web page assembled on the display. Amazingly, the poem he sought appeared for a moment and then vanished in a collapse of pixels. Jhado closed his eyes to allow his memory to reconstruct the words he had seen for a brief glimpse.

In temple darkness
The sangha is enlightened
By a single spark
Monkee

Jhado exhaled a breath of relief. The words confirmed that the Kalacakra throughout Southeast Asia and Australia had been alerted. Each of the poems spoke of groups, "cattle", "moths" and "sangha," which referred to the Kalacakra communities. All of them counterpointed images of darkness with references to light, indicating they had understood his plan to restore the blazing throne of Shambala. Kalacakra temples around the globe would be performing the ceremony of initiation. Every available monk and nun would relive their beginning.

Jhado started to snuff out the oil lamps before leaving his chamber, but hesitated. "I will not extinguish any light today," he said to himself. He tightened his robe against a cold draft and strode from the room. As he passed through his chamber door, Tenzin's empty wooden stool stood in the hall. The old monk was away from his post receiving the last of the Kalacakra who had been recalled from Shambala. Every available adept had to participate in the arduous Kalacakra ceremony, including old Tenzin. He like so many others had given so much already. Jhado feared his people were short on both time and energy.

Gesar watched from the rear of the Senge column as it rode to join the other tapah fighting to clear the barges. On Tara quay, three of the huge catapults were in flames as dakinis circled overhead raining arrows upon the siege engine operators. The dakini attack had at least caused a lull in the steady stream of boulders battering the palace wall. Gesar glanced over his shoulder to assess the condition of the southwest wall. The parapets were gone and the dakini eyrie windows sagged at odd angles. It was clearly in bad shape and Gesar was already devising a plan of defense should the wall collapse. Occupying himself with battle plans helped to avoid thinking about Ane, but despite his efforts his thoughts kept drifting to her.

"Rider, you cannot run in two directions at once." Goba's words intruded Gesar's mind. Until now, Goba had been silent throughout the morning.

"I'm afraid I've been distracted."

"That is a danger to us both." Goba chastised.

"You're right. This could be our last battle. I promise I will make it a good one."

The lead of the Senge column reached the battle line and spread to engage the enemy. Gesar drew his sword and charged into the fray. The tapah pressed forward slowly clearing the barge while some of the men leapt from their horses and started to hew at the lashings holding the logs together. It was a colossal task for the enemy had constructed a broad avenue of rafts held together by complex assortment of chains, ropes, and spikes.

The third row of barges was cleared when the dakinis finally exhausted their arrows. No longer harried by the aerial attack, the nagu engineers quickly reloaded the remaining catapults and released their payloads. The clash of weapons momentarily halted as offenders and defenders turned their eyes to the palace. The boulders hissed through the air before impacting the palace rampart in a thundering cloud of dust. The shining wall of Kalapa, which had stood unspoiled for millennia, appeared to melt and liquefy into uncountable fragments before cascading into the lake. When the dust cleared, a ramp of rubble led up from the barges to a wide gash in the wall. A guttural cheer rose up from Tara quay and the nagu commanders ordered their armies to charge. The nagu frontline was shoved onto the line of tapah spears and swords. Moments later Kalapa's horns sounded the retreat. In disciplined formations, the tapah units fell back and broke off to ride for the Vishvamata gate under the watchful eye of the remaining dakini squadrons.

Amala of the Kra dakini squadron had replaced Ane as first captain. She monitored the retreat and scanned the valley, taking note of nagu positions. Visibility was poor even with amrita enhanced vision. Since daybreak, grey smoke clung to the south valley and clouds obscured the inner mountain ring. Her attention was suddenly drawn to the south where a dark spot over the horizon faded in and out as low lying clouds passed in front of it. For several moments she watched, her eyes straining to make sense of the odd band of darkness. Suddenly, the object emerged from cloud cover and she cried out. "Naga-ta!"

Overspent after a night of battling the flying serpents, Amala sensed spirits falter among the dakini squadrons as they considered the prospect of yet another encounter. With Ane lost from the field, it was up to her to decide whether to engage them or not. She glanced back at the palace. The last of the tapah had reached the Vishvamata gate and the ice bridge had again become dark water. The palace guard was hastily preparing a line of defense along the gash in Kalapa's wall. Like a relentless swarm of ants, nagu warriors rushed over the line of barges and clambered up the ramp of stone to challenge Kalapa's outnumbered defenders. If the naga-ta reached the wall, the palace guard could not hold against both ground and air attack. Amala raised her sword and called out, "Attack formation! For Shambala and the Path!" Dakini squadrons immediately arranged into arrowhead formation and aimed for the approaching naga-ta.

As the dakinis flew to engage the naga-ta, the Senge tapah rode directly to the damaged section of wall to assist the palace defenders. With spears in hand, Gesar and his fellow tapah climbed to the breach, where the battle had reached a crescendo. Men were fighting nagu hand to hand. Driven by Zerden's will, nagu had thrown themselves onto swords simply to disarm Kalapa's defenders.

Captain Jigme ordered, "Tapah, lower spears!" Sorely in need of relief, captains of the palace guard were thankful when the tapah arrived. They immediately fell back to rest as the tapah advanced to take their places.

In the heat of battle, Gesar had lost all sense of time. When had they discarded spears for swords? Had they been fighting for minutes or hours? For most of that unknown time they had held the high ground, keeping the enemy at bay, but the defensive line was weakening. Some of the men, who had been pushed back from the crest of the breach, desperately fought to regain their positions. Outnumbered by a seeming limitless supply of nagu, the defenders knew they would eventually fail.

In a brief moment between clashes, Gesar looked to the sky for any sign of the sun. Instead, a dark shadow swallowed the sky with a dreadful shriek. The huge naga-ta flew low over the breached wall and then banked toward the Diamond courtyard with no dakinis in pursuit. Gesar's only regret was that he had not said good bye to Ane.

When the wall collapsed, Mahakala's eyes widened with eager expectation. Zerden's forces were successfully executing the siege plan he had designed in the event that Shambala's defenders blocked the Vishvamata passage. Though, he had not planned on being trapped himself nor had he anticipated the extent of Palden's power. He was shocked when the phurba dome had allowed her passage while she was in her wrathful form. She had definitely changed, but that was no matter. Once the palace was taken, naga-ta would carry him and his fellows to freedom.

"It seems that Zerden's marshals are not as feeble-minded as I supposed." Mahakala commented. "Our freedom is coming soon."

"Not soon enough!" Yama countered angrily.

Changpa's hind face chimed in, "Mahakala, I have to say that I am disappointed in your strategic abilities. We should never have come charging in here together. By now, the whole of Naraka knows we're trapped like dogs in a pit."

Mahakala shook his head in disgust as he jabbed a barbed sword into the phurba dome eliciting a shower of sparks. "I seem to remember you were quite eager to follow me."

While his other faces remained in mortified silence, Changpa's hind face replied, "We were not in total agreement on that point. It seems some of us are growing a bit dull edged since we restored our old forms."

Though Changpa's hind face was directing his derision at his other personalities, Mahakala had indeed sensed the mental decay in his fellows and was having doubts. Was he too becoming dull edged? Before the Taming, it had never been a concern because he had nothing to compare himself to. Now, he bore memories of his many years as a Guardian of Shambala. He remembered debating with Hayagriva, sparring with Betsge, enjoying the gardens with Palden and creating brush paintings with Yamantaka. Before the Taming,

265

such things were not part of his consciousness. For that matter, his bulky clawed hand could no longer hold a brush.

Mahakala chewed on his conflicting thoughts until he heard the shriek of the naga-ta. "Meaningless, tripe," he growled, discarding his doubts. "I am winning this war."

As sounds of alarm rose from Kalapa's ramparts, the naga-ta circled over the Diamond courtyard several times before landing on top of the broad reflecting wall beyond the reach of the phurba domes. Mahakala's fixed all of his eyes on its rider.

Kubera's obese frame shifted from round to oblong as he stood up in the naga-ta's saddle and jumped off, a surprisingly nimble move considering his bulk. He walked to the edge of the wall and perused his trapped fellows in silence.

Confused and impatient, Mahakala boomed a command at Kubera, "What are you waiting for? Get us out of here!"

"Are you really trapped?" Kubera's god-demon amplified tenor voice pierced the air.

An enraged Yama answered, "You fat lout! Are you blind? Of course were trapped."

Kubera's flabby face broke into a grin and he answered, "No. I'm not blind, however I am amused. Word came to Naraka that you had gotten yourselves into a fix, but how does the human phrase go? Oh yes, I remember, 'seeing is believing'."

"Now that you've satisfied your curiosity, put a rigging on a naga-ta and free us!" Mahakala ordered.

Kubera's manner turned serious. "As much as I would like to, I'm afraid Zerden has instructed me to leave you as you are as punishment for your stupidity. Being the weakest of the four of us, I'm not in a position to defy our new master, so I can only offer my sympathies."

Mahakala roared. The sound shook earth and sky. Changpa and Yama threw their weapons in Kubera's direction, but after causing an explosion of sparks they bounced harmlessly off the phurba dome.

As Kubera climbed back onto his mount and lifted away, Yama turned a scathing look upon Mahakala, "Palden was right. Zerden used us. You were as much a fool as we."

The faithful demon-gods heard Mahakala's muffled roar even in the great temple dome where they held vigil.

"What was that?" Hayagriva asked.

266

"I suspect that was the sound of my former consort gaining more wisdom." Palden answered never taking her eyes from the throne.

Since the Kalacakra had left the Asura realm in response to Lama Zhangpo's command, the flicker of light on Shambala's throne had not changed. Struggling for life, it was so weak that the slightest breeze could snuff it forever. The faithful demon-gods were prepared to defend the meager light from violation for as long as possible, but the future of Shambala and the Path was really in hands of the mortals who had created it.

"Did you see that?" Yamantaka exclaimed, pointing his staff at the throne.

Palden and the others had. For a brief moment the flame flashed brightly and moments later, the great temple doors opened. A ghostly form, even more insubstantial than a Seer, stood in the doorway. Only the eyes of a demon-god could perceive the outline of an old monk with a weather-beaten face and bent back hovering at the door. He blinked his transparent eyes in childlike wonder before floating toward the altar. Silently, he ascended the marble tiers and gently placed an open hand upon the flicker. Instantly, the phantom vanished leaving the tiny flame with a brighter and steadier light. At the temple doorway more ghosts appeared and a procession of phantoms began, each adding their essence to the flame of Sangpo Bumtri. In unison, the four demon-gods dropped to their knees and prostrated themselves before the throne of Shambala.

Chiru pivoted and split the helm of the dron warrior who had challenged him. "They're fighting harder since that naga-ta appeared," he said catching his breath.

"Yeah, I noticed. And it should be coming back soon." Gesar replied as he kicked a nagu dron warrior in chest sending him tumbling downhill and tripping up two other attackers.

As Gesar predicted, there was a shriek and both men looked to the sky. The naga-ta was approaching from their rear and starting into a dive. Its taloned feet would easily sweep away ten defenders on its first attack.

"Well friend, it's been an honor having you as my Senge brother. What you and Goba did in the Diamond courtyard was the stuff of legends. Too bad we won't be around to tell the stories." Chiru said stoically.

As Chiru spoke, Gesar tracked the naga-ta's flight path. "Wait! Something's wrong. It's not coming for us."

The naga-ta flew so low over the wall that the men felt eddy currents about them as the beast beat its wings, but it harmlessly passed over them. As it dropped nearer the lake surface, they saw that the creature was flying without a rider, a rogue. It banked off to the east and disappeared over the foothills of Mount Jetsunmu.

The moment of relief was broken when someone cried, "The line is broken!" Gesar glanced over his shoulder and confirmed it. When the naga-ta had flown over, a company of nagu warriors had penetrated the battle line at the left edge of the breach. They had scrambled over the crest and overwhelmed the sparse rear guard. The defensive line quickly collapsed.

"Withdraw to the outer ring!" a captain ordered.

Gesar and Chiru were among the last to withdraw. They turned and sprinted for the next defensive position. During the battle, units of the palace guard had prepared the second defensive line. The goal was to impede the nagu forces for as long as possible by containing them in a section of Kalapa's outer ring between the rampart and the barrack walls. Each of Kalapa's five levels could be similarly defended until the summit was reached. At each level they had to hold long enough to allow valley refugees, wounded and horses to be evacuated.

Without resistance, a surge of nagu spilled through the breach in pursuit of the retreating tapah. Gesar heard the nagu boots pounding the ground behind him. He was only a few strides ahead of them. Glancing from right to left, he looked for Chiru, but his comrade had fallen behind. Gesar slowed, looked to his rear and saw Chiru tackled by a nagu dron.

"Chiru!" Gesar cried as he spun around to assist his friend. Without thinking, he ran straight into the oncoming nagu force. He reached Chiru just in time to block a nagu spear thrust aimed for Chiru's exposed neck. Another nagu raised a club to strike Gesar from behind, but was struck down by a well aimed arrow from the defensive line. As Chiru struggled to his feet, Gesar wildly deflected blows coming from all sides.

"Back to back!" Chiru shouted as he slashed his way to Gesar.

Surrounded by nagu warriors, the men fought back to back, both resigned to their certain demise.

"Thanks for trying, brother!" Chiru yelled above the fray.

"Sorry it didn't work out!" Gesar cried back.

"You're forgiven!"

For several minutes, the two men worked in perfect harmony, blocking a blur of attackers, but when a sword blow grazed his helmet, Gesar knew that his body was succumbing to exhaustion. "I'm losing it!" he cried.

"Me too!" Chiru answered.

Without warning, the nagu attackers suddenly stopped and parted, opening a space in front of Chiru. A figure twice the height of a nagu dron warrior stood in the opening wielding a massive throwing hammer. The blow struck Chiru squarely in the chest leveling both him and Gesar. A flash of light followed and Chiru vanished. Weaponless, Gesar was sprawled flat on his face, his lips caked with grit. A prodding spear tip flipped him onto his back. The hammer wielding demon-captain looked down at his prize. His indifferent grimace bent into a cruel grin of yellow fangs as he lifted his hammer.

Gesar tried to move, but his arms and legs were pinned under nagu boots. He wanted to say something brave and defiant with his last breath, but strangely he could only think of the first line of the Buddha warrior's prayer. "Let my soul shine with the Light of Illumination to drown the shadow of ignorance."

The demon-captain paused at the words. His feral eyes strayed from Gesar and turned toward Kalapa's summit. The sounds of battle were suddenly silenced as all eyes looked to the great temple. A column of intense light pierced upward from the apex of Kalapa's dome. The column began to spread at its base, opening like an umbrella. Panicked recognition hit the nagu armies and suddenly they dropped their weapons and ran to escape the spreading wall of light.

At once, Gesar arms and legs were free. The demon-captain turned a look of rage upon Gesar and let his hammer fall. Gesar rolled to the side, just as the hammer shattered the pavement. Scrambling to his feet, Gesar ran for the oncoming tsunami of light.

No enemy escaped the spreading Shield barrier as it swept across Lake Shambala and climbed into the valley's foothills. As the barrier rolled over them, nagu warriors crumbled to dust and scattered to the wind like dandelion puff balls. By nightfall, the valley was scoured.

Sitting upon his cushioned chair, Jhado watched the Kalacakra sand painting being swept into a neat pile, all of its colors mingling into a rusty earth tone. What was once finely crushed stone that had served as a window to another realm was now a sacred blend of colors being reverently collected into golden urns. Some of it would be scattered into the streams near Dagpa Akar as a blessing that would flow from the highest land in the world, while the rest would go to Shambala. Sister Kensang held an urn decorated with elaborate lotus motif, while a monk filled it using a funnel. She carried the filled urn to Jhado and presented it for a final blessing and disposition.

Bowing at the waist, she extended the urn with outstretched arms and said, "Your holiness, here is the first urn of sacred earth. What is your will?"

Jhado pulled a hand from a fold in his robe, pressed his palms together in blessing and then answered, "This one must go to Lozang of the Sun Tribe. His people served us faithfully and provided the phurbas that you so wisely employed. Have this sacred earth taken to him and let him know that his people have helped to preserve the Path of Enlightenment. Tell him to use this sacred earth to bless his people, their animals and the grasslands they love, so they will prosper and know the path to true freedom."

"As you wish, your holiness, I will deliver it immediately." Kensang answered.

Jhado raised a palm. "No sister, instruct another to make the delivery, for I want you to take the next jar to Shambala and present it to Lord Hayagriva. The sacred earth of the Human realm has great power in Asura and it will be needed as the Buddha warriors cleanse the mountains of Zerden's strongholds."

Sister Kensang raised her head in surprise. "But, should not a more senior adept perform this task?"

Jhado smiled. "Sister, you have proven yourself more than equal to any senior adept. I can think of no one more qualified than you and I believe that the faithful Guardians will wish to express their gratitude to you in a more formal fashion."

Sister Kensang set down the urn and pressed her palms together and bowed. "Thank you, your holiness. I look forward to the journey."

She was about to take her leave when Jhado raised a palm again to stay her. "Before your leave, I have one question for you sister."

"Yes, your holiness."

"The ease with which you made the journey to Shambala, suggests to me that you are a Tulku, whose feet are familiar to the upper realms. Since I first met you, I sensed the presence of a sacred one. Tell me, do you have other life knowledge and if so, who is it that your body carries?"

Sister Kensang hesitated a moment before replying. "Your holiness, when I was a very young child I had knowledge of another life which I told to my mother. This is the story that I told her.

"I remembered living as a princess by a clear lake. I became a beautiful young woman pursued by many suitors. My first suitor was a vain young prince who took me riding one day. He violated me on the edge of a forest and left me there alone in tattered clothes. In shame I ran away and was captured by a cruel king who added me to his harem. I felt lost, homesick and desperately sad. Everyday, I looked for ways to end my miserable life. One day the king was visited by a handsome lord and I was offered to him as a gift. The king said 'take her, she is my most beautiful consort, but her heart is like iron. Maybe you can do something with her.' The lord accepted me happily, but I only saw the knife at his hip and hoped to plunge it into my belly.

"To my surprise, the new lord did not come to me for favors, but spoke to me of the Enlightened One. He said that he had become a follower of the Buddha and a teacher of the Path and would take me as a disciple and not a slave. My life became a joy, and instead of plunging a knife into my belly, I plunged myself into the teachings as I would plunge into the clear lake by my father's palace. I was provided ancient texts which I drank like water. To this day I remember passages from those texts.

"The day came when my lord instructed me to spread the teachings of the Buddha. I traveled to the mountains of the land that is now Nepal. There, I met a monk named Atsara, who became my partner on the Path. We both vowed to attain awakening in our lifetime and so decided to meditate as hermits in the remote mountains of Tibet. There, we separated and found caves in which to meditate. I faced great hardship and in meditation found my way to the land of god-demons. Despite near failure, I survived and returned with greater strength and became a teacher, spreading my knowledge throughout Tibet until in my later years when I returned to isolation to finally leave my body and transcend the realms. That is what I remember."

Jhado looked at Sister Kensang with an expression of gratified wonder as if he had just found a precious jewel that he thought had been forever lost and said. "You have just described the life of the yidam, Dechen Gyalmo. Are you certain no one told you of her?"

"I am certain, your holiness. I did not know of her story until I entered the sisterhood, but I know far more details of her life then have ever been recorded."

271

Jhado got up from his chair and prostrated himself before Sister Kensang and said. "Then you are truly Tulku. The saint, Dechen Gyalmo or part of her has decided to return to the Human realm in our time of need. We have been blessed. When you return from Shambala, please come to me. I have some questions about some of the termas you wrote in the year seven ninety-five."

Kensang smiled and replied. "And I have some questions about some that you wrote."

Epilogue

Dr. Ashki sat in silence separated from the Navajo elder by a pit of dancing flames. When the old man tossed a log onto the fire, sparks spiraled up through the smoke hole to merge with a star studded night sky. The last of the visitors had gone and the hogan was still close with the comforting scent of sweat, sage and charred mesquite. It was a familiar odor of Navajo communal gatherings and Ashki savored each breath. Family, friends and clan had welcomed him with a grand feast after the long drive from San Francisco to New Mexico. He had come to fulfill promises, but in truth he was renewing his Navajo roots. Now that he was here, childhood memories of being in the safe womb of the hogan were vivid.

"Yéhtso, if you think much harder, you're gonna be too heavy to stand up," the old man jibed.

Ashki tore his eyes from the hypnotic fire dance. The old man had called him by yet another of his nicknames, 'giant one'. "Sechái, I'm not smart enough to think that hard." Ashki replied.

"It's not the smart thoughts that weigh ya down. Just what are ya thinkin' bout?"

Ashki looked back into the fire. "I was remembering being in the hogan when I was kid. I used to think that those fire sparks turned into stars."

Sechái laughed. "I probably told you that story."

"No, I believe you said the stars were the campfires of our ancestors," Ashki corrected.

"That's right and all together they put on a damn good light show, don't ya think?"

"There's no doubt about that." Ashki replied.

Sechái bent his face closer to the flames, accentuating the deep lines in his weathered cheeks. "How are things goin' with your young spirit warrior?"

"He was moved from the hospital last week by those monks I told you about. They put him and the young woman in the same long term care nursing home."

Secháí smiled. "Good, those monks are wise. Those two should dream together. Maybe someday they will wake up together."

"Maybe, but I think they're probably happier where they are."

"As long as they sleep, I will keep singin' a hozhónji for them."

Ashki spread his hands to warm them in front of the fire and said, "You know those Buddhist monks sing blessing chants at their bedsides."

Secháí slapped his thighs. "I told ya! Those brothers and sisters know the blessing way. There's no better medicine than that."

"Are you telling me I wasted my time in medical school?"

Secháí laughed again. "I would never say that. There's nobody better with bones than you, but you're no good with women."

"Don't get started, sani." Ashki countered. "You're worse than my mother."

"Bah! You can't spend your life being a siss-sahkáhd. Lone trees blow over in big winds. Yéhtso, you need a woman. Tonight there was a good lookin' etáhdeh eyein' you up like an ear of fresh corn. Don't tell me you didn't notice her."

Ashki nearly blushed. "I noticed her, but why are you trying to get me a woman?"

"Hey, it's the least I can do for the new truck you gave me."

Ashki laughed and shook his head. "Okay, I'm sorry, next time I'll get the extended cab."

Palden and Kubera enjoyed a spectacular view from the cupola windows of Kalapa's south tower. Snow-capped mountains glowed brightly against a deep azure sky and spring sunshine bathed the palace mount. Other than the scaffolding clinging to its broken south wall, Kalapa palace was mostly whole again. Palden noticed the couple walking in the gardens. With vision more acute than any eagle, she easily recognized Gesar and Ane as they strolled hand in hand among the blossoming trees. The sight stirred a mixture of joy and melancholy in her heart. She felt joy knowing that two spirits had found contentment in each other. Yet the lovers reminded her that her own brief experience with such contentment ended when Mahakala broke his oath.

274

Ane stumbled and was caught by Gesar, who helped her to a bench near a fountain. Her healing is still not complete, Palden thought. Likewise, her kinnara, Brug, was taking only short flights over Lake Shambala, but in time his strength would return.

Averting near total destruction had left many wounds and stretched Shambala's defenders to their limits, especially Ane. After such a long time being strong for others, she deserved a time to be soft for herself. Gesar had brought balance to her life. He had found a way through her steely resolve. He had visited her every day in the infirmary until she was well enough to leave. Not long after, Ane accepted Gesar as her consort; the match being formally blessed by the Council of Guardians.

Kubera, who had been watching the rebel demon-gods who were imprisioned by the ring of phurbas in the Diamond courtyard, spoke, "Look at them, they're still arguing. How long do you think they will stay there?"

"Until they learn to swallow their pride, perhaps a century or two," Palden answered. "It's the Taming all over again for them."

Kubera chuckled and said, "I think, Mahakala will have an especially large meal to digest."

"It will take him a century just to admit what a fool he was." Palden added.

Kubera chuckled again. "He still can't believe that I outwitted both him and Zerden."

"Humility has never been one of our strengths," Palden replied. "I have discovered that we must learn it well, for it is the first step to our freedom."

275

Glossaries

Tibetan and Sanskrit words

Amrita: literally means "nectar of the immortals", a vitalizing liquor made by the residents of Shambala valley

Asura: the Jealous God realm, one of the six realms of Buddhism

Chakpu: a long serrated funnel used for making sand mandalas

Bhikshu: a fully ordained monk

Bhikshuni: a fully ordained nun

Dance of the Earth: initiation dance involving symbolic gestures with the hands and feet

Dakini: Sanskrit for "Sky Dancer"; a female tutelary diety who teaches and tests those on the path of Tantric enlightenment.

Dharma: the path of the higher truths, includes a number of practices or tenants that are in accord with universal order and lead to spiritual liberation

Dhob-Dhob: a specialized class of monks that serve guard and police functions

Dragpo: storm

Drizai: mirage or ghost

Dron: literally means "fang"; the dron are elite nagu warriors

Druk: dragon

Dungchen: a type of Tibetan horn that sometimes can be as long as 14 feet and produces deep tones resembling the sound of a tuba

Dukhang: the main temple assembly hall

Freemane: general term for a warhorse that has yet to choose a rider

Galme: firefly

Getsul: a novice monk

Kinnara: large sentient bird-reptiles that serve as mounts for the dakini

Kra: falcon

Kyilkhor: mandala

Lama: honorific title for a Tibetan religious teacher, may or may not be a Tulku

Lok: lightning, name of the god-demon Begtse's mount

Lung-gom-pa: legendary monks who by means of psychic training had enhanced physical powers and could run nonstop across vast distances of rugged landscape.

Lung-ta: wind horse

Mudras: Buddhist hand gestures used for meditation and healing

Naga: serpent

Naga-ta: a flying serpent horse

Nagu: literally means black, a nagu is a common enemy foot soldier

Phurba: triple-edged knife or blade invested with metaphysical power

Pawo: warrior or hero

Pecha: a Tibetan text, usually of unbound pages held between wooden boards

Preta: the Hungry Ghost realm, one of the six realms of Buddhism

Rinpoche: literally means "precious one", a title generally reserved for incarnate lamas or dharma masters

Sangha: Buddhist monastic community

Senge: lion

Shinga: wooden scraper to straighten lines and fix any errors during sand painting

Skarma: star; the name of Palden Llamo's mount

Sura: the God realm, one of the six realms of Buddhism

Ta: horse; those of Shambala bear a level of sentience

Tapah: horse warrior, derived from Ta Pawo

Thekpu: the special house where the sand mandala is built

Tilug: a long handled spear-sword with a curved blade

Tantra: any of several mystical traditions and practices, some secretive, designed to elicit transcendental experiences leading to enlightenment or true perception

Tulku: a Tibetan Buddhist lama who has consciously determined to be reborn, often many times, in order to continue their Bodhisattva vow to free all sentient beings.

Wa: fox

Wong-khor: initiation or permission to practice Tantra

Yidam: a saint who has achieved enlightenment through meditation

Zhaxika: expasive grassland of eastern Tibet

Zha-xi-de-le: Tibetan for "good luck"

Navajo (Dineh) words

aoo': yes

anaye: evil demons, destroyers of mortals

ch'iidiitah: Navajo hell

chíndi: devils

etáhdeh: girl

hágooné: good bye

hataathli: medicine men and women who are trained in healing and communicating with sacred spirits

hozhónji: blessing chant.

' iikaah: the Navajo word for sand painting, literally "the place where the gods come and go"

sani: old one, used as an honorific

sechái: Navajo name meaning "grandfather" used as an honorific.

siss-sahkáhd: lone tree

tseel: mountain

tséh-ed-áh: rock-with-wings

tsiishch'ili: curly haired

yéhtso: giant.

yeibeichai: spirits with influence over the natural and human worlds

Maps

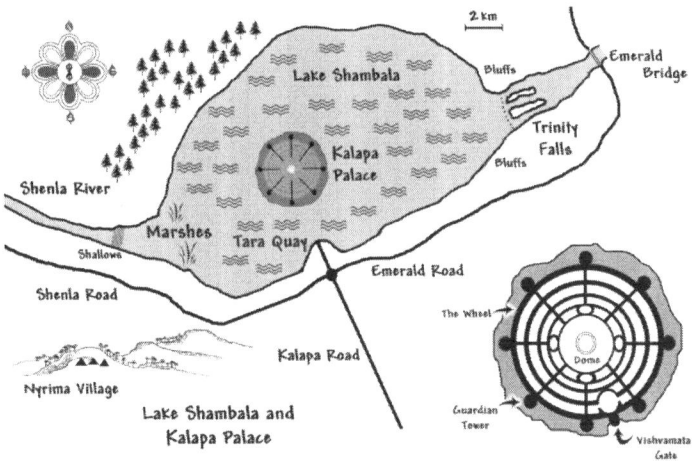

Lake Shambala and
Kalapa Palace

Shambala Valley
and
The Inner Mountain Ring

Mount Rewa

SW Pass

Shenla River

L. Shambala

SE Pass

Trinity Falls

NE Pass

Mount Shiwa

To the
Plains of Asura

Mount Jetsunmu

Northern Range

Mount Jetsun

0 10 50 km

Appendices

The Buddha Warriors and Humans

Amala: captain of the Kra dakini
Ane (Angela Andrakos): captain of the Druk dakini and her mount is
 Brug
Aten Gyatso: Kham horseman and Lozang's third son
Cespa: Dorje dakini and lieutenant
Chandra: Jalus dakini and lieutenant
Chiru: a Senge tapah
Dolma: Druk dakini second in command and her mount is Nam
Dr. Chandron: a neurosurgeon
Dr. Hoskie Ashki: a physician of Navajo descent
Gawa: Kham horseman and son-in-law to Lozang
Gesar Despa: hindmost of the Senge tapah and his mount is Goba
Jigme, (Ben Wilson): captain of the Senge tapah and his mount is
 Dawa
Kara: captain of the Dorje dakini and fallen in battle
Lozang Gyatso: leader of the Kham Sun Tribe
Monlam: Kham horsewoman and Lozang's second daughter
Rinchen: Druk dakini, fallen in battle with Mahakala, and her mount
 is Torma
Second Lieutenant Peng: agent of the Chinese People's Republic
 Army
Shingdong: the Senge tapah stable master
Tashi: captain of the Kalapa palace guard and consort to Dolma
Yeshi Gyatso: Kham horseman and Lozang's fourth son

The Kalacakra

Chongtul: a monk of Dagpa Akar
Geshe: a senior Kalacakra monk of Dagpa Akar
Jamyang: a senior monk of Dagpa Akar
Jhado Zhangpo: Rinpoche and Tulku Lama of Dagpa Akar Temple
Kai: a Bhikshu, an ordained monk of the San Francisco temple
Kasa: code name for a lama of the San Francisco temple
Kensang: a Kalacakra nun or Bhikshuni of Dagpa Akar
Nawang: a senior Kalacakra monk of Dagpa Akar
Norbu: a senior Kalacakra monk of Dagpa Akar, killed by Mahakala
Tenzin Deluk: a monk and personal assistant to Jhado
William: a Getsul, novice monk of the San Francisco temple

Zak: a Bhikshu, an ordained monk of the San Francisco temple

The God-Demons

The Faithful
Palden Lhamo: the Keeper of Beauty and Wielder of the Fire Sword, adopted the form of a divine beauty
Hayagriva: the Keeper of Wisdom, adopted the form of a white-bearded monk dressed in orange robes
Betsge: the Warrior Protector, adopted the form of a tall horse warrior, dressed in armor
Yamantaka: the Enemy of Death, adopted the form of an ancient hermit with a bull's head staff

The Rebels
Mahakala: Defender of the Palace as angelic form; Destroyer of Light in wrathful form
Yama: Protector of the Path as angelic form; Lord of Death in wrathful form
Kubera: the God of Prosperity as angelic form; The Profligate in wrathful form
Changpa Karpo: Protector of the Devout as angelic form; The Plunderer in wrathful form

The Dark Gods and Minions

Munpa Zerden: Master of Eighty-Thousand Negativities, creator of chaos
Gnyan: a demon-god and general of the nagu army
Chidag Nagpo: known as the Black Life Stealing Fiend, demon incarnate as Officer Charles Cutter
Dang Ba: known as the Bearer of Hatred, demon incarnate in Human realm
Na Tsha: known as the Spring of Corruption, demon incarnate in Human realm

Buddha warrior Emblems

The Dakini Emblems

The Tapah Emblems

The Monkey and the Rock Demon

As the Buddha lay on his deathbed, he instructed his disciple, Chenrezig, to carry the Path of Enlightenment to the highest land of the world. The Enlightened One, who could see through lives past and future, knew that from those high mountains and plateaus, his wisdom would flow like rivers to all of humanity. Although the task was daunting, for the land was harsh and ruled by demons, Chenrezig went forth with an open heart to the wild kingdoms of Tibet.

Knowing the journey would be long and hard, Chenrezig packed a donkey with supplies for many days. Under the shade of his master's favorite boddhi tree, he carefully filled his bags and tied them to his donkey. Suddenly, a little monkey jumped from the tree onto his shoulder and whispered into his ear.

"Take me with you and I will help you outwit your enemies."

Normally, the sudden appearance of a talking monkey would have shocked Chenrezig, but there was something of the voice of his master in the monkey's words and having experienced miracles in the presence of his master before, he could not deny the monkey's request.

"Very well, but what nourishment should I pack for you?" Chenrezig asked.

The monkey then jumped onto the back of the donkey and said, "I will need only one boddhi leaf for each day of our journey. In all, that will be sixty-four since the tree will give you no more."

Chenrezig picked sixty-four of the largest and most luxuriant boddhi leaves he could find and sealed them in a bag with a cloth soaked with water blessed by his master, the Buddha, before his death.

The monkey did a joyous flip and landed on the donkey's head and said, "You have chosen well, now let's go."

For many days, Chenrezig and his monkey companion traveled eastward up steep slopes covered with sharp rocks, through deep gorges cut with icy rivers and over high passes blanketed with knee-deep snow. Throughout the journey, the monkey kept to his word, keeping Chenrezig and his donkey safe from danger, which was especially important when his master performed his daily meditations. The monkey was skilled at smelling the approach of snow lions or bears. He even headed off an attack by a group of murderous bandits by cleverly leading them into the maze of a blind gorge.

On each day after his meditation, Chenrezig would reach into his bag and give the monkey one boddhi leaf. After slowly chewing and swallowing the leaf, the monkey would perform his joyous flip and say, "Ah! I understand!"

The journey went without challenge until the sixty-second day when Chenrezig entered the highest and most powerful kingdom in Tibet ruled by a merciless rock demon. Chenrezig was not unfamiliar with demons; his master spoke of demons and other manifestations of the Eighty-thousand Negativities. Such creatures used brutality, deceit, and seduction to dominate, but those who learned the Path of Enlightenment could not be subjugated.

Leading his donkey and its monkey passenger, Chenrezig followed a road that led to a walled fortress built high upon a rocky hill and there he halted at a great closed gate. On the walls overhead, barely human creatures, dressed in horrific armor, stood on guard seemingly oblivious to Chenrezig's presence.

"They have never seen such as us, so they cannot see us," the monkey said. "The unenlightened rarely see what they don't understand. You will have to make some noise for them to notice you."

Chenrezig cupped his hands to his mouth and yelled, "Hey! Hey up there!"

There was a clatter of armor as several helmets peered over the wall looking for the source of the cry. After a few moments search, the guards suddenly noticed Chenrezig and his animal entourage. Hastily, they nocked arrows and pointed them at the strange sojourners.

"What do you want?" A black helmet growled.

"I come to present your king with a great gift of knowledge." Chenrezig answered.

There was a prolonged time of gruff laughter from the ramparts before the helmet spoke again. "I'm afraid we must kill you, since it is unlikely that an ignorant dolt like you can teach our *queen* anything."

At that point, the monkey climbed onto Chenrezig's shoulder and said, "It is time to sit and meditate."

Chenrezig did not question, but immediately sat before the imposing gate and entered a deep state of meditation. During his daily practices on his mountain journey, he noticed that he had reached a deeper awareness of existences and achieved the ability to move between realms like his master. As Chenrezig sat in meditation, the monkey leapt onto the donkey and grabbed the bag containing the last of the boddhi leaves. Before jumping off, the monkey bit the tired donkey on the hindquarters. Offended, the donkey cried "Hee Haw!" then kicked and galloped back down the road. Meanwhile, the monkey scrabbled behind a pile of stones.

The guards on the wall watched the scene with a certain bemusement, but when the excitement seemed over, the black helmed leader ordered, "Shoot!", and a shower of arrows fell upon the place where Chenrezig sat. Miraculously, the arrows either missed, or harmlessly bounced away from an invisible shield surrounding the disciple. When the guards had exhausted their arrows, cries of frustration replaced their jeers of insolence. The day passed and every weapon available to the demon queen's army had been laid upon Chenrezig, including a great vat of burning oil. The night passed and when the sun fell upon the gate the next morning, the guards saw Chenrezig sitting quietly, unharmed and undisturbed.

The monkey watched the whole affair from the safety of his rock pile. Before taking his rest, he slowly chewed and swallowed the sixty-third boddhi leaf and said, "Ah! I understand!" He slept well despite the awful noises coming from the fortress walls and was wide-awake when the black helmets peered over the wall to find Chenrezig sitting comfortably in the morning sunshine.

"Summon the queen!" cried a helmet.

Soon afterward, cries of commotion arose behind the gate, followed by more harsh orders. Suddenly, the gate shuddered and cracked open to the sound of grinding gears. When the gates finally parted, a fearsome woman stepped through the opening. She was nearly twice the height of a man and dressed in bizarrely decorated armor. Her beast-like eyes were set in a sloping forehead above a long nose and jutting jaw set with sharply pointed teeth. A girdle of various skulls hung about her waist and a necklace of bones lay upon her bosom. A crown of gold set with a blood red jewel sat upon her head. In her hands, she held a long, barbed spear, which she pointed at the figure violating her doorstep. Unmoved, Chenrezig remained seated with his eyes half-closed and his face bearing a serene expression.

"I am Daughter of Rock and Queen of Mountains! Leave my realm or die!" ordered the demon in a voice that emerged from the earth.

Chenrezig seemed to smile in response.

Outraged, the queen thrust her terrible spear at the insolent figure only to be blinded by a flash of white light and repelled backward by her own force.

In that moment, the monkey suddenly emerged from the safety of his rock pile and dashed to the open gate. He leapt over Chenrezig and was standing upon the demon queen's bosom before anyone noticed. When the demon queen's vision returned, a small monkey holding a leaf looked into her eyes.

"What is this!" she cried in amazement.

The monkey needed only one word to shove the sixty-fourth boddhi leaf into the mouth of the demon queen.

There was a prolonged silence as the demon queen tasted and swallowed the unexpectedly pleasant meal. Her eyes closed and then opened with a different light within.

"Ah! I understand!" she said.

The monkey jumped down and scurried out of the fortress to perch upon Chenrezig's shoulder and whisper his last human words. "It is time for you to return now."

Chenrezig opened his eyes fully and looked up. The gate that had blocked his way was now open and instead of a demon, before him stood a beautiful queen with jet-black hair encircled by a golden crown set with a single ruby. The jewel and her gown glowed in the morning sunshine.

"Welcome husband," she said.

The children of Bodhisattva Chenrezig and the Rock Queen became the new people of Tibet. To this day, the Path of Enlightenment runs through their land and blood, flowing to the rest of humanity from the highest place on earth.

Other books by the author:

The Zama Codex (2005)

The Angel Maker (2009)

1296901R0

Printed in Great Britain by
Amazon.co.uk, Ltd.,
Marston Gate.